ALTAR
OF
BONES

ALTAR
OF
BONES

PHILIP CARTER

G

GALLERY BOOKS

New York   London   Toronto   Sydney

G

Gallery Books
A Division of Simon & Schuster, Inc.
1230 Avenue of the Americas
New York, NY 10020

First Gallery Books export edition March 2011

GALLERY BOOKS and colophon are trademarks of Simon & Schuster, Inc.

For information about special discounts for bulk purchases,
please contact Simon & Schuster Special Sales at 1-866-506-1949
or business@simonandschuster.com.

The Simon & Schuster Speakers Bureau can bring authors to your live event. For more information or to book an event contact the Simon & Schuster Speakers Bureau at 1-866-248-3049 or visit our website at www.simonspeakers.com.

Interior design by Davina Mock-Maniscalco
Endpaper map by Paul J. Pugliese

Manufactured in the United States of America

10   9   8   7   6   5   4   3   2   1

ISBN 978-1-4516-2879-1
ISBN 978-1-4391-9946-6 (ebook)

For Catherine

ACKNOWLEDGMENTS

I WANT TO give thanks to the following people for their tremendous support and encouragement during the writing and publication of this book:

To my agent, Aaron Priest, for always telling it like it is, both the good and the bad. You're the best in the business. Bar none. And to Lucy Childs and Frances Jalet-Miller for their extensive and well-thought-out editorial critiques, which ended up making the book so much better.

To my publisher, Louise Burke, and my best-in-the-world editor, Kara Cesare, of Gallery Books, and all the others at Simon & Schuster, from the art department to sales to production, who've put so much time and effort into getting the book on the shelves and into the hands of readers.

To CC for your generous advice and encouragement during our weekly lunches at the high-cholesterol factory. You know I could never have done it without you. And to TG, for so much it would take a book in itself just to describe it all. Everyone needs someone they can count on to come bail them out of jail in the middle of the night, and you're that someone for me. (Not that that has ever happened. Yet.) And to my fellow writers of the First Wednesday of the Month Group, for always being there with advice and support.

And finally to my own One, for having put up with me all these years. How lucky I am to have you to go through life with by my side.

PROLOGUE

San Francisco, California
The present

ROSIE KNEW the stranger had come to kill her as soon as he walked into the circle of light cast by their fire.

They were deep in the woods of Golden Gate Park where the cops wouldn't harass them—a small colony of homeless that panhandled on Haight Street during the day and camped out in the park at night. Rosie was new to the group, but it had been her idea to arrange their shopping carts in a circle like a wagon train, then cover them with cardboard and blankets to create a makeshift shelter. Still, she shivered in the bitter February wind as she looked up into the stranger's eyes. His killer eyes.

She'd caught a duck earlier, down by Stow Lake, and was cooking it over the flames using a coat hanger for a spit. The stranger pretended the roasting meat had drawn him, but Rosie knew better.

"Hey, there," he said. His English was good, but the burr of Mother Russia still lay thick on his tongue. "I dove a Dumpster tonight and found this." He held up a pint of Wild Turkey as he came closer. "I'm willing to share for a bite of what you got cooking."

Willard, who was their default leader, put down his beer and stood up to bump fists with the man. "Bring it on, friend."

The stranger—a big, rawboned guy, wearing a greasy brown ponytail and a tough face—sat down cross-legged, close to the fire. He grinned real wide as he handed over his offering.

Willard was tall with a cue ball for a head and prison scratch over every inch of his skin. Even his face was tattooed with a pair of teardrops under each eye. Yet he gave the whiskey bottle a look of childish wonder. "Man, that was some lucky Dumpster."

The stranger smiled again. "A liquor store over on Polk Street caught fire last night, and they wrecked the place putting it out. Most of the shit inside got broken, and the cops and firemen probably ripped off what didn't. Guess I got lucky, huh?"

Rosie had no doubt the burnt liquor store with its Dumpster existed. Men like him usually got the details right.

He had the homeless look down, too: jeans so grimy it was hard to tell if they'd once been blue, crack pipe stuck in his coat pocket, dirt caked in the seams of his skin. His eyes, though, were all wrong. They weren't empty or beaten or lost. They were sharp, focused. The kind that could slide a knife across your throat without blinking, or put a bullet in your head from a rooftop two hundred yards away.

Rosie stayed silent, watching the stranger as the whiskey passed from hand to hand around the campfire: from the transvestite hooker called Buttercup, to the one-legged man with broken teeth known as Gimpy Sam, to Dodger, a tall, stoop-shouldered man with a head of gray dreadlocks stuffed haphazardly under a child's pink sock cap.

Not that I'm such a prize anymore, she thought. *I was pretty once, though.* . . . But a lot of years, a lot of hard living, had come and gone since then, and now none of it mattered anymore because she was dying of the cancer that had already eaten away most of her belly like corrosive acid.

The bottle finally made its way around to Rosie. It held enough booze to give her a good buzz with some still left over for the stranger. She watched him as she finished it all off. Might as well make him pay for the privilege of killing her.

She slipped the empty bottle into her coat pocket, telling him with her eyes to go fuck himself.

He waved a hand at the roasting meat. "Sure does smell good. What is it?"

Rosie pulled her mouth back in a smile that showed her teeth. "Fried rat."

She saw the muscle beneath his left eye jump a little, but he recovered quickly. "Mighty big rat."

Buttercup giggled, then blushed and looked down, scratching at the sores on her neck, the ravages of dirty needles.

Rosie caught the disgust on the stranger's face as he looked away. *Maybe you're not so tough after all, huh, big guy?*

"Dinner's done," she said, and smiled again.

———

THEY SCARFED DOWN the duck with some stale hamburger buns Gimpy Sam had begged from a McDonald's. Nobody had a lot to say, especially Rosie, nor did she eat much. Between the cancer and the pain meds the clinic had given her, her appetite was pretty much gone.

It grew late. Rosie threw some fresh wood on the fire. Maybe as long as the others stayed awake, she would live.

Dodger poked at the flames with a stick, then used it to light up a crack pipe. He drew on the pipe deeply, then passed it over to Gimpy Sam.

Sam took his toke, then held the pipe out to the stranger. "Need a hit, fella? You can have one cheap."

Dodger snatched off his sock cap and whacked Sam upside the head with it. "Don't you be sellin' our crack, fool."

"Hey, now. That's okay," the stranger said. He patted his coat pocket. "I got my own, you know. For later."

If Rosie hadn't already been dead certain the man was only playing a part, that stupid remark would have sealed it. In a world where you could be stabbed through the heart for a pair of old shoes, no real doper would announce to God and everyone that he had a stash.

Dodger and Gimpy Sam stopped their squabbling long enough to exchange a pointed look and then went back to smoking their rock.

Buttercup had left earlier without even eating to take care of some private business. Now she was back with a syringe in her hand. She reclaimed her spot by the fire, scrapped the needle across a rock to knock loose the sediment, then calmly jammed it into her neck.

Rosie pushed to her feet, her old bones creaking. "Gotta see a man about a horse."

She acted like a drunken sot, weaving and muttering to herself. When she was out of the light cast by the fire, she ran.

———

SHE HEARD FEET pounding the path behind her. Wind roared through the treetops, and through her ears. Already she was out of breath.

She'd gotten a head start, but the killer was catching up fast. Her old legs didn't run so good anymore. She could give up—what the hell, she was dying from cancer anyway. But he wouldn't be quick about it, he'd want to make her talk first and she didn't know how much pain she could bear. Everyone had a breaking point.

The stitch in her side was already unbearable. She slowed enough to suck in a deep, ragged breath and rummage through the junk in her deep coat pockets, feeling for a small scrap of paper.

Stupid, stupid, how could you've been so stupid? You should've shredded it to bits soon as you delivered that letter, and now . . .

It was those pain meds. They fuzzed up her brain, made her so forgetful and stupid. Careless.

Got to find it, got to find that piece of paper. . . . Oh, God, if he searches me after he catches me, he'll find it, and then . . .

Where was the damn thing? Whistle, apple core, cigarettes, empty booze bottle, paper . . . She crumpled it into a ball and stuffed it into her mouth.

Off to the left, she heard a branch crack.

Rosie ran.

―――――

SHE WENT FLYING over a tree root and hit the ground, hard. She felt the empty booze bottle smash against her belly, jagged pieces of glass digging all the way through her thick wool coat and into her flesh.

She thrust her hand into her pocket and pulled out a big shard, felt it slice her palm, felt the wetness of blood, but she smiled. She could hurt him now, tit for tat. She wanted to hurt him, even if it was just a little before he did his worst on her.

She pushed back onto her feet. Her ankle gave and she staggered into a tree. A branch slashed across her face, nearly blinding her. She blinked away tears, yet she kept running. He was close, so close. She heard his harsh breathing, the crunch of dead leaves and needles beneath his feet.

Ahead of her she saw moonlight glinting off glass. She knew where she was now—that hothouse place where they grew all those pretty flowers. She thought of it as the petticoat building because it was so white and frilly. A street ran in front of it, and there might be a car, someone to help her—

A hard arm locked around her throat, jerking her back. She felt the point of a knife slide into her neck, not far, but enough to make her blood seep out, hot and thick. The blade slid in a little deeper. She heard his fast breathing, felt his excitement as he dug the tip in a little more.

He flipped her around to face him, held the knife under her chin. "Now, you're going to tell me where it is. And in loving fucking detail."

"I don't—what?" But she knew, oh, yes, she knew what he wanted. She had to hold him off, a car could come any minute, she could yell, she could—

"Talk or I'll slit your scrawny throat like a chicken's."

He'd kill her all right, but not until after she'd told him. Then she would be nothing to him, nothing to those who'd sent him, but an old loose thread to be snipped off. She didn't want to die, not before her time. . . . Now that was nearly funny, so nearly funny she laughed. Only it came out more like a whimper.

He thought he'd won. She felt him relax, heard his breathing lighten.

She stabbed the shard of glass she was holding in her palm deep into his arm.

He screamed, fell back, grabbing his arm, cursing her. She slashed out again, aiming for his eyes this time. He moved so fast his hand was a blur. She felt something slam into her chest. So he'd hit her, it was nothing. She was free of him, free. She'd slash his eyes out, the bastard, but to her surprise her hand wouldn't move. Run, run, then. She had to get away. . . .

She reeled, staggered down the path, burst out into the road. Just a little farther and then a car would come. She couldn't catch her breath.

She looked down and stared. He'd stuck the knife in her. All she could see was the hilt, which meant it was deep, maybe as deep as her heart. But it didn't hurt and that made no sense, and then she realized she couldn't feel her legs anymore.

She fell onto her hands and knees. Blood dripped from her neck onto the ground in front of her. She saw his feet come up, his old scuffed boots, his stupid disguise she'd seen right through. She wanted to tell him he'd lost, that he was a fool, but the words stayed in her head.

She watched his boot come up and push against her chest. Felt the toe of it push into her neck as he flopped her over onto her back.

He squatted down beside her. "You got two choices. Tell me where it is now, and you'll die quick and easy. Make me work for it, and you'll die slow and hard."

She pulled a grin out of her dying heart. "Fuck you, asshole."

She felt the fury rolling off him, the uncertainty, but it didn't touch her. She looked up at the night sky. She wanted to see the moon one last time, but the black clouds had swallowed it whole. Just one more time before she died, just once more—

"All right, you stupid old cow." His breath was hot and sour on her face. "Let's see how tough you are after I take out your eyes."

She saw him reach for the knife hilt in her chest, and she wanted to cry because she wouldn't see the moon now, but just then the black clouds rolled on and she saw not one moon, but two. Two big, round yellow moons just like in the movies.

No, not moons . . .

Headlights.

———

Screeching tires. Running footsteps.

Someone said, "Dude, she's got a knife sticking out of her chest."

"Shut up, Ronnie."

"But, dude—"

"Shut up and call 911."

A stranger's face hovered above her—a little soft around the jowls and bald on top, but she saw caring there and she desperately needed someone to care.

The stranger said, "Help is on the way, so stay with me now, okay? Stay with me."

No, no, too dangerous. Can't stay . . .

Except she couldn't seem to move, so maybe she would stay after all. And there was something she had to tell him. She needed to make him understand.

She tried to lift her hand to pull him closer, and her chest made a funny sucking noise. It felt as if she were trying to breathe underwater.

"I got it back," she said, on a burst of gargled breath that sprayed a bloody mist into the air. "I got it back."

The stranger's hand wrapped around hers, warm and strong, and he leaned in closer. "You'll be okay. You're gonna be okay."

No, no, you don't understand . . .

She tried to shake her head, but it wouldn't move. She couldn't move anything and she couldn't see his face anymore, because the moon was in the way, big and bright, filling her eyes with a beautiful white light. She could hear the sirens now; she was running out of time. *The truth.* She had to make him see the truth. Had to make him see that they—

"They didn't have to kill him," she said on a gush of bright red blood and one last drowning breath. "He never drank from the altar of bones. I got it back."

PART ONE

THE KEEPER

Mother of God, where was Sergeant Chirkov? He should have been here by now. At midnight she and Nikolai needed to be on the other side of the yard behind the latrines, ready to dash across no-man's-land during the forty-five seconds or so the searchlights went dark and the guards on the watchtowers changed shifts. But they couldn't leave the infirmary until the sergeant had done his nightly bed count.

Lena stared at her watch as the seconds ticked away. She had no choice, she would have to go on with her rounds. Pneumonia, dysentery, frostbite . . . The beds the patients lay on were little more than wooden trestles; they had only rough blankets to cover them. And it was always so cold, so cold. She strained to hear the sergeant's heavy tread. Five more minutes passed by. Ten.

She moved to the next bed, to a boy who had tried to commit suicide by cutting the veins in his wrists with his teeth. He'd be dead by morning. And the old man next to him had taken an ax to his own foot—

The door opened with a scream of rusting hinges, and Lena nearly dropped a tray of sterile bandages.

Sergeant Chirkov entered with a blast of cold air, stamping the snow off his boots. A shy smile softened his ruddy face when he saw her. "So it's you on duty tonight. I was hoping it would be . . . that is, I . . ." He flushed and looked away. "Comrade Orlova," he finished with a stiff nod.

"Comrade Sergeant." Lena set down the tray and sneaked a quick look at her watch. Eleven eighteen. They could still make it. The sergeant just had to do his count quickly and be gone.

He ambled over to the stove and lifted his overcoat to warm his backside. The stove—nothing more than a small iron coal pot, really— barely made a dent in the icebox chill of the long, narrow room.

"You heard about the excitement we had this morning?" he said.

"I saw the aftermath of it. Hanging on the front gate."

"Well . . ." The sergeant shrugged as if to say, *What else can you expect?* He began to pull the makings of a cigarette out of his coat pocket, and Lena wanted to scream in frustration.

"That stupid *zek*," the sergeant went on, as he tore off a piece of newspaper and poured some coarse tobacco on it. "Did he really think he could make it over the fence alive? And even if by some miracle he'd managed it without getting shot full of holes—it's Siberia waiting for him out there, not a stroll through Red Square."

Lena looked up from the half-amputated foot she'd been washing. The sergeant had tilted his head away from her while he lit his cigarette. She had a terrible thought he knew what she planned and was giving her a warning. But when he looked around at her again, she could read nothing in his face.

"You're right," she said. "The prisoner didn't stand a chance."

"So why do they do it then? Can you tell me that? Why do they try to escape when they know it's so hopeless?"

"I don't know," Lena lied.

She wound a fresh bandage around the raw stubs of missing toes. The man lay rigid on the cot, his eyes tightly shut, not making a sound even though he had to be in great pain. He had done this to himself. He had taken an ax and tried to chop off his foot to get out of the nickel mines. It had been an act of insane desperation, but Lena had no trouble understanding why.

The sergeant left the stove at last, but instead of doing his counting and leaving, he strolled to the window. She doubted he could see his own reflection with so much ice webbing the glass.

"There's a *purga* coming later. You can feel it in the air. Don't . . ." His voice trailed off. Lena was sure now he was trying to give her a warning. *Don't do this thing you are planning, Lena Orlova. Don't do it. Not tonight. Not ever.*

The silence dragged on, until Lena couldn't bear it. "Don't what?"

"Nothing. Only, you can lose your way in a blizzard just going from the kitchen door to the latrines. If you'd like some company walking back to the barracks after your shift is over . . ."

She managed a smile. "I would like that."

The sergeant grinned, slapped his hands together. "All right then."

Lena looked at her watch. Eleven twenty-seven. *Dear God.* "Sergeant, shouldn't you . . ."

"I know, I know. Duty calls." He pulled a sheet of paper from his pocket. "I see that we have a full house again tonight."

It was a regulation that a prisoner had to be either crippled or running a temperature of at least 101 to be admitted into the infirmary, and the beds were always full. With one glance the sergeant could look down the length of the room and see every bed was full, yet regulations said to count them, and so he counted.

While the sergeant walked down the rows of beds, matching the names on the charts to the ones on his list, Lena dumped the soiled bandages into a bucket and moved on to her next patient.

At last the sergeant was done with his counting. But instead of leaving, he came to stand beside her, watching as she bathed the ulcerous face of an old man near death from scurvy.

"Tell me, Comrade Orlova, how did you come to be in such a place as Norilsk?"

Lena tucked a stray hank of hair behind her ear, then made a note on the patient's chart. *Just go*, she wanted to shout. *Just go, go, go* . . . "I was born here. Or rather near here, on the shores of the Ozero P'asino. And I work in this infirmary because the Revolution in its infinite wisdom says I must."

The sergeant stifled a groan. "Aw, Lena. You shouldn't say such things. And besides, do you think anyone asked me if I wanted to be guarding a bunch of pathetic *zeks* out on the frozen edge of nowhere? But the needs of the collective must always come before the wants of the individual."

She'd known as soon the words left her mouth their flippancy could get her in trouble. He was probably thinking now of reporting her to the *politruk*—well, what did she care if he did? After tonight, she was gone, gone, gone.

A silence fell between them, lengthened, grew strained.

"But are you truly one of them?" he finally said, and she knew that by *them* he meant the Yakuts: reindeer herders with their dark, leathery skin, flat faces, and slits for eyes. "Because your eyes, they are like the sky back home right before a summer storm. And your hair . . ." A stand of it had come loose again, and he reached up to tuck it back behind her ear. "It's the color of ripe wheat rippling in the wind."

She started at his touch, stepping away from him. "I didn't know you had so much of the poet in you, Comrade Sergeant. And you're wrong.

My mother was indeed a Yak, and I am the image of her, as she was the image of her mother, and so on, bound by blood to the beginning of time."

She snatched another quick look at her watch. Eleven thirty-eight. They were never going to make it now, it was too late. No, they still had to try. Tomorrow the commandant was moving her onto the day shift, where she could be stuck for months. By then it would be summer and she would be too . . .

She pressed her hand against her belly, still flat now and showing nothing, but not for long. It was tonight, or never.

She picked up a brimming bedpan. "Pardon me, Comrade Sergeant, but as you can see I've a lot of work to do."

"Yes, of course. I should be going on about my rounds, but I'll be seeing you later? Come morning?"

"Yes. See you later."

She felt a pang of regret as she watched him walk away from her. He would be blamed for their escape, and for his punishment he could spend twenty years in this very prison camp he was now helping to guard.

At the door he turned. "They don't all die, you know. The *zeks*. If you make your quota and you follow the rules, you don't have to die."

He paused, as if waiting for her to say something, but fear froze her throat. *He does know something,* she thought. *He must. Only how could he know, unless Nikolai has talked?*

But Nikolai would never talk, because of the two of them he had the most to lose. If she was caught helping a prisoner to escape, she would be tried and sentenced to twenty years in a woman's camp far away, so deep into Siberia she would never find her way out. But for Nikolai there would be no trial, no sentence. They would simply drag him back here, stand him up next to an open grave, and shoot him.

The sergeant was still standing with the door half-open, letting in the cold, but at last he turned and left.

She waited a few moments longer after the door closed behind him, in case he decided to come back. Then she set the bedpan back down and ran the length of the room, to the last bed on the left, next to the wall, and the man she'd been aware of with every breath and nerve ending since she'd first entered the infirmary.

———————

HE LOOKED LIKE death.

No, no. It was just there was so little light back here, so far away from the lamps and the stove. And he was asleep, that was all. Just sleeping.

Lena snatched up his chart to see what the camp doctor had written when he'd first been admitted that morning. *Nikolai Popov, Prisoner #35672. Fever, some inflammation of the lungs.*

She tossed the chart back onto the bed and bent over him to lay a hand on his forehead. He was indeed running a fever, sweating in spite of the cold, but that was to be expected. He'd had to make himself sick enough to get admitted into the infirmary in the first place, and prisoner lore said you could give yourself a fever by swallowing a dose of cooking salts. Nikolai had joked that anything would be better than taking an ax to his toes.

But a fever could so easily turn into pneumonia.

She touched him again. "Nikki?"

He stirred, and she heard ice shattering as he lifted his head. His sweat-soaked hair had frozen to the trestle board. "Lena," he said, then coughed. "Is this it? Is it time?"

Lena didn't like the soggy sound of that cough, but his eyes, she saw, were lucid, clear. "It's past time. That wretched sergeant. I thought he was never going to leave."

She looked at her watch. They had less than fifteen minutes. *Don't do this thing that you are planning, Lena Orlova. Don't do it. . . .*

Nikolai tossed back the ratty brown blanket and swung his legs off the bed. He grinned up her. "You aren't losing your nerve on me?"

"Never." She found herself smiling back at him as she looked down into his upturned face, so full even now with the dashing bravado that had drawn her to him in the first place. But this time she thought she saw something more behind the dancing light in his eyes.

She wanted to believe it was love.

Nikolai pretended to sag weakly against her as she helped him to his feet. She would say he had typhus and she was taking him to the isolation ward should anyone challenge them. But the blanket-shrouded shapes on the other trestle beds were either all asleep now or pretending to be.

Quickly, she led the way to a storeroom little bigger than a closet. In here, so far from the stove, white clouds wreathed their heads and cold air billowed up from the floor.

The storeroom was crowded: an old desk and chair, stacks of mildewed blankets, rotting file boxes, a set of battered metal instrument cabinets. There was one window just big enough for both of them to squeeze through.

She shifted aside a stack of burlap bags and a box full of moldering newspapers to expose a poster of Joseph Stalin saluting the Soviet worker. She thought she heard Nikolai gasp as she ripped the Great Leader's face in two, and she smiled to herself. *Maybe you're not so much the wild rebel as you fancy yourself to be, huh, Nikki?*

Behind the poster was a panel loosely screwed in, rather than nailed, and behind it a two-by-three-foot hole in the wall. Lena could feel her watch ticking off precious minutes as she pulled out sleeping rolls made of skins, gloves, fur hats, and a *foffaika* for each of them—coats made of the warmest part of reindeer hides. For Nikolai there were trousers like hers, with wool sewn in as padding, and a pair of felt boots.

She handed these things to him in silence, and he began to put them on over his ragged prison clothes.

She dug out the knapsack she'd stuffed full of dried black bread, hunks of fat filched from the staff kitchen, a wire noose for trapping, a tinderbox, a flask full of vodka, and the few hundred rubles she'd managed to scrimp from her small salary. She gave the sleeping rolls to Nikolai and slung the knapsack over her own shoulder.

Next she took out the snowshoes—thin lengths of sapwood bent into bows and strung with interwoven strips of reindeer hide. Any tracks they left, she hoped, would quickly be obliterated by the falling snow.

Nikolai laughed as she handed him his pair. "You mean we're actually going to have to walk out of here? What with all the miracles you've been pulling out of that hidey-hole, I was expecting no less than a sleigh and eight reindeer."

Lena held her finger up to her lips, but she was smiling again. Then she pulled out one last thing: the poorly cured sheepskin that she'd wrapped around the knife she'd stolen from the cook, who was always so drunk on homemade vodka someone could have walked off with his head and he wouldn't have noticed.

It was a *kandra*, a Yak knife with a wickedly hooked, double-edged blade, and Nikolai whistled at the sight of it. Lena started to give it to him, but at the last instant stuffed it into the waistband of her own trousers instead. Then she tied the sheepskin around her hips with a long piece of stiff rope.

She looked up at Nikolai from beneath the rolled brim of her fur hat. "Are you ready?"

He gave her a cocky salute, and in that moment she loved him more than life itself.

———

THE WINDOW WAS frozen shut, but Nikolai broke the glass with his elbow. Lena crawled over the sill first and dropped to the ground, terrified she would hear a guard cry the alarm. A sudden movement by the front gate sent her heart lurching in her chest, but it was only the ghostly silhouettes of the wolves.

Once away from the infirmary, they kept to the deep shadows until they reached the latrines. It was snowing harder now, great wet clots of flakes. The sergeant had been right about a *purga* coming. The cold weighed heavy now and had a metallic smell.

A searchlight beam swept past them, and they flattened against the rough latrine wall.

Lena studied the wide-open expanse of the *zaprethaya zona*—no-man's-land. It stretched between the edge of the camp buildings and a perimeter barbed-wire fence piled six coils high. The area was constantly raked by a pair of searchlights mounted on the guard towers to the right and left of them. Anyone who set foot in the forbidden zone, whether prisoner or a free worker such as herself, would be shot on sight.

It was Nikolai who had first noticed a place where the fence didn't follow the contours of the ground. A dip here behind the latrines made a gap big enough so they could burrow under the wire. And Nikolai had figured out the searchlights went dark for forty-five seconds when the guards changed shifts.

Now, though, bright yellow pools of light crisscrossed the smooth, white snow. Lena looked at her watch through the ice crystals on her lashes. *Past midnight. Oh, God* . . . They were too late. The guards must already have changed shifts while they were still in the storeroom, and now they were trapped out here. Unable to go on, unable to go back—

The searchlights went dark.

Nikolai was already running. Lena followed in his footprints, jerking the smelly, half-cured sheepskin jacket from around her waist, letting it comb the ground behind her to smooth out their tracks and camouflage their scent from the dogs.

Too long, it's taking too long.

Any second the searchlights would come back on, machine-gun fire would cut them down, and their bodies would be hung on the front gate for the wolves to eat.

She didn't realize Nikolai had stopped until she smacked into him, hard enough he grunted and nearly stumbled into the rolls of barbed wire.

He signaled her to go first. She crawled through the gap on her belly, shoving their bulky gear ahead of her, all the while her mind screaming, *Too long, too long.* She was taking too long. The searchlights would flood over them, there'd be shouts, bullets . . .

Then she was free at last, on the other side of the wire. She scrambled to her feet and looked back. All she could see of Nikolai was his head, thrusting up out of the snow. He wasn't moving.

For a moment she thought he'd frozen at the sight of a guard, but then she realized the hooked barbs of the wire had snagged the back of his coat. He shook himself, pulling, pulling, but he couldn't get loose. Little pieces of ice tinkled down the coils of wire. An instant later, Lena heard the snap of a cartridge being levered into the breech of a gun.

"Halt!"

2

H ER HEART nearly stopped with fear.

"Mother of God, don't shoot," she heard an old man's voice whine from over by the latrines. "I'm not escaping. In truth the only part of me running at the moment is my poor bowels."

Lena tried to rip Nikolai's coat free of the barbs, but it was still stuck fast.

"Can't it wait till morning?" the other, younger voice said. The one with the gun.

"In a word . . . no."

"Well, hurry it up then."

Lena jerked on the coat again, harder, and finally it snapped free with another crackle of ice.

"Hurry. Why is it always hurry, hurry, hurry with you people? The State gave me twenty-five years in this paradise, so why should I rush things—?" The old man's voice cut off abruptly as the frozen snow around them exploded into a yellow glare.

The searchlights were back on.

Nikolai burst from under the fence at a dead run. He grabbed her arm, pulling her along with him. Out of the corner of her eye Lena could see a bright arc of light sweeping toward them over the snow, getting closer, closer. Fear shrieked through her. They weren't going to make it—

The night suddenly exploded into a fury of howls and snarls and snapping teeth. The wolves had at last gone after the body of the dead *zek*. The searchlights swung around to flood the front gate. The guards in the towers fired. A man screamed.

Lena stumbled, almost fell, but she didn't look back.

═══════════

WHEN THEY GOT beyond the reach of the searchlights, they stopped just long enough to strap on their snowshoes. Lena listened for the bay of the dogs, for the rasp of the runners on the soldiers' iron sleighs, but there was only the wind.

They'd gone barely a mile farther when the wind began to blow harder, driving pellets of snow into their faces, lashing the loose snow on the ground into ice clouds. Lena stopped to scrub her eyes with her sleeve, knocking the icicles off her eyebrows.

Nikolai staggered up next to her. He leaned over, bracing his palms on his thighs, gasping for air.

"The *purga* will be on us soon." Lena had to shout a little to be heard above the wind. "It'll be hard going after that."

Nikolai tilted back his head to grin up at her. "Hard going, hunh? And what do you call this so far? A nice, warm day at the beach?"

Lena shook her head at him. It would take too much breath to explain, and there was no explaining anyway. A *purga* was something you had to experience to believe, and by then all you could do was pray the experience didn't kill you. Soon there would be no tracks behind them, no horizon in front of them, no ground, no sky. Only snow and wind beyond imagining.

Nikolai's whole body suddenly heaved as a fit of coughing tore through him. When he was finally able to draw a breath again, he said, "It's the damn cold. It shreds your lungs into confetti paper. . . . How far away are we from this secret cave of yours?"

"Not far."

He straightened slowly and looked around them, although she knew he couldn't make out much this deep into the polar night.

"'Not far,' she says. Lena, love, please tell me we're not lost."

She'd heard the teasing smile in his voice, but that cough, the sudden wetness in his breathing, was scaring her. Had the exertion of their escape driven the fever into his lungs?

She pulled off her glove and reached out to touch his face. It was coated with a thin sheet of ice from his sweat freezing instantly in the frigid air.

Still, she felt him smile. "I'll make it, love," he said. "I'm one tough bastard underneath all my surface charm. But how can you be sure you know where we are? It's black as pitch out here, and everything's the same. Nothing but snow and more snow."

"This land is bred into my bones. I can find my way over it blind-folded."

Before they set off again, though, she used the rope from off the sheepskin coat to tie them together, for once the *purga* struck they'd be as good as blind, unable to see beyond the end of their noses. They could lose sight of each other in seconds, and if that happened, Nikolai would be a dead man come morning.

━━━━━━

THE *PURGA* HIT two hours later.

The shrieking wind drove the snow into her eyes and mouth, the cold burned her lungs with every breath. She wondered how Nikolai was managing. She couldn't see him behind her; only a steady pressure on the rope told her he was keeping up. A couple of times she knew he'd fallen, because the rope had suddenly jerked taut, but he'd somehow managed to get right back up again.

They had to have covered at least three miles since they'd entered the box canyon. The canyon was shaped like a boot and at its toe was the lake, the one place she thought of as home. It wasn't the Ozero P'asino— she'd lied about that to the sergeant. The small Siberian lake she'd been born on wasn't on any map. No roads led there, and in winter even the caribou trails were buried deep beneath the snow.

She'd told him other lies, as well. Her mother hadn't been a Yakut. She'd been one of the *toapotror*—the magic people.

I need some of that magic now. Real magic to drive away the purga, *to get us safely to the cave before Nikki—*

The rope jerked taut.

Lena waited, but this time he didn't get back up.

———

SHE USED THE rope as a guide, feeling her way back to him. Only seconds had passed since he'd fallen and already he was nearly buried in snow.

She grabbed him by the lapels of his coat and hauled him half-upright. His head lolled. He breathed and sounded as if he were drowning. "Nikki, get up. You've got to keep moving."

A raw cough ripped through him. "Can't. Chest hurts."

She shook him, hard. "Nikki! Don't you dare quit on me."

"No. Don't want to die. . . ." He grabbed her arms and suddenly his face, crusted with ice, was only inches from hers. "If you love me, you won't let me die."

"You're not going to die."

"Promise me."

"I promise . . . Nikki, please. You've got to get up. It's not much farther now, but I can't carry you."

"*Da, da.* Getting up . . . getting up . . ."

She thrust her shoulder up under his armpit and leveraged him onto his feet. He swayed, but didn't fall back down.

She'd told him it wasn't far, but she wasn't sure anymore. They should've reached the lake by now, but the lake was nowhere, and they were nowhere, lost in a world of snow and wind and cold.

———

SHE LOST ALL sense of time as they slogged on, her arm around Nikolai's waist, holding him up against the blasts of wind.

She needed to get Nikolai to the cave soon, or he would die. She was tired, so tired.

Nikolai's legs gave out beneath him and he lurched into her. She reeled, fighting desperately to keep from falling, screaming as his dead weight wrenched her arm nearly out of its socket. But somehow he got his feet back under him, and they staggered on.

Not much farther now. Just one more step, Nikki. That's it. Don't fall on me. Don't fall—

He fell, and this time he took her with him.

They plunged through black space, hitting deep, pillowy snow and rolling to a stop. They landed in a snowdrift, and it was so warm and soft. She wanted to lie there and rest just a little while.

She knew that to stop was to die.

She thrashed her legs, fighting free of the sucking snow, and realized she wasn't on the snow-shrouded tundra anymore. She was on ice.

They'd found the lake.

———

NIKOLAI STILL LAY in the snowdrift, unmoving. She fell back onto her knees beside him. She shook him, hard. She had no breath left to shout at him, he couldn't have heard her anyway.

She shook him again, felt him move. *Get up, get up, get up,* she willed him, a chant in her mind. And somehow, with her half-lifting him, he got back onto his feet.

Just one more step, Nikki. That's it, one more step.

Her own steps were happening on sheer instinct now. She was as good as blind, moving through a black nightmare of wind and snow. *Just one more step, one more . . .*

They hit a wall of ice.

The waterfall.

———

IN SUMMER, THE runoff from melting snow and swollen streams sent a cascade of water shooting off a tall, steep bluff and into the lake below. In winter the waterfall froze solid.

But no matter what time of year, the waterfall always hid the entrance to the cave. First, you had to know that it was possible to walk onto the narrow ledge between the waterfall and the bluff, but even then all you would see was a flat face of solid rock. Unless you were a daughter of the *toapotror,* the magic people.

A daughter of the magic people knew that what looked like a sheer wall of rock was really two walls, overlapping each other to form a slit barely a foot wide. And if you dared to squeeze yourself into that slit, to inch your way along it, with the space growing narrower and narrower until it seemed that you'd taken one step too many, that you were stuck, trapped forever . . . then suddenly the slit would widen again, opening up into the entrance of a secret cavern.

———————

LENA DIDN'T KNOW how she got Nikolai through the slit to the entrance of the cave, and she would never have managed it if he hadn't battled back through the fever and found the strength to hold himself upright mostly on his own. *I'm one tough bastard*, he'd said, and she loved him for that.

To get inside the cave, you had to climb down steep, shallow steps the magic people had carved long ago into the rock. By the time they hit bottom, Lena's arms and legs were trembling with the effort and she didn't know how Nikolai had done it, even with her trying to bear as much of his weight as possible. The blackness was absolute, and she had to feel around for the pitch torch she hoped would still be in its bracket on the wall.

She found it and lit it with the tinderbox she'd stuffed deep inside the knapsack. The pitch burst into flame, lighting up the round, underground cavern.

And there it was, where it had always been, set into the wall: an ancient altar made out of human bones.

The altar of bones.

She'd started toward it, her aching muscles seeming to move on their own, when Nikolai let out a terrible groan and sagged slowly onto the floor. For a moment longer, she stared at the altar as if mesmerized, then she looked down at the man lying at her feet, and what she saw nearly stopped her heart.

"Nikki! Oh, God, Nikki . . ."

She fell to her knees beside him. How had he even managed to get himself this far? His lips were swollen and blue, his eyelashes frozen to his cheeks. His breathing was ragged, dangerously shallow.

Quickly, she built a fire using pieces of decaying coffins. Once she got the flames hot enough, she used an offering bowl from the altar to make a thin gruel out of melted snow and bread and fat from her knapsack.

"You're not going to die on me, Nikki. I promise. You're not going to die," she chanted, like a prayer, but he was out of his head with fever.

The bowl of gruel trembled in her hands as she looked from Nikolai's face, white as death, to the altar made of human bones. Skulls, femurs, fibulas, the hundreds of bones fitted intricately together to form an elaborate and macabre table of worship. On top of it, among the stubs of hundreds of melted candles, and battered bronze bowls that had once held offerings, sat the Lady—a wooden icon of the Virgin Mary.

The Lady's jewels sparkled in the firelight. Her crown shone and the bright folds of her robes—orange, sea green, and a bloodred—glowed as lush as the day they were painted, nearly four hundred years ago in the court of Ivan the Terrible. And it seemed to Lena that the Lady's eyes glimmered wet with tears over what she was about to do.

"I love him," Lena said. "I couldn't bear it if he dies."

But the Lady was silent.

"I promised him," she said. And still the Lady did not answer.

Lena made sure Nikolai still slept as if already dead, then she brought the bowl of gruel over to the altar and the icon. Because only with the Lady's help could she be sure that her promise would be kept.

WHEN SHE CAME back, she saw the fire had warmed Nikolai enough that she could rouse him some. She slid her arm under his shoulders and raised his head so he could drink. He took a sip. Then another.

His feverish eyes cleared a little and he looked around the cavern. She could see the wonder grow on his face as he took it all in, for this place, macabre and mysterious, had been a burial chamber for her people since the beginning of time. She watched him take in the deep, oily, black pool fed by water dripping from the ceiling, the stalagmites that covered the floor like rows of tombstones, the crude drawings of wolves etched deep in the stone walls.

Finally, he focused on the hot geyser bubbling and bellowing steam beneath the altar made of human bones, and she heard him suck in a sharp breath.

"My God."

Lena set down the bowl of gruel and leaned over him. "Sssh, love. Never mind." She brushed the wet hair off his forehead. "They're just the bones of people from long ago who died during the winter and were put here to be buried in the summer, only some ended up forgotten. And then other people came along and put their remains to another use."

"It's real." His voice was little more than a whisper, his eyes wild. "It's the sketch come to life, I tell you—from the Fontanka dossier. I never believed it, not in my heart. A wild tale told in a tavern by a drunken madman? But it's real . . . the altar of bones."

His gaze came back to her, and on his face she saw not only wonder now, but fear, and a raw, naked hunger. "Give it to me, Lena. Let me drink of the altar. If you love me, you will—"

But then his eyelids fluttered, and he passed out again.

Lena sat back on her heels. She could feel the Lady's eyes on her, but she couldn't bear to meet them. She looked instead at Nikolai's pale, fever-ravaged face.

His lying face.

———————

IT'S ALL BEEN *a lie*. Every kiss, every touch, every word out of his mouth—it had all just been a way for him to find the altar of bones.

Don't trust anyone, her mother had warned her, the day she had brought Lena to the cave and shown her its frightening secret. "You will be the Keeper of the altar of bones, my daughter, after I am gone, and your sacred duty will be to keep it hidden forever from the world. You must tell no one, show no one. Trust no one, not even the ones you love. Especially not the ones who say they love you."

The ones you love . . .

Lena reached out to touch him, then pulled her hand back, balling it into a fist in her lap.

She wondered if Nikolai Popov was even his real name, wondered now if he'd ever been a real prisoner. Most of the men at Norilsk were sent to slave in the nickel mines, but they'd made him the camp "artist" instead, putting him to work painting slogans and red stars outside on the infirmary walls. The infirmary where she conveniently worked, and he had the kind of ravishing good looks to catch any woman's eye.

But it was his defiant courage that had had won her heart. He told her he'd been sent to the gulag for drawing cartoons critical of Stalin and the Communist Party. "They are parasites. They feed off the fruits of our labor, all the while telling us how we should think, how we should be. I refuse to be a happy slave, Lena. There's another world beyond this place, for you and me. For us. A world of infinite possibilities."

He'd made it seem as if the escape were her idea, but she could see now how easily he'd manipulated things, telling her about the gap in the fence, about the forty-five seconds of no searchlights while the sentries changed shifts. And the cave . . . *But is there some place, Lena love, where we can hide until the soldiers give up looking for us?* How eagerly, how stupidly, she'd told him about the cave, how it was so cleverly hidden behind a waterfall on the lake where she'd been born.

What a truly gullible little fool you were, Lena Orlova.

He'd already known about the cave, obviously—not where it was, perhaps, but he'd known of its existence, and that she alone, of all the stupid females in the world, could lead him right to it. She'd been so very stupid. Stupid with love.

And Nikolai? Had he ever loved her, even a little?

Probably not. And, no, he'd never been a real prisoner. He was in the GUGB, surely. The secret police. One of Stalin's spies. He'd been half-delirious with fever, probably said more than he ever should have, but he'd let slip something about a dossier. The Fontanka dossier, he'd called it. Before the revolution, Fontanka 16 had been the infamous address of the headquarters for the tsar's own secret police. So how far back did this dossier go, and what was in it? *Who* was in it? A sketch of the altar, Nikki had said. A wild tale told in a tavern by a drunken madman. But what else? How much did he know?

Somehow he'd found out about the altar of bones. He would never rest now, the men he worked for would never rest, until they got their hands on its terrible power.

"I did love you, Nikki. So very much," she said, but he slept on.

Again she reached out to touch him, and again she stopped herself. One of the times they'd made love had been in the shed where they stored the paints. Afterward he had said, "Do you believe this can last forever, Lena?"

She hadn't wanted to give him too much of herself too soon, so she'd turned the question back at him. "Do you?"

"Yes. And I'm not talking about this," he said, touching her between her thighs. "But this . . ." His hand had moved up to press into the soft flesh just below her breast. "The blood I can feel right now pumping through your heart. And this." Then he'd taken her own hand and put it on his chest. "My own heart's lifeblood. Can you make my heart beat forever for you, Lena?

"Can you make our hearts beat as one until the end of time?"

3

L ENA ORLOVA sat before the dying embers of the fire and watched the man who called himself Nikolai Popov open his eyes. His fever had broken; he would live. His black, treacherous heart would go on beating, if not forever, at least for now.

He smiled at her, and then she knew the instant full awareness came, for his gaze left her face and went right to the altar made of bones, and she saw the greed and the hunger flare in his eyes before he looked away.

He yawned elaborately and stretched. "God, I'm feeling better. Like I might live after all. I'm never dosing myself with cooking salts again, though. I promise you that."

The way he was behaving, still acting the part of the escaped prisoner and her lover, she thought he must not remember what he'd said in his delirium, how he'd given himself away. Good. He would go on with his charade, and she would let him. If he thought she was onto him, he might kill her sooner rather than later.

And he would kill her, she understood that now. *I should have taken out my knife, Nikki, my love, and stabbed you through the heart while you slept.* But then she looked at his face, his beautiful face, and knew she could not have done it. Not while he slept.

He stood up slowly, testing his legs. Lena stood up as well. She slid her knife out of its sheath and held it down at her side, hidden within the folds of her padded coat.

He looked around the cave, careful not to dwell too long on the altar, then his dark, mesmerizing eyes met hers.

"Last night," he said, "I'd never have made it through the *purga* without you."

"I love you, Nikki." It was the simple truth. Still. Even though he was going to kill her.

He smiled. "And I wish I could say I could live on your love, Lena, my sweet, but the truth is I'm starving."

He clapped his hands, rubbed them together. He started to bend over the bowl to see if anything was left of the gruel she'd made, then he straightened, cocking his head, and a wary look came over his face.

"Something's different," he said.

Lena edged a step sideways, away from him. "It's the sudden silence after all those hours of howling wind. The storm's passed."

A new day had dawned, for she could see sunlight filtering through the narrow slit in the stone face above their heads that was the entrance to the cave. It flashed in the Lady's golden crown, shimmered in the black, oily pool of water.

"We should still hide out here for a while longer, though," she said, "until the soldiers give up looking for us. But we're going to need more snow to melt for drinking water."

She tried to make her movements casual as she walked past him and began to climb the steep steps, carved so many centuries ago into the rock. When she reached the narrow passageway at the top, she squeezed through it without looking back, and she felt a small flare of hope for escape because he hadn't tried to stop her.

She came out from behind the frozen waterfall so that she could look out over the snow-blanketed lake. On the distant shore, she saw a streamer of powdery snow. The streamer swelled, became a white cloud, and out of the cloud came an iron sleigh pulled by dogs.

———————

LENA HEARD THE squeak of a boot on fresh snow as Nikolai emerged from the slit in the rock and came up beside her. She turned to look at him, and a movement up on the bluff caught her eye. Last night's storm had dumped a huge mound of snow on top of the bluff, and the wind had sculpted it into a giant frozen wave that now jutted out above their heads.

Nikolai didn't notice; he was looking at the sleigh. It was cutting directly toward them across the frozen lake. "They've found us," he said. "The soldiers. Even with the *purga*, they tracked us here."

Lena still held her knife hidden within the bulk of her coat. She gripped it tighter. She knew, *purga* or not, that the soldiers hadn't had to follow any tracks, since they'd had a good idea of where their prey was going in the first place.

And she knew now why he hadn't killed her yet. He was going to let the soldiers do it for him.

"We have to give ourselves up," Nikolai said. "They'll go easier on us if we give ourselves up first."

"They never go easy on anyone, Nikki. You know that."

"I'll tell them I forced you to come with me. They'll spare you then."

She shook her head. His lies were too monstrous; she thought she might throw up.

The wind gusted, whipping ice crystals off the giant wave of snow above their heads. Lena was sure she'd seen it tremble, the crack at its base widening. Any loud noise now would bring an avalanche down right on top of them and bury the entrance to the cave.

Nikolai cupped the sides of her head with his hands and gave her a little shake. "Love, love, we're not going to make it. If we try to run now, they'll shoot us both and leave our bodies here in the snow for the wolves to find."

"They'll shoot us anyway." *Me. They'll shoot me. But not you, Nikki. Not you.*

The soldiers would know some of the truth, that he was really GUGB for instance, but he wouldn't have told them about the altar of bones. She wondered what tale he had spun for them, to get them out here to the lake with their sleigh.

He let her go and looked out across the lake, squinting against the glare of sun on ice. The sleigh was close enough now to see the soldiers' dark blue uniforms. There were only three of them.

Lena took a step back, then another and another, until she was behind the waterfall again, at the slit in the rocks, and well beneath the huge wave of snow on the bluff above. She could feel it trembling again, a vibration beneath her boots. Surely Nikolai could feel it, too? But, no, all his attention was focused on the sleigh and the soldiers, who were getting ever closer.

He turned around, and she lifted the knife, pointed it toward his heart. Its hooked blade flashed in the sun.

His gaze dropped to the knife, then went back to her face. "You know."

"That you are the secret police, a liar, and a thief? Yes, I know."

"Then you also know you're trapped. There's no way out for you, but you don't have to die."

She could hate him, she thought, if she didn't already love him so deeply. The worst of it was, she knew by the emptiness she saw in his eyes that he would watch her die and feel nothing at all.

"Still lying, Nikki. All the way up to the bitter end."

"Oh, come now. You must have believed me almost all the way up to the bitter end. Or you would never have given me the altar of bones."

"I didn't," she said, but her denial rang so hollow he laughed in her face.

"Of course you did. Otherwise I would not be standing here, feeling, you might say, like a new man—" He cut himself off, shaking his head. "Aw, Christ, Lena. I know what it's cost you. You mustn't think I'm not grateful."

"*Grateful.*" She choked over the word, hating herself because even now a part of her wanted him to go on lying. "I gave up everything for you. My honor. My life." *My heart.* "Did you not care for me at all, Nikki? Not even a little?"

He sighed and looked away. "Lena, Lena . . . does it matter?"

Was there regret in his voice? A twinge of sadness? No, he was right—it didn't matter. And which truth would hurt the least, anyway? Knowing that he loved her, yet had still betrayed her? Or that he'd never loved her at all?

He looked back at her once, for just a moment, then he turned and walked out from behind the waterfall, onto the frozen lake. He lifted his spread arms high into the air, as if he were surrendering. One of the soldiers cupped his hands around his mouth and bellowed, "Halt!"

The soldier's shout carried across the ice like the crack of a rifle shot. For an instant the earth went still, then Lena heard an echoing rumble. She looked up to see the huge, thick snow-wave break free of the bluff above. It plummeted in heavy slabs to hit the ground in front of her, roaring now, billowing in a giant cloud of ice, obliterating her last sight of Nikolai on the lake, obliterating the world.

4

D ON'T SHOOT! I surrender, don't shoot!"
Captain Nikolai Popov lifted his arms higher into the air as the sleigh squeaked to a stop on the ice. One of the soldiers leveled a rifle at his chest. The lead dog growled.

"Don't shoot," Nikolai said again. The camp commandant should already have ordered his men not to open fire, but you could never be too careful.

"Comrade Captain," the commandant shouted as he lumbered his heavy bulk off the sleigh. A wide smile cracked his beefy, wind-raw face. "When I saw that avalanche come down, I thought for a moment there we'd lost you. And what about the girl? Is she all right?"

The commandant used the heel of his glove to knock off the ice caked on his mustache as he looked past Nikolai up to the raw gash in the bluff where the giant wave of frozen snow had just moments before been hanging suspended out over the waterfall and the entrance to the cave. Ice crystals still swirled in the air around them. Nikolai's ears rang from the noise it had made.

"The girl," Nikolai said, as he slowly lowered his arms, "has just been buried under twenty feet of snow and ice. Thanks to your man there." He nodded toward the soldier with the rifle, who was staring at them stupidly now, his mouth agape. "The braying ass. He should be shot."

"But, sir?" the soldier sputtered. "How is it my fault? You said we had to make things seem real. All I did was—"

"Shut up, Private Lukin," the commandant said. "And put down your gun, you idiot. Didn't I tell you he's one of us? Sergeant Chirkov, see to the dogs."

The sergeant who'd been sitting as if frozen to the sled, the reins forgotten in his hands, jerked into life. "But, sir, what about Le—about Comrade Orlova? There's air pockets sometimes. She might still be alive."

The private slung his rifle over his shoulder and jumped off the sleigh. "I for one don't care anymore if we get to fuck her silly before we haul her back to camp. I'm not digging through all that snow even if we had a shovel, which we don't."

"Forget about the girl. Both of you," the commandant said.

He jerked his head at Nikolai and walked farther away from the sleigh so they couldn't be overheard. Nikolai followed, slipping his left hand into his coat pocket to wrap his fingers around the grip of the pistol that had been riding there since just before he'd followed Lena Orlova through the infirmary window.

"Right before the avalanche," the commandant said, lowering his voice nearly to a whisper, "I saw you come out from behind the waterfall. So is that where the entrance to the cave is, then?"

"Where it was."

The commandant made a soothing motion with his hand. "Yes, yes, all right. But it can always be dug out later—I've got a camp full of *zeks* and shovels. The important thing is, did you get inside? Did you see the gold?"

Nikolai shook his head. "This whole thing was a waste of everybody's time. It's a small, circular cavern, no more than twenty feet in diameter, and I got a really good look at all of it, believe me. Nothing's in there but some rotting caskets and a few moldering corpses."

The commandant, Nikolai could tell, did not believe him, and he hid a smile. He wouldn't have believed himself either.

He'd spun the man a tale about how some Party hack back in Moscow had heard a wild rumor that twenty years ago the tsar's army had stashed a treasure in a cave on a secret lake near Norilsk, and that he, Nikolai, had been sent up here to check it out. Now the commandant suspected that Nikolai had found the gold, but was going to keep it all for himself.

"Didn't I tell you it was going to be a wild-goose chase?" Nikolai said. "These Yaks have never had two rubles to rub together. Were they going to leave chests full Romanov gold lying about just for pretty? Lot of bloody trouble for nothing, if you ask me. But then I only do what I'm told."

The commandant forced a laugh. "As do we all."

The dogs suddenly erupted into a frenzy of barking. Nikolai whirled, almost pulling out his pistol, before he realized the dogs were only excited because the sergeant had taken a burlap sack full of dried fish out of the sleigh. The private, Nikolai saw, had walked a few steps downwind and was fumbling with the buttons to his trousers.

"A wild-goose chase indeed," the commandant said. "And we couldn't have picked a worse night for it, could we? What with that bit of a blow we had."

Nikolai suddenly laughed. With all that had been going on this morning, he hadn't fully noticed it before, but he really *did* feel like a new man. It seemed he could feel each separate breath he took, each beat of his heart. And the breaths, the heartbeats, were endless.

"Bit of a blow?" he said, and laughed again. "Fuck your mother. It almost killed me."

Those damn cooking salts—they were supposed to have given him just enough of a fever for the doctor to admit him into the infirmary. He certainly hadn't planned on giving himself pneumonia. But it had all been worth it in the end, because Lena had brought him to the cave. She'd given him the altar of bones.

The altar—Christ, it was real. Every bit of what he'd seen in the Fontanka dossier was real. The lake, the waterfall, the cave, the altar made out of human bones. And the Keeper. She had proven to be real, too.

Lena.

He had thought it would be hard to find her in all this frozen wilderness, but she'd been right there at the prison camp, no more than twenty miles from the lake where she, and all the other Keepers who had come before her, had been born. And her face, it was the very image of the sketch he'd seen of the Lady in the icon. The dossier had been right about that as well.

He wondered now if she'd made it back inside the cave before the avalanche could bury her. And he felt a pang of . . . what? Guilt? Loss? Regret? It didn't matter, she was dead either way. She would starve to death before she could dig her way out.

The commandant, as if he'd read Nikolai's mind, sighed. "Too bad about the girl, though."

"Yes. Too bad," Nikolai said.

Well, he *had* used her badly, and he felt that sharp pang again, like a fist to the chest. He shook it off. You did what you had to do and went on.

He looked around the lake, beautiful in the butter yellow arctic light—a pity it would last only a couple of hours before the sun set again. Time enough, though, for him to get where he had to go.

"Just look at that fool, would you?" the commandant said with a sudden laugh of his own as he pointed to the private, who was writing his initials in the snow with his pee.

"I told you he should be shot," Nikolai said.

The commandant blinked and his smile slipped a little, but then he slapped his hands together. "Well, then, Comrade Captain," he said a little too loudly. "How about a nip of vodka before we head back to the camp?"

The commandant thrust his hand into his coat pocket, but before he could take it out again, Nikolai pulled out his pistol and put a bullet between the man's eyes.

The shot cracked loud over the lake. The private whipped around, his penis still in his hands. He opened his mouth, but his scream died as the bullet plowed through his throat.

The sergeant stood as if stupefied, a dried fish in each hand while the dogs still barked and leaped around him. Then he dropped the fish and ran toward the sleigh. Nikolai shot him between the shoulder blades and he went down hard, his head bouncing on the ice.

Even as the gunfire still echoed in the frigid air, Nikolai was already moving. One at a time, he went to the three men and emptied the pistol into their heads, making sure they were dead. Then he reloaded.

He tucked the gun into the waistband of his trousers. He started toward the sleigh, then turned back. He squatted beside the dead commandant and felt inside the man's coat pocket. He pulled out a flask, silver with engraved initials.

So he hadn't been going for a gun after all.

Nikolai dropped the flask of vodka into his own pocket and stood up. He climbed into the sleigh, smiling. The commandant and his men had served Nikolai's purpose well, bringing the sleigh out here. Nobody in their right mind would try *walking* out of Siberia.

He picked up the reins, but before he drove off, he looked back toward the frozen waterfall, shimmering and sparkling in the sun like a cascade of diamonds.

Diamonds. Nikolai smiled at thought. For what the waterfall hid was more valuable than diamonds, more valuable than any make-believe chest of Romanov gold.

The altar of bones . . . dear God, it *was* real. He'd seen it with his own eyes. He'd drunk from it. Already he could feel its incredible power coursing through his blood, changing him. He felt like a god.

No, not *like* a god.

He threw back his head, and his shout echoed over the raw, frozen land.

"I am God!"

PART TWO

THE BIG KILL

5

Father Dom hated that horrible hiss as oxygen was forced into the failing lungs, but he leaned closer to his father's mouth. The old man was dying and he wanted to confess.

Confess. That was the word he'd used, even though Dom didn't really believe it. Not from his devoutly atheist father, who'd once called religion the greatest con game ever perpetrated on the human race. But "I'm dying and I want to confess," his father had said, then he gave this wild laugh that nearly killed him right there.

"Aw, quit acting like you've been hit with the proverbial thunderbolt," the old man said now. "I'm not gonna start shouting hallelujahs and I haven't gone stupid on you either, if those two afflictions aren't already redundant. I just have something that needs saying and I obviously don't got all livelong day."

"I'm here for you, Dad. But so, too, is the loving and forgiving presence of our Lord."

Dom winced inside at how trite that sounded, but then his father had always been able to make him feel and behave like some ridiculous caricature of a priest. Most days Dom loved being what he was, and he was good at it, but sometimes he thought he'd put on the white bands of the Holy Roman Catholic Church just to spite Michael O'Malley, because he'd known it would piss off the old man for all eternity.

Only now his father was dying, so Father Dominic O'Malley laid his hand on the graying head as he began the last rites. "Through this holy anointing may the Lord in his love and mercy help you with the grace of the Holy Spirit—"

The old man shook his head so hard he nearly tore the oxygen tube out of his nostrils. "Shut up with that ridiculous nonsense. I said confess, not die with the dirge of medieval hocus-pocus assaulting my ears."

"But I thought you . . ." Dom swallowed something that felt halfway between a laugh and a sob, then looked quickly away before his father could rag on him for his weakness. He wished just once the old man could have . . . what? Respected him? Accepted him? Loved him?

"Okay, you win. No more medieval hocus-pocus. Only you know what? You can deny Him all the way up to your last breath, but Christ has never denied you. He's always loved you, and so have I."

The old man blew out a ragged sigh. "You've always been so full of pompous and sentimental certainties. Not only is it tedious, but when paired with your naïveté, it can be downright dangerous. You don't know what I've done."

"Then tell me. Confess. And we'll even leave the Lord out of the conversation, because a godless confession can still be the first step to forgiveness and salvation."

"What baloney. No God worth his salt is going to let puling sinners worm their way back into his good graces just by kissing his ass. Dom"— he felt his father's hand clutch his arm—"quit mouthing religious platitudes for once and focus here."

Such strength still in those fingers, Dom thought. But the old man had always been tough. Texas tough, he liked to brag, like a boot full of barbed wire. Dom stared down now at his father's mouth, bloodless from lack of oxygen, at his watery blue eyes that looked clouded with what?

Fear?

No, Dom thought, that simply wasn't possible. The father he knew had never shown a lick of fear in his life. It was part of the code Michael O'Malley lived by. When things turned bad on you, you sucked it up. You didn't bawl, or whine, or make excuses.

His father released the grip he had on Dom's arm and gave it a surprisingly gentle pat. "Hey, it's okay, son. It'll be okay. It's snuck up on me, this death business. I need you to call your brother, call Ry, and tell him to get down here now. He'll know what to do—" A vicious cough racked the old man, and he let his head fall back on the pillow, closed his eyes. "Call Ry . . ."

"I already did, Dad. He's on his way."

Forgive me, dear Lord for that big honking lie.

They'd often called their father "the old man" even when they were kids, but he really wasn't all that old. Only seventy-five, and when you looked at him, you saw a big, strapping man, still full of vigor and a lust for life, or at least until yesterday.

Yesterday morning Michael O'Malley got up with the dawn, went for his daily power walk on the beach, and ate a breakfast of granola and yogurt. Then he stood up to put the dirty dishes in the sink and was struck by a massive coronary. On his way to the hospital, Dom had called and left a message on his brother's cell, then he'd called again after the doctors had given their prognosis—their dad's heart had been damaged beyond any hope. It would go on pumping for a little while yet, but soon it would stop. Just stop.

As the hours passed, and the old man grew steadily weaker, Dom kept trying to get hold of his brother, kept getting that damn voice mail. Ry not only wasn't on his way to Galveston, God alone knew when they would even hear back from him. He'd been known to drop off the face of the earth for weeks, even months, at a time.

Dom touched his father's hand where it lay, looking waxy and already dead, on the white hospital sheet. "In the meantime, why don't you try to get some sleep. We can all talk later, after Ry gets here." *Or doesn't.*

He saw his father's lips twist with a sudden spasm of pain. "Dad? Are you all right?"

He reached for the morphine drip, but the old man stopped him. "No, don't. That stuff makes it hard for me to think, and we're running out of time. I know I said I had a confession to make, but that was a poor choice of words. I don't have any use for a priest, and if that hurts your tender feelings—tough."

That *did* hurt, actually, but Dom managed to keep it off his face.

"Talk to me as your son, then. Or better yet, as an equal, a fellow human being. Now that would make a nice change."

The old man gave him a ghastly smile. "You live with this thing you call a God, Dom. You preach goodness, turning the other cheek, doing unto others, all that bull, so you think you know all about bad. Only you got no idea. Not the kind of bad I'm talking about. The pure, down and dirty kind of bad that knows no rules and has no stopping point—"

The old man broke off, looked away. His eyes darkened, turned inward, and Dom wondered what they saw. Michael O'Malley had married late, at the age of forty-one, and much of his earlier life had always been a blank slate to his wife and sons. But what he'd just implied—Dom didn't want to believe it. *You're talking about evil, Dad, and you could never do evil.*

Could you?

He saw an odd look come over his father's face. Not dreamy or nostalgic. No, it was too intense for that.

"Katya was her name. Katya Orlova, and from the beginning there was something special about her. In those days Hollywood had more pretty blondes than palm trees, but Katya . . . She had this luminescence about her, this glow, as if the sun was inside her, shining through the pores of her skin. And did I tell you she had the damnedest eyes? Dark gray, like storm clouds."

The old man's mind seemed to be wandering, but Dom got the gist of it: another woman. He might have known. Since he couldn't shut his ears, he shut his eyes and saw his mother's face. The sprinkling of freckles like cinnamon flakes across her cheekbones and nose, those dimples every time she smiled and she'd smiled a lot, even at the very end when the breast cancer finally beat her.

"Aw, Christ, Dom. Quit looking like I'm breaking your heart. Katya Orlova was just a means to an end. I never loved her, not like I did your mother."

Dom blinked away tears, angrier with himself than his father. *Why do I always let him get to me like this?* "So who was she then?"

But his father said nothing more. The watery blue eyes seemed lost now, staring across the foot of his bed at the mint green wall that was empty except for a black-enamel, plain-faced clock.

"Dad?"

"I've been watching that clock," the old man finally said. "Every time another minute goes by, the long hand does this little jump from one hash mark to the next. Sometimes it trembles before it moves, like it's not really sure it wants to go there, but it does it anyway. And it makes this little *click* noise, like it's checking off another minute of eternity, and I've been thinking how one of these times soon that clock is going to do its little tremble-jump-and-click routine, but me . . . I'm going to be too damn dead to see it."

He took his gaze off the clock and looked at his son. "All those rituals and sacraments of yours—what do you really think they're for? In the end we're all the same. We're all afraid of that long dark night, and so we hold sacred the one thing we think can save us."

Dom shook his head. "What are you telling me? That you thought this Katya Orlova woman could somehow have saved your soul?"

The thin mouth opened on a sigh. "Could have given me more time . . ."

Dom leaned closer. "Time to do what?"

The old man shook with another bout of violent coughing that sapped his strength, and the room fell back into silence again except for the hiss and beeps of the machines.

Dom thought his father was done talking, but then he said, "No, not my soul, and it doesn't matter anymore. Maybe it never mattered, because a heart attack from out of the blue or a shot behind the ear from a .22 and either way, bang! You're deader than a doornail."

A shot behind the ear from a .22? That kind of talk was so unlike the man he knew, Dom thought it had to be the painkillers messing with his head.

He was sure of it an instant later when his father tried to grab at the handrails to pull himself out of bed, his eyes wild. "Time . . . we're running out of time, Dom. They'll be coming for you boys once I'm dead, because they'll figure they're safe then. You'll be loose threads to them, just for being my sons. And loose threads get snipped."

He lay back gasping. "They probably already got a man inside the hospital here, waiting for me to croak. Or a woman. Some female doctor I've never seen before showed up to poke and prod at me while you were down in the cafeteria getting coffee. Red hair and that angels-weep kind of beautiful, but I don't like her smile. She's got a killer's smile."

What was he trying to say? That a female assassin was lurking here in the hospital, waiting for Michael O'Malley to die so she could then bump off the man's sons? Dom tried to stop himself from jerking around to check out the open doorway, did it anyway, and felt like a fool. No one was there.

"Who's coming for us? The Mafia? The Columbia drug cartel? Who really does stuff like that?"

A hideous laugh tore out of the old man's throat. "My partners in crime."

Something suddenly seemed stuck in Dom's throat; he had to swallow twice before he could get a word out. "Are you telling me you were some kind of gangster in a past life? I won't believe it."

"Hunh. So says the man who's got no trouble wrapping his head around the idea of a virgin giving birth."

The old man's eyelids fluttered, but then he pulled himself back through sheer will. "You boys've got to find her," he said, his voice faint, raspy. "Find Katya and get it back."

"Get what back, Dad? I'm sorry, but this is just crazy talk—"

"The *film*. The film Katya made of my last kill. Them thinking I had the film is the only thing that's kept us alive all these years."

"What film? What last *kill*, for God's sakes. I know you. You couldn't—"

"Dammit, Dom, get your head around the idea that I'm not who you think I am. I never was. . . ." He drew in a strangled breath and closed his eyes.

Dom shot a look at the monitors. His father's blood pressure was up to 180 over 95, his breathing now so torturous he could barely speak. His hands opened and closed, as if he were trying to grab his strength back out of the air.

"Dad, maybe you should—"

"Shut up and listen to me, boy. I was ordered to do the kill, so I did it. It wasn't like I had a choice in the matter, I was already in too deep. But I knew right from the get-go that once a hit that big went down, they were going to have to kill the killer, if you know what I mean." He grimaced, baring his teeth. "So she got it all in living color, Katya did. It was supposed to be my insurance, the thing that would keep me alive. But a couple of days later, she disappeared on me. And she took the film with her."

Dom looked into his father's eyes and he saw fear, but he also saw sanity. And deep inside where darkness and truth burrowed deep, Dom knew: Mike O'Malley, who'd run a little charter fishing boat off the Gulf Coast, a man who wouldn't even use a pellet gun to chase the jackrabbits out of his vegetable garden, had once been ordered to murder someone and he'd done it. And somewhere there was a film of the crime.

The old man grabbed Dom's arm, but little strength was left in him anymore. "After Katya took off with the film, Dom, I let them go on thinking I still had it. But it was all one big, bad-assed bluff, and now—"

The word ended on another strangled cough. The oxygen hissed, his chest gurgled. "You better pray to that God of yours Katya Orlova isn't long dead, because only she knows where the film really is. You and Ry, you've got to find her and get it back, and you've got to do it fast. Prove to them you have that film and it'll be your life insurance, like it was mine."

Who did you murder, Dad? It was the obvious question, but for some crazy reason the words were all balled up in Dom's mouth, he couldn't get them out. If he said them aloud, they'd be real, and he couldn't do that yet.

"You keep saying *them*," he said instead. "Who are they, these guys who made you . . . ?"

Kill.

The old man shook his head, almost dislodging the oxygen tube again. "The details are for when Ry gets here, because it's a long, ugly story and I've barely got enough life left in me to tell it once. And Ry will understand, he'll know what to do. Call him again, Dom."

"Why can't you for once trust me, rely on me? I don't live in a damn bubble, I know how to do things—" Dom drew in a deep breath, let it out, made his voice calm, soothing. "I'll call him again, Dad, I promise, only I don't think he's going to make it here in time."

The old man gave Dom a smile that froze his soul and nodded slowly, accepting the truth. "All right then," he whispered, phlegm thick in his throat. "It all started with Katya Orlova and the altar of bones, but it ended with the kill."

He laughed again, that hideous noise that shouldn't come from a human mouth. "And not just any kill, but *the* kill. The big kill."

Dom started to take his rosary out of his pocket, then left it there. He picked up his father's hand instead, and this time the dying man let him keep it.

"What big kill?" he asked.

And his father told him.

6

SOMETHING CLATTERED out in the hallway, and Father Dom whipped around. But it was only an orderly, pushing a cart stacked with lunch trays, broccoli and chicken by the smell. He fought down the urge to gag.

He turned back to the bed. His father slept now, so utterly still Dom wondered if he'd slipped into a coma.

He looked at his father's hands, lying flaccid at his sides, at the age spots, the protruding veins, the knuckles only a little crooked and swollen from arthritis. He saw those hands raise the rifle, his father's eyes line up the sights. He heard the shot and saw the bullet smash through flesh and bone, and the blood. So much blood—

"No, you couldn't have done that," he said out loud, but the old man didn't answer. And if he had, Dom thought, it would only have been to sneer at him for not being man enough to accept the truth.

That his father was a monster.

He stared down at the lax face for a moment longer, then he put his priest's sacramental stole around his neck, made the sign of the cross in holy oil on his father's forehead and performed the rite of final absolution. Forgiving Michael O'Malley for his sins, even if he hadn't wanted to be forgiven.

The act, the words, Dom knew, were really for himself.

When he was done, he hesitated a moment, then leaned over and kissed his father's sunken cheek and asked that soulless face, "Who are you?"

Out in the hall an intercom crackled, calling for a Dr. Elder to report to radiology. Dom sat down in the chair next to his father's bed, rested his elbows on his spread knees. He fingered his rosary, but no prayers were in him. He had a sudden, horrible fear he would never be able to pray again.

He didn't know how long he sat there like that, but suddenly he was aware the room felt different. The machines still beeped, the oxygen hissed, but it was quieter somehow. Emptier.

His head snapped up. "Dad?" he said, and knew even before he looked that his father was gone. A split instant later the machines caught up to reality and the steady beeps turned into a screeching alarm.

For maybe five seconds more, Dom stared at the shell of what had once been Michael O'Malley. Then he pushed to his feet and ran from the room.

════════

HE STOOD IN the middle of the hall while doctors and nurses rushed past and the intercom blared, "Code blue! Code blue!" His heart pounded, but already he was feeling foolish. Running from phantoms.

Within moments the hallway emptied, leaving him alone. He rubbed his hands over his face. His eyes burned, but he couldn't cry.

The elevator opened and an orderly with an empty gurney came out, followed by a woman. She wore green scrubs with a stethoscope dangling half out of one pocket, and she had . . .

Red hair and that angels-weep kind of beautiful.

They made eye contact for an instant, then she turned away and went to the nurses' station. She picked up a chart, and although she seemed to be reading it, Dom felt an energy coming off her, like an electric charge, and that energy was focused on him.

The orderly had also stopped at the nurses' station, but now he was pushing the gurney down the hall, disappearing around the corner. Dom's gaze followed for an instant, and when he looked back around, he saw the woman in the green scrubs was coming toward him.

She slipped her hand into her pocket, the one without the stethoscope, and she smiled.

Dom whirled and ran in the direction the man with the gurney had taken, his father's words blaring an alarm in his head . . . *loose threads . . . she's got a killer's smile . . . it's just as likely to be a bullet to the head.*

But she wouldn't dare shoot him here, in front of witnesses, would she?

He rounded the corner, the leather of his black priest's shoes slipping on the waxed linoleum. He spotted a blue restroom sign and ducked inside. It was a single occupancy: one toilet, one sink.

He locked the door, then tested the handle to be sure it held. He leaned back against the wall, his hands flat at his sides. His chest heaved. He strained his ears for any sound out in the hall, but all he could hear was his own harsh panting.

He waited for what seemed an eternity, then went to the sink and splashed water on his face.

He stared at the same face he'd seen when he'd shaved this morning. Brown hair, brown eyes. A fairly ordinary face, really, except for those ridiculously deep dimples that he'd always hated because they belonged on a cheerleader's cheeks, but not on a guy. Guys were supposed to be too tough for dimples, even guys who were priests.

The door handle rattled and Dom froze, not even breathing. The handle rattled again, but whoever was on the other side didn't knock or call out. The silence dragged on and on, then Dom heard footsteps walking away.

He gripped the sink with both hands and leaned over it, squeezing his eyes shut. His father was dead. Michael O'Malley was dead, except there had never been a Michael O'Malley. That man was an illusion, a lie. Or his dying words had been a lie. One or the other, because those two realities couldn't exist simultaneously in this universe.

The big kill.

Dom jerked his phone from his pocket and punched in his brother's cell number on speed dial, praying, praying he wouldn't get shunted off to voice mail again. For long, agonizing seconds there was just dead air, and then Dom heard a ring.

Come on, Ry. Come on, man. . . . Ry would know what to do. Maybe their old man was right, maybe Dom didn't have a gut understanding of evil, but his brother did. Ry O'Malley had been living with it, up close and personal, for years.

The phone rang on and on. *Merciful God in heaven, please—*

The ringing ended abruptly, and Dom nearly sagged to the floor with relief. But when the computer voice clicked in, he cut the connection.

He'd almost done something really stupid. Ry had to be told, to be warned, but not like this. Weren't cell phones like two-way radios? Anyone could be listening in.

So think, Dom. Think . . .

He couldn't stay locked up in this bathroom forever. He heard deep voices, rough laughter, out in the hall. He went to the door, unlocked and cracked it open. A young man with his leg in a cast up to his hip bone was leaving the hospital, surrounded by a rowdy group of uniform cops. Big, tough-looking bruisers they were, with guns on their hips.

Father Dom joined them.

AN IRISH PUB was a block down from the hospital, a favorite haunt of the EMT crews coming off their shifts. The bartender's eyebrows went up a notch at the sight of the white collar, but he gave Dom change for a twenty-dollar bill and pointed out the pay phone, in the hall leading to the kitchen, next to the toilets.

It was dark back there and stank of stale beer and grease, but Dom barely noticed. He punched in his brother's home number. He didn't expect Ry would be there to answer it, but it was a landline with an answering machine. Was that safer than a cell phone? It didn't matter. Ry needed to be warned.

As he listened to the ringing on the other end, he rubbed his face, felt the wetness of tears.

Then Ry's voice, tough and to the point: "Leave a message."

Dom gripped the phone tighter. Over the pounding of his heart he heard the beep of the machine.

"Ry? It's about Dad. He's dead, and—" Dom choked back sobs, then pressed the heel of his hand into his forehead, tried to pull himself to-gether. *You're a grown man, for mercy's sake, and Michael O'Malley's son, so you really should be tougher than this.*

He drew in a deep breath, let it out slowly. Yes, that was more like it. He heard a door open and close behind him, the rap of heels on the pegwood floor, and he jerked around. At first all he saw were black stilet-tos, then the flash of red hair.

He dropped the phone. It clattered and banged against the wall, but the noise it made wasn't as loud as the banging of his heart. He watched the woman emerge from out of the shadows. It wasn't the doctor from the hospital; this woman was older, not as pretty. He thought he'd puke with relief.

She walked past Dom without seeming to see him. He wiped his sweating hand on his pant leg and picked up the phone.

"Ry?"

7

Washington, D.C.

THE TWO men in their designer threads and custom-made shoes quickly crossed the street, jaywalking just so they wouldn't have to meet him on the narrow sidewalk head on. Ry O'Malley gave them a little curled-fingers wave, then laughed to himself as he watched the two suits try to decide whether to wave back or run like hell.

He knew he looked scary as all get out, a real badass with his long hair and tattoos and biker's black leather jacket. This part of Columbia Heights had been flirting with gentrification for years, but enough stubborn pockets of crime and poverty remained so that at cocktail parties the biggest topic of conversation was how to get a permit to carry.

As Ry turned the corner, he heard the stutter and hiccup of an engine badly in need of a tune-up come up behind him. Dusk was just falling, and he paused under a streetlamp to take a pack of cigarettes and disposable lighter out of his jacket pocket. He didn't smoke, but the ritual of stopping to light up was a good way to do a little recon without being obvious about it.

The sick engine, he saw, was under the hood of a small red van with GIOVANNI'S PIZZERIA painted in white script on the side panels. The van chugged past him and pulled up next to a fire hydrant. A kid with spiked hair and a nose ring got out, carrying one of those insulated cases that were supposed to keep the pies hot but left them soggy instead.

Ry watched the kid climb the steps and ring the bell of a brownstone town house, then he tossed the cigarette into the gutter and crossed the street. A lamp also shone in the bay window of his own Queen Anne–style shotgun, but it was set on a timer. No one was waiting inside to welcome him home.

He let himself in, stepping over the pile of junk mail and flyers that had accumulated beneath the slot in the front door. He shut off the alarm and went into the living room, took off his leather jacket and flung it at a leather sofa.

His Walther P99 was tucked gangbanger-style in the small of his back, and he took it out and laid it on the iron-banded Spanish chest he used for a coffee table. The chest was a gift from the prima-ballerina girlfriend he'd lived with for a while, until she'd grown tired of the long separations, of not knowing where he was or what he was doing, or whether the next time she saw him would be on a slab in a morgue.

He sat on the chest and unlaced his boots. They had steel in the toes and one kick with them could cave in a man's ribs or his head, but that made them heavy as hell. It felt good to get them off his feet. He padded barefoot into the kitchen and made himself a very dry and very cold martini. He never drank while on a job and he shuddered now as the icy gin bit the back of his throat.

He had his feet up, Stan Getz on the stereo, and the martini was half-gone before he noticed the blinking red light on his telephone answering machine.

He waited until the last, piercing notes of *Body and Soul* died away before he got up and went to the antique Dickens desk that faced the room's big bay window. Through the deepening dusk outside, he could see his next-door neighbor trying to defy the laws of physics by squeezing his SUV into a parking space three inches too small. And the border collie who lived on the corner was taking her owner out for a walk. He watched as they went from the lamppost, to the fire hydrant, to the tire of the pizza delivery van. His ballerina girlfriend had called it "leaving pee-mails," and the memory almost made Ry smile.

He reached out and pressed the play button, and the machine's hollow voice said, *You have one new message. Thursday, August twelve, four fifty-three p.m.* And then his brother, sounding raw and broken, "Ry?"

The only other word he could make out through Dom's strangling sobs was "dead."

Dad?

Ry's throat closed up, but he shook his head. No way could it be Dad. Ry had gone home over the holidays and the old man had never seemed better. He was still grieving for Mom, sure, and for the loss of their home from the devastation of Hurricane Ike, but otherwise . . . Hell, that game of horse they'd played on Christmas morning—he'd almost kicked Ry's ass.

Had there been some kind of accident? A car crash? The old man liked to take his boat out on the Gulf this time of year, maybe a squall had come up . . .

What had the machine said? August 12? That was two days ago.

Come on, out with it, Dom. What in God's name happened?

He heard a banging noise, as if Dom had dropped the phone, then a burst of laughter, the clatter of billiard balls. His brother said, "Ry?" again, then a mechanical voice cut in demanding seventy-five cents for another three minutes.

He heard coins being fed into a slot, followed by his brother's voice, sounding scared now, "Oh, God, Ry. This woman came out of the ladies' room and she had red hair, and after what Dad said, I thought . . ."

There was a pause as Dom took a couple of deep breaths, then his next words came out clear and relatively calm.

And strange as hell.

"Dad's had a heart attack, Ry. Dad's gone, and now they're going to come after us, because of what he did. The big kill."

"The big *what*?" Ry said, but his gaze was already sweeping the street outside, every molecule of his being alert.

He heard his brother draw in another ragged breath, go on, "I know I'm not making any sense, but I can't . . . not over the phone. You need to get down here fast, Ry, and I'll explain everything—" Dom made a noise, as if he'd started to laugh, then almost gagged. "I mean, I'll tell you what Dad told me, which isn't enough, not nearly enough. But for now just know there may be people out there who are going to try to ki—"

Ry pressed the stop button, cutting off his brother's disembodied voice.

The pizza van.

The red pizza-delivery van that had followed him around the corner, that had pulled up next to the fire hydrant over thirty minutes ago now.

Ry dove for the floor just as the van's side door slapped open and the bay window exploded. *Uzi*, he thought as he rolled, snatched the Walther off the chest, and came back onto his feet. He pressed his back against the room's inner wall, out of the line of fire from the street.

In the kitchen, the door to the backyard crashed open under the force of what had to be either the world's biggest foot or an honest-to-God battering ram. Ry reached around the doorjamb with the Walther and emptied half a clip down the hall. More Uzis returned fire, tearing up walls and furniture. Wood splintered, glass shattered, plaster dust billowed in the air.

Whoever these guys were, they weren't being subtle. And they were professional, taking their time to coordinate their attack, surrounding the house, cutting off any escape route, hitting it hard and fast, and getting out before the cops arrived. Which meant he had a minute, maybe two, before they came at him with everything they had. Ry had another couple of clips in the inside pocket of his leather jacket, but he needed more ammo, and another gun.

The floor plan to his small house was simple. The front door opened into a tiny foyer with a staircase going up and a long, narrow hallway leading back to the kitchen. To the left were the living and dining rooms, separated by pocket doors. Above, was one large bedroom and bath. He had a basement, but the only entrance to it was off the kitchen where the bad guys were, and it was a dead end anyway.

There was no place for him to escape to, no place to hide, and he was fast running out of time.

Ry kept his ammo and extra guns, including a pump-action twelve-gauge shotgun, in a wall safe behind a panel of wainscoting next to the fireplace in the living room. He fired most of the rest of the clip down the hall, then dropped and rolled past the open doorway. He commando-crawled across the floor, picking up his jacket on the way. He slapped one of the fresh clips into his gun and lay down another spray of fire. He got return fire, but it was still coming from the kitchen. He'd slowed them down, but he hadn't stopped them.

He popped the wall panel and spun the dial to the safe. Barely two minutes had passed since they'd blown in the window and battered down the back door, still he strained to hear the distant wail of sirens. The emergency response system had to be flooded with calls by now, so where were the goddamn cops?

The safe clicked open. He jerked up on the handle, swung open the door—

Shit.

Ry's belly clenched into a fist of fear. The guns, the ammo, were gone. In their place were two brick-size packages of white powder wrapped in clear plastic. It could be powdered sugar or flour, but Ry didn't think so. He had to be looking at six kilos of pure-grade heroin.

Jesus. Who were *these guys?* They'd bypassed his state-of-the-art security system, stolen his guns, and planted the smack in his locked safe, then staged what would look like a drug deal gone bad. He knew the D.C. cops weren't coming now. Whoever these guys were, they had gold-plated connections. Federal, probably, and this operation would be completely off the books.

He heard movement out in the kitchen, the squeak of rubber soles on tile, the metallic snap of weapons being readied. There'd be three guys, he thought, maybe four. And figure another couple guys waiting in the street, by the pizza van, in case by some miracle he made it through the front door alive.

A bookcase flanked the other side of the fireplace. Ry jumped to his feet, spun around, and flattened himself against the wall. Now he had the bookcase between himself and whatever came at him from the kitchen, not that a few inches of walnut and bound paper were going to stop the 950 rounds per minute that came from an Uzi submachine gun.

He was also vulnerable to the street here. At least the first shots through the window had blown out the lamp so the room was in darkness. Except for the red light on his answering machine. He desperately needed to listen to the rest of Dom's message.

Dad's gone, and now they're going to come after us, because of what he did.

Going to come, shit—they were already here. He'd been fucked before, but not this fucked.

He reloaded, pointed the Walther in a two-fisted grip at the open door, and blinked the sweat out of his eyes.

Galveston, Texas

AT THE SAME time, in Sacred Heart's peaceful quiet, Father Dom was hearing confessions. He sat behind the thick purple velvet curtain, in the closetlike darkness of the confessional box. He was adrift, empty of all feeling. He'd even stopped being afraid, but then he supposed that was because the human psyche could only live on an emotional knife-edge for so long.

He'd thought about running, disappearing, but he had no idea how to go about it, and besides, he had obligations, duties. A priest could no more abandon his flock than a father and husband could walk away from his family. And so he went on with his life. He'd buried his father, celebrated mass, baptized a baby, read his breviary, tried to pray. And everywhere he looked, every time he turned around, it seemed there was another redheaded woman. Even the woman in the funeral home had red hair, although it was probably from a bottle since she was at least sixty. Who knew there were so many red-haired women in Galveston?

He heard the far-off ring of the telephone in the rectory and then silence. Something wasn't right. It was too quiet. No one had entered the confessional box for a while now, and he could hear no movement out in the nave, no voices. Where were the tourists? They came every evening at this time, drawn by the setting sun, which turned the church's famous giant white onion dome into a brilliant pink.

He parted the purple velvet curtain to peer out. Not a soul. Then a movement by the altar rail caught his eye, and his heart jumped. A woman in a bright yellow sundress and a wide-brimmed straw hat genuflected and made the sign of the cross. Her hair was dark brown, though, not red, and he felt stupid.

He let the curtain fall into place again, but the fear had come back, like a punch to the gut.

Why was the church suddenly so quiet, so empty? Something wasn't right—

The door to the confessional box on the left creaked open, startling him. He heard the rustle of clothing, the hum of an indrawn breath. He smelled jasmine, faint and sweet.

"Bless me, Father, for I have sinned. My last confession . . . rather I should say, my last *real* confession, in a church, before the presence of God, was a long, long time ago."

A woman's voice, low and quiet, and so compelling he turned toward it to look through the mesh screen, but he couldn't make out her face, just a hat and a cloud of long dark hair, and he thought, *Okay. You're gonna be okay.*

"Our Lord is everywhere," he said, "not just in a house of worship. But I'm sure He's pleased you are here all the same."

She nodded and her mouth parted on a soft sigh. "Oh, Father, you are so right. Time is an earthly concept and God is truly everywhere. He sees all. So I guess what I really need to know is, will He absolve every sin? Even the terrible ones? Provided a girl is sorry enough, of course."

"Would I be sitting in this stuffy, dark little box on such a fine summer's evening if I didn't believe in God's mercy?"

Her laugh was delightful, soft, but something about it was off, as if this was some sort of game to her, a play to act out—and he knew then that he was not okay, not okay at all. Had known it instinctively all along.

He went utterly still. He felt her intensity, felt the impact of each separate word as she said, "I have blood on my hands."

"Don't kill me."

"The first time I killed for him," she went on, as if he hadn't spoken, "I used a knife and it was messy. The blood, it got everywhere and later I showed him the blood smeared on my skin, so he would know what I would do for him, the lengths I could go, how I would kill for him. I think it shocked him, but he also liked it. It excited him."

Hot bile rose up in Dom's throat. "Listen to me. You don't want to do this."

"Actually, I do. I really, really do. I've never killed a priest before, and I wonder what it feels like." She sighed. "You know what I've come for, Father. Give me the film, and I promise I'll let you live."

Liar.

"Don't you have it backwards?" Dom was surprised at how calm he sounded now. "As long as I have the film, you can't do anything to me. Right now it's hidden in a safe place, but if anything were to happen to my brother or me—"

"Yes, yes," she said, impatient now. "I know the drill. But the thing is, Father, I don't believe you *do* have it. Shocking, I know—what with you being a priest and saying as much right here in church, in the presence of God. But then some of you guys have been known to diddle little altar boys in the presence of God. So what's a lie or two compared to that?"

Dom gripped his hands so tightly together he could feel the throb of the pulse in his wrists. He had to convince her that he had the damn film, had to or he would die.

"Okay, so you don't believe me, but what if you're wrong? Can you really afford to take that chance? Imagine the film played in an endless loop on every TV set throughout the country. This man you work for, kill for—it would destroy him. And then he would destroy you."

She was silent, and he felt the evil in her like a poisonous cloud. The one tenet of his faith he'd always had a hard time believing in was the existence of the devil, until now.

"Do I believe you?" she began to chant. "Do I believe you not? Believe you, believe you not . . . Swear to me you have it, and I will believe you. But only if you swear on pain of your immortal soul."

Do it, Dom. Come on, man, you want to live, don't you?

He felt her move and he raised his head. He saw her hand come up and he sucked in a sharp breath, but in the next instant he realized that whatever she held was too small to be a gun.

Dom heard a click and suddenly his father's voice filled the confessional: "You better pray to that God of yours Katya Orlova isn't long dead, because only she knows where the film really is. You and Ry, you've got to find her and get it back, and you got to do it fast."

She shut off the recorder and made a little tsking noise with her tongue. "You're a mean man, Father, to go and spoil my fun like that. You see, I planted a bug in your daddy's hospital room. A very good one, actually, state-of-the-art, and I got every word of his so-called confession, so obviously I've known all along that you never had the film."

She laughed again, and Dom couldn't understand how such a sweet sound could come from such a depraved heart. "I wanted to see if I could get a priest to swear to a big fat lie and imperil his immortal soul just as he was about to die, but you wouldn't do it, would you? What a disappointment."

She heaved a mock sigh and dropped her hand back in her lap. "*Such a disappointment.* Why, you've almost gone and ruined my day, Father, and the thing I'm wondering is—do you really believe God is such a stickler for the rules? I mean, don't you think that once you got to the Pearly Gates, you could've just explained that there were extenuating circumstances involved? . . . No? Well, at least now, after I kill you, if you find yourself in heaven, you'll know that you've earned it."

He saw her through the mesh screen, saw her bloodred mouth move as she spoke the familiar words of the Act of Contrition, "Oh, my God, I am heartily sorry for having offended Thee . . ."

He saw her hand come up again, and then he saw the gun.

Washington, D.C.

THEY CAME DOWN the hall from the kitchen as a unit, covering for each other, laying down a field of fire. But one of them was still going to have to be the first through that door, and then Ry would kill him. He knew he was going to die, but he damn well wasn't going to die alone.

Time slowed as it always did in the thickest part of a firefight, when one second felt like a lifetime and every detail seemed etched in glass. He saw the curtains billow from the breeze coming through the busted window, heard the creak of a floorboard in the hall. Broken glass on the shelf above his head tinkled as it settled. His eyes flickered up and he saw—

The grenade.

He'd stuck it on the top shelf of the bookcase, next to a potted fern—

a souvenir from his first operation in Afghanistan, Soviet-made and at least twenty years old. *Was it still live?*

The first guy burst into the room. Ry shot him between the eyes. He reached up and grabbed the grenade off the bookshelf, while shooting the hell out of the doorway. He pulled out the ring pin with his teeth, but kept his thumb down on the safety spoon.

A second guy came through the door, the barrel of his Uzi leading the way, spraying an arc of fire. Ry dove toward the window. Bullets whined all around him, and the whole world seemed to disintegrate into pieces of glass and wood and metal. He let go of the spoon, counted, *One thousand, two thousand . . .*

He slung the grenade sideways, saw it hit the floor and roll. He vaulted over the desk, snatching up the answering machine with one hand and pumping bullets back at the doorway with the other.

He jumped feetfirst through what was left of the bay window, just as the room behind him exploded into fire and smoke and flying shrapnel.

───────

Ry HIT THE ground hard. The spike-haired kid came around from behind the pizza van, firing another damn Uzi. Ry shot wildly back at him and got lucky. The kid spun around in a crazy pirouette, blood gushing from his throat.

As Ry scrambled to his feet, he caught movement out of the corner of his eye. A big guy with a blond flattop and a semiautomatic handgun was darting between two parked cars. Ry fired and kept firing until the hammer of his gun snapped on an empty chamber and the big guy was dead, draped over the hood of a white Prius.

Car alarms shrieked as Ry ran across the street toward the pizza delivery van, cutting the hell out of his bare feet on the broken window glass.

The pizza van still had the key in the ignition. As he drove away, Ry looked back at what was left of the place he'd called home for the last five years.

Dammit. He'd loved that little house.

He drove the pizza truck six blocks to a parking garage, dumped it, and found a car old enough to hot-wire without setting off any more alarms—an '82 Cadillac Seville. Forty minutes later he was off the belt-way and heading for a private runway deep in the hills of West Virginia. He needed to get down to Galveston, needed to find out what in hell was going on, but he had to get off the radar first.

He looked at the answering machine lying next to him on the pas-senger seat.

Dom, he thought. He prayed his brother was still alive.

Galveston, Texas

FATHER DOM FLUNG himself out of the confessional box. He heard a spitting noise and felt a sting, like the flick of a whip end, across the side of his head.

He tried to get up, to run, but the confessional's purple velvet cur-tain was wrapped around his legs. He kicked, twisted, but he couldn't get loose. He could hear the girl laughing and waited for another bullet to hit him, kill him.

He clawed at the curtain with his hands, heard a ripping noise, and he was free. He ran down the nave of the deserted church toward tall wooden doors that shouldn't be closed, but were.

The girl's voice echoed in the vast, vaulted space. "They're all locked, Father. There's no way out, but up, up, up and away into heaven . . . or not as the case may be."

Dom ran between the pews into a side chapel that held racks of burning votive candles and threw himself at the door that led into the sacristy.

"Ixnay on that one, too, Father. When I said they were all locked, I meant them *all*. I'm efficient in that way."

He was trapped beside the small altar within the chapel. She came toward him, moving in and out of the shadows cast by the cathedral's tall columns. She held the gun down by her side now. He still couldn't see all of her face, just that smiling red mouth.

"What kind of monster are you?"

"What a mean thing to say. I just happen to like what I do. Most people hate their jobs, and I imagine that contributes to all manner of the sinning that you, as a priest, have to put up with."

Dom watched her come, his mind racing. He could feel blood streaming down his neck from the gash in his head, saw it splatter on the marble floor.

"Whereas I," she said, "am a purist in everything I do. Like fucking, for instance. And killing."

"*Wait*," Dom cried. "Okay, okay, you're right. I don't have the film, but that makes me even less of threat, not more. Come on, even if I talked, who would believe me? You don't have to do this."

She shook her head. "Father, Father. You just don't get it, do you? But then wusses like you never do. It doesn't matter that you're a nice person, that you don't deserve to die. No amount of pitiful whimpering and begging ever stops people like me. Another gun sometimes does, but then wusses never have guns."

She was nearly upon him now, walking on her high, spiked heels through his blood on the floor. Dom saw her hand come up. He grabbed the heavy bronze candelabra from the altar and threw it at her head.

She flung up her arms to protect her face. Her shoes slid on the blood, and she grabbed at one of the iron votive racks to break her fall. The flimsy racks buckled beneath her weight, and she pitched forward, right into the rows of burning candles.

Dom ran. He was almost past her when he heard a whoosh and saw a burst of flames out of the corner of his eye.

Her screams, raw and terrible, stopped him. He turned back and saw the straw hat and brown wig burning on the floor beside her. And she wasn't screaming anymore, she was laughing. Her hair was the red of sacramental wine.

She raised the gun and pointed it at the space between his eyes. "You should have kept on running."

8

Northern Virginia

R Y O'MALLEY pulled the Caddy onto the shoulder of the road and killed the engine. He was so deep in the Virginia countryside, all he could hear was the wind blowing through the scrub pines. A light ground mist, like old gray lace, drifted past the windows.

He glanced down at the fuel gauge. The tank, barely a quarter full when he'd stolen the car, now hovered on empty. He could add gas to the growing list of things he desperately needed to keep himself alive. When he'd jumped out of his front window, he had all of sixty-three bucks in his wallet and a couple of credit cards, which were now worthless because to use them would be like putting a giant, blinking, neon green arrow above his head.

Dad's gone, and now they're going to come after us, because of what he did.

Well, they had come all right, Dom. But who in hell were *they*?

Ry flicked on the roof light and looked at the answering machine sitting on the passenger seat beside him. At least it had a backup battery, so he didn't need an outlet to hear the rest of his brother's message. Yet his finger hesitated over the replay button.

Dad's gone. . . .

Ry felt the pain of his father's death, hot and deep, and hearing Dom say the words out loud again was only going to make the hurt worse. But it had to be done.

He pressed the button, and his brother's frantic voice once again filled the night, "Ry? It's about Dad. He's dead, and—"

A broken sob, shaky breathing. Then the clatter of Dom's dropping the phone, bar noises, and the operator breaking in, followed by that weird bit about a woman with red hair.

More harsh breathing, then, "Dad's had a heart attack, Ry. Dad's gone, and now they're going to come after us, because of what he did. The big kill. I know I'm not making any sense, but I can't . . . not over the phone. You need to get down here fast, Ry, and I'll explain everything— I mean, I'll tell you what Dad told me, which isn't enough, not nearly enough. But for now just know there may be people out there who are going to try to kill us. Some red-haired woman, maybe. . . . Oh, God, I know how crazy that sounds. But if you'd heard him, if you'd looked into his eyes—he was scared for us, Ry. Really scared . . ."

Dom's voice trailed off, then Ry heard his brother draw in a deep breath and go on, "God knows when you'll hear this, and by then there's a chance they'll already have gotten to me. So as soon as I hang up, I'm going to write down everything Dad said and put it with Lafitte's treasure. For now, just know that a woman named Katya Orlova made a film of what he did. She was a professional, from Hollywood, and Dad said she got it all, their faces and everything. But then she disappeared on him and took the film with her. So we need to find this Katya Orlova, Ry, because if any of this is real, then Dad was right—that film's the only thing that will keep us alive."

Another pause, then Dom, his voice thick and breaking again: "One other thing, Ry, you know, just in case . . . I lo—"

But then the machine beeped, cutting him off. It didn't matter.

"I love you, too, Dom."

———

RY PRESSED HIS fingers into his eyes, as if he could push all feeling back down inside him, tamp it down deep. A terrible fear was in him that Dom was dead by now, too. They'd probably hit the rectory down in Galveston at the same time they'd come after him in D.C., and there'd been five guys, at least, in on the raid at his house, each with enough firepower to wipe out a small village. Against guys like that, his brother wouldn't have stood a chance.

And Dad? A killer? Mike O'Malley had so rarely talked about the first forty years of his life, before he'd met and married their mother, that it was a family joke. The man without a past. Only that didn't seem so funny anymore.

As a father, he'd been tough on his sons, but never mean. Yet even as a young boy, Ry had sensed some secret, some interior life, was buried deep inside the old man that he kept walled off with a cold and pitiless ruthlessness. Like a volcano that looked dormant on the surface, but underneath boiled raging fires of havoc and destruction.

"Just who *were* you really, Dad?" Ry asked aloud, and in the old Caddy's quiet emptiness, the words sounded broken.

He swallowed hard, clenched his eyes shut a moment longer, then forced them open. He had to get a grip so he could think. The first thing he needed to do was get down to Galveston and save his brother.

And please, God, let me not be too late.

———

THREE HUNDRED MILES and six hours later, Ry once again pulled off to the side of the road, this time about twenty yards shy of a tall, padlocked chain-link gate. The gate had razor wire strung along the top. A man stood in front of it, his feet splayed wide, a twelve-gauge shotgun cradled in his arms.

Ry opened the car door and got out slowly, his empty hands spread in front of him. "Nice to see you, too, Clee," he said.

"Well, I'll be a son of a bitch. Lookit what the cat done drug in."

The man stood, grinning, for a moment, then he broke open the shotgun and leaned it against a tree trunk. He came at Ry with his arms spread wide, and Ry braced himself. Cleeland Lewis had a cannonball for a head and shoulders like boulders. Ry was a big man himself—six-four and a shade under two hundred pounds of solid muscle—but when Clee's enormous black hand smacked into his back, it nearly knocked him on his ass.

"Hey, man. Sorry about the welcome party," Clee said. "I wasn't expecting company today."

"You must have one heck of a security system."

Cleeland Lewis had a shady past and an iffy future, mostly having to do with the ragged airfield he'd carved here out of the Appalachian wilderness. The small, twin-engine aircraft that flew in and out of Clee's place did so under the radar, and in more ways than one.

"So you got video," Ry said, "and what else? You got the place wired?"

Clee's grin turned wolfish. He waved a hand at the dusty, battered old Caddy. "Let's just say that if you hadn't stopped that piece of crap where you did, I'd be scrapping what was left of you off the treetops."

Then the grin slid away as he studied Ry's face. "You in some serious shit, bro?"

"Yeah."

Ry didn't elaborate, but then Clee wouldn't expect him to. They'd spent three hellish years together in Afghanistan, running special ops against Al Qaeda and the Taliban. They would have died for each other, no questions asked, and more than once they nearly had.

"What you need?" Clee asked.

"Ammo for my Walther, and enough cash to tide me over until I can get at my own stash. Say, ten thousand, if you can swing it."

Clee nodded. "Better make it twenty. And you'll want more fire-power than just that ol' Walther of yours. 'Cause sometimes you got a tendency to overestimate your talents."

Ry almost smiled. Back in D.C. they'd come after him with everything they had, and he'd not only lived through it, he'd kicked their asses good. Now those fuckers were dead and he was alive, and there was no other feeling like that in the world.

"Also," Ry said, "I'm going to need a plane."

"Figured that." Cleeland Lewis looked down at Ry's feet, bare and cut all to pieces by the broken glass from his living room window. "Gonna need a pair of boots, too."

9

Galveston, Texas

OFFICER BEADSLEY stood on the top step of the Sacred Heart Church, watching a big man come at him fast from out of the wet summer night. He planted his feet and unsnapped his holster.

"Hey, bubba," he called out. The guy slowed, but he didn't stop. The cop's hand rested now on the butt of his Glock. "You see that yellow tape you just stepped over? The one that says CRIME SCENE DO NOT CROSS?"

"I've got a message for the monsignor."

The big guy was close enough now for the cop to make out the black suit and white collar bands. He relaxed, took his hand off his gun. "Sorry, Father, I didn't know it was you. I mean, I didn't know you were a Father. The lieutenant told me to keep out the press and the ghouls, but that it was okay for you all to go on back in. The forensic guys are through in there."

Officer Beadsley pulled open one of the church's massive wooden doors for the priest to pass on through, but the other man hesitated at the threshold.

"They've taken the body away?"

"Huh? Oh, yeah. Long gone. No need to worry about that, Father. And the city'll be sending out a cleanup crew tomorrow, for the, uh . . . blood and stuff."

The priest's face, he thought, looked pale and stark, as if drained of blood. Officer Beadsley struggled for something more to say, but all he could come up with was "We'll get the guy who did it, Father. We'll get him."

Ry O'Malley stood unmoving in the dark, heavy silence. The only light came from a pair of electric sconces flanking the large wooden crucifix at the back of the church, but it was enough for him to make out where more crime-scene tape had been set up around the confessionals.

Was that where it happened, Dom? Was that where they got to you? Ah, Jesus, did you even see it coming?

The only details Ry knew about his brother's death were what he'd read in the *Galveston Daily News:* Dom had been shot in the head while hearing confession, and the police theorized the killer was a drug addict or homeless person because all the alms boxes were broken and empty.

But Ry knew better. He felt light-headed, almost sick, as he took in the signs of a struggle—pews knocked askew, the empty rings on the confessional door where the curtain had been torn off. Dom had fought back, but what chance did a priest have against an armed professional? Ry's hands, hanging useless at his sides, clenched into fists because it was already done, over, and he'd gotten here too late.

Then he saw more tape stretched around a small chapel next to the sacristy. His footsteps echoed in the vaulted space. He breathed in the candle wax and incense before the other smell hit him hard in the face. Blood. It was the smell of his brother's blood, and it nearly drove him to his knees.

He staggered, reached out blindly, and his hand got caught in the yellow tape. He ripped it away with a snarl. A bloodred haze filled his eyes, rage and a terrible, tearing grief. The bastards who did this, the *bastards.*

I'm gonna hunt you down and kill every last fucking one of you.

He fell to his knees, wrapping his arms around his belly, hunching over. His eyes burned and his throat felt raw. He wanted to scream his guts out. He hated that he'd been too late, hated that he and Dom had seen so little of each during these last ten years because they'd taken such different paths.

He hated that he was still here, and alone.

He slammed his fist into the marble floor, so hard he nearly broke it. But the pain was good—it focused him, hardened him.

Slowly, he straightened. He looked at the small altar shrouded in black shadows, at a plaster statue of the Virgin Mary and the large bronze candelabra to the right of her that looked oddly out of place. As if there ought to be another, matching, candelabra on the other side.

He stared at the Virgin's too sweet face for a long time. Then he made himself look at the rest of it. A votive-candle rack tipped over, hardened drops of wax and scorch marks. Blood smears and splatter soaked into the porous marble floor. And something else he still couldn't bear to look at, couldn't bear even to think about: the outline in chalk that marked the place where Dom had died.

It would be at the morgue now, Dom's body. Inert flesh and bones, organs and trace evidence, but not his brother anymore.

Not Dom.

RY SLIPPED OUT the back way through the sacristy door, but he stopped while he was still within the thick shadows cast by Sacred Heart's stone walls. He ripped the priest's collar off his neck, drawing in deep breaths of wet, steamy air, trying to wash the smell of his brother's blood out of his head.

It helped a little, at least enough to get him thinking straight again. Except for the occasional car that rolled by on its way to somewhere else, the streets around the church looked deserted. But the killers, Ry thought—they could still be nearby. They would have been in contact with whoever planned the raid on his house in D.C., they'd know about his escape, and they would figure he'd have heard from his brother. So they'd also figure this would be the first place he'd run to.

They were out there, all right—he could practically *feel* them. Watching the church, waiting for a chance to have another go at him.

They, they, they . . . Who *were* they?

They'd murdered Dom, and they were trying to kill him, and he still didn't know why. But he knew where he might find some of the answers.

Buried with Lafitte's treasure.

So as soon as I hang up, Dom had said, *I'm going to write down everything Dad said and put it with Lafitte's treasure.*

He and Dom had grown up in a small Queen Anne–style cottage a block from the beach on the Bolivar Peninsula, an isolated strip of land that separated the Gulf of Mexico from Galveston and accessible only by ferryboat.

One summer's day, when he was eight, Dom ten, they were exploring the marshes and sand dunes and they came across an abandoned shack, weathered and rotting. Ry was sure the place had to be at least a hundred years old, but Dom said anything that old would long ago have been eaten up completely by the salt water, and they were arguing about that when Ry's foot went through a floorboard and into a hole.

In the hole was a wooden chest, banded with iron, and Ry said it had to be Laffite's treasure chest. Jean Lafitte, the swashbuckling privateer and spy, was one of his heroes, and one story he especially liked had the pirate trying to help Napoléon escape exile only to end up getting his hands on the emperor's treasure instead. Lafitte had buried the treasure, so the story went, near his camp on the Bolivar Peninsula, the secret of its location disappearing along with the pirate into the mists of time.

Dom said a pirate as smart as Lafitte would never bury his treasure in a place where just any old body could stumble across it, and he and Dom argued about that until the moment they broke the padlock with a rock, opened the chest, and found, to Ry's disgust, not jewels and gold doubloons, but a bunch of moldering old newspapers from the 1930s and a single Indian-head nickel.

They got good use out of that old chest, though, using it to stash their own treasure, such as cigarettes and *Playboys*, and later booze and pot and that pack of jumbo-size condoms Dom had shoplifted from Walgreens the day after Lindsay Cramer said she'd go with him to the Ball High School homecoming dance.

Ry started to smile at the memory, then his throat closed up and his belly clenched against a fresh wave of pain. Homecoming. Home.

That little yellow house with its white gingerbread trim was gone now, destroyed by Hurricane Ike along with everything else on the peninsula. Mom, Dad, Dom—all of them gone now. The entire O'Malley family was dead, except for him.

But had there ever really been an *O'Malley* family, or was that name just another part of the lie that had been Michael O'Malley's life? For all of Ry's own life, his father had lived in that little house, making only a so-so living by renting out a small string of fishing boats to the few tourists who made it out to the peninsula. Sometimes, during the lean years, he'd even had to work a few shifts down at the shrimp-canning factory just to make ends meet. Bolivar was hardly a place you'd pick to live if you wanted to get either rich or noticed, it was too isolated, remote; the only way you could even get there was by ferryboat.

No, what Bolivar was, was the perfect place for a killer on the run to go to ground.

A killer such as his father.

———

Ry LEFT THE shadows, walking slowly, even stopping once directly beneath a streetlamp to go through his faux-cigarette-lighting routine, giving whoever might be watching a good look at his face. If the hunters were here at the church, he wanted to flush them out now.

He walked to where he'd parked his ride, a twenty-year-old white Chevy pickup that he'd picked up in a used-car lot near the Houston airport. It was a clunker, but it had the virtue of having come cheap.

This late on a wet Sunday night there wasn't a lot of traffic. He needed to get over to Port Bolivar and see if Dom had a chance before he was killed to write down the old man's confession and bury it as he'd said he would, in that old chest they'd used when they were kids. Lafitte's treasure. But first he drove around Galveston Island, making random turns and flipping U-eys, running red lights and stop signs. A little ditty from when he was a kid kept running through his head: *Come out, come out, wherever you are. . . .* But he saw no sign of a tail.

He idled at a stoplight on the Strand, a part of town that had once catered to sailors and whores, now lined with T-shirt shops, condos, and trendy cafés. Like that cybercafé on the corner, SIP 'N SURF in blinking orange neon.

Ry checked his watch. He still had over thirty minutes before the next ferry, the last one of the night, left for Port Bolivar.

———

THE ONLY OTHER customer in the café was a pimply kid, wearing Harry Potter glasses and a T-shirt that said TALK NERDY TO ME. The barista, a guy with a scraggly goatee, acted put out by Ry's request for a double espresso and a half hour's worth of access to one of the computer stations.

In his message, Dom had said a woman called Katya Orlova had made a film of this "big kill." Ry logged on to the Internet and googled the name. More than eight hundred references popped up. He skimmed through them, but nothing looked even remotely helpful. A dog-grooming business in Des Moines, a Russian gymnast, a Facebook page belonging to a Berkeley coed. Michelle Pfeiffer had played a character of that name in a movie called *The Russia House* . . .

And then he found her. Maybe found her.

It wasn't much, just a few lines in an article, for an academic journal, titled "Women Behind the Camera: The Feminist Struggle in Hollywood, Yesterday and Today."

Still, the following years saw little improvement in the dearth of opportunity for female cinematographers. Even the few kept on salary by the major studios were rarely assigned directive roles on any major projects. Katya Orlova, for instance, put in four years at Twentieth Century–Fox as second assistant cameraman before her name finally appears in the credits as a camera operator for The Misfits. *Other women—*

Outside, a car door slammed. Ry looked up to see one of the island's horse-drawn tourist carriages roll past the window, momentarily blocking his view. Then he saw a woman crossing the street from the direction of a big, black Hummer.

He couldn't see her face clearly through the rain-smeared glass, but he knew she was beautiful just from the way she carried herself—shoulders back, head held high, her hands stuffed deep into the pockets of a swinging, black leather trench coat. Her stiletto boots clicked on the pavement in long, purposeful strides.

She passed beneath a streetlight, and he saw dark red hair that shone like wet blood. *This woman came out of the ladies' room and she had red hair, and after what Dad said, I thought . . .*

Ry dove for the floor just as the café's front window exploded under a hail of gunfire.

———

HE ROLLED BEHIND the counter as more bullets slammed into the espresso machine's big boiler, spewing hot steam down onto his head.

Ry had his gun out, but didn't dare return fire. He heard the barista and the kid screaming, but couldn't see them through the billowing steam. He couldn't see the redhead either, but she suddenly made her presence known again by shooting up the computer he'd been using.

He'd been stupid, almost fatally stupid. He hadn't thought they would come at him in a public place like this, where innocents could get caught in the cross fire.

She started firing again, pumping bullets into the wooden base of the counter. Ry pushed to his feet, put his arm across his face, and plunged into the scalding spray, through a swinging door, and into the kitchen. More bullets thudded into the door as it swung shut behind him—but from a different gun this time.

Ry ran through the kitchen, past tables, a baking oven, pantry shelves, a big stainless steel refrigerator. *Dammit, where's the back door? There's got to be a back door.*

He found it and was through it, standing on a narrow stoop at the back end of a blind alley filled with trash cans, a rusted-out Dumpster, and a pile of rotting lumber.

Across the alley was the solid brick wall of another building. No door, not even a single window, just a wrought-iron fire escape coming down from the roof, partly unfolded but still too high up for him to reach.

He was about to make a dash for the street when the black Hummer screeched to a stop across the mouth of the alley. He heard the swinging door bang open back in the kitchen, and he launched himself off the stoop, out and up, and managed to catch the bottom rung of the fire escape with one hand. He jackknifed his legs hard and got enough momentum to pull himself up, just as a bullet slammed into the brick wall next to his head, so close he felt the heat of it.

He ran up the metal steps, ducking and weaving, while the redhead and a guy in a black-hooded sweatshirt stood on the kitchen stoop. He felt a sting on his neck, a splash of blood. He pulled himself onto the roof, and, thank God, he had a bit of cover for the moment.

He lay there, his chest heaving, listening. He couldn't hear them coming up the fire escape after him, and he couldn't hear any more gunfire from below.

He ran at a crouch over the flat tar and gravel roof of what seemed to be a converted warehouse, wending through brick chimneys and hooded vents until he found a door. He reached up, twisted the knob—

The fucker was locked.

He'd learned a long time ago to always carry a set of lockpicks, but he didn't have time to use them now, and just then, lo and behold, and about damn time, he heard sirens. But could the redhead have some kind of juice with the local cops, such as some kind of federal badge she could flash at them? Shit, if she did, he'd be screwed.

Ry wasn't going to stick around to find out. He ran toward the next building over. It looked like a set of condos, and it had a nice, terraced garden on its roof. It was also convenient that this roof was only a little bit lower than his roof, but shit, fuck, damn, there had to be a dozen feet between them, and it was a long, long way down to the alley below—six stories at least. He might be stupid, but not stupid enough to try jumping over a frigging abyss.

He heard the pounding of feet on the fire escape behind him. He looked back, caught a flash of red hair.

He turned and ran and jumped.

For a moment he seemed to be literally running on air, his legs pumping madly. He'd almost made it across to the other roof when he stopped going forward and gravity won out.

He just managed to snag a drainpipe with his fingertips. He hung there a second, dangling, and of course his fingers started to slip.

He lost his grip, but grabbed at the drainpipe with his other hand, got a better hold of it this time. He hauled himself onto the roof and nearly impaled himself on a tomato stake. He looked up and there she was, her wrists braced on the ledge of the warehouse roof, her gun aimed at his head.

He rolled behind a row of wooden tubs filled with palm trees and came up running.

The condo owners apparently weren't worried about anyone coming in through their roof door because it was, blessed Jesus, unlocked. He took the elevator all the way down to the parking garage, then walked down the rows of cars, banging on hoods, setting off alarms. By the time he climbed the steps onto the street, the cars were playing a loud mad opera.

The Strand was a mess. A half dozen patrol cars ringed the café and one of the cops shouted into a bullhorn, scared that he had a hostage situation on his hands. But Ry would bet only the kid and the barista were still inside.

Ry pushed through the crowd, trying not to stick out while he headed toward his truck. He'd had the sense to park it a few blocks away, over on Seawall, where he could shoot straight down to the ferry, leaving in . . .

He checked his watch. Six minutes, dammit.

He started to run. He heard someone shout, "Hey, you!" and he looked around. But the yell hadn't been aimed at him. He spotted the guy in the black-hooded sweatshirt, though, walking in the street with the Hummer inching along beside him.

He saw the redhead come up the steps from the condo's garage, not even bothering to hide the gun in her hand. He made himself slow down again, tried to blend in—he knew now she didn't give a shit if she killed every innocent in the street as long as she got him.

Dammit, he needed to get to his truck.

Then, music to his ears, he heard a horse's whinny. He waited until the tourist carriage rolled up alongside him, then jumped inside, tossing a twenty into the startled driver's lap.

"How fast can that nag of yours go?"

10

R Y STOOD at the end of the pier and watched the ferry's lights disappear into the night. He listened to the diesel engines die away, then he heard nothing but the lap of water against the pilings beneath his feet.

He'd missed the boat, the very last fucking boat. After getting shot at, scalded, and almost falling into the abyss, he'd gone and missed the damn boat—

Headlights flooded the road behind him.

He'd left his truck idling behind him, the passenger door open, and Ry dove for it just as the whole world exploded into a whirl of noise, bullets splintering the wooden planks of the loading ramp and ricocheting off the metal railing. He sprawled across the front seat, covering his head with his arms as more bullets shattered the back windshield and slammed into the tailgate, shredding the metal into confetti.

The gunfire seemed to last forever, but suddenly there was a lull. He raised his head just enough to get a look out the side-view mirror. He saw that the behemoth black Hummer was blocking the loading ramp, and that really wasn't good at all. They had him trapped—metal railings four feet high on both sides of him, the Hummer behind him, and the empty ferry dock in front of him. And beyond the ferry dock, only black night and blacker water.

More gunfire rocked the truck. He thought of her shooting Dom, and he wanted to take her out right now with his bare hands, but he was outnumbered three to one and they had Uzis and his dying wasn't going solve anything.

He had to save his own ass first, then he'd kill her.

Crouched behind the steering wheel, he saw two men come out

from behind the Hummer, firing their automatics. The whine and ping and thud of bullets were all around him. Save his ass, hell. Who was he kidding? The chances of making it out of this alive were zilch, and that really pissed him off because not only did he not want to die, he didn't want to give the bastards the satisfaction of killing him.

He fastened the seat belt with one hand, while he threw the gearshift into reverse with the other, floored it, and prayed. The truck roared backward so fast the steering wheel bucked. He twisted half-around to look out the shattered back windshield and aimed the truck right for the Hummer. He grinned like the very devil as he got closer and saw the men jump out of the way, their faces white in the Hummer's headlights. He didn't see the woman. Maybe she was still inside, behind the wheel.

Six feet until impact . . . four . . . two . . .

Now.

In the last instant before his truck was going to crash into the Hummer, Ry slammed the gearshift into first instead. The back tires spun on the wet wood, throwing out sparks and smoke, and then, at last, he felt the tires get traction and the truck shot forward. The railings flew by in a blur. The end of the loading ramp loomed ahead, black and empty, closer, closer . . .

Oh, shit, maybe this really wasn't such a good idea after all.

The truck shot off the end of the ramp and out over the water. For one breathless instant it felt as if he were flying.

He plunged down so fast he barely had time to suck in air before the truck smacked the water, so hard his teeth rattled. Water poured through the shattered windows. Down, down. How deep *was* it here? It was pitch-black, so black he felt blind.

Then he felt another jolt, softer this time, as the truck hit the silty bottom.

He pushed up against the steering wheel, but he was wedged in. He nearly lost it then, until he realized the seat belt was holding him down. He felt for the belt's lock and pressed, but it wouldn't open, and he stopped himself just in time from yanking on it and maybe making it worse.

Okay, okay, don't panic. Your chest feels a little tight, but that's all in your head. You know you've still got plenty of time left before you run out of air.

When he and Dom were kids, they used to compete with each other to see who could hold his breath underwater the longest. His brother had always won. The most Ry had ever lasted was about three minutes, enough time if he could get out of the damn seat belt. But the lock wasn't budging.

He grabbed the knife he'd strapped to his ankle and began madly sawing, until finally it busted open, and he was free.

He punched his feet through what was left of the back window and pulled himself out of the truck. His arm snagged on something metal, and he felt a flash of hot pain. The darkness was absolute. He felt his way along the truck bed, the tailgate, back bumper, a tire.

Then he realized he was actually seeing the tire and he looked up. He could see the shine of the Hummer's bright lights cutting through the water, and trails of bullets, looking like flickering silver snakes.

He felt along the tire's rim until he found the air valve, then tore at the pocket of his priest's coat to get at his burglar picks. He was starting to feel light-headed, clumsy, his chest seriously hurting now.

He fumbled with the picks, trying to feel for the slimmest one, and they slipped through his fingers. The picks hit his knee, but by some miracle he caught them before they fell into the silt and reeds. Maybe it was Dom, the spirit of Dom, looking out for him, because he ought to have died ten times over by now.

One more time, though, Dom. Just a little more help down here, because I'm out of air.

White lights flashed in front of his eyes and his ears rang as he fought desperately to keep his mouth from opening to gulp at oxygen that wasn't there. *One more time, Dom, one more . . .*

At last, at last he found the tire's air valve. He popped off the cap, poked the burglar's pick into the valve, pushing in the seal. He closed his mouth over the valve and breathed in the sweet, wonderful air.

He closed his eyes for a moment in blessed relief, then covered the valve with his thumb so that bubbles wouldn't rise to the surface and looked up. They were still there, Hummer lights still shining on the water, but they'd stopped wasting bullets. Soon, he prayed, she'd believe he was dead, but she wouldn't leave even then. She would wait a long while just to be sure, and she would have her two guys watch the shoreline to make sure he didn't swim for it, and then she would wait some more, and he hated her for that.

Yeah, well, he would make her pay for all of it someday, but right now he needed her and the people she worked for to think he was dead. He needed time and the freedom from being hunted so he could find Katya Orlova and the film and get at the truth behind what his father had done. First, though, he needed to get over to Bolivar so he could read what Dom had left in Lafitte's treasure chest, and he hoped to God he was right about that, that Dom had managed to write it all down and hide it away before they'd killed him.

Ry took another breath of the oily, compressed air. He wondered how long he would be able to breathe the stuff before doing serious damage to his lungs.

He breathed again and looked up. The headlights were still there, damn the bitch all to hell.

He breathed and waited. Five minutes, ten. Breathed and waited, and waited some more, and still the headlights were there, shining on the water. Suddenly his stomach cramped, so hard he almost opened his mouth and swallowed water. He hadn't, though. He'd kept it together, and the cramping was probably nothing to worry about, just nausea from the oil in the air he was breathing. Just nausea from the oil.

He looked up.

Still there.

11

Martha's Vineyard, Massachusetts
Sixteen hours later

S HE STOOD naked before him.

The setting sun shone through the bedroom's enormous plate-glass window, burning his eyes and making her red hair look on fire. All he could hear was the surf breaking on the beach below them, and his own harsh breathing.

"Suck it off me," she said, and she cupped her breasts in her hands, lifting them. He saw that her nipples were smeared with something dark red and crusty, and he couldn't stop himself from shuddering.

"Oh, dear God . . ."

"Dear *God*?" she said, laughing. "God's never stopped you before. Is it because of whose blood it is this time? But you knew he was a priest when you told me to kill him, and I blew him away, lover boy. Blew him away right there in his church, and with the Lord Jesus and all his angels looking down."

He shook his head, but he couldn't stop himself from lifting those perfect, bloodied breasts in his two big hands. She was insane, truly mad, and so what did that make him? Because she excited him almost beyond bearing.

She sighed and leaned into him, seemed to melt right into him. "Do you want to hear how he begged for his life?"

"Later. Right now you're the one I want to see down on your knees."

He let go of her breasts to grab roughly at his belt with one hand and her head with the other, snagging his fingers in all that luscious red hair, as he pushed her down onto the floor in front of him.

━━━━━

LATER, SHE SAID to him, "The other one, the priest's brother? He was a lot harder to kill. For a while there it was like we were playing Whac-A-Mole through the streets of Galveston, you know? He just wouldn't go down."

Miles Taylor—billionaire, financial speculator, philanthropist, and political activist—was pouring one of the world's most expensive single malts, a sixty-year-old Macallan, into a pair of Waterford crystal tumblers. And it wasn't so much her choice of postcoital conversation as the *way* she'd said it, with the same tone of voice she might use to order a pastrami sandwich, that made him stop what he was doing and turn to look at her.

Yasmine Poole sat in one of the room's floral, white wicker chairs—a hideous thing his second wife, Laurette, had picked out back in the day and which he'd always hated. Too froufrou he'd told her at the time, but she hadn't really given a shit about his opinion on bedroom chairs or anything else for that matter, which was why he'd eventually divorced her ass.

Yasmine, though, was a whole different kind of woman. He couldn't figure her out. Couldn't figure *them* out, their relationship, or whatever people called long-term and exclusively mutual sex these days. An undercurrent was between them, an intimacy that was nearly unbearable at times, raw and dark. She'd told him once that he indulged in her the need to kill. "You are my pusher," she'd said, "for the dark drug I need to feed my soul."

Lately, though, he was beginning to wonder which of them was really the junkie. Because every time he looked at her, the way he was looking at her now, he was lost in her.

He saw that she'd pulled her hair into a bun at the nape of her neck and was dressed again in the ivory silk Armani suit she'd had on when she'd flown over from the mainland an hour ago. She was reading something off a laptop she had balanced on one knee, and that little crease was between her eyes that she got when she was concentrating. But her mouth was the mouth of a whore, red and wet and swollen.

"You're wearing that moony, doofus look again, Miles," she said, without looking up. "If you're not careful, people are gonna say you're in love."

Miles Taylor could actually feel himself blushing, and it annoyed the hell out of him because he was sure no one had ever succeeded in making him blush before in his life. "I was just thinking how not more than a half an hour ago I was sucking blood off your naked tits, and now you're sitting over there looking so proper and professional. Like a model for a Brooks Brothers catalog."

"I'm a personal assistant to the president of a multibillion-dollar corporation. This is how I always look when I'm not killing for you, or fucking you. And you were so smiling at me, Miles. Lovingly. I could feel it like a warm breath on my skin. I keep telling you we're soul mates. You need to accept that and deal."

"Bullcrap."

Even if he did believe there was such a thing as soul mates, he would never give her that power over him by admitting to it, and the last thing he wanted to do was "deal."

What in hell did that expression even mean, anyway?

Miles Taylor ruled a financial empire worth over $15 billion, more than the gross national product of some third-world countries, and with all the mesmerizing power such an obscene amount of money entailed. He had one child still living, a daughter; five grandchildren, all girls; two ex-wives, both bitches; and he couldn't so much as sneeze without a half dozen ass-kissing toadies springing up to hand him a hankie.

And not a single one of those people mattered to him.

All his life he'd had this aching hole in him that he just couldn't seem to fill. It was like that disease where you're hungry all the time, and you eat and eat, but all the calories and nutrition just go right through you. He could've paid some psychiatrist four hundred bucks an hour to tell him it was all Mommy and Daddy's fault, and the guy would probably be right. But who gave a shit?

All he knew was that ever since Yasmine Poole had come into his life, he didn't feel so empty anymore. And that scared the living hell out of him sometimes, because she was, to put it crudely, crazier than a shithouse rat.

"I'll tell you what it is, Yaz," he said. "You're in love with my money and I'm just a horny old goat, and that's either ridiculous or obscene, because when a man's cock's got some eighty years on it, even a tight pussy and a little blue miracle pill can only compensate for so much reality."

She raised one perfectly shaped eyebrow, although she still didn't look up from whatever she was reading on her laptop. "Notice how all I have to do is drop the word *love* into the conversation, and your mind leaps right to my pussy without even passing go. Yet people call me the gold digger."

He laughed as he went to her, carrying a glass in each hand and trying to hide from her the little hitch in his stride, because if she noticed it, she'd be back on his case again about seeing a doctor and getting it replaced. He'd blown the knee out twice, once years ago on a track field in college, then later on a ski slope in Aspen, and it throbbed nearly all the time now. A low, dull ache. He'd taken two heavy-duty pain pills earlier, but they were wearing off, and he didn't want to take more because he hated what the drugs did to his brain, how they made his thoughts wander.

He set her drink down on the glass-topped wicker table beside her and took a healthy swig of his own. At $38,000 a bottle you wouldn't think it would burn his gullet going down, but it wasn't the Macallan's fault, he knew. It was the damn acid reflux. Christ, he hated getting old.

"The other O'Malley boy," he said. "The one you said was so hard to kill. Are you sure he really *is* dead? Because, baby, if that film ever sees the light of day . . ."

He waved a hand to encompass the whole nightmare scenario. His reputation destroyed, his power shattered, not to mention the possibility of spending the last of his golden years sharing a cell with a sodomizing, drug-crazed biker called Bubba. All these years, all the millions he'd spent on influencing both the marketplace and the ballot box, positioning himself so that he was for all intents and purposes running the party from the inside, and they were finally back to winning elections again, controlling Congress, and starting to change the country for the better. . . . All of that would be down the toilet if the film got out.

"Tell me we've got this under control, Yaz. Tell me you know for sure that he's dead, because first he gets away from a whole frigging commando squad down there in D.C., and then he pops up in Galveston—"

"He drowned, Miles." She made a *glug, glug, glug* sound, bugged out her eyes, and let her tongue flop out the side of her mouth. "We hung around on that dock for almost an hour after his car drove into the water, and there was no way he could've climbed back out without us seeing him, so unless he grew gills, he's dead. Along with his brother and his old man."

"Yeah. Dead like his old man." Miles shook his head. "That fucking Mike O'Malley. He's been like a knife pointed at my throat all these years, and I didn't dare get rid of him because of that damn film. Now he finally goes and dies of a nice, natural heart attack, and it looks like I'm home free. That with him dead and gone, all I got to do is clean up any possible loose ends by whacking his boys, just in case he told them something, you know? And if I can't turn up the film, then it can just go on rotting wherever the hell it's been all this time, some safety-deposit box or lawyer's safe, whatever."

He stopped to draw breath, glancing over at her, and he saw that she was looking up at him, her hands folded in her lap, as if waiting patiently for his rant to wind down. "Only now," he said, "you tell me the prick never had the film in the first place. Or rather that he had it a week at the most, before his woman took off with it. This Katya Orlova person. Hell, up until this deathbed confession of his, I didn't know such a woman even *existed*. Fucking O'Malley. All these years, I could've had him killed at any time and it wouldn't have mattered."

Yasmine breathed out a soft sigh and stood up, closing her laptop. "Well, he's dead now. And his kiddies are dead. And I've already got people out looking for Katya Orlova. If she's anywhere alive on this earth, we'll find her and make her dead, too. After she gives us the film, of course."

"Yeah, okay, okay. Good."

The woman, Katya Orlova—she could be long dead by now, too, Miles thought. And even if she was still alive, she would have to be a withered old crone, all bent over and helpless, maybe even on her merry way to dementia. They were all of them so damn old now.

Miles belched, then tried to rub away the pain in his chest with his fist. He downed another swig of whiskey. It didn't help either.

Yasmine came to him. The material of her suit was soft and clingy, and it moved over her hips like a man's hands. Her eyes were dark and deep and luminous.

"You've still got some of his blood on you," he said, his voice rough.

"What? Where?"

"Here." He cupped his hand around her neck, pulling her to him. "Behind your ear. Jesus, Yaz, what did you do? Dab it on after you killed him like it was some kind of fucking perfume?"

She was batshit crazy all right, but then he'd known that about her, lived with it and relished it, for seven years now. From the first day he'd hired her.

━━━━━━

BEFORE YASMINE POOLE'S résumé came across his desk, Miles Taylor was going through personal assistants at the rate of one a year. He was an exacting—okay, you might even go so far as to say a tyrannical—boss, and it seemed as if no matter how impressive the PAs all looked to him on paper, they turned out to be idiots whose delicate self-esteems got bruised if he so much as looked at them crossways. And he really didn't have the time or patience for that kind of shit.

Yasmine Poole's résumé was also impressive at first glance. A degree from the London School of Economics, followed by a year as an arbitrage trader with F. M. Mayer, then another year as an analyst with Wertheim and Company, and all of this by the age of twenty-eight. Which was young, but that didn't especially bother Miles. It meant she would still be both hungry and malleable—two qualities that seemed to fall by the wayside as you got into your thirties.

His company, Taylor Financials, had never hired so much as a janitor, though, without doing an extradeep background check on the applicant, and it was what came out of the investigator's report on Yasmine Poole that most intrigued Miles.

For one thing, her name wasn't Yasmine Poole, at least not originally. She'd been born Yasmin Yakir, the child of a couple of New York right-wing activist Jews. When she was ten, her parents emigrated to Israel and settled in an illegal West Bank wildcat outpost. Two years later, when she was twelve, a Palestinian rocket destroyed their home while she was at school, making her an orphan. After that she was in a group home in Jerusalem until she turned eighteen, when like the rest of her countrymen she was required to join the army.

But whereas most Israeli women were assigned to support or staff billets, she was selected by Aman, their special ops branch, to be trained as an assassin. She'd served three years, but doing what exactly only God and the Israeli army knew for sure, because as good as Miles's investigator was, he wasn't good enough to penetrate their intelligence files.

"Actually," the investigator told Miles, after he'd been summoned to fill out his report with a verbal and more personal evaluation, "I got the sense she was eased out of the army quietly, you know? After her three years were up. Like maybe she got to liking it just a little too much. The killing, if you know what I mean."

Miles said nothing, and after a long silence the investigator went on, "Her commanding officer couldn't decide whether she was crazy, or she just liked to play at being crazy. But whichever it was, I think she scared the holy bejesus out of him."

The investigator paused again, and Miles still said nothing. Finally, figuring he was dismissed, the guy got up to leave. But at the door he stopped and said, "If you want my recommendation, boss, I say stay away from her."

Instead, Miles had her in for an interview the very next day.

Her beauty literally stole his breath away. He'd long ago lost count of the number of actresses and models he'd fucked, and still he'd never had that happen to him before. Where the very sight of a woman closed up his throat so that he couldn't inhale or exhale, just gape at her like a beached fish.

"So tell me," he finally said, when he got his breath back, "what are you running from, Ms. Yasmin Yakir?"

He expected a gasp or at least a blush, but all he got was a little shrug that drew his eyes down to her breasts. "So, you did your due diligence on me and found a skeleton. Big whoop. We all got them." She crossed her long legs, made sure he was looking, then added, "What are you running from, Mr. Marcario Tavoularis?"

It was so funny, he almost laughed out loud. He'd set out to shock her, and he ended up shocked. Not so much that she knew he'd changed his name from the Greek Marcario Tavoularis to the Waspish Miles Taylor, but that she'd gone to the trouble to find this out about him. He hadn't tried all that hard to bury his working-class origins, but it would still have taken some digging.

But then she'd been in the Israeli intelligence, after all, or a form of it anyway. He was confident, though, that his real secrets, his bodies, were too deeply buried for her to have gotten even a whiff of their stink.

So he leaned forward and put a lot of mean into the smile he gave her. "What's your point, Ms. Yakir or Poole, or whatever? That you're smart and you got a set of balls? You think that makes us even?"

The smile she gave back to him made him hard. "No, Mr. Tavoularis, or Taylor, or whatever. When you kill your first man," she said, "then we'll be even."

He wanted to wipe that smart-ass smile off her face by telling her about the big kill, but he didn't. He told her about it eventually, though. Eventually he'd told her pretty much everything.

"DON'T FROWN AT me like that," she said to him now.

She smoothed the deep crow's-feet around his left eye with the tips of her fingers. "You think too much about things sometimes. Analyze and poke at them. Analyze and poke at *me*. Some people are simply born in love with the taste of blood."

A door slammed down below and someone laughed, too loudly. Miles turned away from her and limped to the window to see what the noise was about.

The sun was long gone now, but enough light was still left in the summer sky to see that it was nothing, just three of the catering crew who'd come out onto the deck from the billiard room for a smoke. To-morrow night he was throwing a party here at his beach cottage, an inti-mate gathering of fifty or so of the world's superrich and famous.

My beach cottage. Hunh. Twenty rooms, stone fireplaces, wraparound verandas, ocean views, and a $12 million price tag—and here at the Vineyard they called it a "cottage."

"Did I ever tell you, Yaz, that I was born and raised right here on the island?" Of course he'd told her, and probably more than once, but he went on anyway. "In a little town called Oak Bluffs. Five of us squeezed into a real honest-to-God New England cottage. Four tiny rooms built by some whaler a couple of centuries ago. It had a lot of gingerbread on the outside so the tourists all thought it was 'cute,' but inside, the linoleum floors were peeling and the old pipes froze and broke every winter. And there was never enough money for anything. My daddy—before he took off on us when I was thirteen—he ran the local gas station. He took care of the fancy cars of the rich summer families who thought of us as townies, when they bothered to think of us at all."

She had followed him to the window and now she slipped her arm through his, leaned into him.

"And yet now those very same people," she said, "are coming to your parties in this big ol' house, their lips in a permanent pucker the better to kiss your ass, and you like it, Miles, and your ass likes it because it feels just so damn *good*."

Miles laughed at the image she'd put into his head, but it was a bitter laugh. Even after all these years, after that dump of a house and his brute of a father, and the rich snobs who came to rub his face in it with their very existence—it all still festered.

They were quiet together a minute, then he said, "I've had this dream the last couple of nights. I'm a kid again, out in the backyard of the Oak Bluffs house, only instead of playing I'm trying to bury a dead body, and it's raining so hard that, no matter how much dirt I shovel in the grave, the water keeps washing it away, exposing the bones."

He turned to look at her. "And, yeah, I know what you're going to say. Sometimes a dream is just a dream."

"No," she said, and something was in her eyes, something hard and cold. "What I'm going to say is that you lied to me."

"About what? And, anyway, are you going to tell me you've never lied to me? Everybody lies. It's in our natures. Hell, the whole world spins merrily along in a circle fuck of lies."

"Your big kill. You lied to me about the reason for it."

"Funny, but that is one thing I haven't lied to you about."

"Call it a sin of omission then."

He shook his head, feeling a little pissed now. "Still not following you."

"The altar of bones."

"The *what*? Yaz, I swear to you I don't know what you're talking about."

Instead of answering, she lifted her left hand and he saw that she was holding one of those miniature tape players. At some point she'd put down her drink and picked up the player and he hadn't noticed her doing it, and that bothered him. Was it those damn pain pills he'd taken for his knee, fuzzing up his head, or was he really losing it?

He knew about the recording she'd made in the hospital, of course. She'd given him the gist of it when she used a burner phone to call him from Galveston on his secure line. How she'd taped the old man right before he croaked, spilling his guts to his priestly son, telling the boy all about the big kill and the home movie he'd had made of it. Only O'Malley didn't have the movie anymore, had never really had the movie, because some woman called Katya Orlova had run off with it and disappeared.

Miles thought Yasmine had told him everything about O'Malley's confession and what had gone down in Galveston, but now she pushed a button on the tape player. He hadn't heard that voice in forty-eight years. Mike O'Malley's voice.

And Yasmine hadn't told him quite everything, after all, because he heard Mike O'Malley say, "It all started with Katya Orlova and the altar of bones, but it ended with the kill."

MILES LISTENED THROUGH it to the end, until that familiar voice, an old man's voice now, faded so it was barely intelligible, saying something that sounded like "I thought she'd died in the cave." Then after a long pause, another voice said, half plea, half prayer, *"Dad? Oh, God—"*

Yasmine turned off the tape player.

"Is that it?" Miles asked.

She nodded. "He didn't say another word after that. He slipped into a coma, and then it was bye-bye, Mikey."

Miles didn't say anything, just looked out the window at a sea that shone silver under the rising moon.

"You really don't know what it is, do you?" Yasmine said. "This altar-of-bones thing." She laughed, and he heard in her laugh the madness that always lived in her, just beneath the surface. "Oh, Lord, this is almost too funny, Miles. You went and killed—"

"No." He thrust away from both her and the window, took a couple of steps, then turned back. "O'Malley did the killing."

"And the Russian, Nikolai Popov, he did the planning. But you conned them into doing it. You were the big mastermind. Isn't that what you told me? Only now it looks like you were the one who got played."

He almost hit her. He got as far as lifting his arm for a backhanded slap, but the way she just stood there, ready to take it, even though she could see it coming . . . He could see she *wanted* him to do it. And that stopped him.

Anyway, the face he really wanted to smash wasn't hers.

It all started with Katya Orlova and the altar of bones. . . . What in hell was that? It almost sounded like a joke. If you didn't know Nikolai Popov.

"You've got to find this Katya Orlova woman, Yaz. Find her, get the film, make her tell you all about this altar of bones.

"And then kill her for me, please."

PART THREE

THE LEGACY

12

San Francisco, California
Back in the present

ZOE DMITROFF looked out the window of her Mission Street law office for any sign of the Impala. Puke brown with a dented front fender, it had been circling the block for over an hour now, slowing down every time it passed her door. It was too misty and rainy for her to see the face of the man behind the wheel, but she knew who it was. Manuel Moreno.

She knew what he wanted, too. He wanted his wife. His obsession. His punching bag.

"Yeah, well, those days are over for you, chump," Zoe said out loud, feeling a little silly, but also more than a little creeped out by the circling Impala. By now the anonymous white SUV carrying Inez Moreno and her three-month-old daughter would be well on its way to a safe house out of state. Something Manuel shouldn't have figured out until five hours from now, when his wife didn't come home after the end of her nursing shift at San Francisco General. Yet here he was, and this was way more than a little creepy.

"It's like he's living inside my head and all I gotta do is even *think* about leaving him, and somehow he knows," Inez had told her once. "He just knows."

Outside, a tire squealed. Zoe tensed, then relaxed once she got a good look at the car that whisked past her window, spraying water. Not the Impala.

Normally the Latino neighborhood bustled with activity, but on this wet and chilly February afternoon few people were out and about. Paco G., who sold fake-leather handbags from a stand on the corner, was already packing it in for the day. Even Tía Juanita, who usually lived in the alley in back of the bodega next door, had given up picking through the trash for cans and bottles and set off to find a shelter.

A Muni bus pulled up to the stoplight, wipers flapping, exhaust belching out a cloud of smoke. Zoe craned her head to look around it. Still no Impala. Maybe he'd given up, too.

Except that men such as Manuel Moreno never gave up.

She turned away from the window and finished clearing off her desk of the case files she'd been studying. When she was done, she put on her black leather bomber jacket and slung the oversize Tumi satchel she used as a combination purse and briefcase over her shoulder. She turned out the lights and headed for the door.

Zoe's office was in a small Victorian-style storefront, sandwiched between the bodega and a T-shirt shop. She got as far as the second step of the front stoop, then the Impala whipped around the corner, nearly knocking down a bike-messenger boy, and screeched to a stop at the fire hydrant.

Manuel Moreno flung open the car door and got out. He was a weedy man, with a scraggly goatee and small, tight eyes.

"Where's Inez?" he shouted, coming right at her, getting up into her face. "Where's my wife?"

"I don't know where she is," Zoe said, and that was no lie. She'd set the system up that way herself because you couldn't be ordered by a court by tell what you didn't know.

Manuel's mouth curled, and he leaned into her, so close she could have counted the individual hairs on his pathetic chin. "Inez is a scared little rabbit. She'd never do this on her own. You know where she's at, lady, and before I'm done with you, you're gonna be beggin' me to let you tell me."

Out the corner of her eye, Zoe saw a silver Ford Taurus pull up, the kind of car that in this neighborhood shouted *la policía* so loudly it might as well have been painted black-and-white. It double-parked alongside the Impala, and two plainclothes cops—a man and an Asian woman—got out.

Zoe knew the man, Inspector Sean Mackey of Homicide, and he never brought her anything but bad news. But right now she wanted to throw him a ticker-tape parade.

"You might want to cool it," she said to Manuel. " 'Cause there's a big, badass cop standing right behind you."

The man snorted. "Yeah, right. What do I got—*stupid* written all over my forehead?"

"Well, since you asked . . ."

Inspector Mackey slammed the flat of his big hand down hard on the Impala's hood. Moreno whirled, almost tripping over his own feet.

"Hey, what the—"

"Better watch it, tough guy," Mackey said. "The lady's got a black belt in tae kwan do. She can kick your ass so bad you'll be pissing blood for a week."

"She can *kiss* my ass, is what she can do."

Mackey stepped into Moreno's space. His voice, though, was soft and smooth as whipped cream. "You might want to go on home now. Take a nice long shower, then pour yourself a brewski and chill for a bit."

Moreno clenched his fists, but he brushed past Mackey and went to his car. He jerked open the door, got inside, and revved up the engine. Then he poked a finger out the window at Zoe. "You tell Inez we ain't finished. Not by a long shot."

"Whoever this Inez is," said the female cop, as they watched the Impala pull out into traffic, "she better not get within a mile of that guy. At least not until he settles down a bit."

Zoe didn't comment. Sometimes the police sympathized with her cases. Sometimes they didn't.

"You okay, Zoe?" Mackey said.

"I'm fine, Mack. Thanks for showing up when you did, though."

"Aw, you'd have taken him."

Zoe shrugged. "Maybe. He was pumped." She held out her hand to the female cop. "I'm Zoe Dmitroff."

"Wendy Lee," the woman said, laughter and curiosity bright in her eyes. "Mack was filling me in about you on the way over here."

"Really?" Zoe looked at Mackey, but he wouldn't meet her eyes. She wondered what he'd said about her. He was a good-looking guy, square-jawed and nicely ripped, and there'd always been this little frisson of attraction between them. But it was never going to go anywhere because he flat out couldn't handle what her mother did for a living.

"And I saw that report Channel 4 news did on you a couple of days ago," Wendy Lee was saying. "About how you've set up an underground-railroad-type service to help get women and kids get away from the assholes in their lives."

"Sometimes she helps them get away," Mackey put in, a little edge to his voice. He didn't always approve of what she did for a living either. "Sometimes they pump a shotgun round into the asshole's chest instead or bury a meat cleaver in his head, and then she helps them walk on the murder rap."

"Sometimes," Zoe said, "when the system fails you, a meat cleaver might seem like your only recourse."

"And who gets to decide when that line's been crossed? Who gets to decide when killing the guy becomes a . . . How did you put it? Oh, yeah. An *only recourse*."

Wendy Lee grinned at her partner. "I think the reporter did mention something about that, too, Mack. Only the way he put it, Ms. Dmitroff not only specializes in battered-wife and partner syndrome as a defense, she works pro bono to free those poor women already convicted and shipped off to prison for murdering their abusers during previous, less enlightened times."

Mackey snorted. "There you go."

"So moving right along," Zoe said. "What brought you guys out here anyway?"

Mackey reached in his coat pocket and pulled out a handful of photographs. "You know this woman?"

Zoe was a criminal-defense attorney; she'd seen crime-scene photos before. And Mackey had only given her headshots so there weren't any visible wounds, just some blood around the old woman's sunken mouth. But something about her, something so vulnerable in those opaque, staring eyes, pulled hard at Zoe's heart. She knew—without quite knowing how she knew—that this poor old woman had died alone and afraid.

"No, I don't think I know her. . . . Should I? What happened to her?"

"She's a homeless woman who was stabbed late last night in Golden Gate Park. On Kennedy Drive near the Conservatory of Flowers. The murder weapon was left in her—some weird kind of knife I've never seen before. This guy and his friend were tooling along in his new Jag when they interrupted the killer in the act. Literally. She died on him before the ambulance could get there, and I know that had to've been tough on him, but now he's got a rant going with the media about poor old homeless women getting shivved on our city streets. There's a real shit storm going on down at the Hall."

Zoe looked at the crime-scene photo again, drawn by those dead, staring eyes, and she felt almost swamped by feelings of sadness and loss. It didn't make any sense. She didn't know this woman, but it felt as if she *ought* to know her. It was her eyes. Something about her eyes . . .

"Do you—" Zoe's voice cracked, and she had to start over. "Do you know who she is yet?"

"Not exactly," Mackey said. "We canvassed the park and found a trannyho called Buttercup who cruises the Panhandle, and who claims they were both part of a colony camping out in the woods behind the Conservatory. He . . . she . . . said the old woman's name was Rosie something."

Zoe tore her gaze away from the eyes in the photograph. She looked up to catch Mackey studying her, concern on his face, but also with a cop's wariness.

"I'm sorry, Mack, but I just don't know her. What made you think I would?"

He reached in his pocket and this time pulled out a clear plastic evidence envelope. "The ME found this caught way in the back of her throat. Like maybe she'd tried to eat it to keep her killer from getting hold of it. It was pretty badly chewed up, but those guys in the lab can do wonders these days."

The envelope held a shredded scrap of paper, scribbled on in pencil. The writing had been chemically enhanced, but even then only part of it was still legible. Zoe could read enough of it, though, and a chill settled over her.

"It's my home address. Not my office. My home."

She looked up at Mackey, who exchanged cop looks with Wendy Lee, then cleared his throat. "You ever hear of something called the altar of bones?"

"No, but it sounds weird. What is it?"

In typical cop fashion he didn't answer. Instead, he produced another plastic evidence envelope and handed it to her. "This photograph was in the pocket of the old lady's coat. We figure it was taken back in the late fifties to go by the clothes and hairstyles. Are either of the two people in it familiar to you?"

Zoe looked down and felt the spit dry in her mouth. It couldn't be, simply couldn't be.

It was an old black-and-white snapshot of a pretty blond woman in her twenties standing with her arm around the shoulders of a little girl of about six. The little girl wore pigtails and a parochial-school uniform and smiled widely for the camera. They stood in front of the entrance to Twentieth Century–Fox studios. Zoe knew it was Twentieth Century–Fox studios because her mother had this same photograph, or rather a larger version of it, in an ornate silver frame on the desk in her library.

"But I don't . . . It doesn't make any sense. How did she get this?"

"So you've seen it before?" Mackey asked. "Or the people? You've seen them before?"

But Zoe didn't really hear him, she was staring at the photograph's crimped corners, at how badly it had faded over the years. Something had been spilled on it at one time—coffee? blood?—staining the sky above the studio sign. But then it had been lived with and loved by an old homeless woman who had been murdered, not carefully preserved in a silver frame.

It began to rain again, fat drops splattering the plastic envelope, as Wendy Lee came up to look over Zoe's shoulder. "Our vic's had a rough go of it and a lot of time has passed since this photograph was taken, but the ME thinks it's the same woman. They're going to run a photo analysis program later to get a more definitive answer."

"But they can't be the same," Zoe said. "The woman in this picture is my grandmother. And her name wasn't Rosie. It was Katya. Katya Orlova. Only she's been dead for almost fifty years."

13

Z OE GUNNED the Babe.

She snagged a yellow light, zipped across Market, hooking a left first chance she got, then right onto Franklin. No way would she stay on Van Ness with its traffic lights turning red at every cross street. She went up, up, through the wind-whipped rain, eyes peeled for cops. A lot of them knew the Babe, and those who didn't would still just love to ticket a vintage baby blue Mustang.

She broke a good-size law, not allowing a pedestrian to waltz out in front of her, drenching him instead, but she had to get to her mother ahead of the cops. She had to find out how an old homeless woman who came to be murdered in Golden Gate Park turned out to be the same grandmother who'd died in an automobile accident years and years ago.

But the only way you ever had a hope of getting the truth out of Anna Larina Dmitroff was to catch her by surprise. If Zoe could get to her mother first, if she could to look into her mother's face, into her eyes, maybe *something* would bleed through that cold, hard mask she wore.

Almost there. Her wipers drug across the windshield, fog piled up inside. The Babe had good rain traction—she cut off a yellow cab, swerved around a big honker Lexus, curses and middle fingers flying in her wake, nearly ended up in the yard of a tall, skinny Victorian. She cut a hard left on Washington, spraying water like a rooster tail, nearly skidded into a parked Toyota, rolled through the stop signs at Gough and Octavia, and two blocks later swung into the driveway of her mother's mansion on the crest of Pacific Heights, the Babe's tires squealing. It was twelve minutes exactly since she'd left Mackey and his partner, Wendy Lee, telling them she was due in court. She'd watched them drive away, then ran around to the alley behind the bodega where she parked her car.

And now she'd beaten them here, thank God, but she had to hurry.

Wind drove the rain into her face as she raced up the steps of the huge granite-and-glass house. But the sight of the tall, ebony double doors, with their sterling-silver handles, stopped her cold.

Thirteen years ago, on the day of her high school graduation, she had walked through those doors and out of her old life with nothing but a duffel bag full of clothes. She swore to herself she would never come back, but she should have known better. You can escape some of your past, but not all of it.

Zoe drew in a deep breath, lifted her head, and pressed the bell. Less than five seconds later it was opened by a man with no neck and hands the size of turkey platters. She shoved past him, probably not smart since she could see he sported a gun in a shoulder holster under his loosely cut black jacket.

"I'm her daughter," Zoe said as he grabbed her arm. "So if you're fond of your hands, you'd better take them off of me."

The man had a weathered face, weary eyes, and fast reflexes. He immediately released her.

"Where is she?" What if she wasn't here? Please, God, she had to get to her mother before the cops, she—

"The *pakhan*," he said, "is up in the library."

Zoe wasn't about to get in the coffin-size elevator. She ran up all four flights of the sweeping limestone stairs, but at the top another door stopped her.

This one was made of solid, shining mahogany, and on the other side of it was Anna Larina's sanctuary. Thirteen years since she'd been inside this house, and two more since she was inside that room. Not since a summer's day when she was sixteen, the day her father had gone in there and sat down at her mother's desk, a giant slab of black marble. Sat down, put a gun under his chin, and pulled the trigger.

Zoe had been the only one in the house that day, the only one to hear the shot. The one who had seen the blood soaking into the ivory silk Persian sarouk and teak floor, who'd seen the splattered bits of gore. The one who'd had to look into was left of her father's face.

━━━━━━━━

Zoe flung the door open with such force it banged against the wall.

Her mother looked up from a laptop computer screen, while her right hand went under the black marble desk to where she kept a Glock 22 on a spring-loaded shelf. Anna Larina Dmitroff had not connived and fought and murdered her way to become the boss of a Russian *mafiya* family by being careless.

"*Zoe,*" she said, and Zoe was surprised to see real shock and concern flash across her mother's face. "Why are you here? Has something happened?"

"Why? Would you care if something had?"

"Don't be ridiculous. Of course I would care." Anna Larina, who'd half stood up, settled once more behind the massive marble desk. "You're looking a bit harried and damp, but otherwise well. All grown-up," she said, assessing her daughter now with cool, indifferent eyes. "But, since in all these years I haven't received so much as a Christmas card from you, I could only assume something dire has happened to bring you here now."

Zoe had to set her teeth to keep from screaming. God, how she'd always hated that light, dry voice that could mock and cut and scar so easily. Thirteen years and nothing had changed. One look at that beautiful but soulless face and all the old bad feelings came rushing back, mixing in her blood like poison.

She needed to pull herself together, to push her emotions down deep. She knew from bitter experience that you couldn't show so much as a flicker of feeling to Anna Larina, show her anything like love or hate or fear, or even anger, because feelings opened you up and then she would eviscerate you. Quickly and cleanly.

Zoe walked toward the great black marble slab of a desk slowly, to give herself time. The room was beautiful but cold, like the woman who occupied it. Shaped like a triangle, it jutted out into the sky like a ship's prow, overlooking the bay and the Golden Gate Bridge. Against the one wall not given over to the floor-to-ceiling windows stood expensive Scandinavian bookcases. They held some books, but were mostly filled with the finest pieces of her mother's antique Russian icon collection. When Zoe was a little girl, it had hurt so much to think these icons mattered more to her mother than she did.

She set the crime-scene photo she'd filched from Mackey carefully down onto her mother's desk. "Look at this and tell me what you see."

Anna Larina laid both hands flat on either side of the photograph and looked down. She studied it in silence, while Zoe studied her. Absolutely no hint of recognition, no hint of shock, no hint of anything.

She looked up, met Zoe's eyes full on. "I see some random old woman who looks dead. Did you expect me to know who she is?"

"Oh, please. Are you really going to try to pretend that you don't recognize your own mother?"

It was a deliberate slap, a hard one. Her mother's head jerked as she stared back down at the death photo. Her hands, still lying flat, turned white at the knuckles. But beyond that small reaction it was still impossible to tell what she was thinking, what she was feeling.

Zoe knew her mother could order one of her enforcers, her *vors*, to whack someone as easily as she could order up a pot of tea, but she didn't believe her mother was responsible for this if for no other reason than it was sloppy, and Anna Larina Dmitroff was never sloppy. Zoe had wanted to rattle her, though, and she had.

She picked up the silver-framed picture on the desk—an enlarged version of the one in the glassine envelope Mackey had shown her—and laid it faceup next to the crime-scene photo. "Do you see the resemblance now? She's got our eyes. Or rather we have hers."

"I don't—" Anna Larina cut herself off. Zoe saw her mother swallow convulsively but she didn't say anything more.

"You don't what—believe it? Because she died in a car accident when you were eleven? Drove off a cliff and into the ocean in bad weather and left you to grow up in an orphanage. Did you actually see her buried, Mother? Or did you just make the whole thing up to keep me away from her?"

Anna Larina seemed not to have heard her. "She is so old here. So

old." She lightly touched the face of the woman in the crime-scene photograph with the tips of her fingers. "All these years I've seen her in my
mind the way she was then. Young and beautiful, so full of life and laughter. She had the sweetest laugh. I always thought of rose petals when she
laughed because of how the sound of it would curl up on the edges. Just
like rose petals do."

Her voice trailed off and her mouth softened a little. "Odd how I
just remembered that, and now she's dead."

"Not just dead, Mother. Murdered. Or don't you know a crime-
scene picture when you see one?"

Anna Larina pushed the photograph away from her. "Yes, of course
I do."

She got up from her desk and went to close the door. The click of
the latch as it swung shut seemed loud in the taut silence.

She stared at Zoe, letting the silence drag, then she said, "I thought
she was dead. I never lied to you to keep you away from her. That's ridiculous. She didn't want me. Why in hell would she want you?"

The words were spoken in that cool, emotionless voice, but Zoe had
seen a dark emotion flare in her mother's eyes. Hurt, yes, but something
more. Guilt? Fury?

Zoe looked at this woman who was her mother. The sculpted cheekbones and high forehead, smooth as a polished seashell. The gray eyes,
wide-spaced and tilted at the corners. Anna Larina's age had always been
a closely guarded secret, but she had to be almost sixty by now. Yet she
seemed not to have aged a day in all these years. *I could be looking in a
mirror,* Zoe thought, and the horror of it twisted in her like a knife in
the guts.

If she'd inherited her mother's face, had she also inherited her black
soul?

Anna Larina's full mouth curved into a wry smile. "What are you
looking for, Zoe? The mark of Satan on my brow? Proof that we aren't
anything alike, after all? That's what you've always been afraid of, isn't
it? It's why you ran away, why you're on that battered-women's crusade
of yours. You're trying to buy your salvation by atoning for my sins."

Zoe felt a sharp pain in her arm. She looked down and saw her fist was clenched in a tight knot. She uncurled her fingers, made herself breathe. "Don't flatter yourself. Right now all I want to know is how the woman who gave you birth ended up homeless, living with the winos and drug addicts in Golden Gate Park."

"I don't—Golden Gate Park?" Anna Larina waved a hand at the photograph on the desk. "Is that where she . . ."

"Was murdered? Yes. It happened in front of the Conservatory of Flowers. She was stabbed with a knife. The cops didn't know who she was at first—"

"And yet they came hotfooting it right to you with their crime-scene photos? So either they're psychic, or you're not telling me everything."

God, the woman is quick, Zoe thought. She needed to remember that. She'd learned in the martial arts not to let the enemy get inside your moves or inside your head; she needed to remember that Anna Larina was her enemy. Her mother was her enemy, and in her heart of hearts, since she was the smallest child, she'd always known that. She just didn't know *why.*

"Before someone rammed a knife up to the hilt in her chest," Zoe said, deliberately making her words blunt, shocking, "your mother managed to swallow a piece of paper. Or half swallow it. It had my name and address on it."

Another cold smile curled Anna Larina's mouth. "Good Lord, how deliciously mysterious of the old woman. She knew where you were, yet she couldn't manage to find the time in between panhandling and urinating in doorways to drop by to see you before she was stabbed? No? Well, what a touching scene we all were spared."

"For God's sake, Mother."

"'For God's sake, Mother,'" Anna Larina mimicked. "What do you want from me, Zoe? Tears? I used mine up a long time ago."

Zoe uncurled her fist again, drew in another deep breath. "I thought maybe she'd been here to see you. Because how else would she have known about me?"

Again Zoe saw something flicker deep in Anna Larina's eyes. *She knows something,* Zoe thought. *She knows what brought her mother here.*

After a moment, Anna Larina shrugged and said, "It's not like either of us has been hiding out in the witness protection program. A three-minute search on Google would've done the trick."

She crossed her arms over her chest and went to look out the wall of glass, although there was nothing to see today, no bridge or bay, just clouds and rain. "So are we done here now, Zoe?"

"No, we are not done, Mother. Not even close. Let's say for the moment I believe you. That this is all such a big surprise to you. Was any of that sappy orphanage story you fed me over the years the truth?"

"Oh, *God*," Anna Larina said in a burst of sudden and genuine exasperation. "What a stubborn little bitch you are, and, yes, of course you got that particular attribute from me. Very well. I'll allow you five more minutes to probe away at the festering childhood wounds you imagine I have, if only you will promise to leave me in peace afterward."

Anna Larina took a package of cigarettes and a gold lighter out of the pocket of her black cashmere pants and lit up. She watched the lighter's flame a moment, before she snapped it closed.

"The orphanage," Zoe said. "Was any of that real?"

"Oh, it was real all right. A big, ugly brownstone run by the Sisters of Charity in a run-down part of Columbus, Ohio. There were even bars on the windows, although I suspect they were more to keep the neighborhood riffraff out then us little Orphan Annies in. It wasn't all gruel and daily beatings, but it was still pretty grim. Only my mother was very much alive when she dumped me off there. Me and one small suitcase of clothes and a cardboard box with a few of my treasures."

"But why Ohio, of all places, when you were living in L.A.? And, besides, no woman would just up and abandon her child. She must have had a reason."

"You surprise me, Zoe. Given whose daughter you are and what you do for a living, you still have a remarkably rosy view of human nature."

"But you must have some inkling of why she did it. If not then, then now, looking back on it."

Anna Larina tilted her head back and blew a perfect smoke ring at the ceiling. "Must I?"

Zoe picked up the silver-framed photograph and returned it to its place on the desk. Anna Larina had cared enough to keep it where she could see it every day. The woman in front of the studio gates with her arm wrapped around her little girl's shoulders certainly looked happy, full of life. But this had been taken a year before the orphanage, if Anna Larina was to be believed.

"You told me she worked for Fox as a cinematographer—"

"More like a cameraman's gofer, I think. Although . . ." Anna Larina trailed off, staring at the end of her cigarette, as if she was really trying to remember now.

"I think the studio was finally putting her to work behind the camera there at the end. I remember she'd already done some actual filming for one picture, and she was all excited because they were about ready to go into production on another. I was worried because it was coming up on my birthday—I was going to be nine—and I was afraid she'd get so wrapped up with her new job that when the big day arrived, she wouldn't remember it. But then we ran off before that could happen, just took off in the middle of the night, or so it seemed to me. She didn't even bother to leave a note for Mike."

"Mike? Who was Mike?"

"Mike O'Malley. My stepfather, or I guess it would be more accurate to call him Mother's husband, since he was hardly much of a father to me. But then they were only married for a couple of months before we took off."

"*Husband?*" Zoe stared at her mother. "This is the first time you've ever mentioned you had a stepfather."

"Like I said, it was only for a couple of months, and even then he wasn't around the house all that much. He was a location scout for the studio and on the road a lot of the time, and before your mind can leap to any movie-of-the-week scenarios—no, he didn't beat her, and he never touched me inappropriately, as they say. He barely seemed aware of my existence."

"Beatings and child abuse aren't the only reasons women leave their husbands."

Anna Larina shook her head. "If you say so. Only I was there, and on our way out of town that night she pulled over at a stoplight so she could bawl her eyes out and moon over his picture—the whole sad, broken-heart drill. So, no, I don't believe she left him willingly."

"Just because she loved him doesn't mean she didn't have a good reason to be afraid of him."

"Again I bow to your vast experience, Zoe. All I know is she threw me and a few things in the car and we didn't stop driving—I mean, we literally did not stop except for taking naps alongside the road until we hit the Scioto River. And now we're back to where we started this little trip down memory lane, with her dumping me in that orphanage full of kisses and promises that she'd be back in a few weeks and me believing her."

"But she didn't come back. So what happened? No, not that tale you told me about her dying in an automobile accident. The truth."

"I don't know what happened to her. There's no reason for me to lie about it now. I don't know. The weeks went by, then months, then years, and during all that time I still believed she was coming back for me. No phone calls, no letters, not even a card on my birthdays and I still believed, and then one day I just stopped believing. Did I think she was dead? I really don't know. Maybe I hoped so. I just knew I was dead to her."

Zoe didn't know how much of that to believe, except for those last five words. *I knew I was dead to her.* They sounded as if they had truly come right from the depths of Anna Larina Dmitroff's soul.

"Did she ever tell you anything about her past before she was born? About her family? Where she came from?"

Anna Larina uncrossed her arms, turning away from the window. "She never said so outright, but from what little I know, she was probably illegitimate. Like I am. She used to tell me she was her mother's only child, like I was her only child, and that her mother always crooned to her about how she was born a blessed girl child, from a proud long line, and she couldn't be the last. Like it was supposed to be a special thing, to mean something, although what I haven't a clue."

But she did have a clue, Zoe thought, for again she'd caught that sheen of secret knowledge in her mother's eyes.

"It sounds sweet," Zoe said. It certainly didn't sound like anything else Anna Larina had ever said to her, and Zoe felt a deep ache from the loss of this grandmother she'd never known. "What else? Was she born here or in Russia?"

Anna Larina gave Zoe an impatient look, then she shrugged. "She was born in Shanghai, of all places. On the very day the Japanese invaded. She used to tell this crazy story that her mother, whose name was Lena, Lena Orlova, had escaped from a prison camp called Norilsk in Siberia and walked all the way to China, if you can believe that."

Anna Larina paused, shrugged again. "At some point after the war, though, Lena hooked up with a gem dealer from Hong Kong, and he brought her and my mother to live with him there. A few years later Lena went to buy some fish off a sampan, slipped on the gangplank, hit her head, and drowned in the harbor. I think my mother was fifteen, maybe sixteen at the time. Old enough, anyway, to make it on her own."

Zoe had never heard any of this before. It sounded exotic, adventurous. Until you really thought about what life would have been like in a Siberian prison camp and a city ravaged by war.

"Did she ever tell you how she got from Hong Kong to L.A.?"

"No, she never did. Although she had plenty of stories, full of the most amazing details, about her own mother, Lena. And that miraculous escape out of Siberia."

Her mother's words dripped with their usual sarcasm, but Zoe got the feeling that some small corner of Anna Larina's shriveled heart was as fascinated with this family history as she was.

"Like what sort of details?"

"Oh, how Lena walked only at night, so that her fur-wrapped silhouette wouldn't stand out against the snow-shrouded tundra, and how she built snow huts for shelter and made fires with moss scraped from rocks and tree trunks. And how she fed herself by milking reindeer and fishing from holes cut in the ice.

"Finally, after months of walking she ended up on a grassy hill overlooking the river that separated Russia from Mongolia, eating wild potatoes she'd dug up from a field and staring at the red poles that marked the border. The poles, topped by round metal signs painted with a hammer and sickle, were spaced every quarter mile or so, and she watched for two days and two nights, but she never saw any patrols. So in the end she simply walked from one side of the poles to the other, just one more step in a life of thousands that she'd taken since escaping from Norilsk."

It seemed impossible to Zoe to even imagine the courage and the strength of will that must have taken, and she felt small in comparison to this great-grandmother that she'd never heard about until now.

"So then what happened?"

"She kept on walking. Until one day she came across a shriveled old man with a rotting sampan, who took her downriver with him as far as he could, then turned her over to a great-nephew who gave her a ride on his vegetable cart. The great-nephew had a friend who worked as a brakeman on the railroad, and the brakeman had a brother, and so on, and she was passed from one person to another down the length of China. Until she found herself floating into Shanghai on a garbage scow and going into labor with my mother."

"Katya."

"Yes." Anna Larina stubbed her cigarette out in a crystal ashtray on the desk. "And God alone knows who the father was. . . . Is this really all that important, Zoe? Who cares? Lena's long dead, and now her daughter is, too, and from the looks of her, she was homeless, pathetic. Old. Someone probably knifed her for the pint of cheap whiskey she had in her pocket."

"God, what is wrong with you? She was your *mother*. All those years missing, cut out, a mystery—and now, suddenly, she's here and someone kills her, and you act like you couldn't care less. It's obvious she's been running from something all this time."

"Is it?"

"You know it is. So what scared her so badly that summer and then kept her scared for so long? Who would want her dead, and why?"

"I don't *know*," Anna Larina shouted, slamming her fist down on the desk so hard the lamp rocked. But it wasn't anger. Zoe had seen her mother angry before and this wasn't it.

Zoe picked up the crime-scene photograph and tucked it back into her satchel. "I'm going to the morgue to see her. Do you want to come?"

Her mother didn't bother to answer, just gave her a look.

"Then I take it you won't mind if I make the funeral arrangements."

Her mother laughed at that. "Really, Zoe. You can't shame the shameless—you should know that by now." Anna Larina waved a hand. "Do whatever you like with her. Although if it matters, she was Russian Orthodox. You may send me an announcement after you decide."

The room fell into a heavy silence. Zoe stood in the middle of the ivory silk rug. She felt suddenly lost, drained. She could think of nothing more to say to this woman.

But then, on her way to the door, she did think of something else. "Have you ever heard of the altar of bones?"

Anna Larina was back in her designer chair behind the black marble desk, closing up her laptop. She looked up and said just a shade too casually, "No. Why?"

"Never mind. It's not important."

Zoe started to turn away again, but her mother's voice stopped her. "It was your father's choice to put that gun to his head, Zoe. His choice to pull the trigger. He *left* you, deliberately took himself out of your life forever, but you couldn't accept that. You had to blame someone, and so you blamed me."

Zoe fought back the pain. Even after all these years, it was still an unutterable pain. "Daddy loved me."

"Oh, I have no doubt he believed he loved you. He simply loved himself more. He was a vain man, and he was weak. He turned the family business over to me, and then he hated me for doing the very things he wanted done but didn't have the guts to do himself."

"He loved me," Zoe said, shaking inside. "And that's always been your problem, hasn't it, Mother? You're jealous. Jealous of your own daugh—"

A sudden, sharp knock on the door cut her off. Her mother stared at her a moment longer, the color for once high on her pale cheeks. Then she dismissed her with a turn of her back. "Come in."

The door opened and a big man walked through it. Black, black hair, violent blue eyes, cruel mouth. He didn't look much older than Zoe, only in his midthirties. But the brutality in him was two lifetimes older.

He looked from her to her mother, than said in Russian, "Two cops are at the front door."

"Thank you, Sergei."

Zoe looked him up and down. A gun in a shoulder holster worn over a black T-shirt that clung to every well-buffed muscle. Black jeans and steel-toed boots. A colorful tattoo of a dagger dripping blood ran the full length of the inside of his thick forearm. It was Russian prison scratch, the tat your fellow cons gave you inside on the day you became a made man.

Zoe said, "Are you running so low on homegrown *vors*, Mother, that you now have to import them from the old country?"

The violent blue eyes flickered, swung back to her, dismissed her.

"Good-bye, Zoe," Anna Larina said.

On her way out, Zoe found Mackey and Wendy Lee standing in the middle of the enormous white, marble-tiled foyer. Wendy was admiring a sculpture of twisted bronze that shot up all the way to the top of the cathedral ceiling. Mackey was fuming.

"I saw your frigging car in the driveway," he said. "I'm calling Traffic. They should've jumped on your ass."

14

ANNA LARINA Dmitroff stared down at the blank screen of her laptop, but what she saw were other images playing out in her mind.

Her mother kissing her good-bye on the steps of that orphanage, and her sad, pathetic, little-girl self, clinging to her cardboard box of useless treasures, watching her mother go down those steps, turn the corner, and walk out of her life forever.

Until now.

So imagine my surprise, Mama, when you turn up here alive after all these years. Alive until last night, that is, when someone finally killed you. Now who could that have been, dear Mama?

Never mind. The who didn't matter, and the why Anna Larina already knew. They'd killed her for the altar of bones, of course.

And that serves you right, dear Mama, because I know why you came, and it wasn't for me. I don't exist for you, I haven't existed for forty-nine years. So of course you wouldn't come for me. You came for Zoe.

Anna Larina snatched the framed photograph from her desk and almost flung it against the wall, stopping herself just in time. She had to control the soul-eating rage that filled her, but it was so hard sometimes. Higher and higher it would rise until she thought it would choke her and she would die, strangling on her own fury. It was stronger some days than others, but it was always there, in her very bones, she sometimes thought. In the marrow of her bones.

The altar of bones.

You promised it to me, Mama. It's mine. Not Zoe's. Mine.

Okay, okay. She could handle this. She could handle Zoe. She'd fed the girl such a clever stew of truth and lies, so clever she'd almost lost track herself at times of what was fact and what was fiction. But Zoe . . .

Zoe, Zoe, Zoe. Have I been underestimating you? You're such a righteous little crusader, charging out into the world to do your good deeds to make up for all my wicked sins—it's saccharine enough to make my teeth ache. But maybe you have some of me in you, after all, huh, Zoe? A little of the hard and selfish and merciless bitch?

How much do you know, child of mine? Not everything obviously, but more than you were letting on.

She needed to think, to plan what do. Starting with Zoe—

"*Pakhan?*"

Anna Larina looked up, startled. Sergei Vilensky, one of her enforcers, still stood at the door, apparently waiting for her to say or do something. Oh, yes, the cops. They were downstairs, and no doubt fairly brimming with questions about dear Mama.

"Those *menty,*" Sergei said, using the vulgar Russian slang word for the police. "Do you want me to get rid of them for you?"

Anna Larina almost smiled. "This is America, Sergei. Here you don't 'get rid' of the cops by bonking them over the head and dumping them in the river, much as you might be tempted. For one thing, they'll only come back at you with a blizzard of warrants and subpoenas. Besides, it's nothing important, so I may as well talk to them and get it over with."

He nodded and turned to go, but she stopped him. "Sergei?"

He turned back, and she looked at his face, into his hard eyes. He was from the gutter, a brute, but he'd been with her for over a year now and she was beginning to realize that he had far more cunning than her other *vors,* whose usefulness tended to stop at the end of their fists.

"Do you know how I came to be the *pakhan?*"

If he was surprised by her question, he didn't show it. "The one with the most brains and balls always ends up as the *pakhan.* Eventually. But I did ask around when I first got here. Who wouldn't?"

"And what were you told?"

She thought he nearly smiled. "I was told your husband was a connected member of the Dmitroff outfit down in L.A., the boss's favorite nephew and would-be heir apparent if he ever got his shit together, while you were a high-priced call girl working the star circuit in Hollywood.

He paid you a thousand bucks to spend the night with him and ended up on his knees the next morning, proposing marriage with a two-carat diamond ring."

"It wasn't the next morning, it was a week later, and it was only a one-carat ring. He'd just been dumped, you see, and was on the rebound. Go on."

He looked at the big honker diamond she now wore on her left hand and raised his eyebrows, and she laughed. "I upgraded. Go on, Sergei."

He shrugged. "It turned out one of the loan sharks who worked for your husband was skimming off the top, and you spotted it right off soon as you took a look at the books. The next thing anybody knew the shark was found dumped in an alley, every bone in his body broken, and you'd taken over the loans and numbers business from your husband. After that you branched out into hookers and heroin, moved up here to San Francisco, and started encroaching on the Dmitroff family's northern territory. Only you took it high-tech, with computer-stock and banking scams, and by the time they figured it out, they were too late."

She said nothing to that, but instead made him stand there while she took her time lighting up another cigarette. And he did stand there, big and unmoving, so self-contained she couldn't even see him breathing.

"Well," she finally said, on an exhale of smoke, "you left out most of the blood and gore, but essentially you got it right. And do you know why I had you repeat that little story?"

This time he did smile. "You got a job you want me to do, something delicate, and you want me to understand what could happen to me if I fuck it up."

The smile she gave back at him was calculatedly mean enough to make his bowels water. "I don't just want you to understand it, Sergei Vilensky, I want you to *know* it. Know it in your gut—how far I've come, and how far I'm willing to go."

She paused, but he said nothing, his face showed nothing, and she thought she could trust him. At least as far as she intended to trust him.

"Because the 'delicate job,' as you put it, has to do with my daughter."

15

ZOE LOOKED down at the white plastic body bag that lay on a stainless steel gurney in the morgue. Too small surely to hold even the shrunken remains of an old homeless woman.

"Do it," she said.

Christopher Jenkins, the assistant medical examiner, studied her face, a worried look on his own. "Are you sure you wouldn't rather go through with this back in the viewing room, by video?"

"I want to see her. I need to see her, Chris."

"I don't know . . . ," he said, although he was already reaching for the bag's zipper, "I could catch all kinds of grief for breaking protocol, even though most of the guys around here know you." He pulled the zipper open just far enough to expose the head.

Zoe had steeled herself, yet she still wasn't prepared for the gut punch of seeing her grandmother like this.

Katya Orlova's face was like gray putty, the bones sunken, nothing left of the pretty young woman in the silver-framed photograph. But in her gut and in her heart, Zoe knew her. This was the woman who'd given her own mother life. Zoe had never realized before how primal were the ties of blood. She felt something for this woman. Not love—that was both too deep and too shallow a word. A bond, perhaps. A blood bond.

Yet this was also the woman who'd dropped her daughter off at an orphanage and disappeared. For forty-nine years. What loving mother could do such a thing? Had she been running even back then from whatever had finally killed her?

"Why?"

Zoe hadn't realized she'd spoken out loud until Jenkins said, "We'll get the bastard, Zoe. It's early yet."

Zoe stepped back and turned away from the body. The morgue was supposed to have an excellent ventilation system, but she would swear the smell of death hung in the air like an oily cloud.

"It might help to know . . . ," Chris Jenkins said, as he zipped up the body bag. "I don't think she was homeless for long. She had some fairly expensive dental work done recently, and she didn't have lice or any of the other parasites you can't help but pick up living on the streets. Also, if she hadn't been murdered, she would only have lived another month or so at the most. She was riddled with cancer."

Her grandmother had been dying of cancer? Was that why she was here? Zoe wondered. Had finding out that she was about to die driven her to reach out to the family she'd abandoned so long ago? Except she hadn't reached out. *Surely, she meant to, though. She had a piece of paper with my name and address on it.* A piece of paper she'd tried to swallow right before she died. To keep it from her killer? But why?

And whatever the reason, did it go all the way back to that young woman in the photograph? Had the seeds of her death been sown that long ago?

"Inspector Mackey said the murder weapon had been left in the body," Zoe said. "Can I see it?"

Jenkins hesitated a moment, then shrugged. "It's in the lab."

He led the way, holding open the door for her. "Did anyone ask you yet about giving us a DNA sample? It would give us a pretty definitive answer on whether the vi—the woman is your grandmother."

"Whatever I can do to help."

The cops would need the DNA test to compile their case, but she didn't. She knew the murdered woman in the body bag was her grandmother. Katya Orlova.

The blood bond.

━━━━━━━

"WE DUSTED THE weapon for prints," Chris Jenkins said, as he snapped on a pair of latex gloves. "Nothing. Not even a smudge. There were fibers, but they were all consistent with her clothing. Nothing extraneous."

He opened a manila envelope and upended it so the knife slid hilt first into his hand. He held it out, twisting his wrist back and forth like Darth Vader wielding a light saber. The dull gray blade was long, double-edged, with a hooked point.

"You don't run across a knife like this everyday," he said. "It's Russian, called a *kandra*. It took some digging, but I got the manufacturer nailed down to a small, nameless reindeer herder on the slopes of Siberia. . . . Zoe, that last bit was a joke."

But Zoe couldn't even manage a smile. In some dark corner of her heart, she'd been afraid there'd be something about the murder weapon to connect it with her mother. That it was some rare Russian knife was probably not good.

Jenkins rebagged the weapon and held up a cotton swab. "Open please."

Zoe opened her mouth and he swabbed the inside of her cheek.

"I don't know how much you know about maternal-lineage testing," he said, "but it uses a unique form of DNA found in the part of our cells responsible for energy called mitochondrials. They're passed down directly through the maternal bloodline."

"A blood bond," she said, marveling again at the thought.

"Yeah, you got it. Mitochondrials mutate so rarely over time, theoretically we could trace every woman alive today back to the first female homo sapien."

He held up the swab. "We're talking one hundred and seventy thousand years' worth of evolution, and on the end of this little piece of cotton I've got Eve."

IT WAS DARK by the time Zoe left the Hall of Justice. The rain had fizzled into a thick mist. She zipped her black leather bomber jacket and turned up the collar against the winter cold, but it didn't help her insides.

She'd parked the Babe farther down on Bryant, underneath the freeway. It wasn't the best part of town, and so she kept a wary eye out. The streetlamps barely penetrated back here among the concrete stanchions, and the wind whipped empty food wrappers against her legs.

There was little traffic, the only other pedestrian a ponytailed man who was chaining his bicycle to a row of mostly empty newspaper vending machines. She made eye contact as she passed. He nodded back at her and smiled.

She stepped off the curb to go around to the driver's side of her car, digging in her purse for her keys, then heard a footstep behind her. She caught a blur of movement out the corner of her eye—

The ponytailed man, swinging the bicycle chain at her head.

She ducked and spun around on the ball of her foot, but not quick enough. He whipped the chain around her neck, jerked her off her feet, and dragged her deep beneath the overpass. The chain dug into her throat, cutting off her air. She threw her satchel off to the side, but his eyes didn't even follow it.

Not a mugger. One of the abusers then, looking for his woman? Or . . . Oh, God, is he going to rape me?

His hot breath blew against the side of her face. "Where is it, bitch?"

What?

Zoe went limp, trying to draw the man off-balance, but he didn't fall for it. Instead he tightened his grip on the chain, and black spots danced before her eyes.

"Now you listen," the man said, in a heavy Russian accent. "I am going to ease up on this chain a little and you are going to sing for me like tweetie bird. The old lady wouldn't cooperate and she took a knife in the heart. How about you not being so stupid?"

Her chest heaved, and she fought back panic as her lungs strained for air. This was the man who'd killed her grandmother and now he was after her. But why? What did he want?

Hot breath again. "Now, I want the altar of bones, and you are going to have just one or two seconds to tell me where it is. If you don't, I'll choke you with this chain until you black out. When you come to, I'll have a knife pointed at your eyeball, and if you don't tell me then, I'll pluck out your eye like a wet grape."

As soon as Zoe felt the pressure of the chain ease, she slid her right leg back and twisted sharply away from him, whipping her fist across her body and smashing it into his throat.

He reared back, gagging.

She pivoted, lashed out with her right leg, and kicked him hard in the groin. It was only a glancing blow because he moved so fast, but it was enough to double him over. He hugged himself, cursing her, cursing the pain.

A siren cut through the night. Red and blue lights flashed.

The suddenness of it stopped Zoe for a split second, just long enough for the ponytailed man to turn and hobble away.

She started after him, screaming, "You bastard! Why did you kill her? What do you want?"

Tires squealed. Feet pounded behind her. A man's voice bellowed, "Police! Both of you, stop right now!"

Zoe—not sure how clear the cops were on who had been assaulting whom—stopped. But the ponytailed man kept going, still half-crouched over, but picking up speed.

Zoe pointed and yelled, "He's the one. Stop *him*."

The ponytailed man was running full out now. Zoe started after him again, but one of the cops grabbed her arm. "Oh, no, you don't, lady. You stay right here until we can get this sorted out."

Zoe watched as the cop's partner took off after the ponytailed man. But he was at least fifty pounds overweight and he ran like a Teletubby, and she thought he had a better chance of having a heart attack than of catching the perp.

———————

A COMPUTER SALESMAN had called 911 on his cell to report a woman being mugged beneath the overpass, and the patrol car had been idling at a stoplight only a block away over on Ninth Street.

Zoe let the beat cops go on thinking it was a mugging, and she gave a statement saying she hadn't gotten a good look at her attacker.

After the cops left, she got in her car and looked up Inspector Sean Mackey's cell number on her PDA. He answered halfway through the first ring.

"It's me. Zoe. Zoe Dmitroff. I—"

"Where in hell are you? Never mind. I'm parked outside your loft. Get over here—we need to talk."

She opened her mouth to tell him what he could do with his attitude, then suddenly she was back under the overpass, a chain digging into her throat, cutting off her air.

"Zoe?"

She closed her eyes, drew in a deep breath. "I'll be there in five minutes."

She lived six blocks away, off South Park, in a turn-of-the-century brick bakery that had been converted into lofts and apartments during the dot-com boom. In the nineties the neighborhood had bustled with purple-haired programmers and venture-capital highfliers, but they'd disappeared with the bust. At least now, Zoe thought as she pulled the Babe into a space behind Mackey's silver Taurus, it was easy to find a place to park.

He had his butt hitched up on the hood, his arms crossed over his chest, a frown on his face.

When she opened her car door, he unfolded his arms and straightened. The frown stayed. "I really ought to slap your ass in jail for interfering with a homicide investigation—" He cut himself off when she walked up to him and he got a good look at her face. "What happened?"

Her throat closed again, the smell of oily metal chain filled her nostrils. She wanted to gag. She started to reach up and touch the raw bruises on her neck, but stopped when she saw how badly her hand shook.

"What?" Mackey said.

"I just met my grandmother's killer, Mack. Up close and personal." Then she started laughing a little hysterically because it sounded so crazy. "He tried to strangle me with a bicycle chain."

Mackey gave her a long, hard look, then reached out and tilted her chin up and to the side to get a better look at the marks on her neck. "You really did meet up with him."

She nodded, swallowed around the tightness in her throat.

"Tell me."

She told him, feeling stupid that she'd been distracted and allowed herself to be taken by surprise. She gave him as many specifics as she could remember, such as the man's breath had smelled of wine and garlic, and that he spoke English with a Russian accent.

"And his shoes looked Eastern European. You know—thin leather and pointed toes, with the heels kind of built up to make him look taller."

Mackey nodded, writing it down in his notebook. When she was done, he called in to have an all-points bulletin put out on the suspect, then he took her through it again, and then a third time.

He said, "What's this altar-of-bones thing he wants so bad that he's willing to kill and torture an old woman and her granddaughter to get his hands on it?"

"I have no idea. None, Mack. I swear."

"You sure? No clue?"

She shook her head. "Wait, I just remembered something else. He was wearing this thick brown sweater and there was a rip—no, a cut on the sleeve, and I could see a bloody bandage through it. I hope my grandmother did that. I hope it hurt."

"Yeah, she did slice him up some," Mack said. "The ME found a cut on her palm, and blood that wasn't hers on the front of her coat and on a piece of broken bottle at the scene. We'll run the DNA through CODIS, but that always takes time." He thrust his fingers through his hair. "Do you think this could have anything to do with your family business? That this guy is one of your mother's Russian goons . . . what're they called?"

"*Vors.* You don't seriously think she up and decided yesterday to start whacking her nearest and dearest one at a time? Why would she do that?"

Mackey shrugged. "You tell me. I mean, we're talking about the woman who had the head of her brother-in-law's top enforcer delivered to him in a ten-gallon bucket of butter pecan."

"It was her cousin-in-law. And the head belonged to a guy who'd killed more people than Ted Bundy, but I get your point. I know she can be ruthless, but this afternoon when I showed her the crime-scene photo and told her who it was, she was shocked, Mack. I really think she believed her mother was already dead all these years."

"She said your grandmother had a husband." He took his notebook out of his pocket again and flipped it open. "A Mike O'Malley. You know anything about this stepfather of hers? Your mother claimed not to remember much."

Zoe shook her head. "Until today I never even knew he existed. But the ponytailed man can't be him. He's much too young. Late thirties at the most."

Mackey said nothing more, only looked at her, and his face softened. "Look, I know you're beat. But if you could come back down to Homicide and give a description to our sketch artist, maybe go through some mug books?"

Zoe brought her hand up to her neck. She kept thinking she could still feel the chain there. "Can I at least take a shower first? I feel filthy."

"Yeah, okay. I got a shitload to do back at my desk, anyway. You go on up, shower, have a cup of tea. Or better yet a stiff drink. We can hook up later on the mug book."

Zoe tried to smile, but her face felt tight. So she nodded instead and started for the door to the bakery. Then she stopped and turned back. "You asked me about the altar of bones earlier, when you first told me about my grandmother. How did you know it was what the killer was after?"

"I didn't. It was something else . . ." He hesitated.

"Come on, Mack. I know you guys like to hold things back, but he was going to cut out my eye."

"Your grandmother lived for a few minutes after she was stabbed. Long enough to talk to the guy who found her. The guy thought she told him, 'They didn't have to kill him. He never drank from the altar of bones. I got it back.'"

"*Kill* him? But that sounds like somebody else was murdered, too. Oh, God, Mack, do you think it's . . . ?"

"Somebody connected to you? Another long-lost relative, maybe? I don't know."

Zoe tried to think what it all meant, but she couldn't. She was too shaken, too scared. "And how do you drink from an altar of bones? It doesn't make any sense."

"Nothing about this case makes sense."

THE DOOR TO the first-floor rear apartment opened as soon as Zoe entered the bakery. A tall Hispanic woman with blue-black hair and a priest's eyes stepped out into the foyer.

"Hey, Maria," Zoe said. "How's it going?"

Maria Sanchez was hardly recognizable from the woman Zoe had saved from a murder rap five years ago. Zoe had been fresh out of law school then, working for the public defender's office and getting all the dregs cases, the sure losers, when the night-court judge had assigned her Maria's case: an immigrant woman from Nicaragua, who had put a shotgun to her husband's sleeping head and blown it off.

Zoe would never forget the first time she'd seen Maria, sitting on the narrow cot in a city jail cell. A woman whose soul seemed more battered than her face. A woman whose eyes were dead. But as they spoke, Zoe realized that what she thought were dead eyes, what she thought was a loss of hope, was in fact its exact opposite. Deep inside her Maria Sanchez had a human dignity so pure and strong, Zoe had never encountered its like before. In spite of all the evidence against her client—fingerprints, gunshot residue, even a well-Mirandized confession—Zoe had never wanted to win a case so badly.

To this day, she wasn't sure how she pulled it off. She thought that in the end Maria Sanchez herself had most swayed the jury, simply by taking the stand and telling her story. And when Zoe walked out of the courtroom that day with a free Maria by her side, she'd known what she wanted to do with the rest of her life.

For years Maria had sold hot tamales and burritos from a handcart on Mission Street during the day and waitressed tables at night, but just last month she'd finally opened up her own taqueria down by the Giants' baseball park. Usually Zoe wanted to talk and let her hair down with Maria, but not tonight. Not when she felt so battered herself.

"Did that policeman find you?" Maria asked. "He wasn't after one of your *chicas*, was he?" Maria always called the women Zoe rescued *chicas* no matter what their age.

"No, it's not that. I was sort of a witness to a case. . . . Listen, I'm going to go on up. I'm not feeling so hot tonight and—"

"*Sí, sí*, you go on up. . . . Wait a minute, though. The mailman left something with me for you. He said he found it stuck in the bin beneath the mailbox, where he leaves all the catalogs and magazines. But it never went through the postal system. See—no stamps and no postmark."

Maria handed her a brown padded envelope the size of a paperback. Zoe's name and address were printed on the envelope in block letters. There was no return address.

"That's odd." Then she thought, *Grandmother.* She hefted the package in her hand. It was light. "Thanks. I gotta go, but I'll call you later."

She walked past the elevator—a creaky, old metal cage a person would have to be insane to get into—and headed up the stairs. Her loft was at the top of six flights and usually she liked to see how fast she could run up them before she became winded, but not tonight.

Tonight, she walked slowly, holding the envelope tight, as if it were a magic talisman.

═══════

She couldn't believe it, simply couldn't believe it. Her front door was wide-open. The lights were on.

She ran into her loft without stopping to think the intruder could still be in there. The place was a shambles, but—

My cats.

God, oh, God. They were indoor cats, they'd spent their whole lives in this one big room. If they'd gotten out, if someone had hurt them . . .

She dropped her satchel and the envelope on the floor. She ran to the bed, flung up the quilt that was now dragging on the floor. Two sets of yellow eyes peered at her from deep in the corner. Her own eyes blurred with tears of relief.

Bitsy, a calico sometimes too brave for her own good, came right out at the sound of Zoe's voice. Barney, big and black and fat, wouldn't budge and hissed at her when she reached for him.

She had to resort to the cream cheese. Barney was a sucker for cream cheese and he had the potbelly to prove it.

The crinkle of the tinfoil wrap did the trick. His whiskers emerged first, followed by the enormous rest of him. He waddled over to lick a dab of the cheese off her finger, in between meows to let her know what he thought of this fine state of affairs.

Zoe sat on the floor and gathered her babies into her lap. She buried her face in their warm fur.

When her heart had finally quieted, she looked around her loft. Whoever had done this had not only searched the place, he'd savaged it. Shattered china, split sacks of flour and sugar, broken wine bottles, ripped cushions. The lock on her door was the best out there and it was the only thing that hadn't been broken. It had been picked.

A professional then, of some sort, but one who'd been angry. Angry enough to take it out on her things.

She scratched Barney under his chin. "What did he look like, babe? Did he have a long brown ponytail? Do you think you could pick him out of a mug—"

Out beyond the open door, a board creaked. She'd climbed up and down those stairs every day for five years. It was the fourth flight, third tread.

Barney heard it, too. He leaped out of her arms and shot back under the bed, Bitsy right behind him.

Zoe quickly and quietly got to her feet and picked up her satchel where she'd dropped it on the floor. She eased open the zipper, took out her gun, released the safety. She reached for the padded envelop nearby and slid it under the bed. Barney hissed.

She went to the door, thought about closing it, then didn't. She flicked off the lights instead.

She pressed her back against the wall, holding her gun two-fisted, barrel pointed up, and waited, her heart beating fast and hard.

A shadow crossed the threshold first, followed by the silhouette of a man. Zoe pressed the gun muzzle into his head, right behind his ear.

"Don't even breathe."

16

T HE SILHOUETTE didn't move, but he did breathe, a sharp intake that ended with her name. "Zoe? It's me."

Zoe pulled back the gun as her own breath whooshed out of her and she sagged against the wall. After a moment, she reached behind her and turned on the lights.

Inspector Sean Mackey stepped farther into the loft, his hands spread, half-raised in the air. His chest heaved with the adrenaline shooting through his system. "Dammit, woman. Are you nuts? I could've shot you."

"Yeah? You were the one with the muzzle of a Glock pressed against your ear."

"So will you put it away, for Christ's sake?"

Zoe looked down and saw she still had the gun pointed at his heart. "Sorry. I'm a little jumpy here."

"No shit." Mackey lowered his hands as he looked around him. "Jesus. What happened? It looks like a bomb went off."

"I'm guessing it was the ponytailed guy looking for the altar of bones—whatever that is. What are you doing back here anyway? I thought you were on your way to Homicide."

"I came to tell you that I've radioed for a patrol car to give you a lift. In case that asshole decides to come after you again. Now I'm thinking after we do the sketch and go through the mug books, you oughta spend the night in a hotel somewhere."

"I'll be okay. I doubt he's coming back—for one thing he already knows that what he's looking for isn't here. And I got a bar I can put across the door on the inside. The only way anyone can get through that is with a battering ram. . . . Mack, I really, really have to take a shower."

He waved a hand. "Okay, okay. I'm going. The patrol car should be here in five minutes tops, but I'm going to stick around outside until it gets here, just in case. And I'm sending the lab guys to go over this place with a fine-tooth comb."

After the door closed behind him, Zoe lowered the iron-reinforced bar and latched it into place. She watched out the window until she saw Mackey emerge and go to lean against a lamppost to wait for the patrol car. Feeling safe now, for the moment at least, she dropped to her knees and wriggled under the bed, feeling for the padded envelope.

She couldn't find her scissors in the mess, so she used a steak knife to slice carefully through the glued-down flap. She wet a towel and wiped flour, sugar, and some unidentifiable brown, gooey stuff off her flea-market table, and if the lab guys didn't like it, they could lump it. She found one chair that wasn't in splinters, pulled it up to the table, and sat down.

Barney and Bitsy joined her, purring and rubbing against her arms and generally getting in the way. For a moment longer she simply held the envelope in her hand. She felt excited and she wanted to cry. Her grandmother had left this in her mailbox not long before she was murdered, Zoe was sure of it.

She opened the envelope and emptied its contents carefully onto the table: a postcard, a key, and a couple of folded-up pieces of lined tablet paper.

The postcard, worn at the edges and bent in one corner, was of a famous medieval tapestry, one of those with a unicorn. She turned it over.

It wasn't addressed, but in the space for the message her grandmother, or someone, had written what looked like a poem in Russian:

Blood flows into the sea
The sea touches the sky
From the sky falls the ice
Fire melts the ice
A storm drowns the fire
And rages through the night
But blood flows on into the sea
Without end.

It didn't quite scan like a poem; it was odd all the way around. The words were simple, they conjured up clear images in her mind, but she couldn't make sense out of the whole. She read it twice more. Got nothing.

The small print at the top of the postcard identified the tapestry as *The Lady and the Unicorn:* À *mon seul désir.* Musée de Cluny, Paris, France. She flipped it back over. A woman stood in front of a tent with her maidservant beside her, holding open a casket. A unicorn lay on the ground next to her. But there was nothing in the tapestry of flowing blood or falling ice or a raging storm.

She tucked the postcard back into the padded envelope and picked up the key.

It looked old. No, beyond old—it looked as ancient as the beginning of time and felt heavy, like bronze. And strangely warm in her hand, as if it still held captive the fire from the forge that had fashioned it. One end was in the shape of a griffin, an animal with the head and wings of an eagle and the body of a lion. But the key's teeth were particularly strange—like Ferengi teeth, jagged and angled in a crazy way. Zoe couldn't imagine what kind of lock such a key would fit into.

She put the key back into the envelope with the postcard, then picked up the sheets of notebook paper and unfolded them. It was a letter, also written in Cyrillic, the words ragged and shaky.

To my beloved granddaughter,

They say you can disappear completely, living homeless on the streets. I pray this is so. That I will be able to get this letter to you without the hunters finding me first.

I regret so many things, but my greatest sadness is that I will never have the joy of looking on your face. To save you from the hunters, I've kept away for so many long and lonely years, but last week I was told that I have inoperable, incurable cancer. I am dying. It is the reason I am here now, the reason for this letter.

If only I could take all my secrets to the grave, but ignorance is a poor shield against danger, and doing one's duty despite the cost is still a noble thing, is it not? Yes, I must believe it is, or else for me there will be no salvation.

I'm running out of time, and there is always the danger this letter could fall into the wrong hands and innocent lives be lost, so I dare write no more, but this . . .

The women of our line have been Keepers to the altar of bones for so long, the beginning has been lost in the mists of time. The sacred duty of each Keeper is to guard from the world the knowledge of the secret pathway, for beyond the pathway is the altar, and within the altar is the fountain of life.

Upon my death you must become the next Keeper. I know you're probably asking, What about my mother? And you're right, the honor and the burden should have been hers, but—

Here, Zoe saw, were a few words had been heavily crossed out, before the letter went on.

You better than anyone know of Anna Larina's true nature. So the altar of bones must be your legacy. I cannot be there to guide you, instead I can only leave you these ridiculous riddles to unlock. No, I malign the past by telling you the riddles are ridiculous, for they were devised by earlier Keepers who understood all too well the altar's dark power and how the place of its existence must always be kept safe from the hunters.

For you see, there will always be hunters of one sort or another. Oh, their names and their makeup will change with the generations, but one thing has and will always remain constant. Somehow they learn of the altar's existence, and once they do, they are driven to harvest its power for themselves.

When my own mother first told me about the altar of bones, she warned me to trust no one, not even those I love. But I was a fool. A terrible crime was committed because I betrayed the altar's secrets, making the danger to you, my granddaughter, all the greater. Now, should the hunters ever find what they search for, *they will kill you and all who come near you simply for knowing too much.*

God forgive me, I should never have done what I did, yet without free will we would be a soulless species. So may the Lady advise and preserve you in the choices you too will have to make.

Look to the Lady, for her heart cherishes the secret, and the pathway to the secret is infinite. But when you arrive there, be sure not to tread where wolves lie.

Your loving grandmother, Katya Orlova, who is the daughter of Lena Orlova, who was the daughter of Inna, who was the daughter of Svetlana, who was the daughter of Larina, and so on back through the centuries and bound by blood to the year of the altar's discovery and the anointing of the first Keeper.

Then at the bottom, the words darker, sharper, as if fear had made her grandmother press the pen deeper into the paper:

Remember, trust no one. No one. Beware the hunters.

━━━━━━━━━━

"THE ALTAR OF bones," Zoe said out loud, and she shuddered as if she were looking down into an open grave. Her grandmother had died with those words on her lips.

She shivered again as she got up quickly and went to the window. Inspector Mackey was gone, but the patrol car was here now. A uniformed cop stood next to it, talking into his shoulder radio.

She read over her grandmother's letter again. The altar of bones, becoming the next Keeper, a secret pathway and riddles to unlock—it should seem silly, like something out of a Russian folktale, yet her grandmother was dead, murdered.

The ponytailed man. He was close by still, Zoe could feel him, and her throat burned as if the chain were still wrapped around her neck, choking her.

She looked around at the shambles he'd made of her loft. Surely he hadn't expected to find an altar made out of bones in here? But maybe it wasn't really an altar, or maybe it was an altar but it wasn't really made out of bones.

The riddle was making her head hurt. Whatever the altar of bones was, the ponytailed man had killed her grandmother trying to get his hands on it.

Well, to hell with him. Zoe wasn't going to allow her grandmother to have died in vain. If Katya Orlova wanted her granddaughter to be the next Keeper, then her granddaughter would do whatever it took to become just that, even though she had no earthly idea at this point what it even meant, let alone what it would entail, beyond—

Look to the Lady . . . She took out the postcard of the lady and the unicorn to study it again.

"Beyond a trip to the Musée de Cluny," she said to Barney, who was pawing through the mess on the floor for more cream cheese.

She took another quick glance out the window—the patrol car was still there, but the cop was gone. He must be on his way up. She would have to hurry.

She looked for her jewelry box and finally discovered it dumped upside down in her bathtub. She sorted through the tangle, looking for a sturdy chain, and found a silver one that would work. She threaded the chain through the key, then fastened it around her neck and hid it beneath her sweater.

A fist pounded on the door. "Ms. Dmitroff?"

"Just a minute," she called out. "I'm not quite dressed yet."

"Sorry, ma'am. I'll, uh, be right out here in the hall."

She tucked the postcard and her grandmother's letter into a zippered compartment inside her satchel. Then went quickly to her rolltop desk and opened the secret cubbyhole. Her passport was still there, thank God. She put it into her bag as well, then checked her wallet: $85 in cash, plenty for a cab to the airport. If she couldn't get a direct flight to Paris tonight, she would try to go through Chicago or New York, or even Atlanta. Once she landed, she could get euros from an ATM.

She would text Gretchen, her paralegal, while she was in the cab, have her apply for a continuance on the one court case she had scheduled for next week. She also needed to file an amicus brief on behalf of a custody case, but Gretchen could deal with that, too.

Zoe felt a sudden pang at the thought of her grandmother lying in that white plastic body bag in the morgue's refrigerator. She didn't want her to be buried as an indigent, and she didn't trust Anna Larina to care enough to make the proper arrangements. Maybe she could get Gretchen to at least start the paperwork for her if she didn't get back from Paris in time.

Another knock on the door, gentler this time. "Uh, ma'am? How you doing?"

"Coming . . ."

She grabbed up fresh underwear, socks and panties and bra, stuffed them in her satchel. She really would've loved to shower and change. The clothes she had on, black jeans and black cashmere turtleneck, had been through hell today. But there was no time.

She got Barney and Bitsy in their carriers—they were cooperative for once. Then she unbarred and opened the door.

She gave the young, fresh-faced man who stood on the other side of it her brightest smile. "My poor cats are so terrified I thought I'd leave them with a neighbor while I was gone. I'll only be minute. If you could maybe wait here by the door, keep an eye on things?"

———

Maria Sanchez practically had her door open before Zoe could knock.

"Are you sure you're not in trouble, Zoe? All these cops here tonight, coming and going—"

"Could you take care of the critters for me?" Zoe said, the words tumbling out in a breathless rush. "I have to go out of town for a few days."

"Of course. Anything. You know I would die for you."

She said it as if she meant it, and it didn't sound silly or melodramatic. Besides, Zoe trusted her with her babies, and that was pretty much the same thing.

They hugged, then Zoe said, "Thank you, Maria. And don't worry,

I'm going to be fine. In a few minutes a nice young patrolman is going to be down here asking you where I've run off to—"

"So don't tell me. It will be better that way."

Outside, the elevator clanged into motion, going up. Maria made shooing motions with her hands. "Go, go. Call and let me know you're safe."

Zoe would call. She thought it might be a while, though, before she was safe.

17

New York City

A FIRE ROARED in the library of Miles Taylor's four-story Upper East Side brownstone, but it wasn't helping the cold he felt in his bones. He sat in his favorite tufted leather chair, nursing a glass of whiskey. A Laphroaig this time, not the sixty-year-old Macallan. The Macallan was only for celebrating the good times, and this was not a good time.

The cell phone in his pocket vibrated, and he jumped as if he'd just been goosed. Damn things. He couldn't decide whether he loved them or hated them.

He fumbled around with the phone for a moment, trying to remember which button on this model he was supposed to push, then he barked, "Taylor, here," a little too loudly.

"Hey, lover boy," Yasmine said in his ear. She sounded breathless, and more than a little crazy. The kind of crazy she got right before or just after she killed someone. "We've found Katya Orlova."

"About goddamn time." It had been a year and a half since Mike O'Malley had breathed his last, and since then an army of investigators had been scouring the world over for the woman, with not even a nibble. Until now.

"Yes, well, don't pop the champagne just yet," Yasmine said. "Because there's good news and there's bad news."

"You know how I hate it when people do that. What's the bad news?"

"Not over the phone. Where are you—at home? I got a call to make. I need to nail down a couple of things, then I'll be there in . . ." There was a pause, and he imagined her checking her watch. It would be the

$100,000 Patek Philippe he'd given her for Christmas. "An hour," she said, and hung up.

Miles folded up the phone and dropped it back into his pocket. He wanted to get up and pace the room, but his knee already ached like the devil and he didn't want to pop any more pain pills. And, besides, he suddenly felt drained, limp. Good news and bad news. Why did it always seem that the bad news was more bad than the good news was good?

Yaz said they'd found the woman. So what was the bad news—that she didn't have the film anymore? Or maybe Mike O'Malley had been lying on his deathbed? Miles wouldn't put it past the son of a bitch. Maybe she never had the film in the first place. But if she never had it, and O'Malley never had it, then who did?

Dammit, this was making him nuts.

He started at a knock on the library door, spilling whiskey into his lap. He half stood, hoping it was Yasmine, even though it was too soon.

It was his butler instead, bearing a magazine on a silver tray. "I believe you were expecting this, sir. Next month's *Vanity Fair* delivered by messenger. Hot off the presses."

"Thank you, Randolph. Leave it here by the lamp, will you?"

Miles waited until the man left the room before he picked up the magazine. He held it out at arm's length, squinting because he didn't have his reading glasses handy. His own face looked back at him, and beneath it, in black boldface type, the subhead MILES TAYLOR, AMERICA'S KINGMAKER.

He had to flip through what seemed to be twenty pages of ads before he got to the table of contents and found the page number for the article. There was another picture of him, standing in a wide-legged stance with his arms crossed over his chest. Only this one had been photoshopped, so that it looked as if he were a giant, straddling a miniature stock exchange and Wall Street.

Miles's eyes scanned the article, not really absorbing it, just a few sentences popping up here and there.

Few people outside of this country's elitist of the elite have even heard of him. And in this camera- and video-hungry age, he shuns the media as if we were the proverbial plague. Yet his few friends and many enemies alike all agree he has more money and more power than God. What they don't say, at least not for the record, is that unlike God, Miles Taylor is not afraid to get his hands dirty in the day-to-day running of the world.

His first real money—and by real money, I'm talking billions here—was made when he was only thirty. When he shorted $500 million worth of Thai bahts, profiting from Bangkok Bank's reluctance to either raise interest rates or float their currency. At the time a reporter asked if it bothered him that whole companies had gone under and people's life savings were wiped out in an instant. That because of him, little old mama-sans had been thrown out on the street and were now living off dog food.
His infamous reply was "Yeah? Well, fuck 'em."

A certain haughtiness creeps into his voice when he talks to you about politics. He blames the world's economic inequalities on market fundamentalism, and he talks about how we need a strong central, international government to correct for the excesses of self-interest, and you find yourself agreeing with him, thinking: Yeah, yeah, ain't that the truth. But you're also hating him too, for his utter, self-righteous conviction that only he is right about these things.

Miles Taylor is a kingmaker in Webster's sense of the word: he has the utmost influence over the choice of candidates for political office. If anyone can make a president in this country—if any one man can own a president—it is he.

MILES WAS THINKING it wasn't bad, was kind of liking it actually, when a paragraph toward the end caught his eye:

One has to wonder, though, at the hubris of a man convinced he can save the world, when he could not save his only son from

ending up a near parody of the spoiled rich kid who had it all
and was destroyed by it. Jonathan Taylor died in a crack house at
the age of 22 after injecting an eight ball of heroin into his veins.
Suicide or accident?

MILES SLAMMED THE magazine closed. He started to throw it into the
fire, then dropped it on the floor instead. He nudged it under the chair
with his foot, as if out of sight was out of mind. Well, who read Vanity Fair
anyway? These days if it wasn't on YouTube, it was as if it never happened.

Accident or suicide—what difference did it make? He'd tried it all
with that boy: counseling, rehab, begging and pleading, even bribery.
Only as a last resort did he do the tough-love thing, cutting off all the
money, cutting off the sugar tit. Had they put that in the article?

It had been a snowy night like this one. Him in this very chair; Jonathan, white and shaking, pacing the rug in front of the fire. Begging for
money. "Just a twenty. Just to get a burger and a coke, I swear. Come on,
Dad, you could use twenties for toilet paper and it wouldn't make a dent
in all you've got."

And Miles saying, "I don't know which of us is more pathetic. You
for being stupid enough to think I'd fall for your bullshit, or me for listening to it."

Then Jonathan, whirling away from the fire to face him, and Miles
seeing his boy, really seeing him for the first time, and realizing that the
shine he was seeing in his son's eyes wasn't from tears. It was hate. Pure,
unadulterated hate.

But what had shocked Miles even more than seeing the hate in his
son's eyes was the realization inside his own heart that he just didn't give
a fuck anymore. Had he ever loved the boy at all, or had he just been
going through the motions?

He'd taken out his money clip that night, peeled off a twenty.
"Here. Take it and go stick a needle in your arm. And leave me the
hell alone."

It was the last time he saw his son alive.

HE MUST HAVE dozed off, because Miles was suddenly startled awake by the feel of cold lips against his cheek. He opened his eyes. Yasmine Poole's white face floated in front of him, flames from the fire dancing in the sheen of her dark eyes.

He blinked and croaked something, and she straightened and took a step back. She had on tight black pants with stiletto-heeled boots, and a short, fuzzy white jacket that looked sexy as hell, and his guts did that funny crimping thing that happened when he looked at her.

"You got snow in your hair," he said.

"It's pretty out there tonight. The flakes are big and fat and soft."

The room fell into a silence that was electric, not soft, and the air around her seemed to vibrate, sucking him in.

"So?" Miles said, when he could bear it no longer. "Katya Orlova—you found her?"

Her red mouth broke into a smile. "Ding-dong, the bitch is dead," she sang. "The wicked bitch is dead."

"Will you quit playing games and tell me what's going on?"

"Katya Orlova is dead, Miles. As in deader-than-a-doornail dead. Deader than roadkill. Deader than hell in a preacher's backyard. That kind of dead."

Miles felt a flash of relief so strong it made him dizzy. "And the film? What about the film?"

"Yeah, well, see, that's where the bad news comes in."

"Dammit, this shit isn't funny, Yaz."

"You're right. I'm sorry. As you know, the high-powered private investigator's agency we hired was never able to pick up diddly-squat on the old woman herself, but they found her family easily enough. A widowed daughter and a granddaughter living in San Francisco."

She was prowling the room now, running her hands along a row of leatherbound books, giving the big globe in the corner a spin. *The killing crazies are on her,* Miles thought. *She's smelling blood, tasting it.*

"So for the last eighteen months, the PIs have been keeping tabs on both the daughter and granddaughter," Yasmine was saying. "Just in case she ever showed up, you know? When lo and behold she did show up—as an old homeless woman who was stabbed in the chest in Golden Gate Park last night."

Miles grunted, feeling suddenly ill. "God*damn* it. I don't believe in coincidences. Whoever killed the bitch now has the film. Nikolai Popov—it's got to be him."

"Well, not him personally. Because he'd be way too old to be running around stabbing people."

"And here's another thing," Miles went on. "If she's stayed away from her family all these years, why does she suddenly turn up there now, right after Mike O'Malley kicks the bucket?"

"It wasn't *right* after, Miles. It's been a year and a half. Besides, the PI firm got a look at the autopsy report. She was dying of cancer. She probably wanted to tell them good-bye."

Miles grunted. "Okay. I'll buy that part. But her getting murdered— that's got to be Popov's doing. I might not have known that she's had the film ever since the big kill, but you can bet that Popov sure as hell did. He's probably had men watching her family for decades, waiting for her to show up."

"Maybe," Yasmine said. "The ME's report did say she was stabbed with a Siberian knife."

She'd circled the room and was behind him now, and not for the first time Miles was a little scared of her. Of what she might do to *him* one day, when one of the blood frenzies seized her.

"The thing is, Miles, this guy who killed the old lady? He probably was one of Popov's men, but I don't think he got the film. Because the granddaughter suddenly dropped everything and caught a plane for Paris tonight, and what do you want to bet it wasn't to climb the Eiffel Tower?"

"You need to go after her." Miles tried to crane his head around to look at Yasmine, to see what she was doing, but the back of his chair was too high.

"I've already booked a flight to Orly. With the time difference, I might even get to Paris a few minutes ahead of her."

In the meantime, Miles thought, maybe he should give the Russian a call, poke at him the way you do a rattlesnake to see what trouble you can stir up. It had been such a long time since they'd last talked. Years.

Nikolai Popov had fallen far since his glory days with the KGB. He was nothing but a gangster now, pimping girls and selling drugs and running numbers. Well, supposedly he had a son who did all the dirty work, but Miles had no doubt Nikolai wielded all the power behind the scenes.

And, yeah, his face was on the film, too, but who was left alive to recognize him after all these years? And why would he give a shit anyway if the whole world found out what he'd done? Hell, it would probably give him the Russian equivalent of street cred. You couldn't be brought down when you were already as low as you could go.

Miles heard, or maybe just felt, a movement behind him, then Yasmine's hands reached around the back of his chair and began to knead his shoulders. Her fingers were strong, almost too strong, bringing him to the edge of pain.

Her voice was soft in his ear. "I've still got an hour before I need to leave for the airport."

He clasped her wrists in his two hands and drew her around in front of him. She knelt at his feet, and her face was beautiful and so white, except for the bloodred lips. He had a sudden, profane thought that he wanted to marry her. He wanted to live happily ever after with her, maybe have a child with her. Another son.

"This is all going to be over," he said. "Soon."

"I know. I know."

He reached out and rubbed his thumb across her full bottom lip. "The granddaughter . . ."

"Zoe Dmitroff."

"Whether she can get her hands on the film or not, she could already know what's on it."

"We can't take that chance."

"No. But talk to her first. Show her a photograph of Nikolai Popov. I want to know if he's ever approached her, and if he did, what was said."

"And then?"

"Then you will do what you do best."

Her eyes darkened, and her mouth parted open. He felt her hot breath on his hand.

"With pleasure," she said. "As always."

PART FOUR

THE LADY

18

*L*ook to the Lady, her grandmother had written. Well, Zoe had looked, and looked and looked and looked. She'd studied every square inch of these wretched tapestries until they felt imprinted on her eyeballs, and she'd come up with nothing. So what had she missed? What was here that she couldn't see? Surely her grandmother had put the postcard in the envelope to bring her to this place, but what good did it do if she couldn't figure out what it all meant?

Look to the lady.

She circled the round, dimly lit room yet again to gaze up at the sixteenth-century wall hangings, vibrant as a spill of jewels. The Lady, *her* Lady, starred in all of them, with her unicorn and a lion, but no griffin.

The tapestries were supposed to depict the world of the senses. In *Taste* the Lady was taking candy from a dish held by a maidservant. In *Smell* she was making a wreath of flowers. In *Touch* she was stroking the unicorn's horn, and in *Hearing* she was playing an organ. In *Sight* she held up a mirror and the unicorn knelt on the ground beside her with his front legs in her lap while he stared at his reflection.

Zoe stopped to look up at the final tapestry, the one on her grandmother's postcard. *À mon seul désir*, to my sole desire. Here, the Lady stood in front of a tent with her maidservant beside her, holding an open casket. The Lady was putting the necklace she'd been wearing in the other tapestries into the casket.

But there was no altar of bones here, no altar of any kind. So what did it mean? Damn it, what was she supposed to see?

The women of our line have been Keepers to the altar of bones for so long, the beginning has been lost in the mists of time. The sacred duty of each Keeper is to guard from the world the knowledge of the secret pathway, for beyond the pathway is the altar, and within the altar is the fountain of life.

A ridiculous riddle, her grandmother had called it. Okay, it might be ridiculous, but it was also obtuse, even more obtuse than that other riddle written on the back of the postcard. Or rather she was obtuse, because if the answer had been woven into the tapestry, it was beyond her—

A guard poked his head in the doorway, startling her. He tapped his wristwatch and said, *"Madame. Nous fermons en cinq minutes."*

Zoe started to nod at the man, when suddenly her eyes filled with tears. She wasn't ready to go, she wasn't done here. Until yesterday her grandmother had meant little more to her than a smiling face in an old photograph. Maybe it was only those shared mitochondrials, but in this place, standing before the tapestry in the postcard, Zoe felt connected to Katya Orlova on some deeper level. Connected, too, to those women named in the letter going back through the generations to the first Keeper. Her grandmother had said they were bound by blood, and Zoe was screwing up, she was letting those women down.

Look to the Lady, for her heart cherishes the secret, and the pathway to the secret is infinite.

The women of our line have been Keepers to the altar of bones for so long, the beginning has been lost in the mists of time.

So the altar of bones must be your legacy.

Only she was so stupid, she couldn't even figure out what the damned thing was, let alone how she would "keep" it.

Zoe looked one last time at *À mon seul désir,* at the Lady putting her necklace into the casket.

The museum guide said this meant the Lady had renounced the passions aroused by the other senses. After four hours of staring at the Lady's face, though, Zoe wasn't so sure. Passion was life, and this was the face of a woman embracing life, not renouncing it. And if you began your journey through the senses with this tapestry, then the Lady could be taking the necklace out of the casket, not putting it in.

Maybe, Zoe thought, feeling punch-drunk with jet lag and museum

torpor, she should write an article on this insightful discovery and sub-
mit it to some art magazine. She could call it "The Lady Is a Hedonist,"
and to support her thesis she could point to the expression on the unicorn's face, a smug smile if ever there was one, as if he'd just been fed
an especially yummy bucket of oats. And then there was the lion—a
strange-looking beast, but not a griffin, his mouth open wide in a big
roar. Or maybe it was a belly laugh.

"All right, give it up, you guys," Zoe said, out loud because she was
the only one left in the room. "What is this altar-of-bones thing, and
where is it when it's at home?"

The lion laughed, the unicorn smiled, but the Lady only had eyes
for her jewels.

———————

ZOE WALKED OUT of the museum and into a whirl of lights and noise
and people. It was dark, a cold drizzle misted the air, wetting the pavement and haloing the streetlamps. She turned up her face, let the rain
wash over her. It didn't help.

She wanted to weep and curse, both at the same time. Here she was,
wearing the same clothes she'd put on in San Francisco more hours ago
than she cared to count, so tired her feet kept moving only because they
knew they should. She needed a hotel room, and maybe some food, except she was too tired to eat.

She wasn't even sure where she was in relation to anything else.
She'd told the cabdriver at the airport to drop her off at the Musée de
Cluny, and after that it was a blur. She looked for a street sign and found
one finally, embedded in the wall of a cream-stone apartment building
with a gray dormer roof—Boulevard St.-Michel.

Which would be a useful bit of knowledge if she had a map, and if
she knew where she wanted to go from here in the first place.

She turned around and nearly bumped into an in-line skater with
purple spikes in his hair who didn't even notice her as he whizzed by.
The street was jammed with traffic—motorbikes, every one of them
with a hole in its muffler, and all those small European cars that honked
for no reason and looked ridiculous, and so many voices, all of them

speaking French. She didn't understand a single word and she didn't care.

The tapestry. She'd focused every brain cell in her head on it and gotten nothing. She really wasn't all that stupid, so that meant there'd been nothing to get.

Let it go for now. Let it go.

So many French voices, most of them happy, most of them young, and if she'd had a gun, she would've shot the lot of them. Her head ached so badly that if she didn't get some aspirin soon, it would explode. She looked for a drugstore and saw only bistros and restaurants and cafés.

Zoe searched through her limited high school French for the word for drugstore, but it hurt to think. She had a vague memory, though, that their pharmacies—yes, that's what it was, *une pharmacie*. And you were supposed to easily spot *une pharmacie* because of the universal symbol of a bright green neon cross they all had over their doors.

She looked up and down the street for a green neon cross. No luck.

No, wait . . . The rain had thickened and it was hard to see, but was that a wedge of green light across from the museum and down a side street?

Zoe dashed through the stalled traffic to make it across before the stoplight changed, weaving through Peugeots and Vespas, barely beating out a taxi driver with manic eyes who tried to run her down.

A huge McDonald's loomed in front of her, bursting with people. But down the narrow cobblestoned side street, it was deserted. The wedge of green light was still there, a pale luminous green, though, not the cross of a *pharmacie*.

No, it was something else entirely.

Zoe's breath hitched. She had to be seeing things. She walked slowly toward it, wondering if her brain had finally shorted out on her.

The wedge of green light sliced through a small shop window and lit a wooden signboard swinging in the night wind. It seemed to be an antiques store. Or rather, more like a junk shop, or maybe a pawnbroker. That sign, though, that gently swinging wooden sign . . . It was carved in the shape of a griffin.

And not just any griffin.

It was an exact replica of the one on her grandmother's key.

———————

ZOE RAISED HER hand, almost afraid to push at the narrow door with the sign in it that said OUVERT. She could see no one inside, only a tall, green-shaded belle epoque streetlamp that had been placed directly in the bay window. As if the shop's owner had known all along she would leave the museum with a headache and go looking for the green neon cross of a pharmacy.

Zoe thought of all the stories she'd heard growing up about Russian sorcerers who could divine the future, and she shuddered.

But, no, she was being silly. If she'd been paying more attention when she first got here, not so out of it from jet lag, and if it hadn't been raining, she would have spotted the griffin signboard right off, as soon as she'd stepped out of the cab in front of the museum. This green light in the window was a coincidence, nothing more.

But however she'd come to be here, this was the place her grand-mother had meant for her to find, Zoe was sure of it.

She pushed open the door.

A bell above the lintel jangled loudly and she paused, but the shop was deserted and no one came out of any back room to help her.

She looked around. The place was like something out of a Dickens novel. Floor-to-ceiling shelves crammed with what could only be de-scribed as "stuff." Clocks—lots and lots of clocks—but also paintings, busts, flowerpots, lamps, candlesticks . . . In one corner was a ship's fig-urehead, a bare-breasted floozy with a trident in her hand and a lascivi-ous grin on her face.

"*Bonjour,*" Zoe called out. But the shop remained quiet, except for the tick of the clocks.

She looked for something that might take her key, but the trouble was there were too many somethings: chests and jewelry boxes by the dozens, several bureaus, and even a couple of armoires.

Just then a blue velvet curtain half-hidden behind an ornate floor mirror flared open so dramatically Zoe expected nothing less than a vampire to step out from behind it.

Instead, an old man came into the shop. Only a few wisps of white hair dusted his pink scalp, and the teeth behind his smile probably spent the night in a glass on his bedside table. He'd been whittled down by time, yet he had quite the dapper air about him with his argyle sweater vest, polka-dot bow tie, and rimless bifocal glasses.

"*Bonjour, monsieur,*" Zoe said.

"*Bonsoir, madame,*" he said, neither rude nor friendly, but he couldn't help correcting her French.

Faced now with having to explain what she wanted in that language, Zoe's head had emptied of almost every word she knew, and there hadn't been all that many in there to begin with. "*Parlez-vous anglais?*"

The man blew out a "No" between his lips, lifted his shoulders, spread his hands.

On impulse, Zoe asked him if he spoke Russian.

The man beamed, said in beautiful Russian, "How ever did you know? I've lived here so many years I might as well be French. . . . Well, Parisian—there is a distinction. But I was born ten years after the Bolshevik Revolution." He turned his head aside and spat. "In a reindeer herder's hut on the frozen tundra near what they now call Norilsk. You will not have heard of the place, and for that you should count your blessings."

Zoe kept her voice light, but her gaze didn't leave the old man's face. He had the darkest eyes she'd ever seen. More than black, they were opaque.

"Actually, I have heard of it, *monsieur*. My great-grandmother was . . . well, maybe she wasn't born there like yourself. I really know so little about her. Just that she escaped from a Siberian prison camp called Norilsk, back in the 1930s. Her name was Lena Orlova and she had a daughter called Katya. Maybe you know the family?"

The old man's smile stayed in place, but Zoe thought the tiniest spark of a light had come on deep in those dark eyes. "Truly what a small and intimate planet it is we dwell on. I have a nephew who works in a bank in Chicago."

Zoe laughed. "I'm from San Francisco, but I get your point." She waved at a particularly cluttered stack of shelves that seemed to have a Russian theme going on. "I was wondering, though. . . . Ever since I first heard my great-grandmother's story I've wanted to go to Norilsk. To trace my roots, as we Americans like to say. Do you have some artifacts, antiques, or whatever, native to the region I could look at? Maybe buy."

"You do not want to go to Norilsk, trust me on this. She is the frozen armpit of the universe, never mind the season. Or, if you want to save that epithet for Mother Russia herself, then Norilsk is a puss-filled pimple on the frozen armpit of the universe.

"So," he went on before Zoe could get another word in. "Sadly, I've nothing from Siberia at the moment. Not even a necklace made of wolf's teeth, which is more common than you might think. Can I show you other things? A clock, perhaps? I have many clocks. Cuckoo, grandfather, turret, water, repeater, pendulum, marine—and every one keeps perfect time." He pulled out a pocket watch, flipped open the lid. "If you care to wait for twenty-one minutes and sixteen seconds, you will hear them all strike the hour simultaneously. It is a symphony, trust me. Stay, listen, your ears will thank you."

"Your clocks are beautiful." Zoe pulled the silver chain out from underneath her turtleneck and over her head. "But I was wondering if you have something in your shop that might be opened with this key."

The old man went very still. He started to reach up to touch the key, then let his hand fall back down at his side. He said, his voice barely above a whisper, "If you have that, then Katya Orlova is dead."

"So you did know my grandmother."

"I knew them both, Lena Orlova and her daughter, Katya. Her death, was it a kind one?"

Zoe's throat got tight, so that she ended up blurting it out more harshly than she'd meant to. "She was murdered."

"Ah." He bowed his head, shut his eyes. "It never ends."

"Were you very close friends?"

"Katya and I? No, not in that way. But I have been waiting many years for her to walk through my door again. Or for the one who comes after her."

Zoe had so many questions, she didn't know where to begin. "I'm sorry. I should have introduced myself. I'm Zoe. Zoe Dmitroff."

She held out her hand, and the old man bent over it in an old-fashioned bow. "And I am Boris. A good Russian name, no?"

He kept her hand while he stepped closer, to peer up into her face. "Yes, it is still as it should be. One Keeper passes, but another is there to take her place. I saw it was so the minute you walked through the door. I only thought I should wait for you to produce the key. But I saw it."

He stared at her, but with faraway eyes, as if he were lost in another time. "But then I am of the *toapotror*. The magic people."

"The magic people?"

He sighed, letting go of her hand. "Do you not know? Well, the years pass by, and with them goes the knowledge of the old ways. We *toapotror* are a tribe of native Siberian families whose duty it is to help the Keeper preserve the altar of bones from the corruption of the world. Sadly, we are mostly all gone now, either dead or strewn to the four corners of the world."

His flat black eyes glimmered with his sudden smile. "But then the real magic has always resided within the altar, not in us."

"Yet it was the green light you put in your window that brought me here. I would never have found you otherwise. That was magic of sort, wasn't it?"

"Yes. . . . Yes, perhaps it was." He smiled again. "And I suppose it was magic of another sort at work that day I spotted Lena Orlova in a Hong Kong noodle shop. That two war-weary exiles from so far a place as Norilsk should both happen to take hungry at the same time, to walk into the same noodle shop in a city full of noodle shops—coincidence or magic, who indeed is to say? And I knew her the moment I laid eyes on her. How could I not? For although we were both only children when last I saw her, she had grown up to be the very image of the Lady. As you are."

Zoe's blood quickened. *Look to the Lady* . . . "What do you mean I'm her image?"

He held up a finger. "You will see in a moment, but first . . ."

He went to the front door, poked his head out, and looked up and down the street. He shut the door, hung out a FERME sign, and turned the lock bolt.

He turned back to her, his voice barely above a whisper. "Were you followed?"

"I don't know," Zoe said, feeling stupid now that the possibility hadn't even occurred to her.

The old man turned off the green-shaded lamp, peered out the window, then pulled down the shade. "We *toapotror* have served the Keeper for generations, since ever there was a Keeper, and we do so with loyal hearts. But sometimes it is dangerous. We learn to take precautions, even when we look like old fools for doing so."

He went back to the blue velvet curtain behind the mirror and pulled it open. "Come."

Zoe followed him through a narrow door into a small room. It looked, she thought, like a stage set for a séance. A round, cloth-draped table was surrounded by five hard-backed chairs. A tin-shaded lamp hung from the ceiling. The plaster walls were bare of paintings, the old peg wooden floor of any rugs.

The old man pulled out a chair. "Please . . ."

Zoe sat.

"It will be a moment," he said, then left to go back into the front of the shop.

Zoe heard the scrape of wood against wood, the creak of a hinge, followed by a sneeze and *"Merde!"*

The curtain swirled open, and he came back into the room. "I'm afraid I've allowed things to get a bit dusty."

Zoe felt a jolt of pure excitement when she saw the wooden casket he carried so reverently in his outstretched hands. It was an exact replica of the casket in the tapestry. The one the unicorn lady had used to keep her jewels.

This one was large enough, though, to hold a good-size loaf of bread. It was banded with studded iron strips and had a domed lid. It also had two locks, one at each end.

The old man set the chest on the table in front of her. He whipped a cloth from his coat pocket and wiped away the dust. "We *toapotror* like to tell a story of how many, many years ago, so long ago the truth has been lost in the mists of time, there lived a people who practiced the ancient arts of sorcery, and whose shaman was possessed of a magic so powerful he could bring the dead back to life. One day this shaman took himself a wife, who was as fair as the first snowfall of winter. Alas, she could bear him only daughters, although each daughter she bore him was as beautiful as their mother."

"Did he care?" Zoe asked, her feminist hackles on the rise. "That she gave him only daughters?"

The old man laughed softly and shrugged. "If he did, it is one of those truths now lost in the mists. But to go on with the story . . . On another day some evil men, who were jealous of the shaman's powers, set upon him in a snowy field. They stabbed a spear into his side so that they might drink his blood. But the taste of it drove them mad. They fell into fighting amongst themselves, killing each other until none was left alive."

The old man gave the casket a final buff, then took a step back to admire his handiwork. "It was nearly nightfall when the shaman's wife and daughters came upon him there in the field, his red blood staining the snow. They wailed and tore at their hair, and their hearts broke into pieces. Then they gathered up his shattered body and bore it away to a secret cave behind a waterfall of ice, where they guard it to this day and will for all eternity. . . . But, my dear, why are you crying? It is only a story. One story among many that are told around the fire during the long and cold Siberian nights."

"Sorry," Zoe said, feeling a little silly as she wiped the tears off her cheeks with the back of her hand. "I honestly don't know where that came from. It must be the jet lag." She also thought, though, that there was something more to this particular story than what the old man was letting on, but she let it go. "So tell me what happened after you met up with Lena in the noodle shop."

"Why, I offered her my services, of course. As was my duty."

The old man's eyes had lit up with a look of wistful memory, and Zoe wondered if he and Lena had been lovers for a time. It was hard to imagine, looking at him now, but he would have been a young man after the war.

"After Lena died," he went on, "I kept in touch with her daughter, Katya, over the years, and in the fall of 1962 Katya came to me here and asked for my help in safeguarding the altar's secrets for the Keeper who would come after her. She never told me the nature of the danger she was in, out of fear perhaps that with too much knowledge the danger could rub off onto me."

The old man stuffed the cloth back in his coat, then removed a pocket watch from his vest, and Zoe saw that instead of a fob on the end of the chain, there was a key. With a griffin on the end of it.

"It takes two keys to open the casket," he said. "Mine and the Keeper's. Your grandmother Katya designed it. Clever, is it not? But then over the centuries you Keepers have always been clever at devising riddles to keep the altar safe from the world."

"It's like a safe-deposit box in a bank," Zoe said, feeling more than a little intimidated. She couldn't even solve the old riddles. God help them all if she ever had to come up with any new ones.

The old man pushed his key into the lock on the left end of the casket, then motioned for Zoe to do the same with her key to the lock on the right.

He met her eyes and actually winked at her. "Now we must both turn our keys simultaneously for the mechanism to work."

"Okay," Zoe said, feeling both a little silly and so curious she was about to burst.

The old man said, "One, two . . . now," and they turned their keys. There was a soft click and the casket lid sprang open a quarter inch.

Zoe reached for it, but the old man stopped her.

"Not yet. For this I must not be present. There is only one Keeper, and she is always a she. But then you knew that, of course."

Zoe nodded, thinking of those names in her grandmother's letter, Lena, Inna, Svetlana, Larina . . . And then she remembered something Anna Larina had told her only yesterday in San Francisco. How Lena Orlova liked to sing to her daughter when she was little, about being a blessed girl child from a proud, long line who wouldn't be the last.

"Thank you, Boris."

He crossed one arm over his waist and bowed slightly. "I wish you God speed. I fear that you will need it."

He turned and pulled aside a smaller velvet curtain—purple this time—to reveal a plain oak door. "When you are ready to leave, it is best if you do so through here. You will find yourself in a small courtyard. To your right will be a wine bar, and if you go through it, you will emerge onto the Boulevard St.-Michel. If you're of a mind to pause for a little libation and without making your wallet squeal too loudly, I can recommend the house Bordeaux."

Zoe smiled. "May I buy you a glass after I'm done?"

He bowed again. "Thank you for the offer, but, sadly, I find that at my age the grape gives me the heartburn."

He opened the blue curtain, said, "Good-bye, Katya Orlova's granddaughter," and disappeared behind it.

———

Zoe was so excited now she was humming with it as she pushed open the casket's domed lid and looked inside.

She saw something square, about the size and thickness of a hardback novel, wrapped tightly in a sealskin pouch. She lifted it out slowly, unwinding the thick, oily skin, and she gasped.

Inside the pouch was a Russian icon, and although her knowledge didn't run nearly as deep as her mother's, even she knew this one was exquisite and rare. And very old.

It was painted on a thick piece of wood, the image unlike anything she'd ever before seen. It filled her with both wonder and a supernatural fear. The Virgin Mary sat on a gilded throne with her hands folded around a silver cup fashioned in the shape of a human skull. But the Virgin's face . . . Zoe couldn't stop staring at her face. It had been painted centuries ago, but it was the same face Zoe saw looking back at her in the mirror every day of her life.

She could see now how the old man knew Lena Orlova was a Keeper the moment he saw her in that noodle shop. *She was the very image of the Lady. As are you.* The thought gave Zoe chills.

Could this icon be the altar of bones? Certainly in centuries past, from superstitious peasants to the powerful czars, it was believed some icons could heal and work miracles. But surely no one would buy into such a thing today—at least not enough to kill for it. The icon was priceless, though, like a buried treasure, and if a clerk in a convenience store could be shot over twenty bucks, Zoe supposed an old lady could die trying to protect the secret of an icon worth millions.

Suddenly the shop seemed quiet, too quiet. Except for the ticking of the clocks. Zoe opened her mouth to call out to the old man, then shut it. She *felt* alone.

And she didn't like it.

She looked at the icon again. It was starting to creep her out now, how the Virgin had her face. The skull cup was creepy, too. The Virgin and her throne seemed to be floating on a lake. On one side of her was a waterfall, on the other something that looked like a jumble of rocks. And the painting had been studded with jewels, but it was odd the way they were laid out, as if the artist had stuck them on with no plan of either symmetry or logic. Except for the ruby, which he'd put right in the middle of the skull's forehead.

Ruby, sapphire, aquamarine, diamond, fire opal, iolite, onyx. Seven jewels, and no two of them the same. She didn't know enough to assess their quality, but the ruby was as big as her pinkie. The other stones were smaller, though.

She stared at the Virgin's face a moment longer, then wrapped the icon back up into its waterproof sealskin pouch and slipped it in her satchel. She was about to close the casket's lid when she saw something else inside. It must have been lying underneath the icon.

Not until she took it out, though, did she make sense of what it was—a round, gray tin can of the type that was used for storing reels of 8 mm film. And sure enough, that's what was inside it.

She unspooled the film a little and held it up to the light. She thought she could make out a little girl blowing out the candles of a birthday cake. She would need a projector to be sure, but she thought the little girl was her mother.

Zoe closed her eyes against the burn of sudden tears. To think this could be all Katya Orlova had left of the daughter she'd been forced to abandon when she'd gone on the run for her life. Why hadn't she just given up the icon? Zoe wondered. Surely no material thing, no matter how old and rare and valuable, was worth such a sacrifice.

Zoe put the reel of film in her satchel and stood up to go. Then she sat back down to check the casket one more time, to be sure it was empty. She ran her fingers over the bottom and sides and was only a little surprised when she exposed the corner of a photograph peeking out from a slit in the black satin lining.

She pulled the photograph out carefully, for it felt brittle to the touch. Oddly enough, though, it wasn't all that old.

It was of a man and two women, both blondes, sitting in the booth of a restaurant somewhere. Zoe recognized the woman on the left as her grandmother, and it looked as if it had been taken a year or so after the one in front of the studio gate, for in this one her hair was longer, worn in a soft bob just past her shoulders. Zoe was also sure she knew the woman sitting next to her grandmother, but she couldn't place her. The man in the photograph was extraordinarily handsome, with dark hair and a charming, bad-boy grin. He, too, looked familiar to Zoe, although much less so than the second blonde.

She turned the photograph over and saw writing on the back. *Mike and Marilyn and me at the Brown Derby, July '62.*

Marilyn . . . Zoe turned the photograph over, looked at it closer. The other woman in the booth had most of her platinum blond hair wrapped up in a scarf and she had little makeup on, but she looked like . . .

My God, it is. It's Marilyn Monroe.

Had her grandmother actually known Marilyn Monroe? Known her well enough to sit in a restaurant with her? But then she *had* worked for a movie studio, after all. . . . Still, it just seemed so amazing.

Zoe put the photograph into the sealskin pouch with the icon and the reel of film and stuffed it all back into her bulging satchel, then scraped back her chair and stood up.

"*Au revoir, monsieur,*" she called out. She got no answer.

But as she pulled back the purple curtain and opened the door to the courtyard, the front of the shop exploded into a symphony of gongs and chimes and tinkles and bells.

19

Z OE WOULDN'T have known she was being followed if it hadn't been for the fire-eater.

She came out of the wine bar back onto the Boulevard St.-Michel, as the old man had promised. A juggler and a man with a burning torch stood in front of a sidewalk café on the corner. The juggler tossed a balloon, a billiard ball, and a bowling ball from hand to hand, and he'd drawn quite a crowd. Zoe watched the street performance without really seeing it, while she tried to think what to do. She needed a hotel and some food. She needed sleep.

At least for the moment it had stopped raining.

She thought she saw what looked like a hotel farther down the block on the other side of the museum. She'd taken about a dozen steps toward it when from behind she heard a loud "Ooooh!"

She whirled instinctively, to see the man with the torch pull it out of his mouth, then breathe a gust of fire, and the crowd went "Ooooh!" again.

Zoe's eye had caught a sudden movement farther down the street, though—a man jerking around too fast to look into the window of an umbrella store. His build was big and ropy, and he had a long brown ponytail, like the man who had attacked her with the chain in San Francisco.

She pretended to watch the fire-eater, while he admired the umbrellas. He didn't turn his face her way once, kept his attention right on those fascinating umbrellas no matter how many times the crowd oohed at the fire-eater's antics. He was the man who'd killed her grandmother, she was sure of it. He'd followed her from San Francisco, followed her to the museum and then to the shop, just as the old man had feared.

Zoe started walking again, just another tourist admiring the brightly lit bistros and shops, the cream stone buildings with their gray dormer roofs and lace iron balconies. She stopped at a newspaper kiosk and pointed to a copy of *Le Monde*.

She dug into her jeans pocket for a couple of euros, then deliberately dropped them on the sidewalk. She bent over to pick them up, and as she straightened, she looked into the side mirror of a parked car.

The ponytailed man was only a half a block behind her now, closing fast.

The guy must've figured he was made because suddenly he gave up all subtlety, running full out now and right at her.

He got within a couple feet of her and made a wild grab for her satchel. She swung around, slamming her elbow under his chin, and sent him reeling into a parked car.

Then she gripped the straps of her satchel with both hands and ran.

———————

SHE DASHED ACROSS the wide street just as the light was changing. Behind her she heard the screech of brakes, horns, curses in French.

The shops, the cafés, they were all open, full of people. Maybe she should run inside one, shout for help, for a gendarme, but it would be a nightmare. She didn't speak French, and what could she tell them? The whole altar-of-bones thing sounded insane, and the icon . . . What if they confiscated the icon? She was the Keeper now, she couldn't let them have the icon.

She glanced back over her shoulder. She'd put a little distance between herself and the ponytailed man, but he was still coming fast. She had to lose him, but how?

She ran faster, everything around her a blur of lights and faces. Couldn't they see a man was chasing her? Ahead of her she could see the bell tower of a church, thought about trying to hide inside, then changed her mind. She could just as easily end up trapped.

She twisted her head to snatch another look behind her and knocked into a hot-chestnut cart. She tripped, nearly fell onto her hands and knees. Pain shot up her thigh.

She stumbled around a corner and onto a narrow street jam-packed with an outdoor market and throngs of shoppers. She cut around a fish stand and nearly fell again when her heel slipped on a piece of rotting kelp. She wove in and out among the marble-topped tables of a *salon de thé*, bumping into them, not caring.

Her coat sleeve caught on the wheel of a wagon full of yellow flowers. She tugged, couldn't get loose, couldn't get loose . . . She felt panic, hot and terrifying, blur her eyes. She gave one more hard tug, and her sleeve pulled free.

She looked behind her. Bobbing heads, so many heads, but she didn't see him. She turned back around just in time to keep from slamming into a woman pushing a baby carriage.

Suddenly he was there, lurching out from behind a rack of handbags. He was smiling at her and she'd never been so afraid in her life.

Zoe made a little juking move. He bit, twisting right while she went left. He lunged at her, grabbing for her satchel again. She dodged to the side at the last second, and his momentum carried him into a pyramid of oranges.

Zoe ran past him, leaped over rolling oranges, and darted in one door of a pastry shop, then out the other. She could hear a lot of yelling behind her, but she didn't look back.

━━━━━━

ZOE RAN DOWN a street—no shops or cafés here, only a few people. Ahead she could see the lights of a bridge and a tourist boat below on the Seine.

The street that followed along the river was wide, the traffic murderous. She raced across it just as the light changed, setting off a flurry of horns, shaking fists, and more French curses.

I've lost him. Please, God, let me have lost him.

She slowed to a walk, panting, her heart pounding in her ears as she

took a crowded footbridge. She looked downriver and finally saw something she knew—the massive lit towers of the Notre Dame cathedral
thrusting into the night sky.

The cathedral would, surely, be full of tourists and tourist buses.
Maybe she could sneak onto a bus and ride it to a nice big hotel with
a staff who spoke English. And room service. What she wouldn't give
right now for some room service.

NOT ONLY WERE there no tourist buses, the big square in front of the
cathedral was practically empty of people, too.

The floodlights cast the side streets in deep black shadows. She felt
exposed out in the open, in the light, but the dark streets leading to who
knew where seemed worse. She hadn't lost him; she couldn't see him but
her skin crawled with the feel of him. She strained her ears, listening,
listening . . .

Running footsteps slapped the pavement behind her.

Zoe ran.

THE STREET SHE ran down spilled onto another bridge. A large group
of Japanese tourists was crossing over, coming toward her. Zoe plunged
in among them.

But she was too tall. She could still see the ponytailed man, and if she
could see him, he could see her.

She wasn't going to escape him. Maybe she should just toss him the
satchel and be done with it. But the letter . . . *they will kill you and all who
come near you simply for knowing too much.* The bastard had left his knife
in her grandmother's chest, but he could also have a gun. Would he dare
to use it on a Paris street? Probably.

A hand grabbed her arm, startling her so badly her heart jumped up
into her throat. A smiling man got in her face, pointing to the camera
he held in one hand. "Take picture?" he said. Zoe shook her head, tried
to get around him.

She looked ahead of her, toward the other end of the bridge. Another man stood there, just stood there as if waiting. For her. He was dressed all in black and it was too dark to see his face, but she was so scared of him she wanted to vomit.

He took a step toward her, then another and another. He reached into his coat pocket and—

A gun. He had a gun.

She looked over her shoulder. The ponytailed man moved through the oblivious Japanese tourists like a shark, smiling, closing in on her.

Zoe backed up until she was pressed against the wrought-iron railing. She was so afraid, so frozen with it, she couldn't think. *Please, God, please, what am I going to do?* The ponytailed man was coming from one end of the bridge, and the man in black was coming from the other, and she had no where to go but . . .

She looked down at the rushing, black, icy waters of the Seine. She was standing on a low bridge, and the water was running high, but it still looked like a long way down. Then she saw the bow of a barge, coming out from underneath the bridge, moving fast, with bound newspapers piled on it as high as a house.

Zoe didn't think, didn't hesitate. She grabbed the railing with both hands and vaulted over it. She hung by her fingertips for one long, agonizing second.

Then she let go.

━━━━━

SHE HIT THE bundles of newspapers hard, driving all the air from her lungs.

Finally her chest heaved and blessed air came rushing in. She lay there, shuddering, praying she hadn't broken anything, afraid to move and find out. Then she smiled. She'd jumped from a bridge and landed on sodden piles of *Le Monde*, and she'd survived.

Maybe, just maybe, some *toapotror* magic was going on here. She still didn't move, though, even after it began raining hard, splashing her face, getting in her eyes, up her nose. She shifted one leg, then the other. Thank God her arms worked, too. She felt as if her chest had gone through her back, but nothing was broken, and she smiled again.

She sat up slowly and looked back up at the bridge, fading now into the distance, the rain veiling it, but she could still see the ponytailed man where he stood at the railing, looking down at the river. The man in black was gone.

I'm alive, you bastards, I'm alive. The Keeper's alive and she's still got the icon.

Then her euphoria died as she saw the streets and buildings float past her. Where was the barge going? Would it stop even once before it got all the way to Le Havre?

The river flowed between quays, sheer and steep as cliffs. About every twenty yards, shallow steps carved into the stone laddered up to the street. But to get to them, that was the thing. The water whipped by, fast and cold and treacherous. She had a horrible feeling she'd used up her share of luck.

Okay, think. The barge wasn't going down the river on its own. She saw the green glow of an instrument panel through the window of a small pilothouse. Somebody had to be inside doing the steering. Maybe whoever it was would put her ashore, or more likely he'd have a radio and he'd call the gendarmes and she'd probably be arrested, but at this point she didn't care. At least the cops wouldn't shoot her, she hoped.

She pushed to her feet. The newspapers were wet and slippery and squished beneath her feet so that she wobbled and staggered with every step.

Suddenly the door to the pilothouse crashed open. Zoe opened her mouth to shout a hello and screamed instead when a huge black mastiff burst out, teeth bared, snarling.

She turned and ran, the dog right behind her, growling, snapping at her heels. He got her pant leg, but she jerked free. She didn't even think about it. She leaped over the side.

20

S HE PLUNGED deep, deep, then shot back up, gasping, her lungs on
fire with the hideous cold.

The satchel's strap was strangling her. She struggled to pull it off
over her head, choking, swallowing water, then got it off at last. The
satchel was supposed to be waterproof and the icon was wrapped up
tight in the sealskin pouch, but she wasn't taking any chances. She held it
up as best she could out of the water while doing a lame sidestroke with
one arm. The current was fierce, pulling her downstream.

She looked up to see how far she was from the quay and the steps.
Too far, and past the steps nothing but sheer stone as far as she could
see. Maybe the steps stopped here. Maybe this was the end of it for her.
No, no . . . She kicked out hard with her legs, trying to burst free of the
vicious current.

She saw the steps coming up fast, then suddenly she was sweeping past them. She flung out her hand, barely caught the bottom one.
Her fingers slipped. She grabbed again, held on this time with all her
strength, which wasn't much now. She was cold, so cold she couldn't
breathe.

She clung to the step with numb hands while the rushing river pum-
meled her. She knew she needed to get out of the water now, but she was
so cold and so tired.

She looped the satchel's strap back over her head and hauled herself
up the narrow, steep steps hand over hand. She climbed over the lip of
the quay and fell flat on her face. She lay there, shivering to her bones,
black water streaming off her. She didn't want to move, but she had to.
She simply had to, no choice.

She struggled to her feet, staggered forward, fell to her knees, and crawled up a dirt ramp to the street above. Saw a lamppost and crawled to it. She wrapped her arms around its iron base, shuddering. Her wet clothes felt like a shroud. She was cold, so cold, but she wasn't going to give up now. She wasn't about to die. She wasn't. She needed more *toapotror* magic, though, and didn't she deserve it? After all, she'd kept the icon safe from those two men, and a killer dog, and a mad dunking in the Seine.

She dug deep, pulled herself up. She was shaking so hard her eyes blurred. The icy rain thickened, and wasn't that just perfect, the wind driving it sharp as needles into her face.

Through the bare branches of a tree on the corner she saw a light shining in a window with red-and-white checkered curtains. A restaurant? *Please, God, let it be a restaurant.* Because there would be a phone inside. Or someone willing to call her a taxi. She needed to hide somewhere, anywhere, it didn't matter so long as it was warm and she could get herself together again until she could catch a plane home. She wanted to go home. *Home.* It sang in her like a mantra.

She took a staggering step, then another, aimed for the tree and that beautiful light beyond it.

A man's shadow crossed in front of her, looming out from behind the tree's thick trunk. A big man, dressed all in black. The man from the bridge.

He was on her in a second, so fast she didn't have time to scream. He poked the barrel of a gun in her ribs.

Slowly, Zoe looked up into a pair of familiar blue eyes. What in hell was *he* doing here?

"Sergei," she said, but she was so cold, her teeth chattering so hard, she hadn't even understood herself. She said it again, clearly this time, "Sergei."

"Give it to me," he said in her ear. He sounded out of breath, and for some reason that really made no logical sense, that made her feel better. She hoped he was good and cold, too. She hoped he was freezing his balls off.

"Give me the film, and then you're coming with me. Nice and quiet."

The film?

She was really losing it because that made no sense at all. Why did her mother want the film and not the icon? And what about the ponytailed man? He'd killed her grandmother. She knew to her soul her mother hadn't known about that, but suddenly he shows up in Paris with Sergei? Something was very wrong here. Her brain squirreled around, she was too exhausted and cold to make sense of it.

He pushed the gun harder into her side. "Have you fallen asleep? Give me the film, and don't even think about trying any more comic-book heroics. My God, I still can't believe you actually jumped off that bridge and didn't break your neck. And then you added stupidity to insanity by jumping off the barge and into the river. I thought I was going to have to go in after you, and that, lady, would really have pissed me off. So quit pushing your luck and give me the damn film."

The film, the icon, it didn't matter. She was the Keeper and the Keeper kept.

Zoe fumbled with the satchel, tugged at the zipper, tugged again. He grunted with impatience and leaned forward to pull it out of her shaking hands—

She rammed her elbow straight into his chin, so hard she heard his teeth crack together. Then she pivoted on the ball of one foot and lashed out with the other, kicking him square in the gut.

The air whooshed out of him. He staggered backward, holding his belly. But before the thought *Run!* could even enter her head, he had his gun back up and pointed at her chest.

"Don't move," he said. "Don't you dare fucking move another inch, and Jesus God, woman, that hurt. I ought to shoot you now just for the hell of it. Give me the film."

He saw the intent in her eyes and took two more steps back. But he kept the gun pointed at her chest. It wasn't fair. She was alone and soaked to the bone, her legs felt like lead, and she was so cold she was beyond bearing it. She was going to walk to the restaurant and call a taxi, and if he didn't get out of her way too bad for him because she wasn't born yesterday. If he was going to shoot her, he'd have done it by now.

"You want it so bad, cowboy"—she beckoned to him with her curled fingers—"then come and get it."

He raised his face to the sky. "Why can't things ever be easy?"

"What? You don't think you can take me one-on-one? Why don't you give your ugly partner with the ponytail a jingle then? Maybe he can drop on by and give you a hand."

"I don't have a partner. And that guy, you don't want to get near that guy."

"Oh, yeah, and you're such a prize."

He bared his teeth at her. "Enough of this. Give me the fucking film or I'm going to shoot you."

"Sure. Right. You're my mama's pet goon, no way would you shoot me."

He shot her.

21

She opened her eyes on a white plaster ceiling. It was a tall ceiling with a brown stain in one corner. A vague panic filled her, but she couldn't name what she was afraid of. Something to do with a river. And ice.

Then it all came back to her in a rush—the ponytailed man, the Japanese tourists, the barge, the dog, the river.

Sergei with a gun.

Had he shot her? Was she in a hospital?

She didn't feel hurt anywhere, but then she hadn't tried moving yet. She turned her head and saw a red-beaded lamp sitting on a table next to an ornate silver clock. Beyond it a walnut armoire draped with a fringed Spanish shawl stood against a red-and-gold-flocked wall. Definitely not a hospital then, unless the French furnished their hospitals to look like Victorian bordellos.

She jerked, struggling against a heavy pile of quilts to push herself up onto her elbows. Pain stabbed her head so fiercely she gasped out loud from the shock of it. Her blurred eyes focused on a brass footboard, then beyond to Sergei.

He straddled a chair with his arms folded over the back. His face was in shadow so she couldn't see his eyes, but she felt them.

"What did you shoot me with?"

"A tranq gun."

Zoe flopped back onto the pillows and shut her eyes. She had to think, but it hurt to think, so she just lay there and shivered. It felt as if she'd been shivering for years.

"Cold," she said. The word sounded as if it came out around a mouthful of marbles.

"Cold is what you get when you go swimming in the Seine in February. You would've croaked from hypothermia if I hadn't saved your ass after all those stupid, gutsy stunts you pulled. I had to hold you propped up under a hot shower for a good hour to get your body temperature back to something even close to normal."

"Don't hold your breath waiting for a thank-you card." There, that was better. She could get words out now without her teeth knocking together. His teeth had sure made a nice cracking sound when she'd smacked him in the jaw. Too bad she hadn't laid him out cold.

Something about him was different, though. For one thing, he was speaking perfectly good English, as before when he—

The film.

Zoe jerked back up and nearly blacked out from the pain that shot through her skull. "What've you done with my stuff?"

He nodded to a chair upholstered in purple cabbage roses. Her satchel was in the chair, but Zoe saw that he'd taken out the reel of film. He'd set it on a round table, between an old-fashioned black telephone and a glass vase of tulips.

Zoe lay back and closed her eyes again against a fresh wave of dizziness. He'd gotten what he wanted, so why hadn't he just tossed her back into the Seine and left her to drown? She decided she wasn't so scared of him anymore. Not as scared as she probably ought to be.

"Will you tell me just one thing?" she asked him. "What is there about a home movie of a little girl blowing out birthday-cake candles that makes it worth killing for?"

He said nothing.

"Okay, I get it. You're just a dumb *vors.* A goon who follows orders, no questions asked. Mr. Stepin Fetchit."

He still said nothing.

"Are you here on a job for my mother?"

"The *pakhan* believes your life is danger."

"My mother sent you along to protect me?" Zoe said with a snort. "Yeah, right."

More likely Anna Larina wanted for herself what her own mother had kept hidden away in the casket. That meant she'd known of its existence, but probably not where it was all these years. Had she known, she would have sent someone to the griffin shop to take it by force a long time ago. She didn't have the fancy key to open it with, but a crowbar would've done the job.

But, no, that still didn't make sense. The thing of value in the casket should be the icon, especially to Anna Larina, who collected the things. Yet with Sergei, her hired thug, it was all about the film.

He'd gone quiet again. Zoe's head hurt too much to lift it and check out what he was up to.

"Are you working with the other man who was chasing me? The guy with the ponytail?"

"I already told you no."

"But you do know who he is?"

"I got an idea."

"Mind sharing it?"

He said nothing.

"Damn you, he killed my grandmother," she said, suddenly so furious she was near tears with it.

She heard the chair scrape across wood; a moment later he came into her view. He went to a lace-curtained window and looked out. From her perspective all she could see was blue sky and a couple of cotton-ball clouds. Apparently while she'd been sleeping off the tranquilizer, a new day had dawned in Paris.

"Where am I, anyway?" she asked.

"A friend's apartment on the Île St.-Louis."

"You have friends? Who knew?"

She looked around the place again. It was just the one room with a tiny bathroom between the window and the armoire. A microwave and an espresso machine passed for a kitchen.

Sergei hadn't bothered to respond to her snark. He stayed with his back to her, his gaze on the street below, as if he were waiting for someone.

The telephone rang.

He quickly crossed the room to the table to snatch up the receiver on the second ring. He carried on a conversation in rapid French. Zoe couldn't understand a single word.

He hung up the telephone and came right at her. She met his eyes, and inside she felt a lick of fear.

He reached into his coat pocket as he leaned over her, and she braced herself to be shot again with the tranquilizer gun. Instead he took out a pair of handcuffs, snapped one end around her right wrist and the other end around one of the brass pipes on the headboard.

"Oh, for God's sakes, gimme a break."

He startled her by laughing out loud.

Then he left her.

ZOE CALLED HIM every filthy name she knew while she jerked and wrenched at the handcuffs, but they were the real deal and weren't going to pop open no matter how much she tugged at them.

She thought for a while that maybe she could fold her hand in upon itself and slip it out of the rigid cuff, but she wasn't small-boned enough. She tried shaking the brass pipe loose from the crossbar on the headboard, but it was welded solid.

Damn the man. Damn him, damn him.

She had to get out of here before he came back. She was the Keeper now, and even though she still didn't know what it all meant, she figured she at least had to "keep" everything that had been in the casket out of the hands of men like Sergei. Was the film the altar of bones? No, she was being stupid again. Her grandmother had said the women of their line had been Keepers for so long the beginning had been lost in the mists of time. Yet the film had been made in the early 1960s.

Zoe lay back, stared at the ceiling, and tried to think through the pounding pain in her head. A cloud passed over the sun, and the room darkened. She looked at the lamp sitting on the table beside the bed. A lamp with a shade made of hundreds of red glass beads strung on wires.

SHE COULDN'T REACH the lamp with her free hand, and the silver clock on the dresser was ticking down the seconds like an ominous metronome. She doubted Sergei would be away long, he could come back through the door at any minute and she'd have no more chances to escape.

She kicked off the heavy quilts and jackknifed her legs sideways, grabbing at the lamp with her feet. The lamp teetered and almost fell to the floor. At the last instant, she managed to snag it by the fringe with her toes.

She pulled it back onto the bed within reach of her free hand. It was harder to strip the beads off the wires than she had thought it would be. She ended up using her teeth.

She stripped six wires and wove them together until they were about an eighth of an inch thick. She wanted to make it thicker, but there wasn't time.

She struggled one-handed with the pick, poking it into the cuff's lock, jiggling it, poking, jiggling. . . . It wasn't going to work and the damn clock was ticking louder than a drum now, louder than the pounding in her head—

The lock on the cuff snicked open.

Her nerves were screaming at her, *Hurry, hurry, hurry.* She jumped off the bed, and the floor tilted beneath her feet. Her muscles felt as mushy as overcooked spaghetti, her head throbbed.

She snatched up the film and stuffed it back in her satchel. The icon and the postcard with the riddle were still there, wrapped up in the sealskin pouch, but oddly the Marilyn Monroe photograph was gone. She checked her money, passport, and credit cards—all still there.

She was about to run out of the apartment when she suddenly realized that all she was wearing was her bra and panties. All this time she'd been half-naked, she thought, laughing out loud, and she hadn't even noticed.

She found her leather jacket, boots, and socks next to the radiator, her jeans and sweater hanging over the towel bar in the bathroom. They were damp and clammy and smelled of the river, and she shuddered as she put them on.

Something was in her jeans back pocket . . . two soggy sheets of— *Oh, please, God, no* . . . But it was. Her grandmother's letter.

Sudden tears burned her eyes, her chest ached. She must have stuck the letter into her back pocket when she'd left the museum, and then she'd gone and jumped in the Seine. Her grandmother's words were gone now, just smears of blue ink and—

Downstairs a door slammed, and she froze. Then she heard footsteps walking away out on the sidewalk and she let out a long, slow breath. She put her grandmother's letter into her satchel, even though it was ruined now, and headed for the door.

———

SHE WALKED INTO the first bank she came to and rented a safe-deposit box. She wanted to put the icon and the film where no one could get at them.

While she was in the room with the safe-deposit box, she started to enter into her PDA the parts of her grandmother's letter she could remember, but then it occurred to her that the battery might run out before she could recharge it, so she wrote it all down on a piece of the bank's notepaper instead.

She left the bank with her satchel feeling a thousand pounds lighter. A trendy boutique blasted throbbing hip-hop music next door. She went inside and bought another pair of black jeans, a black wool turtleneck, some more underwear, and finally a new, trendier black leather jacket that was going to put a serious dent in her bank account.

The clerk was young, and friendly, and wanted to practice her English. Zoe asked her where she could get a taxi to take her to the Musée de Cluny.

Now that she was thinking again, she realized she should go back to the griffin shop and talk with Boris some more. He'd recognized Lena as a Keeper the first time they met because of her resemblance to the Lady. Surely there was some history, some more folklore, to go with the icon that he could tell her.

———

ZOE ASKED THE cabdriver to let her out across from the museum. But when she rounded the corner of the little side street, she was shocked to see a crowd gathered in front of the old man's shop, along with an ambulance and two cop cars with whirling red bubble lights.

She pushed through the crowd, her heart pounding slow, dull beats. *Please don't let him be dead. Please don't let him be dead.*

She wedged herself between a young couple, and a man wearing a stained butcher's apron, just as the door to the shop opened and two EMTs in white smocks came out carrying a body bag on a stretcher. She heard the young man say in English to his girl, "One of the cops just said the guy's eye was cut out."

The ground lurched beneath Zoe's feet, and she almost fell. She spun around, hot bile rising in her throat. She put a hand up to her mouth and pushed back through the crowd.

Oh God, oh God. This was all her fault. She must have led the ponytailed man right to the griffin shop yesterday, and now he'd killed the old man. But not before cutting out his eye, and there'd been no reason to do that. Boris didn't have the icon anymore, and he had no way of knowing where it was.

She wove blindly down the jostling sidewalks, not knowing or caring where she went. Once she almost stepped off the curb and into the path of a bus.

She passed a huge multiplex movie theater and thought about losing herself inside, yet she walked on. She needed to find a hotel, a place with a shower and a bed. A place to lie low and think about what to do.

She found one that looked promising off one of the narrower side streets. It had a threadbare carpet and a half-dead palm tree in the lobby—definitely not a hotel you'd expect American tourists to flock to.

The man behind the front desk had a pathetic mustache and a snooty nose. He claimed to have only one vacancy, a small room on the top floor, facing the street and with only a shower, no bathtub. Was *madame* sure . . . ?

Madame was sure.

The elevator was smaller than a phone booth. *Madame* took the stairs.

━━━━━━━━

NOT UNTIL SHE sat down on the bed did she realize how badly her legs were shaking. She was hungry, but she was afraid if she tried to eat now, she'd be sick. She couldn't get the image of that body bag out of her head.

She curled up in a ball on the bed, hugging a pillow to her chest. She knew she ought to go to the French police and tell them about the ponytailed man, but she was afraid they would make her turn over the icon and the film because those things came from what was now a crime scene. She could even become a suspect herself, and she hadn't heard very nice things about Parisian jails.

She lay there for a while, until hunger pangs penetrated her numb brain and she could smell the river on herself. She wanted to stay on the bed, curled up in a ball, but she made herself get up, shower, and change into her new clothes.

She left her ruined things in the hotel, but brought everything else along with her in her satchel. She took a table at the first café she came to, sat beneath a green-and-gold awning, and ordered a *salade Niçoise* and a bottle of Evian.

She knew she needed to make herself think, but she sat there, numb, still cold and feeling so very alone. A big old stone church was across the street. She wondered if churches still offered sanctuary for the hunted. The streets around her were jammed with cars and people, and she watched the bustle while she wolfed down the salad and half a loaf of bread. There were supposed to be over 2 million people in Paris. She could lose herself among so many, surely.

Except you couldn't make a move in today's world without leaving a trail of numbers. Credit card, passport, driver's license, Social Security. Even her library card had a bar code and a number. If Mr. Ponytail had a source in the French police, he might already be waiting for her back at her hotel. Sergei, as one of her mother's enforcers, would be even quicker to find her, with contacts in the Russian *mafiya*, whose tentacles reached into every major city government throughout the world.

A shadow fell over her table.

22

It was a woman, a stranger. Okay, a beautiful woman in a to-die-for red designer suit, and because they'd made eye contact, Zoe smiled at her, then scooted her chair closer to the table, thinking the woman wanted to squeeze by. Instead she pulled back the chair opposite Zoe and sat down.

"Ms. Dmitroff—no, don't pop up like a jack-in-the-box, for heaven's sake. That's the last thing you want to do right now." The woman placed a black leather Chanel bag on the table, folded her hands on top of it, looked carefully around her, then leaned in close. "After all, we don't know who else might be watching."

The woman looked all around her again, then opened the Chanel bag, pulled out a matching wallet, and flipped it open long enough to flash some sort of laminated ID card with her picture and a government seal on it.

"My name is Yasmine Poole. I'm an operative with the Central Intelligence Agency."

Zoe snorted, because all this nightmare needed right now to make it complete was the CIA. "And I'm Batgirl. Sorry, I'm afraid I left my decoder ring back at the hotel."

"Oh, puh-leeze, Ms. Dmitroff. You're intelligent enough to know that not all secret agents run around on Jet Skis and flying motorboats like James Bond, saving the world from master villains. I've worked for the Agency for over ten years, yet most days you will find me sitting behind a desk at Langley analyzing what affect a half-a-tael rise on the price of rice in Mongolia will have on the world's economy."

She smiled, Zoe didn't smile back.

"Most days," Zoe said, "you would find me on the phone in my cubbyhole of a Mission Street law office, trying to wrangle a plea bargain out of an ADA who thinks defense attorneys rank somewhere below pond scum. Yet here I am and here you are—so how did that happen?"

"I followed you just now from your hotel. We had you located fifteen minutes after the man at the front desk ran your credit card."

"I guess it's nice to have a fancy badge. Beats a decoder ring any day of the week." Zoe finished the last of her water and patted her mouth with her napkin. "So what do you want with me?"

"This is going to sound all melodramatic and surreal to you, but we believe a certain item has fallen into your possession which could have grave consequences on national security. It's vital that you turn the item over to me now, before it falls into the wrong hands."

Zoe's mouth had gone dry, even though she'd expected something like this. From here on out she was going to have to be careful. Somehow she was going to have to get as much information as possible out of this woman without revealing her own ignorance. For as her grandmother had warned her, ignorance was a poor shield against danger.

"I'm in possession of a lot of 'items,'" Zoe said. "You'll have to be more specific."

Yasmine Poole—if that was her real name—pursed her very red lips as if she'd just kissed a lemon. "A film. A reel of eight-millimeter film, to be exact. Don't waste time denying you have it, Ms. Dmitroff. We both know better."

The film again, not the icon. What was it about that damn film?

"Wow, I've got a home movie of a little girl's birthday party. Our nation is in peril. Arrest me now."

Yasmine Poole's beautiful face turned hard. "Pretending to be stupid isn't something I would recommend, given the circumstances. Because I *can* arrest you, and Guantánamo Bay really sucks. Trust me on that."

Zoe said nothing, and the woman took her silence for some sort of surrender. "Your country really would be grateful for your cooperation in this, Ms. Dmitroff, because there are others who will stop at nothing to get their hands on that film, and they are not nice people. Not nice at all."

Yasmine Poole opened her bag again, removed a photograph, and held it out to Zoe. "Have you ever seen this man before?"

The photograph was of a man standing next to a wrought-iron lamppost on a snowy, cobblestoned street. He looked to be in his midforties, and he was extraordinarily handsome, with intense, hooded eyes, flaring cheekbones, and an aristocratic nose.

"His name is Nikolai Popov," the woman said. "He was a very senior echelon officer in the KGB during the Cold War, a vicious, ruthless man, responsible for too many deaths to count. He's long retired, of course, enjoying his Crimean dacha. We figure he's got to be in his nineties now, but his power and influence hasn't waned."

"And you think he's after the film?"

"Zoe . . . Can I call you Zoe? He's had his agents out trying to track it down for years."

"Why? What's in it for him?"

Yasmine Poole pursed her lips again. "Oh, dear. See, I knew you would ask me that. Unfortunately the answer is classified. Top secret, and all that."

Zoe looked down at the photograph one last time, then handed it back to the woman who called herself Yasmine Poole. Zoe didn't trust her as far as she cold spit. Somehow, she needed to find a way to look at the film, because it obviously had something more on it than just a little girl's birthday party.

She gave Yasmine Poole the earnest look she used on juries. "I just want to do the right thing."

The woman patted her hand. "Of course you do."

"Only I don't have it with me anymore."

"I know that, Zoe," Yasmine Poole said, and again Zoe heard that tinge of malice in her voice. "I searched your hotel room and your possessions while you were showering. You've obviously put it somewhere you think it's safe. Just tell me where, and I'll be out of your life. Then you can enjoy the rest of your vacation in this beautiful city. You don't look like the club-hopping type, but there's always an art fair at the Grand Palais this time of year."

Laughter, coming from the next table, distracted Zoe. She looked over and saw a couple, dressed in matching hooded sweatshirts, holding hands between two steaming cups of espresso.

When she looked around again, the butt of a Glock was protruding out of the expensive designer handbag. "You see, I really didn't want to go to a bad place where there are guns and threats of violence," Yasmine Poole said. "But you made me. Hand over the film, Zoe, or I'll be forced to play hardball, and you really don't want that. Trust me."

"I'm not being deliberately obstinate, Ms. Poole. I put the film in a safe-deposit box. So I'm afraid you'll need my signature in order to get at it."

Yasmine Poole stood up. She shut her handbag, slipped its strap over her arm, and tugged at the bottom of her suit jacket. "Then let's do it."

"The bank is by the opera house," Zoe lied. She hadn't a clue where the opera house was, but she figured Paris had to have one and she was gambling that it wasn't right around the corner. "We'll have to take the metro."

"Honey, I'm really not the metro type. And I have a nice expense account. We'll take a taxi."

"Sorry, but the only way I can find it is to retrace my steps from this morning, and this morning I took the metro."

Yasmine Poole really didn't look at all happy about this, but she followed Zoe across the street and down into a subway station next to the big old stone church. It was the tail end of the midday rush hour, so the platform was crowded. But the woman stuck to Zoe like an African river leech.

The train pulled in and they got on together. Yasmine Poole started to take a seat, but she stopped when she realized Zoe had stayed by the door. "We transfer at the next stop," Zoe said.

Yasmine Poole nodded, but Zoe saw that she was checking out the route painted on the wall of the car.

Zoe counted off the seconds as more passengers squeezed on.

Yasmine Poole pointed to the map. "If the bank is near the Place de la Bastille, then shouldn't we be on the Porte d'Orleans train? Or were you talking about the old opera house. Still—"

Zoe widened her eyes. "Oh, my God, it's that man again. The man who killed my grandmother."

Yasmine Poole's head whipped around. "Who? Where?"

"There." Zoe pointed. Then she jumped off the train just as the door slid shut.

Yasmine Poole whirled back again, but it was too late. She pounded her fist on the door, tried to pry it open with her fingers, but the train was already moving.

Zoe waved bye-bye to the woman's furious face as the train pulled away from the platform, gathering speed and disappearing into the black tunnel.

SHE TOOK THE steps back up to the street at a run. She figured she had fifteen minutes to disappear in the crowded Parisian streets before Yasmine Poole could double back. Unless the woman had an accomplice she was in touch with by cell phone. In which case Zoe was dead meat.

She shot out of the metro station at a run and slammed into a man's chest so hard she nearly knocked herself over. He grabbed her arms to steady her. She didn't even have to look up; she knew who it was.

There were over 2 million people in Paris, so how come she was so easy to find?

"Come on," said Sergei. He kept hold of her left arm, leading her toward the big stone church. "Let us pray."

HE TOOK HER to a pew tucked away in a corner behind a marble column, next to a wooden confessional box.

They sat down side by side. Zoe said, "Fancy meeting you again so soon, Sergei."

He said nothing, just reached in his pocket. She half-expected him to pull out a gun.

He pulled out a wallet and flipped it open to show a gold shield that glittered even in the dim light. "My name isn't Sergei. It's Ry O'Malley. I'm an undercover agent for the DEA."

Zoe laughed, although she thought she sounded hysterical even to her own ears. "That woman who called herself Yasmine Poole flashed a CIA badge at me. And now you with the . . ." She peered closer at the gold shield. "Ryland O'Malley. The Drug Enforcement Administration. For all I know you could both be fakes."

"Sometimes you got to go with your instincts on who to trust."

"And in what universe would my instincts be telling me to trust you?"

"I think you know you should at least listen to what I have to say."

"Okay, then you can start by telling me how you found me so easily. Do I have a tracking device planted on me somewhere?"

A corner of his hard mouth actually twitched in a smile. "When a person's being hunted and that person is an amateur, they run to ground in a place that's familiar to them. I figured you'd eventually go back to the shop across from the museum where you first picked up the film. And, sure enough, you showed up there just about the time they were carrying out the body."

Zoe hadn't been able to cry earlier over the old man's death, but now tears suddenly flooded her eyes and she had to look away. "Do you have to say it like that, like it's just another day on the job? His name was Boris, and he was sweet, and the ponytailed man cut out his eye."

Sergei, or Ry, or whatever his name was, said nothing.

"Maybe you were there, too. Maybe you helped him do it."

"You don't believe that."

She leaned back so she could study him again, from head to toe. "You really aren't a true *vors*, are you? In spite of your gutter Russian and that tattoo you've got on your arm."

"The tat's real. I earned it in a Tajikistan prison cell, but that story is for another day. What did you do with the film? Put it in a safe-deposit box?"

"Such aptly named things—safe-deposit boxes. As in safe from guys like you and Ms. CIA and Mr. Ponytail. Well, it's the icon that he seems to want." She waved a hand. "But details, details."

"We need to take a look at that film, Zoe."

"I'm beginning to wonder if it isn't like that movie from a while back—the one with Naomi Watts. *The Ring*? Once you look at it you die."

"You don't have to look at it to be killed."

Zoe said nothing. The church was dark and silent and cold, like the proverbial grave, she thought.

"You know what's on it, don't you?" she said. "On the film."

"Yes. But I need to see it."

Zoe blew out her breath in a sigh. "Oookay. So why don't we just bop on down to the nearest video store? I'm sure they have one of those old-fashioned projectors we can rent. On the shelf right next to all the Betamaxes."

His mouth did the twisting thing again. "It so happens I know a guy whose hobby is collecting prints of old, uh, movies."

"Porn, you mean?"

"Not all of it's porn. Anyway, he owns the kind of projector we need, and that's where I went this morning—to his place to pick it up."

"And left me handcuffed to the bed."

"Using the best, state-of-the-art handcuffs, by the way. And being stupid enough to leave the film behind, too. Man I waaaay underestimated you there."

"I'll choose to take that as a compliment."

"It was meant as one. . . . Look, I'll make you a deal. We go back to the apartment and watch your grandmother's movie, and afterward if you want to take it and walk out the door, I won't stop you."

Zoe sat in silence a moment, then said, "I wouldn't even make it as far as the airport alive, would I?"

"Probably not."

━━━━━━

ZOE GOT THE film and her icon out of the safe-deposit box, and they crossed the river to the Île St.-Louis and the apartment of Sergei's . . . of Ry O'Malley's friend. The projector was there. He'd told the truth about that at least.

They took a couple of hunting prints off the wall to clear a space. Zoe let him handle the film, since he seemed to know what he was doing, threading it through sprockets and around spools. She pulled the shade down over the window, darkening the room.

She felt an odd mixture of excitement and dread. She knew what she was about to see would probably change her life forever. But her life was already changed, her life was already in danger, and at least now she would be getting some answers.

And once she saw what was on the film, maybe she'd know better how to handle Sergei . . . Ry. And all the rest of the hunters.

The projector was noisy, with a whirring fan, and the film made a clatter as it fed through the sprockets. Black marks danced on the wall and suddenly there was her mother's face, close-up, a big grin splitting her small mouth. Her eighth birthday party, according to the brightly penned banner across the wall behind her. She pointed to her cake with its flaming eight candles, frosted white, but Zoe knew it was chocolate inside, her mother's favorite, her own favorite.

And there was her grandmother Katya, so pretty, so happy, almost dancing around the table. It was like seeing herself, dressed up in a play, how much she looked like the two of them.

They watched the girl blow out the candles on her birthday cake and open her presents. Katya was always there, helping to untangle a bow, adjusting a paper hat. Zoe tried to imagine what awful thing had driven this seemingly adoring mother to abandon her child, but she couldn't. And who was the person behind the camera? The stepfather Anna Larina could barely remember?

The birthday party faded to white, more black sprocket marks danced on the wall.

Then suddenly, a splash of color. Blue . . .

23

THE CAMERA *pans along a wide boulevard, buildings on one side, a park of sorts on the other, the sun shining beneath the big blue bowl of a sky. And there are people and they're cheering, although you can't hear them. Motorcycle cops and cars are driving slowly toward the camera, a cavalcade.*

Suddenly the lens zooms in on a dark blue stretch Lincoln convertible with American flags flapping on its fenders. Two men are sitting in the front seat, a couple in the middle seat, and another couple in the back, and they're smiling and waving to the crowds lining the sidewalks.

The camera closes in on one face. His thick hair is shining in the sun, his large white teeth are flashing.

It is John Fitzgerald Kennedy.

The camera moves slowly as Kennedy turns his head and looks at the woman beside him. It is the first lady, Jackie, wearing a pink suit and her trademark pillbox hat. They seem to share a moment of what? Intimacy? Triumph? The camera rests on both their faces and they are so alive, so beautiful. They look on top of the world.

But the camera is veering away from them now, leaving the motorcade in the distance, panning over a curved, white pergola, its columns looking classically Greek and a bit strange under the bright Texas sun. Then leafless early-winter trees come into sharp focus, and globe streetlights along an open grassy knoll. The crowd is sparser here, almost eerily calm as they wait for the motorcade to pass by.

The camera lingers awhile on a handsome, bareheaded man, all dapper in a dark suit, standing next to a freeway sign. He carries an umbrella in the crook of his arm, odd for there is not a cloud in the sky, but now the camera is leaving him, moving on to an all-American family who could have walked straight out of the pages of the Saturday Evening Post. *The mother looking Jackie-like in her red, sleeveless shift dress and matching red heels, the father holding his boy on his shoulders, telling him, maybe, how he is going to remember this day forever. The day he saw the president of the United States of America.*

The camera jumps now, over to a wooden picket fence that separates the grassy knoll from what looks to be a parking lot near a railroad yard. Stopping suddenly to focus on a man in a brown suit and a hat who is standing behind the fence, using it as a blind, because he has a rifle in his hands.

The camera is resting on his profile, studying his thoughtful expression, when the man suddenly turns and stares directly into the lens, and his eyes light up, as if he knows he's the star in this macabre home movie and he wants everyone else to know it, too. But after a moment his face hardens, turns cruel, and he looks away, back toward the grassy knoll.

Slowly, he brings the rifle to his shoulder and sights down the barrel.

Then it's all a blur—pergola, trees, grass, asphalt, people—nothing but a whirling kaleidoscope of color until the camera freezes again on the dapper man with the umbrella. The man seems tense, waiting for something. Suddenly, he snaps open the umbrella and raises it high above his head. Is it a signal to the man with the rifle? Because the camera is jumping now, down the street, and the president's car is coming into view, closer and closer. The camera zooms in on that famous, smiling face, locking in so close it fills the apartment wall.

He looks happy, he's playing to the crowd, loving the adulation, the cheers. Then his hand stops in midwave, and he half turns to Jackie. Has he heard something? Seen something?

Suddenly, he reaches up and clutches at his throat with both hands. He looks so surprised, and Jackie is reacting now, too, glancing over at her husband, not understanding what has already happened, what else is going to happen soon now. Then she understands and horror twists her face.

The driver, too, is turning to look over his shoulder and the car is slowing, slowing, stopping . . .

And the president's head explodes in a red mist and pieces of something white—is it his skull?—are flying through the air.

The camera jerks, then quickly moves over the crowd, recording the hysteria, the terror, the screaming mouths making no sound. Then the camera shifts back to the Lincoln as it madly picks up speed, and a Secret Service agent is running alongside it, jumping onto the trunk, where a piece of the president's skull has landed, and where Jackie, in her bright pink suit and pillbox hat, is climbing out to get it, as if all she has to do is stick it back on and he will be whole again.

The camera closes in on the president, slumped over onto the seat, no longer moving. It lingers on him, almost lovingly, almost with a mad flourish, as if to show—Look, he's dead, just look, the back of his head is gone.

And then the camera, as if suddenly repelled, jerks away from the carnage, back to the killer just as he is stooping to pick up the spent shell casings. As he straightens, he looks directly into the lens, and he grins really big, like, Fuck you, I got it done, didn't I?

Then he spins away and runs toward another man who's standing, waiting, a man in some kind of uniform. Not a cop, though, for he has on pin-striped overalls and a beaked cap, like a railroad worker in a children's book. The assassin pitches the gun to him as he passes, then he disappears out of the scene.

The camera records every movement of the man in the overalls as he breaks down the rifle, smooth and fast, putting it in a toolbox, and then he is walking along the railroad tracks toward some parked boxcars.

Slowly, the boxcars fade to white.

24

Z OE STARED at the blank wall, as the tail end of the film flapped around and around on the spinning spool. Her brain refused to work, but her mouth did.

"Holy bejesus."

She kept looking at the wall, as if expecting it to show her more, to continue with the carnage, to show her Lee Harvey Oswald's arrest and his murder by Jack Ruby, maybe show LBJ getting sworn in as president with Jackie in her bloodstained pink suit standing blank-faced beside him.

But there was nothing more. It was over and she'd witnessed history. The real history, not the cooked-up report of the Warren Commission.

She looked at Ry, who stood motionless, staring just as she had at the now blank wall. Then his hand came up, startling her, and she jerked back. But he was only reaching for the switch on the projector to shut it off.

The cold, empty look on his face terrified her.

Carefully, slowly, she said, "What in hell is going on here? How did you know my grandmother had this film? Why *did* she have it? I know it's real. Nothing like that could be faked . . . could it?"

Ry put the film back into its can and tossed it on the bed. "No, it's real."

"I want to look at it again," Zoe said, as she watched him pack up the projector. "That man with the rifle, the assassin, I think I've seen him somewhere before. And there was another guy, the one with the umbrella? He's the spitting image of this photograph Yasmine Poole just showed me back at the café. She said his name is Nikolai Popov, and that he was once a big muckety-muck in the KGB. Of course she could've been lying through her teeth."

"That's always possible," Ry said, though he didn't seem at all surprised to be told that the KGB might have been behind the Kennedy assassination. "We'll talk it through later. Right now we should get out of here."

She took a long, hard look at him. "You know, I had a real nice life back in the day. All I had to worry about was some wifebeater or deadbeat dad going all postal on me, and then the next thing I know my long-lost grandmother turns up murdered, some guy is threatening to pluck out my eyes, I get a letter that sends me to Paris, where I find this icon and end up jumping off a damned bridge and land on piles of soggy newspapers before I nearly drown, and then, just to put the cherry on top of the sundae, I'm lucky enough to meet up with you. But that's not the grand prize, oh, no. I've just found out there really was a second gunman on the grassy knoll. It's like I went to bed and woke up in the middle of some moonbat conspiracy theory, and right about now I'm thinking you can take your silent act and . . . well, I won't be indelicate. Who are you? Just who in hell are you? What is going on here? Spit it out now or I'm going to kick you in the balls."

"I told you who I am."

"Right. Ryland . . . no, let's get all cozy here. It's Ry O'Malley with the DEA. But what does—my God, are you telling me Kennedy was killed over drugs?"

"*No.*"

He snapped the lid on the projector case and pushed to his feet, his eyes dilated, wild. She half-expected him to pull out a gun and shoot her.

Instead he shoved his fingers through his hair and spun away from her. She saw the muscles of his back expand as he drew in deep breaths, got himself back under control. Then he turned to face her again.

"Technically I'm not working for the DEA at the moment. I took what you might call a leave of absence a year and a half ago."

"And decided wouldn't it be fun to join the Russian *mafiya*? You must be quite the agent to come up with a cover story good enough to fool my mother and her security investigators, because she's no dummy. She's many other things, but no dummy."

"If you have the means and the know-how to do it, it's easy enough to create a background for yourself—a Social Security number, false immigration papers, a prison record. Get some skell to vouch for what a badass you are. Stuff like that. It's called creating a legend. We do it all the time in the DEA."

"I bet. So somehow you discovered that my grandmother Katya had the film, and when you couldn't find her, you went undercover as one my mother's *vors*, hoping to pick up a lead from her that would put you on Katya's trail. Have I got that right?"

"Yeah, that's about it in a nutshell."

She waited, but he said nothing more. "Okay. Then there's one or two other things I'd like to know. How did you know my grandmother had the film in the first place? How did you know it even existed? And the man with the rifle, the killer? You know who he is, don't you?"

"Yes, I know." His eyes met hers. The violence was still there, but it was being banked by something that looked oddly like pain.

"Then tell me."

He reached into his coat pocket and pulled out a photograph. It was her photograph, or rather her grandmother's, the one she'd found tucked inside the casket. The one of Katya Orlova and Marilyn Monroe and—

"Hey, that's where I've seen the shooter before!" Zoe took the photograph to study it more closely. *Mike and Marilyn and me . . .* "Yesterday in Boris's shop, I was so focused on my grandmother and how cool it was that she knew Marilyn Monroe, I didn't really look at this Mike guy in the booth with them, but it's him, it's Kennedy's assassin and—oh, my God, I can't believe I didn't put it together before. *O'Malley.* My mother's stepfather, Katya's husband, his name was Mike O'Malley and . . ."

She looked from the photograph to Ry O'Malley's harsh face, back to the photo again.

"Yeah," Ry said. "I look like just like him, don't I?"

Ry WENT TO the window, lifted the shade, and sunlight filled the room. He pulled aside the lace curtain to check out the street below. She knew what he was feeling. She was the *pakhan*'s daughter, after all.

"The kil—the man in the film . . . He's your father."

Ry said nothing, so Zoe went on, "And Yasmine Poole wasn't lying, was she? I could tell by your reaction when I told you about the photograph of Nikolai Popov. He really was in the KGB, which means your father probably worked for the KGB, too. The KGB killed Kennedy."

"Apparently so."

"Why?"

Ry gave a short, bitter laugh. "That's the million-dollar question, isn't it?"

She stared at his back. She was sure he knew way more than he was telling, and it was starting to piss her off because while his father may have been the killer, it seemed to be her neck on the line here now.

"That was no home movie taken by some random person who showed up to watch the president of the United States drive by that day in Dallas. Whoever had that camera in his hands—no, scratch that. The camera was in *her* hands, wasn't it? My grandmother's. That's how she ended up with the film of the assassination. She was *there*."

Ry said nothing, so Zoe went on, "And your . . . the assassin. He knew she was there. You could tell by the way he was mugging for the camera. But why film it in the first place? Certainly it wasn't to show that he'd pulled off the job, because Kennedy's death would've been proof enough for that—"

"Life insurance," Ry said, cutting her off. He let the curtain fall back into place and turned to face her. "Because once the assassination went down, the triggerman would be a loose end to whoever ordered the job, and loose ends get whacked."

Whacked. That sounded like something out of *GoodFellas*, except it wasn't funny.

"I guess that's what I am now. A loose end," Zoe said, not trying to hide how scared she was. "I think I want to go home now."

"Hey." His face softened, his eyes squinting into his version of a smile. "For an amateur, you've been handling yourself pretty well. Don't wimp out on me now."

"Thanks, I guess. . . . The one thing I'm not getting, though, is where the ponytailed man fits into this. He's got a Russian accent, so you'd think he'd be working for this Popov guy and the KGB, or whatever they're calling themselves these days, trying to get his hands on the film. But, no, he kills my grandmother, then he comes after me with a bicycle chain, but with him it's all about the altar of bones—"

Ry closed the distance between them so fast, Zoe didn't even know what was happening until it was too late. He grabbed her shoulders, spun her around, and pushed her against the wall. He spoke softly, but each word was distinct and deadly. "What do you know about the altar of bones?"

She tried to knee him in the balls, but he had the whole length of his body pressed up against hers and she couldn't get any leverage. She said, "I'll give you two seconds to put me down, and then I'm going to scream so loud they'll hear me on top of the Eiffel Tower."

He put her down.

She went to the bed, picked up the film, and put it into her satchel. "You're a bully, and you're probably a liar, and I'm outta here."

"Don't be stupid." He stepped in front of her, blocking her way. "You try to handle this on your own, and the wolves out there are gonna eat you alive."

"And what are you? You claim to be one of the good guys, and maybe you are and maybe you aren't. So far you haven't shown me much reason to trust you."

"Maybe because I'm still trying to figure out if I can trust you. I—"

He cut himself off and turned toward the door. Then Zoe heard it, too—the creak of a board outside on the stair landing.

Ry yelled, "Get down!" and knocked her to the floor just as the door burst open.

25

A SEMIAUTOMATIC WEAPON spat bullets, stitching the wall high above Zoe's head as she rolled and kept rolling, all the way into the tiny bathroom.

She came up onto her feet in a half-crouch and whirled in time to catch the big black pistol that came sliding across the floor at her from Ry's outstretched hand. The studio apartment was too small, and there'd been no time for him to make it to cover. So he lay flat with his arms above his head, and Zoe waited with horror for bullets from the gunmen in the doorway to riddle his body.

But the shooting stopped abruptly, and then it was eerily quiet except for the soft tinkle of glass falling from a busted picture on the wall and the pounding of her heart.

Zoe's hands shook a little as she checked the ammunition clip of the pistol Ry had tossed her, a Walther P99. She pressed her back to the wall between the toilet and door, held the Walther two-fisted out in front of her, and waited.

From where she was, she could see Ry lying in frozen stillness on the floor, but the half-closed bathroom door blocked her view of the shooters. She thought there were two of them, though, men with hooded sweatshirts, one in black and one in blue. They'd looked familiar. The lovers from the café, maybe? And they'd fired high, which meant they hadn't been aiming to kill. Yet.

The floorboard out in the hallway creaked again.

"Well, well," said Yasmine Poole, in that soft, smirking voice. "Why, if it isn't Agent Ryland O'Malley. What a hard man you are to kill. I was certain, back there in Galveston, that I was staring down at your watery grave and yet here you are again, the proverbial bad penny.

"And Ms. Dmitroff, I know you're back there in the powder room. Give me the film, and I'll let you walk out of here alive."

Ry met Zoe's eyes and he shook his head a fraction of an inch, but she didn't need the warning. They lived only so long as they had the film.

"Do you hear those sirens, Zoe? Your name has been put on the terrorist watch list with both the FBI and Interpol. So you see, there's nowhere for you to run to now, nowhere to hide. But if you give me the film, I can make it go away. Bygones and all that."

The whoop-whoops were growing steadily louder, coming closer. Zoe thought the imminent arrival of the French cops was probably the only thing keeping Ry O'Malley alive. He still lay on the floor, unmoving, completely vulnerable to a single bullet from Yasmine Poole or her two hooded thugs.

Think.

She noticed a bucket full of cleaning supplies under the sink. One was an American brand she recognized—a spray cleanser with bleach. She started talking, to cover any sound she made as she shifted her weight so she could reach it.

"It seems to me we've all landed in a bit of a pickle here, Yasmine. I could wait until the French cops arrive and turn myself and the film over to them, which would leave you with a lot of explaining to do, starting with what the CIA thinks it's doing carrying out covert operations on French soil."

"You win some," said Yasmine Poole, "you lose some. I'm willing to take my chances."

"Yeah?" The bottle of cleanser was full. Zoe checked to be sure the nozzle was in the "on" position. "But imagine what the reaction will be when they actually take a look at the film. *Quelle horreur. Quelle suprise.* The images of the second gunman on the grassy knoll would be all over the evening news. Would the guys you work for call that a win, Yasmine?"

Zoe set the cleaner on the floor between her feet and took the film back out of her satchel. It was hard to open the tin can one-handed, but she didn't dare set down the gun.

"By the way, just who *do* you really work for? The CIA, or the people who killed Kennedy? Or are we talking about the same thing?"

At last, at last, the can popped open. Zoe quickly dumped the film back into her satchel and pressed closed the now empty can. She shifted her weight again and craned her head so she could look through the crack between the jamb and the half-open door. She could see Yasmine Poole now, and the two hooded guys who flanked her on either side, their semiautomatics still pointed at Ry. Yasmine herself was unarmed, but Zoe remembered the gun she carried in her purse.

"Agent Blackthorn," said Yasmine Poole, "shoot Agent O'Malley in the kneecap."

"No, wait!" Zoe cried out, and she didn't have to fake the panic in her voice. She was running out of time—both with Yasmine and the French police. The sirens blared so loudly now, they had to be on the next street over and rounding the corner. "I'll give you the film. Don't hurt him."

She caught Ry's eye one last time, and she thought he might have winked at her, even though the blue-hooded guy was now standing over him, his weapon pointed down within inches of Ry's knee.

"It's just . . . I'm scared, Yasmine. Do you promise to let us go?"

"Of course, Zoe. After all, you could blab to the press all you want about some nameless guy on the grassy knoll, but without the film itself, they'd just think you were another tinfoil-hatted whack job. So slide the film out the door now, please, and we won't hurt your boyfriend."

Outside tires screeched, the whooping sirens cut off abruptly.

"The film, Zoe. Now."

Zoe shot the film can like a hockey puck through the half-open door, toward the far corner of the room and under the purple cabbage-rose overstuffed chair.

Either she was too smart or she didn't want to risk ripping her gorgeous red suit, but Yasmine Poole didn't dive for the can as Zoe had hoped. The black-hooded guy did, though, and the distraction was enough.

Ry jackknifed his legs and kicked the gun out of blue-hooded guy's hand. He sprang to his feet just as Zoe flung open the bathroom door, firing with one hand and tossing the bottle of cleanser to Ry with the other. He caught it in midair and sprayed blue-hooded guy in the face with it. The man screamed and clawed at his eyes.

Zoe shot up the rose-cabbage chair, where the black-hooded guy was still frantically trying to fish out the empty film can. Blood sprayed the wall behind him, as he went down with a scream, clutching his thigh.

Zoe swung the barrel of the gun onto Yasmine.

The woman stood still in the midst of the carnage, with her hands held out to her side, her eyes wild and full of a sick excitement, as if daring Zoe to shoot her in cold blood.

Zoe smiled. "You lose."

Ry knocked her arm aside just as she squeezed the trigger. The bullet hit the iron bedstead with a *ping* and ricocheted up into the ceiling. Yasmine Poole didn't even flinch.

Ry pushed Zoe toward the door. "Cops," he said. "Let's go."

━━━━━━━━

ZOE COULD HEAR men shouting and the slap of leather soles on the flagstone courtyard below. She started down, but Ry grabbed her arm and pulled her up a narrower set of stairs, toward the roof.

"Always," he said, "have a plan B."

The stairs ended in a trapdoor that opened up into an attic with huge, exposed beams, sectioned off into storage units for the building's tenants. It smelled strongly of mothballs. Zoe didn't see a window, which wouldn't have done them much good anyway, as high up as they were. Ry led the way to the back, deep beneath the sloping roof, where a midget-size door with a small white knob was set low on the wall, almost at floor level.

He turned and grinned at her. "Laundry chute."

"Great," Zoe said. "Only the thing is . . ."

But Ry had already turned back to open the little door.

It was a laundry chute all right. A dark and narrow laundry chute.

Ry took both the Walther and her satchel out of her suddenly lax hands. He stuffed the gun into an inside pocket of his jacket and zipped up. "You go first," he said.

"The thing is, I'm kind of claustrophobic."

She heard a door bang right below them, and someone shouting, "*Arrêtez! Arrêtez!*"

"Don't think about it," Ry said. "Just do it."

Zoe set her jaw. She swung feetfirst into the chute, shut her eyes, and held the doorframe with a white-knuckled grip. *How hard could this be? You just let go and slide.* But what if the chute got narrower as it went down? It was barely wider than a coffin as it was. A coffin . . . Oh, Lord. What if she got stuck? Unable to go up or down, trapped with the walls squeezing her chest, tighter and tighter, and the air black as death, growing thinner and thinner, running out, until she . . .

"Nope," she said. "Sorry, cowboy, but ain't no way—"

His hand smacked her hard in the back.

It was a long, long way down.

26

S HE LANDED flat on her back on a cement floor, her blood hammering in her ears.

She heard Ry coming down after her—it sounded as if someone were beating a tin can to death. She scrambled out of the way just before he exploded out of the chute. He landed and rolled up onto his feet in one smooth movement.

"You okay?" He helped her to her feet. He gave her back her satchel, then brushed her cheek with the backs of his knuckles. "You did great."

Zoe was humming, her adrenaline shooting through the roof. "I did it, Ry. I was so scared coming down that thing, I thought was gonna pass out, but I made it. And we were like the A-Team, the way we took them down. I had that bitch Yasmine Poole nailed, too."

"Zoe, we need to—"

"And I've still got the film, Ry—the can was empty. I thought I could fool them and create a diversion at the same time."

"I figured as much. Now—"

"Not that I wouldn't have given it up if I had to, to save your life. But I don't get it, why didn't you let me shoot her? I wasn't going to kill her, just make her bleed a lot, so you should've let me do it, Ry."

"We'll get her, don't worry about it. But right now—"

"Because you know she's gonna come after us, and if I never see the woman again in this life and in every reincarnation thereafter, it'll still be too—"

He clapped his hand over her mouth. His palm was hard and dry. Her heart was still pumping madly, and she was bouncing up and down on the balls of her feet. She realized suddenly that she could hear boots pounding on the stairs, shouts and whistles, the crackle of radios. Blue and red lights strobed though a narrow window set high in the basement's wall.

She breathed hard through her nose, then her eyes slowly focused on Ry's face. He lifted his hand.

She breathed, swallowed. "We're still in big trouble, aren't we?"

"Yeah. Take another breath. Good, you're coming down a bit."

Zoe took another breath and looked around. The basement was small, barely room enough for a deep sink and a row of three chipped and dented coin-operated washing machines.

She saw that Ry had found the door that led out onto the street. It was up a narrow half-flight of stairs, made of a thick gray metal, and dead-bolted from the inside. Ry slid back the bolt and eased the door open a crack. He looked out for a moment, then quietly shut it.

"It opens into another stairwell, six steps, leading up to a dead-end alley," he said, heading back to her. "They're working on the gas main, or something, out in the street right in front of the building, and that's kept the squad cars from parking close. But we can't just stroll on out because there are two cops within sight of the door, armed with MAT-49 submachine guns."

"Wonderful. So how do we get out of here?"

"We need a diversion to distract the cops away from the alley. Something involving noise and smoke and flames would be nice."

Zoe looked around the basement again, but besides the ancient washing machines and the sink, all she saw were enough cobwebs to weave a small tapestry. "Well, unless they're arachnophobics, I don't see anything down here that could create much of a distraction."

Ry was bent over, rummaging through the detergents and cleansers under the sink. "Hey, we just got lucky, Zoe. They got Drano. We can make us a bomb."

"You can make a bomb out of Drano?"

"Mixed with chlorine bleach and ammonia. It creates hydrogen gas. Nothing big or deadly—it's all smoke—but it'll get their attention." He set the bleach, ammonia, and can of crystal Drano on top one of the washers. "Look through that trash can over there for a liter-sized glass or plastic container. A Coke bottle would be perfect, but make sure it has a cap."

Zoe could hear more sirens turn up the street outside as she pawed through empty detergent boxes, take-out containers, spray starch—

"How about an Evian bottle?"

"That'll do."

A door slammed above their heads, so hard the whole building vibrated. Heavy boots pounded down the inner stairwell, only two or three flights above them now. "Ry, they're coming!"

"We'll make it. They'll want to search the main floor first." He went back under the sink again and came out with a rusty wrench.

"Okay," he said, handing her the wrench. "Here's how it's going to work. As soon as I add the Drano to the bottle and cap it, we'll have about fifteen seconds before it explodes. I want you to throw this wrench through the window and yell for help—'*Aidez-moi! Aidez-moi.*' Wait for me to throw the bomb before you go out the door, though, and let me go first in case there's shooting, okay?"

Zoe nodded, even though her knees had gone wobbly.

She watched Ry pour the bleach and ammonia into the Evian bottle, spilling some because he didn't have a funnel. Then he poured in the Drano crystals and capped the bottle fast.

"Hit the window now," he said to Zoe, just as a man out in the street yelled, "*Arrêtez!*" and a woman screamed.

Zoe pulled her arm back and flung the wrench at the window, suddenly terrified that she would miss.

The wrench crashed through the glass. Zoe shrieked, "*Aidez-moi! Aidez-moi!*" at the top of her lungs, and ran for the door. Out the corner of her eye she saw Ry toss the Drano bomb out the shattered window, then he ran past her and up the steps. He slapped open the dead bolt and slammed through the door, Zoe on his heels.

They were up the outer stairwell and into the alley when a terrible explosion ripped the air.

ZOE FELT THE building's stone walls shudder on their foundations. Windows rattled and shattered, shouts and screams rent the air.

The street was chaos. A water main had broken, blowing off a man-hole cover, and water geysered into the air. Bricks and cobblestones littered the sidewalks, and where they'd been working on the gas main there was now a giant hole in the street.

They started to go right, saw a squad of riot police and their parked cruisers at the corner, so they veered left. They ran by a cop who was barking into his radio, but by now everybody was running so they didn't stand out.

They dodged around a taxi that had jumped the sidewalk and plowed into a wine shop. Wine from dozens of broken bottles ran like rivulets of blood along the gutter. Zoe saw an old man with a loaf of bread tucked under one armpit try to scoop some up with his beret.

Ry grabbed Zoe's arm and pulled her toward a lamppost, where a red motorcycle was parked with LUIGI'S PIZZERIA emblazoned across its fuel-tank cover. The delivery boy was nowhere in sight, but he'd left the bike's engine running.

Ry jumped on, kicked up the stand, and peeled away, so fast Zoe barely managed to swing up behind him, straddling saddlebags that were stuffed full with boxes of hot pizzas. As she looked back as they careened around the corner and through the downpour of Parisian tap water, she caught sight of the fiery red of Yasmine Poole's designer suit.

———

ZOE WRAPPED HER arms around Ry's waist and yelled into his ear, "You said nothing big or deadly!"

He was actually crazy enough to laugh. "The Drano bomb must've rolled down into the gas main, and there must've been an open flame down there. It lit the hydrogen gas, and *boom*."

They tore across the river and up the Left Bank, weaving in and out through traffic that seemed to have no concept of lanes or turn signals or even, occasionally, the laws of gravity.

She wanted to ask him where they were going, but it was impossible with the noise. So she looked at the Paris scenery whizzing by and tried not to think about her not wearing a helmet.

Dusk was falling, the streetlamps coming on, the booksellers along the quays packing up their stands. The damp February cold cut through her leather jacket, chilling her to the bone. Across the river she could see a landmark she recognized—the Louvre, and the point of I. M. Pei's glass pyramid thrusting through the skeletal trees. A tourist boat floated by, shining a spotlight on the cream, cut stone walls and gray mansard roofs. As they idled at a red light, sandwiched between a diesel-belching bus and a beer truck, Zoe twisted around for another look at the famous museum and saw a flash of red sitting behind the wheel of a silver BWM, a half a long block behind them.

No, it can't be.

The Beamer suddenly swerved up onto the sidewalk, shooting around the bumper-to-bumper traffic, squeezing between cars and a mammoth granite building, scattering pedestrians like bowling pins. Its side-view mirror scraped sparks from stone as it bore down on them.

Zoe jabbed Ry in his side with her elbow and bellowed, "Gun it!" in his ear, but his head was already snapping around to see what the commotion was about. The Beamer squealed to a stop, blocked for the moment by a moving van parked in a driveway, but it was close enough now for Zoe to see easily through its window. It was Yasmine Poole, all right, and she looked pissed. She also looked as wet as a sewer rat, and Zoe would've smiled if she hadn't been so scared.

The backseat window rolled down and a hand emerged, holding a semiautomatic. The long, gray muzzle slowly swung around until she was looking right down the bore, big and black as the mouth of hell.

"Gun!" she screamed.

"Gun it where?" Ry shouted back at her. "I got a goddamn red light—"

"*A* gun. Pointing right at—"

A bullet buzzed past Zoe's ear and pinged into the body of the bus alongside of them. The next one plowed into the bulging saddlebags, killing Luigi's pizzas.

Then the light changed and Ry finally gunned it. The motorcycle, small-framed and light, shot forward with such force it leaped off the pavement, and for a few terrifying seconds Zoe was stretched out parallel to the street and only her one-handed grip on Ry's belt saved her from falling. Even so, her head almost smacked into one of the bus's giant front tires, coming so close some of her hair got caught up in the fender guard and was pulled out by the roots.

Then another bullet plowed a groove in the asphalt right before her terrified eyes.

She barely managed to haul herself back upright before Ry cut sharply across the front of the bus and a taxi, then jerked the handlebars so hard to the right that their back tire fishtailed, and Zoe nearly went flying again. They jumped the curb up onto the sidewalk, barely dodged a quayside stand loaded with stamps and postcards, then dropped down onto an arched bridge and headed for the other side of the river.

Zoe glanced back over her shoulder in time to the see the silver Beamer U-turn across four lanes. Tires screeched, horns blared, and there was the clanging crunch of metal slamming against metal, but miraculously the BMW emerged unscathed and hot on their tail.

Where were the damn traffic cops? Zoe wondered, then an instant later heard the whoop of a siren.

They hit a green light at the end of the bridge, and for a moment Zoe thought Ry was going to turn up into the three lanes of one-way traffic, but he jumped another sidewalk instead, threading through a row of bollards and cutting into a park.

The pebbled pathway was crowded with people out taking their evening constitutional, but Ry barely slowed down as he plowed through them, leaving a wake of screams and curses and shaking fists, but, thankfully, no dead bodies.

Zoe heard lots of sirens now and saw whirling blue lights, but given the number of traffic laws they'd broken, she wasn't so sure she wanted the cops anymore.

They flew past rows of plane trees, rosewood hedges, and geometric flowerbeds. They careened around a colonnaded fountain, where a boy was trying to sail his toy boat through a pool choked with miniature icebergs, then shot out of the park and into the biggest square Zoe had ever seen in her life. Or rather it was an octagon, with an enormous Egyptian obelisk in the center of it.

Eight streets spoked in and out of the square, and they were all jam-packed with rush-hour traffic. Cars, buses, trucks, motorcycles, bicycles, all whirled in seemingly haphazard abandon and dizzying speeds. Ry cut in and out, like a skier slaloming down a mountain, ignoring stoplights and traffic cops—doing things that would have gotten him shot on a L.A. freeway.

Zoe searched through the kaleidoscope of swirling headlights for a silver Beamer and a flash of red hair. *We've lost them*, she told herself, and wished she could believe it.

A quarter way around the enormous square, Ry peeled off, taking one of the wider spokes. They were still moving along at a pretty good clip, but he'd stopped breaking all the laws in the good-driver's manual. It was a miracle they hadn't been jumped on by every traffic cop in Paris by now.

The street they were on pulsed with neon-lit nightclubs, shops, and cafés. Ry rolled the motorcycle to a stop at a red light. Ahead of them was a square with a church built to look like a Greek temple. It was half-covered with scaffolding, but its doors were open and a man in a business suit sat on its marble steps in spite of the cold, eating a McDonald's burger and reading a newspaper.

Suddenly a cacophony of car horns blared into life behind them. Zoe twisted around and saw the silver BWM whip out from behind a Japanese tourist bus. The blue-hooded guy with his semiautomatic was leaning far out of the backseat window, making sure that this time he wouldn't miss.

"They're back!" Zoe screamed.

27

R Y JUMPED the light, scooting between a truck loaded with terra-cotta bricks and a yellow Mini Cooper. Brakes squealed behind them, horns shrieked, but Zoe's horrified eyes were riveted on the bakery van, double-parked and blocking the street ahead of them.

Two men walked toward the van's open rear doors, carrying a seven-tiered wedding cake between them, their eyes wide at the sight of the pizza cycle hurtling toward them. They stopped short, and the cake swayed dangerously. They sidled two steps backward; the cake swayed even more.

Ry started to pull around them, into the oncoming lane of traffic, but that way was blocked by yet another smoke-belching tourist bus. So he throttled back and aimed right, for the impossibly skinny space between the bakery van and the row of cars parked along the curb. A space that was now filled by the bakers and their cake.

A gun popped behind them, sounding close and loud, like a string of firecrackers going off, and the window of a parked Fiat exploded in a shower of glass.

The bakery men dropped the wedding cake and ran, and Ry plowed right through it. Silver and white frosting sprayed up in sticky globs, splattering their faces. They shot past the van, knocking its side-view mirror askew, and out into the square.

An outdoor flower market, lit up by strings of white twinkling lights, lined the church's east colonnade. They ducked under a low-hanging orange canopy, and Zoe looked back. Lots of flashing blue police lights, but no big silver BMW, no hooded men with guns.

They rounded the back end of the church and nearly slammed headfirst into the Beamer.

Ry swerved, and they went into a violent, fishtailing U-turn, clipping a cart full of cellophane-wrapped bouquets and snagging a watering can when its spout got caught up in the bike's spokes. They dragged it behind them, trailing sparks, and it acted as a brake, slowing them down. But then it fell off, and the bike surged with a roar of released speed—aiming right for a shop with a plate-glass window full of fancy chocolates and bonbons.

At the last second Ry jerked the handgrip hard, and the bike popped up over the sidewalk, through an arched art deco doorway, and into a shopping arcade. Hanging globe lanterns, café tables, and startled faces whipped past them in a blur, then they burst back out through another arched doorway and into a narrow, one-way street zipping with traffic.

━━━━━

No SIGN OF the silver BMW, and Zoe started to breathe again. But then, incredibly, she saw it—the Beamer, barreling out of the side street *ahead* of them.

It sent a taxi swerving into a light pole, and within seconds the narrow street was a chaos of locked bumpers, blaring horns, and screaming bystanders. Ry gunned the cycle's engine and aimed for the narrow gap between the Beamer's front bumper and a green kiosk plastered with posters.

But the gap was closing fast, too fast. Only five feet wide, and they weren't going to make it. The Beamer's headlights flooded the kiosk. The gap narrowed some more, only four feet wide now. Zoe gripped Ry hard around the waist, felt the sweat and tension of him through his clothes.

Three feet.

Two and a half.

They shot through what was left of the gap, shaving it too close. The Beamer slammed into the kiosk. Metal crunched, glass shattered, someone screamed, and a car alarm started shrieking.

They turned the corner at a skid, taking out a newspaper stand, and barreled right into the oncoming flow of traffic, going so fast the little motorcycle whipped back and forth like a snake.

The street ended in another open square, this one full of buses and taxicabs and a massive stone railway station straight out of the gaslight era. Ry cut through the snarl, ignoring traffic signs and crosswalks, hurtling down the length of the station until they could see the peeked-roofed platforms. And then at least a dozen set of tracks, crisscrossing a wide and open expanse that was latticed with electrical wires and littered with switch boxes and signal poles.

Ry twisted his head around, and she saw his mouth open. She couldn't hear him over the noise, but she thought he yelled, "Hold on!"

Zoe held on. Although if she'd known what he was going to do, she might have jumped off instead and taken her chances with the bad guys and the French cops, whose sirens she could now hear again, closing in behind them.

They bounded up onto the sidewalk and went flying up and out, through the air, out, out, out, and Zoe screamed, sailing over a skein of wires that looked hot enough to fry an elephant.

They hit the ground so hard she felt as if her teeth had been driven through the top of her head, and something fell off the back of the bike with a loud clang. But by some miracle the tires didn't blow.

Ry poured power into the sputtering engine, and they bounced and lurched over the web of rails and crossties, tires grinding, spewing gravel. Zoe looked toward the platforms and saw a bright, white headlight burst out of one of the dark tunnels.

This time her scream was swallowed by the shriek of a train's warning whistle. It bore down on them with a hammering roar that rent the air. The whole world seemed to be shaking.

They leaped over the last of the tracks, just as the train blew by them in a buffeting gust of wind and another earsplitting shriek of its horn.

———

RY TOOK THEM on a twisted route through a warren of narrow one-way streets. Zoe had no idea whether he knew where he was going and she didn't care. They were climbing now, the cobblestoned streets taking on a bohemian charm, but she barely noticed. She kept twisting around to look for the silver Beamer.

She heard it before she saw it—the rev of its powerful engine. It came roaring around the corner behind them, and this time the hooded guy wasn't being careful of innocent bystanders by trying to take aim. Bullets bit into the cobblestones, shattered glass, and ripped into a pile of garbage cans.

"How is she *doing* it?" Zoe cried. It seemed impossible—after the shopping arcade, the one-way streets, the railway tracks—that Yasmine Poole could have found them again already.

Ry opened the throttle as wide as it would go and they shot forward, putting some distance between them and the semiautomatic weapon. Even so, Zoe thought, it was a good thing it was harder than it looked to hit a moving target from another moving target.

They careened up a winding street, using the buildings as a shield. But the street ran out at a small square studded with leafless trees and the few straggling artists still packing up for the night. They ripped past colorful restaurants and galleries, and then Zoe saw before her the white dome and turrets of an enormous basilica lit up against the night sky.

The forecourt of the basilica's great bronze doors was full of tourists and Arabs selling knockoff handbags spread out on blankets over the paving stones. The bike slashed through faux Gucci and Chanel, its headlight pointing right at a low stone balustrade. Beyond the balustrade the city's rooftops and shimmering lights spread out for miles below them.

Far below them.

———————

BULLETS SPRAYED THE stone railing in front of them, kicking up a blizzard of stinging pellets.

For one terrifying instant, Zoe thought Ry was going to drive them over the balustrade to die, impaled on the point of a gray mansard roof. Then she saw the long flight of terraced steps, lit by a string of globe lampposts.

They dove down the stairs, hurtling, bouncing, and rattling, and more pieces of the pizza cycle fell off. They reached the end of one flight of stairs, cut hard right, under the framework of a funicular, and started down another, longer flight.

Ry yelled, "When I say *now*—jump. I won't be slowing down, Zoe. You got it?"

Zoe nodded, unable to shout back she was so scared.

They bounded past a row of poplar trees, then Ry yelled, "Now!" and they jumped. The bike kept going without them, faster now, careening wildly out of control with no one to steer it.

Her momentum carried Zoe into some kind of holly bush, whose prickles scraped the side of her face. She landed hard on her left side, jamming an elbow into her chest and winding herself.

Ry was suddenly there, leaping out of the dark. He grabbed her hand, hauled her back onto her feet, and they ran down the steps, following the path the empty pizza cycle had taken. Zoe could still hear it, clattering and roaring, but far below them now. They didn't run all the way after it, though, and thank God for that, because after the eternity on that thing with its rotten shock absorbers and padless seat, Zoe could barely feel her legs.

Ry pulled her down onto a stone bench and reached for her satchel. "Give me your bag."

Zoe clutched it to her chest. "Why?"

"This afternoon, back at the café, Yasmine Poole must have dropped in a tracking device when you weren't looking. That's the only way they could be keeping up with us the way they have."

Zoe was already dumping out the satchel onto the bench between them. The sealskin bag with its priceless icon first, then the film, which without its can was unspooling into a wiry mess. Then lipstick and compact, hairbrush, eyeliner, a couple of pens, wallet, passport, keys, a petrified PowerBar, sunglasses and sunscreen, a small box of tampons, a handful of old credit-card receipts, cell phone and PDA—both probably dead now . . . an expired coupon for a free cup of Peet's coffee, a can of Mace and a whistle . . .

"Jesus, the things you women—"

"Don't say it."

Red lacy bikini panties and matching bra . . .

"Nice," Ry said.

Zoe quickly tucked the underwear inside the half-open zipper of her leather jacket. "Down, dog," she said, and Ry laughed.

She got to the bottom and turned the satchel upside down. Crumbs and lint and dust fell out, but no tracking device.

"Oh, God, maybe it's stuck on me somewhere. . . ." She jumped up and ran her hands through her hair, over her jacket and jeans, searched her pockets.

Then Ry spotted it, caught among the bristles of her hairbrush. He held it up—it had the size and shape and creepy look of a wolf spider, and a tiny red light that was blinking like an evil red eye.

"This is the very latest technology," he said. "I've never even seen it before, just read about it. I wasn't really buying her tale before, but maybe Yasmine Poole really is CIA. In which case we are seriously . . ."

"Screwed," Zoe said. "I'd use another word, but I don't speak French."

She expected Ry to throw the tracker into the bushes or squash it to smithereens beneath his bootheel, but instead he wrapped it up in his big fist and jumped to his feet. "Let's go," he said, and started at a jog back down the steps.

Zoe shoveled her stuff back into her satchel and ran after him.

―――――

AT THE BOTTOM of the steps, they passed a garbage truck idling at the stoplight. Ry tossed the tracking device onto the mound of trash.

Zoe watched the truck disappear around the corner. "We didn't just put that garbage man's life in danger, did we?"

Ry shook his head. "Soon as they catch up with the truck, they'll know they've been had."

They caught a cab going in the opposite direction. Zoe leaned back against the cracked black leather seat and shut her eyes. A moment ago she'd felt as if she had a half dozen double espressos shooting through her bloodstream; now, suddenly, she didn't think she'd ever be able to move again. Ry would have to pry her out of the cab with a crowbar when they got to where they were going.

And where *were* they going? She'd heard Ry say something in French to the driver, giving him an address presumably, although it had sounded like gibberish to her. If she'd known one day she would be running for her life over and over again through the streets of Paris, she would have studied more French in school instead of Spanish. She would have . . .

———

THE CRACK OF a gunshot startled her awake.

She jerked upright and looked around wildly for the silver Beamer, but except for a ratty old Citroën idling at the red light in front of them, the street was deserted.

She felt a hand on her knee, and Ry said, "It was only a car back-firing."

She tried to laugh, but it broke coming out. Her heart was still pumping hard. "Sorry. I guess I get kind of jumpy when people are try-ing to kill me."

She thought she caught the flash of a smile, but it was dark in the back of the cab. "You're doing great, Zoe. Better than great, you're kick-ing ass and taking names."

She knew he was just being a good leader, rallying the troops, but his words were still nice to hear. His hand on her knee also felt nice.

She was trying to think what to make of that when he said, "We're almost there."

Zoe looked out the window. The streetlights were few and far be-tween, but she could make out a quaint, old-fashioned tobacco shop complete with a wooden Indian in front, a tailor shop with a nude man-nequin in the window, and a ramshackle garage. This was a poorer neigh-borhood than any she'd yet seen, the buildings lopsided and grimed with the soot of centuries.

"So where is 'there'?" she asked, just as they turned the corner onto an even narrower side street and rolled to a stop.

Ry leaned into her, and this time she was sure he smiled. "Come with me," he said in a really bad Pepé Le Pew imitation, "to the casbah."

28

I T WAS the casbah. Literally, in the sense that THE CASBAH was written in purple neon script above the front door.

It was a theme nightclub, Zoe supposed, and the theme was glaringly obvious. The building was built like a mosque, decorated with Moorish-like tiles and mosaics. It had no windows, just an iron-banded wooden door framed on each side by a pair of green neon palm trees.

The door had no handle that Zoe could see, just a grilled spy hole set dead center and at eye level. Ry pressed a buzzer, and a moment later the spy hole shot open, then closed.

Then the door itself was flung wide, and Zoe expected to see a guy in a fez or maybe a belly dancer in harem pants. But instead a woman of a "certain age" stepped across the threshold and into the green light cast by the neon palms. She looked straight out of the 1930s, a chanteuse with straight, bobbed black hair and dramatic cheekbones, a black pencil skirt, a red silk blouse, and a long ivory cigarette holder pinched delicately between two fingers.

"Ry*lushka*?" she said, in Russian roughened by too much bad vodka. "I do not see or hear from you in two years, now suddenly you are banging on my door? You must be in big, bad trouble."

"BUT THEN WHEN are you not in trouble?" the woman said, switching to English so thick Zoe was afraid she would choke on it. She held up the hand with the cigarette before Ry could answer. "No, better to say nothing, *lapushka*, tell me nothing. That way I can keep my—what is it you Americans call it? My 'plausible deniability.'"

"We thought we'd drop by for supper," Ry said, and turned to Zoe. "Madame Blotski makes the best borscht west of the Urals."

"He lies." The woman smiled at Zoe, but the dark eyes narrowed and looked her up and down, as if sizing up a potential rival. "I cannot even boil a potato without burning it. But there is always the takeout, no? So come in, come in." She stepped aside and waved the cigarette at the open door. "But no *Madame* Blotski. You must call me Anya."

"*Ochen priatna*. Nice to meet you. I'm Zoe—"

"*Nyet, nyet*. Say no more. Plausible deniability, remember? How nice, though, that you speak Russian. And how polite of you to let me know of this accomplishment, before I gave myself the red face by letting slip a little insult here, a little indiscretion there, thinking you were—what is the word you Americans say? Clueless. Ry*lushka*, wherever did you find this girl?"

"I fished her out of the Seine."

"Hunh. You make the little joke. Still, she does have the look of the drowned *krysa* about her. Never mind, I have bathing facilities, and for that she should be thankful. And for why are we all still out here on the stoop? What if someone is to see you and starts to shoot?"

Zoe looked nervously up and down the street. She didn't want to bring trouble down on this woman. "Thank you, Madame Blotski, but maybe we should—"

"Anya," Ry cut in, "likes to pretend she is living inside a John Le Carré novel. If you told her we had the KGB hot on our trail, it would make her day."

Madame Blotski laughed. "Listen to yourself, Ry*lushka*. It is you who must always be playing at the good guys, bad guys."

Zoe looked at Ry. Earlier, when she'd woken up thickheaded and nauseated after he'd shot her with that tranq gun, she'd thought he was one of the bad guys. She didn't think that anymore, but she knew there were still a lot of things he wasn't telling her.

Then again, she hadn't told him everything either. *Remember, trust no one. No one*, her grandmother had warned. Zoe had been the Keeper for barely forty-eight hours, and already she was contemplating breaking rule number one.

Anya Blotski was laughing as she took Ry's arm and pulled him inside, leaving Zoe to follow. Anya leaned into him and her breast brushed his arm. A clue, Zoe thought, as bright as the neon palms outside the front door, that the two of them had a history, and she smiled to herself at the thought.

———

ZOE LOOKED AROUND at the potted palms, art deco stenciling, and the gilt on the cobalt blue walls and thought Humphrey Bogart would have felt right at home.

They wended their way through wicker chairs and small, round tables with crisp, white cloths, each table with its own little red-shaded lamp and onyx ashtray. Then crossed a small parquet dance floor in front of a slightly raised stage that was already set up for a jazz band, with the instruments out of their cases, the sheet music on the stands. Zoe didn't see any musicians, though; in fact there wasn't a soul in the place. But then it was early; things probably didn't get hopping here until after midnight.

Anya Blotski led them through a swinging door in the back, down a short hall to another door, which she opened with a key. "This is the singer's dressing room, but since I am the singer, I say you may use it. Please to make yourselves at home. That chest over there is really a refrigerator—clever, no? And there is vodka inside. Meanwhile, I go send for takeout." She brushed Zoe's cheek with a cool, dry hand. "Poor darling. You looked half-starved and blue with the cold." Then Anya left on a cloud of Opium perfume.

The dressing room reeked of it. In here, Zoe saw, the decor was faux Turkish harem. The wooden floor was laid with overlapping Turkish rugs, the mirror above the dressing table was gilded, and there was a chaise longue loaded with beaded, fringed pillows. A samovar burbled on a nearby table.

"I should be doing the dance of the seven veils," Zoe said.

Ry came up to her and tucked a loose strand of hair behind her ear. "You okay? You looked really wiped."

She smiled, but she took a step back. She'd felt his touch all the way to her toes, and she didn't want to go there. She'd be a fool to go there.

"Apart from my insides feeling scrambled for an omelet, I'm fine. Only next time you go to steal us a getaway vehicle, would you mind staying away from the pizza bikes?"

His eyes crinkled up at the corners. "I could go for something classy, like a Beamer."

"As long as it's not silver. If I see another silver Beamer, I might just jump back into the Seine."

"Isn't your mother's Beamer silver?"

"Thank you for making my point."

He laughed as he went to the table with the samovar. She watched him pour tea into a pair of tall, curved Russian glasses, then place two sugar cubes on the little lips meant for that purpose. How did a guy named O'Malley come to speak better Russian than she did? And he'd played the part of a *vor* so well, he'd even fooled her mother, a *pakhan* in the Russian mafia. No way could he have picked that up in DEA school. There was simply too much she didn't know about him—she'd be nuts to trust him. Okay, so he'd saved her butt multiple times today, but still . . .

She walked to the chaise and collapsed. The strap of her satchel cut into her shoulder. Her eyes felt gritty, and every bone in her body felt pulverized. Her stomach was now so empty, its growls were echoing.

She ran her fingers through her hair and they came away sticky. She couldn't for the life of her . . . Then she remembered the wedding cake Ry had plowed into on their mad dash through the streets of Paris.

Ry turned around with the tea glasses in his hand and must have caught her smiling because he said, "What? You're sitting there grinning like an idiot."

She laughed. "I was remembering the looks on those two guys' faces when you drove through their wedding cake. That was some wild ride you took me on, O'Malley. I thought—"

She was interrupted by a knock on the door, and Madame Blotski came in bearing a tray with silverware, glasses, and a half dozen white takeout cartons.

"From Igor's deli," the woman said. "We have chicken *tabaka* and pickled cabbage, and *kotleta*, which he promised to me is stuffed with lamb, not horse, so you need not to worry. The bread is pumpernickel. You like?"

"We do," Ry said. "*Spasibo.*"

Zoe's mouth was suddenly so full of water, she was afraid she'd actually start drooling. "It smells wonderful. *Spasibo.*"

"You are most welcome. And, please, help yourselves to the vodka."

The woman set the tray on the chest that doubled as a refrigerator, brushed Ry's cheek this time, and said, "Eat, eat. Meanwhile, I take hint you are too polite to give me and give you kids some privacy."

Zoe waited until the door had shut behind her, then she looked at Ry and they shared a smile. "Us 'kids'? What *is* this place, anyway?"

"The Casbah? It's a nightclub that was started by some White Russian émigrés way back before World War Two, although it's changed hands several times since then, obviously. Anya was a singer in a Moscow nightclub when the Soviet Union collapsed. She emigrated here and bought this place."

Probably with a little *mafiya* seed money, Zoe thought, but she was too hungry to pursue the subject, even if it were any of her business. As she started to reach for a steaming carton that smelled of potato soup, she caught sight of the condition of her hands and shuddered.

As Zoe came out of the bathroom, she saw that Ry had his back to her and was talking on his cell phone. She heard him say, "Yes, *pakhan*. No, *pakhan*," before he flipped the phone closed.

"You were talking to my mother," she said, suddenly feeling so sick that if she'd had any food in her stomach, she would have vomited.

Ry turned to face her, tucking the phone into his back pocket. "She thinks I'm working for her, remember? If I don't check in every day, she's going to get suspicious."

"What—" Zoe's voice broke, and she had to clear her throat. "What did you tell her?"

"That some guy tried to kill you last night, but I saved your life and now you trust me."

"Is that what you think? That I trust you now?"

"I don't know, Zoe. You tell me." He heaved a sigh, thrusting his fingers through his hair. "Look, we need to talk."

"I'd rather eat."

"We'll talk, then we'll eat. You need to sit down, though. You look dead on your feet."

Zoe could feel her anger and mistrust slipping away. She was almost too tired to care anymore, and besides, he was right about Anna Larina. Her mother was going to get suspicious if he didn't call in.

She went over to the chaise while he pulled up a chair whose arms were carved to look like serpents and sat down facing her.

"Tell me about the altar of bones," he said.

Zoe said nothing, just looked at him. His face was tight with strain and fatigue, but then he'd been the one whipping the motorbike in and out through cutthroat traffic, flower markets, and shopping galleries, while she'd just been along for the ride. And he'd gotten even less sleep last night than she had. She remembered him talking about having to hold her propped up under hot water so she wouldn't die from hypothermia.

"I was thinking maybe we could arm wrestle to see who has to go first," she said.

He blinked, looked at her dumbfounded a moment, then laughed. "You are the wackiest woman I've ever met in my life."

"*Wacky?* All the adjectives in the world you have to pick from and you go for *wacky?* What's wrong with *gorgeous, brilliant, charming, sexy?*"

"*Vain?*"

He did that squinting thing with his eyes that was his version of a smile, and she couldn't help smiling back at him. "Oh, all right. If you're going to laugh at me and call me names, I guess I'll go first."

She drew in a deep breath, shutting her eyes for a moment. She prayed she was not making a terrible mistake and plunged in. "It started with my grandmother getting murdered in Golden Gate Park."

She told him about Mackey coming to her because her grandmother had tried to swallow the piece of paper with her name and address before she died. About the photograph, and her grandmother's dying words to the man in the park, and the whole nightmare scene with her mother.

"The first I'd ever heard of the altar of bones was when Mackey brought it up. I mentioned it to my mother as kind of a parting shot, and she was so careful not to react that she gave herself away by not reacting. Do you think she also knows about the film?"

"It's possible, but I don't think so. What she wants is your icon. I didn't tell you all of the truth before. Your mother did send me after you for your protection, because she thought you could be in danger. But she also told me that if you got hold of an icon, I was supposed to seduce you and steal it from you."

Zoe felt her face grow hot. "You weren't really going to . . ."

He leaned over and took her hands, and she hadn't realized until then that she had them clenched into a fist in her lap. Or how cold to the bone they were.

"I'm on your side in this, Zoe. I always have been."

His hands were big and hard, his palms calloused, yet their touch was gentle. She started to lean into him, then pulled away fast and reached for her tea.

"I'm thinking we could use something stronger," Ry said, getting up and going to the refrigerator.

Zoe blew out a big breath. "Boy, could I ever. . . . So, anyway, after that typically aggravating conversation with Anna Larina, I went to the morgue to see my grandmother's body. I had to *see* her, you know, to make her real to me. Then when I left, I got attacked the first time by the ponytailed man. He wants the altar-of-bones thing so bad, Ry, he was willing to cut out my eye to get it out of me."

While Ry poured them glasses of vodka from out of the bottle in the refrigerator, she told him about how she got away from her attacker, and then came home to find her grandmother's package, with the key and the postcard, and a letter full of warning and mystery.

She stopped to take a big swig of the vodka, shuddered hard as it burned all the way to her toes and made her eyes water. "And that's how she led me to the old man in the griffin shop, where I picked up the film and the icon, and it's been one damn thing after another since then, pardon my French."

"I didn't see any letter when I went through your bag," Ry said. "Sorry about that, by the way, but—"

She waved a hand, slopping vodka onto her wrist, which she licked off not to be wasteful. "Bygones, as Yasmine Poole would say. You were after the Kennedy film, which is totally understandable, given . . . Well, we'll go down that road later. The letter was in my pocket when I jumped into the Seine, and it ended up a soggy, illegible mess, but I'd read it so many times that a lot of it was carved into my brain cells. I wrote what I could remember down on the bank's stationery."

She dug the notepaper out of her satchel and handed it to him. He read it through, sat in silence a moment, then said, "Okay, so you're the Keeper of this altar of bones, but it's so dangerous your grandmother didn't want to risk giving you the details in the letter, in case it fell into the wrong hands, so she gave you a postcard with a riddle on it and a key—"

"Which opened a chest that had the icon, the Marilyn Monroe photograph, and the film of your . . . the Kennedy film."

"You don't need to keeping tiptoeing around the subject, Zoe. I've come to terms with the reality that there really was a second shooter on the grassy knoll and the son of a bitch was my father."

Not hardly, Zoe thought, *since your face closes up tight as a fist every time we do tiptoe around the subject,* but she said, "Right. Sorry."

She watched him prowl the small dressing room, then he startled her by whirling around. He looked hard and mean and deadly, and Zoe stiffened as he came at her.

"Let me see the icon again." Then he added, "Please," no doubt because of the look on her face.

Zoe took the sealskin case out of her satchel, unwrapped the icon carefully, then gave it to Ry. He sat back down in the serpent chair to study it, turning it over in his hands.

Seeing it again, Zoe was struck by how exquisite and rare the icon was. The jewel colors of the oil paints looked as bright as if they had been applied only yesterday. And the facets of the real jewels twinkled in the lamplight like crystal tears.

"It's uncanny how much you look like her," Ry said.

"I'm not the expert my mother is, but I'm pretty sure it's at least four hundred years old."

"Did they always paint them on blocks of wood this thick?"

"Most of the time."

He hefted the icon in his hand. "It's thick enough that it could be hollowed out on the inside."

Zoe jumped up and leaned over him for a better look. "Hollowed out to hide something else, you mean? Like a set of Russian nesting dolls, where one fits inside the other?"

He shook the icon gently, but there was no rattle. He turned it over in his hands again, and they both searched for a seam or a hinge, first on the back and then on each side, but they found nothing. The wood looked and felt solid.

Ry said, "Okay, so it was just a thought. But if this thing's as old as it looks, and if these stones are real, it's got to be worth some big bucks. Maybe it's nothing more complicated than that—a valuable artifact some unscrupulous collectors are trying to get their hands on. Like your mother for one."

"But there's also the riddle Katya wrote on the back of the postcard," Zoe said, reaching back on the chaise for her satchel. "I thought at first it had something to do with *The Lady and the Unicorn*, but that whole tapestry thing was just a way to get me to the griffin shop. What if this riddle is a clue to the altar of bones? What the altar is maybe. Or where it is."

She gave the postcard to Ry, and he translated it into English he read out loud:

Blood flows into the sea.
The sea meets the sky.
From the sky falls the ice.
Fire melts the ice.

A storm drowns the fire
And rages into the night,
But the blood flows on into the sea
Without end.

"So what do you think it means?" she said.

"I have no idea."

She studied his face, trying to read if he was telling the truth, but he was an expert at hiding his thoughts.

"And on top of everything else," she said, "somehow the Kennedy assassination has to fit into all of this. I refuse to believe my grandmother could be involved in two separate top-secret conspiracies that have nothing to do with each other. Nobody's that unlucky."

This time some brutal emotion did cross Ry's face, although still too quick for her to read. She opened her mouth to tell him it was now his turn to come clean, when he said, a little too casually, "Are you sure there wasn't anything else in the chest?"

Zoe shook her head, but she kept her eyes riveted onto his face. "After I found the Marilyn Monroe photograph tucked in the lining, I really checked it over carefully. There was nothing else. Why? You think there should've been something else in there? Like what?"

Finally his eyes met hers, and she saw again the deep, black pain that had been there back in the apartment, after they'd looked at the film. "An amulet," he said.

"Wait a minute. The altar of bones is an amulet? How do you know? And what—?"

He held up a hand. "I'll tell you everything I know, Zoe. Like we agreed going in. But I need to start at the beginning. With my father's confession and how my brother, Dom, was murdered."

———

ZOE WATCHED RY prowl the floor as he talked, but when he got to the part about seeing the chalk outline of his brother's body on the floor of the church, she had to look away because she couldn't bear what she saw on his face.

He threw himself back down in the chair, braced his elbows on his spread knees, and looked down at his clasped hands. His voice sounded calm, but his knuckles were white. "Now you know why I didn't let you shoot the bitch. Yeah, we need her alive until we can find out who she's really working for, but mostly I wanted the privilege of killing her myself. That hour I spent at the bottom of the Gulf sucking air out of a tire—that's all I could think about. That and getting over to Port Bolivar, so I could dig up what Dom had written down of Dad's so-called confession."

He gave a harsh, bitter laugh. "I could've stayed down there at the bottom of the Gulf and thought about it for a hundred years and still never come up with anything close to the truth of what kind of man my father really was."

"I'm so sorry, Ry," Zoe said softly. "I can't imagine what it must be like to lose your brother like that. And then to find out that your father . . ." Her voice trailed off. She had a hard time putting it into words herself.

He was quiet for a moment, looking down at his fisted hands, then he said, "Growing up, it never occurs to you your dad might not be the man you think he is. He was supposed to have been born on a small ranch in east Texas, near the Louisiana border." Ry breathed a hollow laugh, shook his head. "We even drove out there once to take a look at the old place, but now I've no idea whether any of that was true. I suppose that place could've belonged to anyone."

"Ry, you don't have to—"

"No, you really do need to know the rest of it." Ry reached around for his jacket, which he'd slung over the back of the chair. He took a mud-splattered plastic envelope out of an inner pocket and handed it to her. "But I'll let my father do the talking."

Zoe took a thick sheaf of papers out of the envelope. She unfolded them, looked up once at Ry's white, tight face, and then began to read.

Ry, this is everything Dad told me before he died. The only way I could even get myself to write it down was to put it in his own words as best as I could remember them, and after a while it felt like he was telling it all again, through me to you. You were the one he wanted with him at the end, anyway, but he had to make do with me. How much of this is really him talking now and how much is me, I don't know. I'll let you be the judge of that.

But this is what he said. . . .

29

It all started with Katya Orlova and the altar of bones, but it ended with the kill. And not just any kill, but *the* kill. The big kill.

You see, I was the man on the grassy knoll.

Yeah, you heard me right. I'm the guy who shot President John Fitzgerald Kennedy. Well, Lee Harvey Oswald shot *at* him, and maybe he hit him, or maybe his was the bullet that wounded the Texas governor. Christ, what was that guy's name? Connors? Connelly? Something like that. Funny that I can't remember it, considering . . . But then I never cared about him. What's important to know is that mine was the head shot, and that's what killed the President. Lee Oswald got the blame, of course, though most folks never believed he acted alone, and which goes to prove you really can't fool all the people even some of the time. But good ol' Oswald? He was just a Commie punk we set up to take the fall.

The killing shot was all mine.

But I'm getting ahead of myself here, because it really started one July night a year before the Kennedy killing, the night I first heard about the altar of bones. We were sitting in a red leather booth at the Hollywood Brown Derby, eating Cobb salads and drinking a passable but overpriced '59 St.-Émilion. We being myself, my bride, Katya, and Marilyn Monroe.

Yeah, *that* Marilyn Monroe. The movie star.

Funny how those two simple words both describe her to a T, yet fail to do her justice. Just like all the other millions of words written about her, before or since her passing, have failed her. Maybe that's because we all keep looking at her through the screen of our own delusions and lies.

I know I did.

BEFORE THAT NIGHT, I'd been spying on Marilyn Monroe for the past seven months, and by that I mean official, sanctioned spying.

I had a day job as a location scout for Twentieth Century–Fox, but that was just a cover set up by my employer, the Central Intelligence Agency. In spite of the McCarthy fiasco, the powers that be back in Langley were convinced Hollywood was a seething hotbed of anti-American activity. My mission was to make friends with the locals so we could separate the dangerous Communist wheat from the chaff.

Personally, I thought the assignment was bush league from the get-go, and a waste of my time and talents. My previous posting had been the Congo, where I'd been sent to assassinate a couple of people who will have to remain nameless, so the L.A. gig felt really tame to me.

Although things did get more interesting once the president of the United States began engaging in reckless national security pillow talk with an actress who ate barbiturates like cocktail peanuts. The powers that be really got their panties in a bunch when they found out about that, probably because Marilyn also happened to be the ex-wife of the playwright Arthur Miller, who'd once been denied a passport for "supporting the Communist movement."

So getting close to Marilyn's good friend Katya Orlova, asking her out on a date, had been just part of the job, a way for me to get close to Marilyn herself. It was my own idea to marry the girl, and I still don't know why I did. Maybe I was just bored, stuck out there in Tinseltown.

But I think it was more complicated than that. In years I was still young, only twenty-six, but I'd been knocking about my whole life. I came into the world an orphan, so I never had a family, and I was too secretive to have any friends. My only women were either whores or one-night stands. Katya was the first person to tell me she loved me and mean it. She made me feel something I'd never felt before. I guess the word would be *cherished*.

Anyway, the truth was I liked being married to Katya. We had fun together.

She had this eight-year-old kid by another lover who was long out of the picture, and so we made up this little family together, just the three of us, which I kind of liked. Anna Larina—that was the kid's name—had almost died when she was four, of leukemia, I think, but somehow she'd gone into remission, and Katya spoiled her some because of that. She wasn't a bad kid, though. She was just tough to get to know.

So Katya and her kid, and my "job" at the studio where I got to hob-nob with glamorous movie stars—all those things were good. But that wasn't the best part. The most interesting, the most deliciously ironic twist to the whole thing was that the CIA—so busy seeing a commie behind every actress's bush and under every director's bed—didn't have so much as a clue that Mike O'Malley, their dashing guy in Hollywood, was himself a mole for the KGB.

Why? you ask. Why was I a mole who sold out his country's secrets to the Communist enemy?

Well, it started with a small thing. I overdid it betting on the po-nies and got in deep with a loan shark who was threatening to shoot out my kneecaps if I didn't pay up. And about the time I was starting to feel desperate, this guy comes along and offers me a thousand bucks for the name of a double agent down in Mexico City. And the thing you don't realize at the time is that if you do it once, you got to keep on doing it, because you're compromised then, you can't go back. And after that, the hole you've dug for yourself just keeps getting deeper and deeper.

I don't think I was born with much of a conscience, though, because giving up that guy in Mexico City, knowing he'd be killed—it never really bothered me. And the things I did afterward? They didn't bother me much either.

And as long as I'm confessing, I'll tell you something else. I loved the spy game—the disguises and the lies, and the double-dealing. I even loved the killing. It was all I game to me, and I loved to play it.

━━━━━━

So WE WERE at the Brown Derby one night in the summer of '62. Katya, Marilyn, and me.

Marilyn was in what she liked to call her "disguise," and I'll admit, it actually wasn't a bad disguise at that. She had covered up her platinum hair with a scarf, hadn't put on any makeup, and she didn't look quite so luscious to me then, with her freckles and plain brown eyes. And she was wearing this dress, some cheap thing with little pink flowers on it. God knows where she'd gotten it—probably off the discount rack in Macy's basement. Yet, even so, on her it still clung in places so sexy that in some states she would've been arrested for indecent exposure.

But the best part of her disguise, the genius of it, I thought, was how she could change the way she walked. She'd lose her swivel—that hip-swaying, butt-undulating thing she could do that was pure, one hundred percent sex appeal. That was pure Marilyn Monroe. If the woman could have patented the move, it would have sold like the Hula-Hoop, and she'd have made a mint off of it too.

And the funny thing was, she could've used the money. She was only getting a hundred K for starring in *Something's Got to Give*, which might seem like a lot for those days, but when you figure Liz Taylor was paid a million for *Cleopatra*, and when you're a movie star, you got to live like a movie star . . .

So, anyway, Marilyn was in her "disguise" that night, but she had the maître d' seat us close to her place on the "Wall of Fame"—these framed caricatures of famous and maybe not-so-famous movie stars and other Hollywood big shots that went all the way back to 1929. And she made sure it was a booth with a phone jack, so the waiter could bring a telephone over should an important call come in. Also, no sooner do we sit down then some girl with a cigarette tray and a camera comes along and offers to take our picture for a buck, and Marilyn says, "Sure, honey. Why not?"

I didn't get the logic of this, going incognito to a place where everyone was sure to recognize you anyway. All that time I spent around the woman, and I never understood the first thing about her. But then I'd probably never seen her when she wasn't acting.

"You look at her and see a world-famous movie star," Katya told me once. "But inside she's feeling like a scared little girl, afraid that if you stripped away her blond hair and breasts, she'd just be a nobody. She wants to be loved for herself, unconditionally, and not as a sex object."

Unconditional love. Yeah, it sounded good all right, but I'd discovered long ago that there were conditions attached to just about everything. Still, maybe that explained how a world-famous movie star ended up being best friends with a cameraman's gofer.

Because when Katya Orlova loved you, she did so unconditionally.

——

So THAT NIGHT at the Brown Derby, over our Cobb salads, Marilyn started talking about sex in that breathy bedroom voice of hers.

"If they gave out Oscars for faking it," she said, "I'd have so many on my mantelpiece it would crack right in two. I've done some of my best acting convincing my lovers I was in the throes of ecstasy."

"I doubt they took all that much convincing," I said, thinking that all the guys she'd slept with probably hadn't given a rat's ass if she came or sang the "Hallelujah Chorus."

She made a face at me, but her eyes were fairly dancing with delight because she liked being teased, and she liked the idea that right at this very moment I was probably imagining what a romp in the sheets with her would be like, and, yeah, I was. I'm not dead.

But then the smile turned brittle, and an awkward silence fell over the table. So Katya, ever Marilyn's rescuer, said, "You haven't eaten much of your salad tonight, darling. Only rearranged it on your plate. You need to eat. You're getting too skinny."

This pleased Marilyn so much she held out her forearm, gave her flesh a good squeeze, then laughed again. "Jack likes me skinny. He never came out and said it, but I think he thought I was too fat there for a while. He likes me to pose in front of him wearing nothing but a fur coat, and then I do this thing with my shoulders and the coat slides off . . ."

Katya and I exchanged a look, but neither of us said anything. To Marilyn, it was as if we weren't there, or she was just too dense to realize how really bizarre it was for her to talk so nonchalantly about screwing the president of the United States.

"To tell you the truth, Jack makes love like a boy," she went on, "but it's still kind of sweet, and it never matters because he actually talks to me about politics and things. He treats me like I have a mind, that I'm not just all tits and ass."

I blinked at that, couldn't help it. I held a forkful of salad halfway to my mouth while my mind tried to process this remarkable piece of self-delusion. I thought of the secret files I'd read on the President's sexual exploits. The orgies in the White House swimming pool, countless one-night stands, or rather more like thirty-minute stands, a near endless stream of women, both classy and low, and the way he talked about them. He called them "poontang." Tits and ass.

Yet here was Miss Sex Appeal Personified thinking the man valued her for the wonders of her mind.

"James Joyce could really penetrate the human soul, don't you think?" Marilyn was now saying, and don't ask me how she got from fucking the President to English Lit 101. "I've been reading Molly Bloom's mental meanderings—see, I can be clever with words just like you, Mike. . . . Now, here is Joyce, a man, writing about what a woman thinks to herself, but he got it, didn't he? All our pain and insecurities. And I've been reading Shakespeare too, memorizing whole chunks, because I've been thinking I could produce and act in the Marilyn Monroe Shakespeare Film Festival. I'll approach all his major plays from the female point of view."

"Oh, darling, I like it," Katya said, and I knew the enthusiasm in her voice wasn't faked, bless her. She had the most generous heart—when she believed in you, she believed all the way down to her toes. "A woman's Shakespeare. And think how it will show everyone what a really fine actress you are."

Marilyn beamed. "I feel certain I'll win an Academy Award for one or more of my Shakespearean woman. Don't laugh, Mike."

"I'm not," I said, and if anyone deserved an Oscar, it should've been me.

"Oh, Kat," Marilyn said to my wife, "you don't know how I've so wanted to talk to Jack about this, to get his opinion too, but when I tried to get hold of him, I found out they'd changed his number, the special one he gave me for the Oval Office. So I called the main switchboard, only they wouldn't put me through."

Well, well, well, I thought. *Now, this was interesting.*

I remembered the Democratic fund-raising tribute in Madison Square Garden a few weeks ago, of course, with Marilyn in her fur stole and a $12,000 Jean Louis beaded gown, oozing sex and singing "Happy Birthday, Mr. President." She couldn't have declared more boldly and plainly to the world what was what than if she'd gone on *What's My Line* and said, "I am having sex with John Fitzgerald Kennedy."

So it was hardly a wonder if the President's handlers had reacted to that night with a dawning horror, and better late than never in my opinion. The affair had started back in December, and everybody who was anybody in Washington knew about it. The press corps sure knew all about it, but they kept that kind of stuff off the front page, not wanting to tarnish the image of the office, or so they said. Hell, maybe they just liked Jack, wanted to see him get reelected, and, besides, more than a few of them, especially the *Washington Post* guys, got invited to those White House pool parties.

But then Marilyn had to go and smack everyone in the face with it. And what with brother Teddy's senatorial primary looming in September and the administration still reeling over the Bay of Pigs fiasco, they sure didn't need the scandal of a White House love affair of any sort to tarnish the Camelot image, let alone one with the most famous woman in the world.

"At least I've been able talk to Bobby about it," Marilyn went on. "I met him that night I sang 'Happy Birthday,' and he's been such a big help through everything these last few weeks. He's a wonderful person to tell your troubles and your dreams to."

I swallowed a snort along with a piece of bacon and nearly choked. Katya was making little soothing sounds in the back of her throat, but a worry crease was now between her eyes.

Marilyn planted her elbows on the table, leaned into us, then cast a furtive look around the restaurant as if eavesdroppers lurked behind the potted palms. "I guess you've probably heard the rumors about Bobby and me. It seems like suddenly all Hollywood can't talk about anything else."

"Now there's a puzzle," I said. Katya kicked me in the shin.

"Well, they aren't true. Sure, we've made love, but when I hear about some of the stuff we're supposed to have done—well, it isn't true."

Robert Kennedy, the President's brother and Attorney General of the United States, had been out here in Hollywood a lot this summer to drum up financing for the filming of *The Enemy Within*, his bestseller about his crusade against organized crime. I knew for a fact there'd been some pretty wild parties at this Santa Monica beach house belonging to Bobby's brother-in-law Peter Lawford. The place had lots of bedrooms, but the scuttlebutt going around was that Bobby and Marilyn's favorite place to get it on was in the bathtub.

"I think all these awful rumors are getting to Bobby," Marilyn said. "Because now something funny's going on with him too. It's like they're all trying to shut him off from me, just like they're doing with the President."

I opened my mouth, and Katya kicked my shin again, so I shut my mouth.

But Marilyn seemed to have read my thoughts as if they'd appeared in a comic-strip bubble above my head.

"I'm not stupid, Mike, so quit thinking I am," she said, and looked both wistful and tough at the same time. Quite a feat, I thought. "I think they've got him convinced I'll go blabbing about us in a press conference, because he told—"

She'd been all set to come out with something really juicy before she cut herself off, I was sure of it, and I nearly swore out loud. But then she said instead, "Jack sent someone out to my house to tell me it's over. He should have at least had the courage to tell me good-bye to my face."

"Oh, Marilyn." Katya reached out and touched her arm. "You know how men are. They don't like scenes."

"Is that how men are, Mike?"

I had a tough time looking her in the face. It was like her heart was on the verge of being broken. Really broken, and that surprised me. Surely any girl who'd been around as many blocks as she had knew the score. I mean, it's not like she ever believed Jack would divorce Jackie and marry her, did she?

I said, "Honestly? We'd rather be boiled in oil, skewered on a spit, and then flayed alive. When it comes to women, we're all cowards. Every one of us."

Marilyn nodded solemnly, as if I'd revealed the answer to one of life's great mysteries, and for the first time I, Mike O'Malley, felt sorry for her. Katya had told me about Marilyn's childhood, born a bastard, her mother in and out of insane asylums while she was shunted off to orphanages and foster homes, unwanted and unloved, and so she'd created a sex goddess, a woman no man could ever possibly leave. And now here she was being dumped like yesterday's garbage, and, yeah, it was stupid of her not to have seen it coming, but it was also sad.

Then she said something out of the blue that floored me.

"I can survive this, though, because for the first time in my life I feel strong inside myself. Oh, I know that what I have might not last forever—fame is fickle, as they say. But if it goes, then it goes, and I'll survive because I know my true worth. Not only do I know what I can do, I know what I must do."

This time Katya reached across the table and took her hand. "You've always been a strong person. No one could get to where you are without being strong inside. And tough."

Marilyn gave her a smile that trembled at the edges. "And you've always seen the best in me, Kat. That's why I love you. But I haven't always seen the best in myself. Until now. So they don't need to worry about me, those switchboard operators and those men with their dark suits and hard faces. I'll never embarrass him."

"I know it will be hard, but you really are doing the right thing," Katya said, but she still looked worried. Or maybe, like me, she wasn't sure where all this was going, but she had an inkling it wasn't to a happy place.

"Oh, I am," Marilyn exclaimed. "I know I am. Because Jack needs me now more than ever. This is a man who can change our country. He shared his vision with me, so I know. If he has his way, no child will go hungry, no person will sleep in the street and get his meals from garbage cans . . ."

There was more, and all of it sounding like the worst sort of campaign-ad dreck, so I tuned her out and amused myself by trying to see how many of the caricatures on the wall I could recognize.

And then I heard her say to Katya, "That's why I'm going to give him your magic amulet, Kat. Your altar of bones. To do all he needs to do. At least I can help him in that way."

Altar of bones?

It was such a non sequitur, and a really weird one, that I almost missed Katya's reaction. And I'd only ever read about this in books, but her face actually drained of blood, like someone had come along, whipped out a knife, and slit her throat.

When she could finally speak, her voice was a strangled, harsh whisper. "Marilyn, please. It was to be our little secret. You promised."

"I know, and I was going to keep my promise, really I was. But that was before. He's not well, Kat. He's sicker than most people know. The Addison's disease is killing him, he's in pain all the time. So I've got to give it to him, because there's no end to what he will achieve if he's given the chance."

Katya's hands were lying flat on the table, pressing so hard her knuckles were white. I reached out and wrapped my fingers around one of her wrists. I squeezed, hard enough to get her attention. "What is this altar of bones?"

Katya didn't look at me, she didn't even blink. She said, "Marilyn, listen to me. You cannot under any circumstances give the . . . the magic amulet to President Kennedy."

"But why not? Look at what it's done for me. First, it helped me over that little trouble I had last month."

The "little trouble," I knew, had something to do with a long weekend Marilyn had taken on the spur of the moment out of town. The day after she left, Katya got a call in the middle of the night and took off, without telling me why or where she was going, and when she got back two days later, she looked white, shaken down to her core, but she still refused to tell me what it was all about no matter how hard I pushed. I had my suspicions, though, that Marilyn's little trouble was an abortion that had somehow gone wrong.

"Then it got rid of that sinus infection that wouldn't go away," Marilyn was saying. "The studio and Mr. Cukor told me I was just being lazy for missing so many shoots. With them it's like you don't even dare get a cold. And then they made it out like I was mentally ill because I'd flub my lines, when I was so sick I couldn't hold a thought in my head. But my mind feels so sharp and focused now. I told you I've been memorizing Shakespeare? And I've lost the flab, you said so yourself. I'm thin and fitter than I've ever been in my life. I'm even sleeping most nights. Oh, Kat, you can't imagine how good it is to sleep."

I said again to Katya, "What's she talking about? What did you give her?"

Katya didn't answer, but Marilyn unbuttoned the neck of her dress and reached inside to pull out a silver chain with a tiny bottle-green glass amulet, about the size of a thumbnail, dangling at the end of it. I leaned over for a closer look and saw that the amulet was shaped like a human skull and had an itty-bitty silver stopper. Strange marks were etched into the glass, almost like rune characters.

Marilyn said, "It's a funny thing to call it, the altar of bones. Like something out of a B horror movie. But then I got to thinking—your skeleton is your inner framework, like the steel beams on a skyscraper—and the altar of bones makes you strong from the inside out, so it's the perfect name for what it is."

I relaxed then and let go of Katya's wrist. She cradled it to her chest, rubbing the red marks I'd left on her, and I felt mean for having hurt her. This altar-of-bones thing was just one of those old Russian folk remedies she was always going on about whenever I got so much as a sniffle. Some witch-doctor hoodoo her mother had brought out of Siberia with her. Eye of newt and hair of the toad, or some such nonsense, with maybe a little feel-good, peyote-like mushroom thrown in.

Trust Marilyn, I thought, to have actually swallowed some of the stuff, and then she goes and has herself a good day and, presto-chango, it's magic and she decides to make a federal case out of it. Literally.

Still, it wasn't something you could go passing along to the president of the United States without having all kinds of federal agencies crawling up your ass. No wonder my poor Katya just had the fright of her life; she probably envisioned the Secret Service descending on her with handcuffs and an arrest warrant.

She seemed to have recovered, though, and I was relieved to see the color back in her face. Even the worry line was gone from between her eyes.

She slipped her arm around Marilyn's waist and gave her a hug. "You're such a generous person, too generous for your own good sometimes. Only you should put it away now, before someone in the restaurant here misunderstands and goes to the press, and then tomorrow there'll be screaming headlines in all the tabloids about how you're mainlining heroin."

Marilyn laughed and tucked the little glass vial back between her boobs, and like a fool I figured that would be the last I'd ever see or hear about the altar of bones.

———————

LATER, THE THREE of us stood beneath the restaurant's red awning, waiting for the valet to bring our car around.

I looked out at Hollywood and Vine; the neon lights were buzzing in the still air, the sidewalks humming with life. I watched a Cadillac convertible with giant tail fins cruise by, its radio blaring Little Eva's "The Loco-Motion." The Caddy was full of girls with teased hair and tight sweaters and dreams in their eyes about being a star, and I thought of something Marilyn had once said, about Hollywood being a place where they pay you a thousand dollars for a kiss and fifty cents for your soul.

I turned to look at her then, but she and Katya had stepped away from me and were talking, their heads together, and I wondered again about their strange friendship. Something, I thought, bound them together, something beyond Marilyn's loneliness and my wife's exaggerated sense of loyalty, but I couldn't for the life of me grasp what that something was. I guess there are some things in this world that simply defy explanation.

"I have no regrets, Kat. None," I heard Marilyn say, and the streetlamp caught the glint of tears on her face. "I know I say that all the time, but I mean it. It's just, wouldn't it have been nice if Jack and me could be together?"

Katya's eyes were wet as well. "It wasn't meant to be, darling. He's the President, his life is not his own. But you know you made him happy."

Marilyn drew in a deep breath, bit her lip. "It's just . . . it's lonely out here, isn't it?"

I watched her, and I have to say I was a little sad as well, because I liked her in that moment. I liked the core of courage I saw, but I wondered about the resiliency.

My Impala rolled up to the curb, purring. A kid with big ears and freckles got out and opened the passenger-side door with a flourish, grinning shyly up at Marilyn. She gave him a brilliant smile in return and started to get in the car, then she straightened and looked up. She pointed up to the red tile roof, to the sign with the restaurant's name written in neon, and to the moon, full and fat, that seemed to be sitting right on top of the hat's crown.

"Look at the moon," she said. "So big and round and yellow. Just like you see in the movies. It's almost too perfect, isn't it? Like you should die right in this moment, because every moon you'll ever see from here on out will never measure up to this one."

30

A FTER OUR trip to the Brown Derby, I wrote out two separate reports. One was a banal and heavily edited account of that night,
mostly having to do with what Marilyn said about the President and his
brother, but nothing about any amulet called the altar of bones. This
report I filed with my boss, the head of counterintelligence for the CIA's
Los Angeles field office, where it presumably would be read and duly
digested. And then perhaps, depending on the current turf wars, for-
warded on to Langley.

The other report was much longer, more detailed, covering not only
that night at the Brown Derby, but everything else I'd seen, done, and
overheard in the last three months, including all the state secrets I'd
been privy to. This report I put in a plain brown envelope. On the following Tuesday morning, at precisely ten minutes after ten, I was deep
in the stacks of the Los Angeles public library, sliding that envelope between two dusty tomes—a history of the Roman legions and a lengthy
dissertation on Cato's works.

After that I started reading the used-car ads in the *Los Angeles Times*,
not really expecting much, because my report had been pretty thin, truth
to tell, full more this time of innuendo and gossip than hard intelligence.
But I read the ads anyway and then, lo and behold, a week later there
it was: For sale, a '47 Ford Sportsman, $1,300. Followed by a phone
number.

It was a coded message from my cutout man, the KGB intermedi-
ary, who passed whatever intelligence I collected on to our superiors in
Moscow. I was to meet him at the top of the Hollywood Bowl on August
4, at one in the afternoon.

━━━━━━━━

I GOT THERE early.

The Hollywood Bowl is this enormous outdoor amphitheater, and that day the sun was beating down so hot I had to take off my suit coat and sling it over my shoulder. But sweat still drenched my shirt by the time I'd climbed the last set of the steps to the very top row.

I sat down on a bleacher, huffing like a beached whale and thinking I ought to start hitting the gym more often. I took off my hat, mopped the wet off my forehead with my sleeve, and admired the view. This far up, I could see the HOLLYWOOD sign in the distance, those famous white letters stuck into a hill above the town, a siren call for so many Marilyn wannabes and never-would-bes.

The rumble of a car's engine reached my ears long before it came into view. You could see and hear for miles in the Hollywood Bowl, which was why, I knew, my KGB cutout had chosen this spot for our meet.

I watched a man who looked no bigger than an ant get out of the car and begin the long, hot climb. In the two years I'd been working out there in la-la land, I'd only met with him twice face-to-face. He never gave me a name, but if he had, it wouldn't be the one he was born with, so what would be the point?

By the time he'd climbed all the way up to the next-to-the-last tier, though, I could see whoever this was, it wasn't my cutout. This guy was taller, leaner. And he carried himself differently, like a soldier on a parade ground.

I half stood up, then sat back down. It was too late to run, and there sure as hell was no place to hide. The stranger must have left his suit coat in the car, because he too was in shirtsleeves. He wasn't wearing a gun belt or a shoulder holster, but I could see that he carried a good-size paper sack in one hand. If a pistol was inside that sack, then Mike O'Malley was a dead man.

Then the stranger began to whistle the Russian song "Black Eyes," and my breath left me in such a rush of relief I felt weak. I tried to whistle the next few bars, but I had trouble getting my dry mouth to pucker up enough.

"Never mind. Myself, I've never been able to carry a tune," the stranger said as he sat next to me on the bleacher. His English was so thick with Russian consonants and vowels it came out half-strangled. "It is all rather silly anyway, do you not think so? Grown men playing at spies."

"Don't look at me," I said. "I don't make up the rules."

"This is true." The man's lips twitched in a fleeting smile. He was extraordinarily good-looking, with indigo eyes and cheekbones sharp as stilettos. He had the "blood and milk" complexion you found in some Russians. Skin so pale you can see the veins beneath.

And he must have a hell of workout routine, I thought, because he was barely breathing hard after climbing a couple hundred steps in the heat of an August-afternoon sun.

He reached into his paper sack, and even though I was trying to play it cool, I might have stiffened up a little, because he gave me a mock wide-eyed look and said, "What? Do you think I would come six thousand miles just to shoot you?"

Yeah, yeah, and everybody fancies himself another Bob Hope, I thought.

The man took out a blue-and-white-checked napkin and spread it out on the bleacher seat between us, followed by pickled herring and black rye bread. "You won't faint if I reach into my pocket? I assure you I have no gun in there."

"Very funny. You outta think about taking your show on the road."

The Russian took a silver flask out of his pocket. He unscrewed the fat cap that was also a cup and filled it with what was surely vodka. He handed me the cup and kept the flask for himself.

"*Na zdorovye,*" he toasted, and took a long, healthy swig from the flask.

"Cheers." I took it more slowly and was glad I did. The vodka was loaded with pepper and other spices I didn't know the names of except that they were hot as hellfire.

I blinked the tears out of my eyes and said, "Now that I've drunk to your health, how about letting me in on who the fuck you are."

"My name is Nikolai Popov. I am Procurator General of the Komitet Gosudarstvennoy Bezopasnosti in Moscow."

And I thought, *Holy Christ*, because this guy was like a KGB big cheese, big enchilada, and big kahuna all rolled into one. I seriously wondered if I was supposed to snap to attention and salute.

I let a long, slow beat pass while I decided how to play this, then opted for my fallback position—the smart mouth. "You're a long way from home and in case you haven't noticed, there's a cold war going on. Aren't you afraid you'll be picked up as a spy and shot?"

"Hunh. Your country would not be so rude. I have papers proving I am a vintner from the Georgia Socialist Republic, here to tour the wonderful vineyards of California. It is part of the cultural exchange, an effort to ease the tensions between our two great nations."

He took another drink of vodka from the silver flask, and I noticed it was monogrammed with the Cyrillic equivalent of the letter *P.* For *Popov*, I supposed, but maybe not. Maybe he wasn't really who he said he was at all. I'd heard the name Nikolai Popov before, usually spoken in tones of awe and fear, but this guy looked way too young to be in such an exalted and powerful position within the KGB hierarchy.

The Russian had taken out a pack of Marlboros and lit up. He took a drag, then exhaled the smoke along with a deep sigh. "You have excellent cigarettes in your country. That is not a criticism of the direction the Revolution has taken back home with regard to tobacco production, mind you. Merely an observation."

He took another drag, then changed directions so fast, I nearly got whiplash. "I have read your reports, Mr. O'Malley."

"I'm flattered."

"You ought to be. You are but a small, insignificant cog in the engine that propels the Revolution. Now I want to hear again from your own lips about this dinner you had with Miss Monroe at the Blue Derby."

"The Brown Derby."

"As you say." He waved his cigarette through the air. "Please proceed."

It had been three weeks since that night, but I had an excellent memory. When I was done, I asked, "Are you going to expose the affair?"

"Which affair? Or should I say, with which brother?" The Russian thought a moment, then shrugged. "We have other irons in that particular fire."

I'd heard about one of those irons, a young German socialite in Washington who had recently caught the President's eye. She was also, like myself, a Soviet agent. Unlike with myself, however, the FBI had gotten wise and deported her.

"And Miss Monroe?" the Russian said. "Is everything still coming up roses in her life?"

"You could say that. And which I did, at length, in my report. The studio fired her last month from the set of *Something's Got to Give*. For always being late and muffing her lines because she was stoned up to her eyeballs. Then they agreed to take her back, probably because Dean Martin, the film's costar, insisted on it."

The Russian's eyes lit up. "Ah. Dean Martin. He is one of the Rat Pack, no? Deano and Sammy and Mr. Blue Eyes."

I hid a smile. Hollywood. No one was immune to its magic.

"And Miss Monroe, she attributes this good fortune to the magic amulet your wife gave her? The . . . what is it you called it?"

I had a feeling the man knew damn well, but I said, "The altar of bones."

The Russian looked out at the vista for a long moment, then said, "What do you think, Mr. O'Malley?"

The question floated out there just a little too casually for my peace of mind. A guy in Popov's position wouldn't travel all this way to hash over a routine report filed by a low-level operative like myself. Something weird was going on here, but I was damned if I could figure out what.

"It's bunk. Like I put in my report, my wife said she bought it off this old White Russian émigré who works in the corner deli. Scratch any of those babushkas and underneath you'll find an old fool who fancies herself a witch. For a couple of bucks, she'll tell you your fortune and give you something to cure your warts."

The Russian nodded pensively. "Tell me more about this new wife of yours. This Katya Orlova. Is she Russian?"

"Her mother was, but she was born in Shanghai. On the day the Japanese took over the city. It's kind of a remarkable story, actually. The woman walked all the way there from Siberia after escaping from one of those gulag camps—"

"The gulag does not exist, has never existed. It is a piece of filthy propaganda spread by the West to discredit the Soviet empire."

Yeah, right, I thought, but I let it pass, because what was really interesting was the look I'd seen flash across Popov's face. I would say I'd just given him the shock of his life.

"So your Katya," Popov said after a moment, "she gave the babushka's magic amulet to Miss Monroe, and now Miss Monroe believes it has cured her of all of life's ills."

"Miss Monroe has chronic insomnia, for which she pops Nembutal like it's going out of style. After which the studio gives her amphetamines to counteract the effect of the barbiturates, and on top of that, she's a lush. If you told her wearing a dead skunk around her neck would chase away all the bogeymen she's got rattling around her closets, she'd do it."

"Then you do not believe she has given the amulet to your President?"

I laughed at that, although I wasn't sure why. "She hasn't had the chance," I said. "Not since the 'Happy Birthday' fiasco."

The Russian stood up. "Good. Then we will go and get it from her."

I felt like I'd suddenly been knocked on my ass by heatstroke, like I wasn't hearing things right. I stared up at the tall Russian, blinking the sweat out of my eyes. I drew in a deep breath—

"No, don't bother to ask why, Mr. O'Malley. How do you say it in your CIA? It is on a need-to-know basis and you do not need to know."

"Okay, forget why. Let's try for a how. Are you going to walk right up to her and rip it off her neck?"

"If necessary." The man who called himself Nikolai Popov smiled, but the cold in his eyes was cut right out of the snow-covered steppes of Siberia.

He shot the cuff of his silk shirt to look at the time on a gold Rolex. A pretty damn expensive getup, I thought, for a Communist. "At nine o'clock tonight I will pick you up on the corner of . . . What is that famous place where all the sexy starlets hang out? Hollywood and . . ."

"Vine," I said, only it came out as a squeak.

"Yes. Hollywood and Vine. Do not be late."

31

So how are we going to play this?" I asked later that night, as we turned off San Vicente with its huge coral trees and into the area of Brentwood known as the Helenas. Not la-di-da mansions by any means, but they'd still set you back a pretty penny.

"It is not nuclear physics," Nikolai Popov said. "We go in, we get the amulet, we leave."

The retro globe streetlamps cast intermittent pools of light on the eucalyptus trees, but the houses were shrouded behind high walls, and the streets and sidewalks were deserted. Nobody was out walking their dog or putting the garbage in the can.

I expected Popov would drive by Marilyn's cul-de-sac and park somewhere farther down on one of the other streets. Instead we turned down Fifth Helena Drive and headed right toward number 12305, with its bougainvillea-draped whitewashed walls. I was surprised to see the big, green front gates yawning wide-open, as if she'd been expecting us.

Popov slammed the car door getting out, and I nearly jumped out of my skin. A dog started barking, somewhere out back, but no lights sprang on. The night air felt balmy, with just the barest breeze stirring the tops of the tall eucalyptus trees.

"Here," Popov said, as he pulled out of his pocket a wad of what turned out to be a couple pairs of a doctor's rubber gloves. "Put these on."

It was funny, I thought, as I snapped the gloves on over my sweating hands. Not ha-ha funny, but ironic funny. Here I was a traitor, a double agent. I'd been stealing my country's secrets for the Russians for years, yet tonight was the first time I'd ever felt like a thief.

The front door was locked, but Popov popped it open with a set of burglar picks.

He clicked on a penlight as we stepped into a living room of thick white carpeting, textured alabaster walls, and dark-beamed ceilings. There was little furniture, just a wooden bench along one wall, a red couch along the other, a plain wooden coffee table flanked by four Mexican-style stools. But stacks of records sat in corners next to piles of magazines and cartons of books.

"This does not look like the house of a movie star," Popov said.

"She bought a bunch of furniture in Mexico," I said, for some strange reason feeling suddenly defensive of her, like I owned her in some way. Owned her sins and her foibles. "The stuff's taking its own sweet time getting here from the land of mañana."

Through the window that opened out back, I could see moonlight glinting off the water in the pool she rarely swam in. A stuffed toy tiger lay, as if abandoned, alongside one of the patio chairs. It wasn't the kind of thing Marilyn went in for, and I wondered what it was doing there.

"She will most likely have it with her in the bedroom," Popov said. "We will go there first."

The bedroom door was locked, but again the Russian picked it easily.

It was pitch-dark inside, the air cloying and sweet with the scent of her Chanel No. 5 perfume. I heard the scratch of a needle circling around the end of a record, and the soughing sound of her drugged breathing.

The beam of Popov's flashlight played around the room, picking out a pair of black stilettos on the floor, a pile of dirty clothes, and more stacks of records, a brass wall sconce.

Then, as if the Russian had been prolonging the moment, savoring it, the flashlight beam found Marilyn on the bed.

Her white telephone lay beside her, dangling half off the hook. The light found it first, then moved over her body. She lay on her side, her arms and legs sprawled. She was drooling a little, and I felt embarrassed for her. She was nude except for a brassiere.

She wasn't wearing the amulet.

The flashlight beam jumped over to a bedside table barely bigger than a dinner plate, overflowing with more stuff than I could make out. A lot of pill bottles. A stack of papers. Letters? A box of Kleenex.

Popov started toward the table, tripped over a carton of books, and swore out loud in Russian. Marilyn didn't even stir.

He flicked on the lamp, and although it was a small lamp, light seemed to flood the room after the utter darkness of before.

"There, that is better," he said. "No sense groping around like blind men in a whorehouse." He looked around the room, his lips curled in disgust. "What a pigsty."

"She gets bad bouts of depression sometimes," I said, still whispering, and again feeling stupidly like I had to defend her.

I went to the phonograph and turned it off—the scratching was grating on my already raw nerves. Frank Sinatra, I saw, from the label as the record spun slowly down and stopped.

Popov pawed through the stuff on the table; he picked up the bottle of Nembutal and shook it. Nearly full, I thought, although I saw the corpses of several empty capsules sitting nearby. She often pulled open the pills and swallowed the powdered barbiturate neat, to speed up the effect.

Popov was now flipping through the pages of what looked like a black leather diary, and I caught sight of her childish bubble handwriting.

He tucked the diary under his arm. He picked up an earthen jug, tipped it over, and shook it, but no amulet fell out. I thought I should probably be joining in the search, but my legs and arms felt stiff, I couldn't seem to move. A pounding in my ears sounded louder the Pacific surf.

"Mike? What are you doing here?"

I spun around so fast all the blood left my head.

Marilyn was half-sitting up among the sprawl of white silk sheets, her eyes blinking against the light. Her platinum hair was tousled, her pale skin glowed with a fine sheen of sweat.

She was the stuff wet dreams are made of.

I opened my mouth, but nothing came out. I could think of no plausible way of explaining what the Russian and I were doing in her bedroom at ten o'clock at night.

It didn't matter. She was so out of it from the Nembutal, she was lucky she remembered her own name. She sat up a little straighter, but she moved as if underwater.

"Tell Kat I'm okay now," she said, and her voice whistled strangely. "I guess maybe when I called her earlier, I sounded like I might do something crazy, so she sent you over. But I'm all right now. Bobby came to see me this afternoon, and we got in this big fight. I told him I felt used and passed around, and then I told him to get out. It felt good to say that, Mike. So good. Only after he left, I got to feeling like I'd never sleep, so I took a few pills, but I'm okay now. I'm okay."

She didn't look okay to me, but I wasn't feeling so hot either at the moment. I still couldn't seem to coordinate things between my head and my tongue.

From beside me, Popov said, "Ask her where it is."

And this was the weirdest thing of all, but Marilyn didn't look at the Russian or react to him in any way. It was almost as if she didn't see him, or didn't want to, or maybe she thought he was a figment left over from a nightmare that would dissolve if she just ignored it.

I swallowed, wet my lips. "Marilyn, do you remember that night at the Brown Derby?"

A childish, yet strangely sweet, smile lit her face. "The moon was soooo big."

"Yeah. You showed me the magic amulet. Remember? You called it the altar of bones."

She frowned, then combed the hair out of her eyes with her fingers, as if that would help her think better. "I told Bobby that I would never embarrass his brother, I just wanted to help him. Help the president. So I gave it to Bobby, to give to Jack."

"You gave the amulet to Bobby?"

She nodded slowly. "I did it today, but don't worry. Bobby knows it's not for him, that it's a present from me to Jack. A good-bye present.

I told Bobby, I said, 'It's not for you, it's for the commander in chief. Because he's going to change the world.'"

And then in the next instant everything did change. My whole life, and Katya's life, even Popov's life, I suppose—it all changed. The Russian moved so fast, it was like there was a five-second delay while my brain caught up with what I was seeing. One moment, he was standing beside me, the diary in one hand, the other hanging loosely at his side. In the next, the diary was on the floor and he was on the bed, straddling Marilyn, and she was making this harsh panting sound.

At some point she must have made a grab for the telephone because she had it in her hand and was flailing at the air with it.

I think I might have shouted, "What are you doing?" Or something like that, although what I was thinking was that the Russian had really lost it, that he was going to rape her.

"Why do you stand there like a poleaxed bear?" he said to me. "Hold her down."

I don't know why I obeyed, but I did. She lay face forward on the bed now, no longer moving. But she was still breathing. I could hear it, that harsh panting louder now than the surf of blood that had been pounding in my ears.

And then I watched with growing horror as the Russian reached slowly into his pocket and pulled out a small enema.

─────

IT DIDN'T TAKE us long, probably no more than five minutes, but it was an ugly thing to watch. I held her down while Popov thrust the enema tube up inside her, then he pumped her full of chloral hydrate.

At least that's what he told me it was, as my numb hands held her down. Only as the seconds passed there was less and less need, but still I held her down.

When he was done, he got her Nembutal from the nightstand, dumped the pills into his pocket, then put the now empty bottle back where it was. He picked her diary up from off the floor and tucked it back under his arm.

His gaze slowly swept the room, then stopped at me, and he smiled. "We are done here."

I realized I was still pressing into Marilyn's shoulders and I flung up my hands as if they'd suddenly caught on fire. I stumbled away from the bed and followed Popov, who was already halfway out of the room.

At the door, though, he paused, then he turned and went back to the bed. He unhooked her brassiere and rolled her over. He pulled off that pathetic bit of armor, just a few strips of cotton and elastic, and tossed it on the floor. He stared down at her a moment, then positioned her back the way she was before, lying facedown, with the phone tucked underneath her.

Then he came strolling back to where I waited at the bedroom door, and moving so damn nonchalantly, too, as if we hadn't just murdered Marilyn Monroe, that I couldn't help myself, I had to ask.

"Why did you do that?"

Popov shrugged. "I wanted to see her tits."

━━━━━━

BACK IN THE car, Popov was quiet, not scared quiet, just *focused*. I felt like I'd just popped a half dozen uppers. I was so jittery, my leg was twitching.

I kept seeing Marilyn the way we'd left her, sprawled naked on her white satin sheets, her hand clutching the telephone as if there were still time for her to make one last, desperate call for help. That poor, pathetic hand, with its cracked nails and chipped polish.

She would've hated the thought of dying like that, not looking her best. And I thought then that I ought to be feeling worse about what we'd done to her, but I was beyond that now. All I cared about was getting away with it.

I flicked on the radio, half-expecting for one insane moment that her death would already be all over the news, but it was Shelley Fabares singing "Johnny Angel."

I shut it off, twisting the knob so hard it snapped off in my hand.

I could feel Popov's eyes on me, but he said nothing, so I said nothing. All I had were questions, and he wouldn't have answered them anyway.

But then I couldn't help myself. "What in hell did we just do back there? Why did we just kill Marilyn Monroe?"

"She was much too famous, and she was not going to shut up. All this talk of hers about the altar of bones, giving it to the Kennedys—questions might be raised, and that would not be good. Not good at all. The altar belongs to Russia. And if your president does drink from it . . ." To my surprise he actually shuddered. "That could be a very bad thing for both our countries."

He paused a moment, then shrugged. "Also, she saw our faces."

When we were back on Santa Monica Boulevard, Popov heaved a very Russian-like sigh and said, "It doesn't matter now. What is done is done. Now we must go and have ourselves a conversation with Katya Orlova."

———

KATYA AND I were renting a little Victorian bungalow on Bunker Hill, near Angel's Flight, the inclined cable railway that had advertised itself as "The Shortest Paying Railway in the World," when it opened back in 1901.

Popov drove right to the place without any help from me, and that got me to wondering what else he had in those pockets of his baggy Russian suit. A gun, probably. A knife? Another enema filled with chloral hydrate? He was like a fucking Boy Scout—always prepared.

We didn't have a garage and parking was tight in that neighborhood, even back then, so he pulled up next to a fire hydrant. The windows were dark, but then it was past midnight now, and I figured Katya and Anna Larina were probably asleep in bed. Only I didn't see her car parked anywhere on the street, so maybe she wasn't home after all.

We got out of the car and started up the steps to the front door. There were a lot of them. Twenty-nine, to be exact, and they were too narrow for us to walk up side by side. So Popov went first and I followed. Katya had set out a few geranium pots, and I thought about picking one up and bashing him over the head with it, but I didn't, and eventually we were on the stoop and he was waiting for me to fish out my key and let us in.

"You won't hurt her?" I said. Then I winced at how pathetic that had sounded, even to myself. And how useless. He'd just killed Marilyn Monroe, for Christ's sakes, over this altar-of-bones thing. And *she* had gotten it in the first place from Katya.

But I looked him straight in the eye and let him get away with the lie.

"Of course we will not harm her," he said. "She is your wife."

———

"Honey, I'm home," I called out just like they did on TV in those days, and, believe me, it sounded hokey even then, but I also figured Popov wouldn't know any better.

I needn't have bothered, though. The house *felt* empty.

We stood in the middle of the small living room that was all Katya, decorated with odd, whimsical pieces she'd picked up from flea markets and Chinatown.

"Where is your bedroom?" Popov said.

I pointed down the hall. "Ours is the one on the right."

While he went that way, I headed straight for the kitchen table, where she usually left a note for me propped up against the sugar bowl if she had to go out unexpectedly. But there wasn't one.

I went back into the living room and waited, and a couple of minutes later Popov rejoined me. "She is gone," he said. "With the child. The closets are empty of their things."

I started down the hall to our bedroom, but Popov grabbed me by the shoulder and flung me up against the wall. I felt his grip all the way to the bone, and for a moment there I was seeing my own death in his eyes.

"What did you tell her?" he said.

"As far as she knows, I'm a location scout for the studio. She has no idea what else I am."

"Then why has she run?"

"I don't know," I said, and I didn't. Then.

I couldn't have known it that night, of course, but Katya Orlova would come back to me because she couldn't stay away, or so she said, and I believed her. Like I said, when she loved you, she loved unconditionally.

She came only three times during that year between Marilyn's murder and the other, bigger kill, appearing in our bedroom with no warning, in the dead of night, and she was always gone by dawn. She wouldn't tell me who she was hiding from, or why, or where she and her kid were living now. And I was too deep in my own lies to force any sort of truth out of her. She came back three times, and that was one thing I made sure to leave out of my reports. I figured what Nikolai Popov didn't know wouldn't hurt him.

The last time she came it was a chilly November night in '63, and by then Popov had told me the KGB was going to assassinate the President, and that I was the lucky bastard he'd picked to do the job. "Your Jack Kennedy has to die," he'd said, "because he drank from the altar of bones, and that makes him dangerous to the world."

At the time, I didn't know what the hell any of it meant—what had been in that damn amulet, and why drinking from it meant Kennedy had to die—but that was the moment when I realized I would need Katya to film the kill for me if I wanted to keep my own sorry self alive. So when she came to me a few nights later, I took the chance. I laid it all out for her, the whole rotten, duplicitous tale, and when I was through, she told me a tale of her own.

She told me what was in the amulet.

———

"I loved Marilyn like the sister I never had," Katya said that night. "I gave her the magic amulet to save her, because I thought it was her only hope. I should have known that in spite of her all her promises she wouldn't be able to keep herself from talking about it."

She made a small sound in the back of her throat, like a caught sob, then went on, "That night at the Brown Derby, when I realized . . . I should have run then, but I couldn't bear to leave you. So I watched and waited, and a week or so went by, and I began to think I was safe.

But then a man in a red cap followed me home from the studio, and later, while I was fixing supper for Anna Larina, I saw out the kitchen window the same car pass by three times. And there was a man at the bus stop who sat reading a newspaper, and two buses came but he didn't get on."

She shuddered in my arms, turned her face into my shoulder. "I didn't know then who those men worked for, only that I had to take Anna Larina and run far away. But now you've told me his name. Nikolai Popov." And she spat it out like a curse.

I made soothing noises and stroked her hair, but I was thinking the surveillance techniques of Popov's men left a lot to be desired. But then he must have arranged for it on the fly, right after our chat at the Hollywood Bowl.

"There is another thing you should know," Katya was saying. "Years ago, when my mother worked in the prison-camp infirmary, she fell in love with a man and he used that love to trick her into taking him to the altar of bones. She gave it to him to drink, and so he thought he knew all its secrets. He thought he would be able to find it again, but he was wrong, and he's been searching for the altar ever since. Hungering for its power."

She sat up and gave me a look I couldn't read. Her voice, though, was sad and serious. "The man who hunts me now, the man who will make you shoot the President—he's the same man who seduced and betrayed my mother. Nikolai Popov is my father, Mike, the man who gave me life, and yet I know he would kill me in an instant himself if that meant he could possess the altar of bones."

I have to admit I was more surprised by this than I should have been. But then, while I was still digesting that bombshell, she dropped another one on me, and here's the funny thing, or maybe it's a tragedy. . . . She told me that President Kennedy could never have drunk from the altar of bones, because she got it back. She said the morning after our dinner at the Brown Derby, she brought a second amulet over to Marilyn's house, one that was identical to the first except that it had toilet water in it instead of the altar of bones, and while Marilyn was taking a bath, she switched them out.

So what Marilyn gave to Bobby the day we murdered her was not the real altar of bones, and, no, I never told Popov that inconvenient truth. I couldn't think of a way to do it without betraying Katya.

Over the next couple of weeks, while Popov mapped out the detail of the big kill, Katya and I figured out the best way to save both ourselves from Popov. And it all went according to plan.

Until the end.

She filmed the kill from a natural blind and with a zoom lens, so she not only got the killing, she got all our faces in some of the frames. Afterward, we made still prints off it, the shots with their faces in them, and I gave them the prints, so they'd know what I had. I told them as long as both Katya and I stayed fat and sassy and alive, the film would stay buried.

We were home free then, and yet I couldn't stop thinking about the altar of bones. I had to have it. I *needed* it. But she wouldn't give it to me, damn her soul to hell. She'd given it to Marilyn, but she wouldn't give it to me.

After a while she began to suspect I wanted it bad enough to kill her for it, and God help me, but she was right.

So she ran. And she took the altar of bones with her to protect herself from *me*.

But all of that was still over a year in the future. At the moment I was more worried about talking Popov out of killing me in the here and now.

"If you are lying to me," Popov said, "I will rip off your balls and make you eat them. Now, think. Is there a friend she could have gone to? A relative?"

"I don't know." That was the truth. Her only real friend had been Marilyn.

"I could destroy you." I knew Popov would, too. Without breaking into a sweat, or without an instant's regret.

"I still don't know anything. Hell, I don't even get what this is all about."

I edged my way down the hall, back into the living room, Popov with me every step. Suddenly his gaze sharpened and focused, and I whirled, half-expecting to see Katya standing there.

But there was no one, and then I realized he was looking at the framed photograph on the fireplace mantel, a larger copy of the one Katya always carried in her purse—of her and Anna Larina standing in front of the studio gates. He went to it and picked it up, stood looking at it for a long time.

Then he said what I thought was the strangest thing at the time.

He said, "I thought she'd died in the cave."

32

He said, "I thought she died in the cave."

Those were the last words Dad spoke, Ry. He was having such trouble breathing by then, and I didn't want to hear more, yet I knew I had to know it all. I had to know what kind of Devil's temptation was in the amulet, that he'd actually thought about murdering his own wife to get his hands on it. And what kind of man would travel willingly down a path that would take him from that Brentwood bedroom to a grassy knoll in Dallas with a rifle in his hands? What kind of monster was our father? But he never spoke another word, slipping instead into a coma, and within a half an hour he was gone. I gave him the last rites, may God forgive me if I did it to spite him.

I hope that while you're reading this, I've been sitting across the kitchen table from you, nursing an Irish whiskey and waiting for you to finish so we can hash it out and decide what to do. But if you're alone instead, then know you were the best little brother a guy could ever have, and that I loved you.

ZOE WIPED THE tears off her cheeks and closed her eyes. She felt a movement beside her: Ry wrapping a throw blanket around her shoulders.

"You're so cold your teeth are chattering," he said.

She looked down and saw that she held the pages of Mike O'Malley's story clenched so tightly in her fist she was wrinkling them.

She smoothed them out on her lap. "They shot Kennedy for no reason, Ry. My grandmother got the amulet back—we know that part is true, because she said so with her dying breath. So they shot him for no reason. And what they did to poor Marilyn. It's the *way* she was killed that seems so awful, to be violated like that. And now they've killed your brother, too."

When Ry didn't say anything, she looked up to see that he was back to prowling the room. He stopped in front of the dressing table and leaned over, bracing his fists on it to look into the fanciful gold mirror, but she didn't really think he was seeing his own reflection.

"I know it might seem almost obscene to say this," he said, "but I think we need to look at it from Nikolai Popov's point of view. If he didn't know your grandmother got the amulet back, then it wasn't 'no reason' to him."

"Yeah. I see your point," Zoe said.

Ry straightened and spun around. "So what in hell was in that thing to make the KGB kill a president of the United States just because they believed he drank from it?"

Zoe couldn't help shuddering. "I don't know, but I think we'd better figure it out fast before not knowing gets us killed. And where's the amulet now? Katya got it back, so you'd think it would have been in the chest with the icon and the film."

Ry sighed as he pushed his fingers through his hair. "Maybe the disastrous consequences of her giving it to Marilyn spooked her so badly she threw it away."

Zoe shook her head. "She would never do that. She might give it to someone out of love, but she'd never just throw it away. It's the altar of bones, and she was the Keeper."

Ry came and sat down on the chaise next to her. He wasn't crowding her, yet she could feel the ferocity in him, the barely leashed violence. Had his father been like that? Is that what had attracted her grandmother to Mike O'Malley?

"Do you think they were really married?" she asked. "Your dad and my grandmother?"

Ry was quiet a moment, then he said, "Yeah, they were. After Galveston, when I new I had to track down Katya Orlova, to get some answers and see the film, I looked for her in the one place where I knew for sure she had once lived—the L.A. area. I found a record of their marriage in the Holy Virgin Mary Russian Orthodox Church in Hollywood. A Michael O'Malley married Katya Orlova there on June twenty-third of 1962. Anna Larina's birth certificate and her own marriage license to your dad were there, too. That's how I was able to track your mother down so easily once I ran out of other leads. I was hoping that somehow Anna Larina would lead me to Katya."

"And your plan worked," Zoe said. "In a crazy sort of way. It seems weird to think of them being married, though. Katya and your dad, I mean. It's not like that makes us blood relatives or anything, but still, it seems weird. Two strangers with a connection neither of us knew about, and now here we are."

"Getting shot at."

"There is that," Zoe said, and they shared the kind of grim smile she imagined soldiers in a foxhole did during a lull in the fighting. "And to top it off, now I gotta come to terms with the idea that this Nikolai Popov monster is my great-grandfather." She gave a bitter laugh. "But then it's not like I had a normal family to begin with."

Ry said nothing, but he reached over, took her hand, gave it a gentle squeeze, then let it go.

A silence fell between them then that was almost poignantly intimate, yet fraught with so many conflicting emotions, Zoe didn't know what to make of it. Maybe it was because of this newly discovered past they now shared, a past full of such dark and ugly secrets, but it felt as if this man understood her, knew her, better than anyone else ever had. She wondered if he felt the same.

"What are you thinking?" she asked.

He leaned back, lacing his hands behind his head. "That it's like a jigsaw puzzle made up of all these pieces. I keep thinking if we can just put the pieces together right, we'll be able to see the whole picture."

Zoe leaned back against the sofa cushions alongside him and stared up at the ceiling. "Well, we know that somewhere there exists, or existed, an amulet filled with this stuff called the altar of bones. Stuff so scary that when the KGB thought the president of the United States drank it, they killed him."

"But not right away," Ry said. "They murdered Marilyn in August of 1962, on the day she gave what they thought was the altar of bones to Bobby to give to the president. Yet Jack wasn't assassinated until November of the following year, a whole fifteen months later. If Popov and the KGB really believed his drinking from the altar made him a danger to the world, then why did they wait so long?"

" 'Danger to the world' . . . ," Zoe echoed. "That makes the altar sound like something downright evil. Yet Popov and your dad were both willing to betray the women who loved them just to get their hands on it."

"A two-bit pimp told me a story once, about taking a knife to one of his whores who'd gotten out of line. He said the power he felt while he was cutting her made him feel like a god. For some people, Zoe, the mere act of doing evil can be a seductive thing."

Ry leaned forward, bracing his elbows on his spread knees. "Anyway, we might not know yet exactly what the altar of bones is, but we got an idea how it fits into the Kennedy assassination—they killed him because they believed he drank from it. So that's at least one part of the puzzle. And we also know we've got two separate bad guys after our asses. Mr. Ponytail, who wants the altar of bones, and Yasmine Poole, who wants the film."

"They could both be working for Nikolai Popov, though," Zoe said. "Katya got his face on the film, remember? He was the guy with the umbrella, which he used to signal your father that the president's limousine was coming. So he's got a good reason to keep the film from ever seeing the light of day. At the same time we now know that he was after the altar of bones from as far back as the 1930s, so—" She stopped as a thought suddenly struck her. "Which was what? Eighty years ago? So that means Popov would have to be old as dirt now, and I think I just shot a big hole in my theory, didn't I?"

Ry gave her a tired smile. "Actually, he'd be pushing a hundred and ten or so, if he were even still alive. While I was trying to find your grandmother, I did some research on the Nikolai Popov, who was a procurator general for the KGB in the early sixties. As you can imagine, there wasn't a lot to be found, but as near as I could tell, he was born in St. Petersburg sometime around the turn of the last century. He wielded a lot of power behind the scenes until Leonid Brezhnev's death in 1982. Apparently, once he found himself out of favor with the new regime, he retired to his dacha to live out his golden years. There was no mention of him anywhere after that."

"Not even a death certificate?"

"Not that I could find, but then a lot of records got lost or were tossed after the Soviet Union collapsed."

"Well . . . ," Zoe sighed, and straightened, stretching out her legs and the kinks in her muscles, "it was a good theory while it lasted."

"Actually, you might have been sort of right. At least as far as the ponytailed guy working for a Popov, I mean. Back in the early eighties, when organized crime really got going in Russia, a man calling himself Mikhail Nikolaiovich Popov emerged as the *pakhan* of a big *mafiya* outfit in St. Petersburg. He claimed to be the old master spy's son, even produced an official birth certificate to prove it, and supposedly he's the spitting image of his dad. Whatever, this guy's into some real serious shit now—prostitution, extortion, murder for hire, drug trafficking. Especially crystal meth."

"How delightful. Yet another *pakhan* in the family. If Nikolai Popov was my great-grandfather, then that would make his son my . . . what? Great-uncle or something? You don't think it could be genetic, do you?" she said, only half-joking.

Ry cupped the side of her face, turning her head so that she would have to meet his eyes. "You are your own person, Zoe. You've already proved that a thousand times over."

She nodded, swallowed. "I know. It's just . . . I know."

He stroked her cheek once with his thumb, then let her go. "So I'm thinking Nikolai Popov could certainly have told his son about the altar of bones, and your ponytailed guy does have the look and feel of a typical *vor*. But as for Yasmine Poole?" Ry shrugged. "Maybe she works for him, too, but I don't think so. She doesn't fit the *mafiya* picture. As far as I can tell, the Popov crime outfit only operates inside of Russia, a country that's chauvinistic to the max. No insult to your mother, Zoe, but I can't see a true Russian *pakhan* trusting a woman to do his enforcement work, especially someone as flamboyantly out there as Yasmine Poole."

"Remember there was that other guy in the film?" Zoe said. "The one in the railroad uniform who took the rifle from your dad? Katya made sure to focus in tight on his face for a good ten seconds. With your dad dead and Nikolai Popov most likely dead by now, too, and his son a criminal—that guy in the railroad uniform might be the only one left with everything to lose. He could've been another KGB mole, like your dad. Maybe Yasmine Poole really is with the CIA, and they're doing all this to keep the scandal from getting out."

Ry grunted in agreement. "If it turned out the CIA was involved with the Kennedy assassination, even as dupes, and they covered it up, there would be so many spook heads rolling down Capitol Hill, it would dam up the Potomac."

Zoe picked up the icon to study it some more, and another thought struck her. "All those icons my mother collected through the years, I bet it was all a front, a way to get her name out there as a serious buyer. *This* is the only one she's ever really wanted, Ry. Anna Larina knows about the altar of bones, all right. Maybe not everything, but she knows enough to believe this icon is a clue to finding it."

Zoe brushed the tips of her fingers over the embossed silver skull cup that was cradled in the Virgin's hands. So unlike anything she'd ever seen on an icon before. "I'm the one who's supposed to guard the altar from the world, to keep it safe from the hunters, including my own mother, it seems, yet I don't even know where, or even what, it is. All those Keepers who came before me—I don't want to be the first one to fail, Ry."

She hadn't realized she was crying again until he cupped her neck to wipe a tear off her cheek with his fingers. "No way are you going to fail. *We* won't fail, because we're in this together now. From here on out I've got your back, Zoe. Trust me on that."

He spanned the back of her neck with his hand, and this time he didn't let her go. His palm was hard, calloused, yet warm. She saw his eyes darken, and she thought, *He's going to kiss me.*

But then he looked away, and a moment later he let his hand fall away as well, and her neck felt strangely cold and naked now without his touch.

━━━━━━

ZOE DIDN'T REALIZE how hungry she was until she started eating, and then she couldn't stop. The soup had grown cold, but it still tasted wonderful and she had to restrain herself from licking out the inside of the carton. And she would have arm-wrestled Ry for the last lamb pastry, if he hadn't snatched it up when she wasn't watching.

Out in the nightclub, she could hear the hum and crackle of conversation and laughter, the clink of glasses, a melancholy pianist, and Madame Blotski's husky alto singing "La Vie en Rose."

Zoe said, "You know, Ry, I've been thinking . . ."

"Jesus. Should I duck?"

She searched through the take-out cartons for something to heave at his head, but they'd eaten everything except the cardboard. Then she spotted a crust of pumpernickel under a napkin, but instead of throwing it at him, she popped it into her mouth instead.

She looked up and caught him grinning at her. "What?"

"Nothing. I just like to see a girl with a healthy appetite. I lived with a ballerina for three years and all I ever saw her eat was lettuce. She'd get so hungry, I swear there were times she looked at me like she wanted to slather me with ketchup and—"

He cut himself off, but he wasn't quick enough. Zoe felt a big grin splitting across her face, but before she could open her mouth, Ry covered it with his hand. He was laughing, though, and she thought how much she liked his laugh.

She also liked his fingers on her mouth, probably too much, but he pulled back and raised his hands, palms out, in an attitude of surrender. "Okay, okay. You probably got a good half dozen smart-ass zingers just bursting to get out, so lay them on me."

"Naw," Zoe said, blushing a little. "I think I'll pass up on the temptation. This time."

Ry laughed again as he poured them more vodka from the bottle that now had a good-size dent in it. "So you were thinking . . ."

"Huh? Oh, just in her letter to me, my grandmother said, 'Look to the Lady, for her heart cherishes the secret, and the pathway to the se-cret is infinite'. . . . 'The Lady' is what Boris, the griffin shop man, called the icon, and the icon is what Anna Larina seems to be after. So maybe the icon, or rather the composition of the painting itself, is the riddle that's supposed to lead us to the altar."

"Hey, that is a good point. We should find an expert on Russian icons. Get him to take a look at it under the guise of getting it appraised, and see what he's got to say about it. . . ." His voice trailed off, but she could feel his intensity as he stared at her. "You really are something else, Zoe. You know that, don't you?"

Zoe's cheeks felt hot, and she couldn't meet his eyes or get her mouth to work. She finished off the last of the vodka in one gulp and stood up slowly, brushing off her jeans. "I, uh . . . think I'll take a shower. I've got wedding cake in my hair and I smell like I've been soaking in diesel fumes for a month."

———

WHEN SHE CAME back out of the bathroom, all clean and deodorized and wearing fresh underwear, the dressing room was empty. The icon and the postcard that she'd left lying on the brass table were gone.

No, goddammit, no. And God damn you to hell and back, Ry O'Malley.

He couldn't have done this to her, he just couldn't. Not after all they'd been through together. She'd trusted him, spewed her guts out to him, told him everything. He wouldn't do this to her because she knew him, knew he was honorable—

Yeah, right, Dmitroff. Who are you kidding? You didn't know jackshit, except that he's gone.

She crumbled slowly back on the chaise. She wasn't going to cry, dammit. She would *not* cry. The smell of the empty food cartons was making her sick. She gathered them up to throw them away and saw the note he'd left her, scrawled on a napkin.

GONE TO SEE A GUY ABOUT A THING.

She lay back on the chaise, grinning like a fool. Then out of nowhere, she burst into tears.

She snatched up one of the gaudy, fringed pillows and buried her face in it so no one could hear her. Ry had said she was something else, but she didn't feel like something else right now. What she felt was scared, and she wanted to go home.

———

SHE CAME AWAKE with a start. It felt late, deep into the night. The room, the whole nightclub, was quiet, still. The small lamp on the dressing table was lit, but its soft pink light barely penetrated the shadows. Everything was so quiet, but she knew she wasn't alone.

She half sat up. "Ry?"

Something huge and heavy slammed her back down onto the chaise, a hand clamped down hard over her mouth. She saw the tip of a knife, pointing at her left eye.

PART FIVE

THE RIDDLE

33

"You're gonna give me the altar of bones, bitch," said the ponytailed man as he straddled her, his hand clamped tight over her mouth. "But to save us both time and trouble, I'm taking one of your eyes out first. That way you'll believe me when I tell you just what you gotta do to save the other one."

The dim light glinted off steel as the knife touched her eyelid. She grabbed his wrist with both hands and twisted her head aside, felt a sting on her forehead, a splash of blood. He'd cut her, but not her eye yet. Not her eye.

The knife was coming back at her face again, and he was so strong. She pushed against his wrist with all her might, and still the knife tip came closer, closer.

She tried to ram her knee into his balls, but she couldn't get any leverage. She couldn't breathe, couldn't move, and she could feel the strength melting out her, all her muscles turning to mush, and the knife was so close now.

She squeezed her eyes shut, felt the tip prick her lid.

Something wet and hot splashed her face. He let go of her mouth, and she screamed and screamed.

SHE COULDN'T SEE. Oh, God, what had he done? Was she completely blinded? Why couldn't she see?

Suddenly the weight lifted and she stopped screaming to gasp and suck in air. She felt something soft wipe at her eyes, and then she was looking up into Ry's face. She was *seeing* his face.

"Hey, hey, you're okay," he said. "You're gonna be okay."

"He was going to . . ." She shuddered, closing her eyes, then she opened them again right away. She didn't like the world being dark.

Her forehead burned. She touched it, looked at her fingers, and saw blood.

"It's not yours," Ry said. "Mostly not yours. I guess we did kind of let things get a little too close for comfort there."

His voice sounded tough, matter-of-fact, but as he leaned closer to her, she thought his eyes were dark with violence and something else she couldn't read. His mouth was white.

She was afraid that if she blurted out all the things she wanted to say to him, she'd sound all emotional and embarrassing, so she said, "Hey, O'Malley, don't get too full of yourself. I had things perfectly under control in here. Couldn't you tell?"

He laughed. "Yeah? What I heard, Dmitroff, was you screaming like a girl."

"Well, if the shoe fits . . ." She was laughing herself as she sat up on the chaise. She felt weak and dizzy, but at the same time she had so much adrenaline shooting through her veins she felt as if she'd burst into a million pieces.

She tried to stand up and her foot knocked against something thick and heavy. She looked down and saw the ponytailed man sprawled on his back on the floor, half his head blown away.

She stared at the body, at the big, ugly-looking knife in his hand. It looked just like the knife he'd left in her grandmother's chest. A Siberian knife. This was her grandmother's killer and he was dead. *Good*, she thought. *Good.* She was glad he was dead, he deserved to be dead.

She picked up the knife. It was heavy, wickedly sharp, and she was going to keep it. She would use it, too, on the next asshole who came at her from out of the dark.

She looked from the knife in her hand back up to Ry. He still knelt in front of her, a blood-soaked pillow in one hand, his Walther in the other, but she noticed now that it had a silencer attached, which explained how the ponytailed man had suddenly keeled over dead on top of her and she hadn't heard the shot.

The weird thing, though, was that Ry had been right—she'd screamed her head off. So where was everybody?

"I thought you'd left me," she said to Ry. "When I came out of the bathroom and saw that my stuff was gone and you were gone. But then I found the note you scribbled on that napkin, so you're forgiven. Sort of. I mean, 'Gone to see a guy about a thing'? Way to overwhelm me with the details, O'Malley."

"I had to call a couple of guys, see if they could give me a lead on a Russian-icon expert. Then I arranged to meet another guy who can make us some fake passports, since we can't go on hiding in here forever. It ended up taking a lot longer than I thought it would. I took your stuff because it didn't seem smart to leave it unguarded while you were in the bathroom."

"No, it wasn't very smart." She dropped the knife in her lap and lowered her head in her hands, feeling suddenly exhausted, and way, way, way out of her depth. Ambitious DAs, prickly judges, deadbeat dads, abusive husbands, stalkers—all those she could handle. But not this.

She pushed her hands through her hair and felt something sticky. What the . . . ? She thought she'd washed out all the wedding-cake frosting, and then she realized it was the ponytailed man's blood, and maybe some of his brains, too, and she shuddered.

"He wanted me to give him the altar of bones, but he was going to torture me first just for the hell of it." She looked back up at Ry's face, into his eyes. He looked serious and tough, but a tenderness was there, too, and she wasn't sure what she ought to be making of it. "You had my back, Ry. I should've thanked you sooner."

He brushed back the hair that was stuck to her forehead with the ponytailed man's blood. "Most people who went through what you have would be curled up in the corner in a fetal position by now, so cut yourself some slack. And in the world where I come from, when a guy tells you he's got your back, he's also saying he knows you've got his."

Zoe felt tears well in her eyes and she looked away, embarrassed. But she also felt full up to bursting inside with a mess of feelings she couldn't name. Pride, she supposed, but also something strangely like faith, a deep, lasting faith in the man kneeling in front of her, and also faith in herself.

"Really?" she asked. "You really trust me to have your back?"

"All the way."

She cleared her throat. "Okay, then. Good." She poked at the body again with her toe. "I guess we won't find out now if was working for Popov's son or not."

Ry got to his feet. "What I'm wondering is how, out of all the gin joints in all the world, this guy knew he'd find us here."

"How do you think he knew, Ry*lushka*?"

Madame Blotski stood in the open doorway. She had a gun in her hand.

34

YOU ARE to bend over slowly and set your gun onto the floor, please," Anya Blotski said. "With the barrel pointing towards yourself. . . . Yes, yes. Very good. Now you will push it over to me."

Ry did as she asked. The Walther didn't slide well on the thick Turkey carpet, but it went far enough that it was now out of his reach.

He straightened, his hands hanging empty now at his sides. "Since when are you working for the bad guys, Anya?"

"There are no good and bad guys, only the living and the dead. Was it not you who once told me that, *lapushka*?" She pointed with her gun toward the table with the samovar. "Now, you will be so kind as to move over there. . . . No, that is far enough. I want you separate from your little friend, yes? Yet not so separate that I cannot watch the both of you at once."

But the Russian woman's eyes, her whole being, Zoe saw, were really focused all on Ry. So she stole the chance to pull one of the pillows from the chaise up onto her lap to hide the ponytailed man's knife.

She looked from the barrel of the woman's little Ruger back to Ry's face. He didn't seem surprised, rather disappointed, and Zoe realized he had figured right off that the only way for the ponytailed man to have found them here at the Casbah was through Madame Blotski.

"So who did you sell us out to?" Ry asked, and Zoe wondered if he was as relaxed as he sounded. Because with his gun now halfway across the room, she couldn't see where he had a plan to get them out of this mess once he got what information he could out of the woman.

"I only ask," he went on, "because maybe I can top their offer."

Madame Blotski shook her head, and Zoe was surprised to see the gleam of tears in her eyes and on her cheeks. The gun in her hand trembled a little. "There is no amount of money to buy what he can give me."

"He?"

"This afternoon a telephone call comes to me from a man, a stranger to me. He says only one thing at first—a name. Oksana."

She shook her head again, crying more openly now and not caring if they saw it. "Oksana. It is the name of my niece, Ry, and she is only five. She lives in St. Petersburg, and she loves dinosaurs and your silly SpongeBob SquarePants, and she wants to be an Olympic ice-skater when she grows up. This man, he gives me a cell phone number and he tells me I must call it if you come here, and I knew even as he was telling me this, even as he was telling me how I must betray you, I knew I would do it, because of the way he said her name."

She choked on a sob, squeezed her eyes shut. "Then he says to me, 'Life can be cruel, madame. Little girls, especially the lovely ones like your Oksana, are disappearing from the streets of St. Petersburg every day. Where do they go? Who knows? But I have heard that in Bangkok there are brothels where one can buy, for a price, a child of either sex and any age.'"

Ry drew in a deep breath. "I'm sorry, Anya."

She gave him a wry, sad smile. "This man—he must know a lot about you, if he knows who are the few in this world you would trust with your life. Is he *mafiya*?"

"We think so."

She nodded slowly. "They are like vampires, these *mafiya*. They live in the dark, they suck your blood dry, and they cannot die."

The word *die* echoed in the empty nightclub. Zoe slid her hand under the pillow, wrapping it around the hilt of the knife.

Madame Blotski's gaze flickered over to Zoe, then back to Ry. "I am so sorry, *lapushka*, but it is the girl he wants. Not you. If I thought you would give her up without a fight . . . but, no. I know you too well."

She raised the gun higher, pointing the barrel at the middle of Ry's chest.

And Zoe threw the knife at her head.

MADAME BLOTSKI DROPPED the gun and threw her hands up in front of her face as she tried to duck the flying knife. Zoe dove for Ry's Walther at the same time that he did. They bumped heads so hard she was knocked back onto her butt, nearly senseless.

By the time the world stopped spinning, and she'd blinked the tears from her eyes, Zoe saw that Ry's gun was trained on the Russian woman and he was picking up her little Ruger.

"Zoe?" he said. "Are you all right?"

Her ears were ringing and she thought she might be sick. "Your head's as hard as concrete, O'Malley. I feel like I've just been kicked by a—"

"I know, I know. Get your stuff now, okay? Fast. We need to get out of here."

She looked wildly around the room for her satchel, which only made the world spin again. Then she spotted it, leaning up against one end of the chaise. She tried to stand up, but that wasn't working so well quite yet, so she ended up crawling to it on her hands and knees.

"Okay. Got it," she said. Only now her words were coming out all woozy, too.

"Are you sure you're all right?"

"In a minute. I just . . ." She drew in a deep breath and that seemed to settle her stomach down, although it did nothing for the ringing in her ears.

She took another breath and stood up slowly, slowly. The world spun, settled, spun again, then settled again and stayed settled. She took a careful step, then another, and when the world stayed put, she decided she was going to live after all.

She saw the ponytailed man's knife—her knife now—lying on the floor in front of Madame Blotski. In the end it had fallen short, but it had come close enough to do the trick.

Zoe picked it up and started to shove it into her waist as she'd seen them do in the movies, but that didn't seem like such a good idea after all, so she stuffed it into the bulging satchel instead.

"Okay, I'm ready now," she said, and looked up at Ry. He had a stunned look on his face, as if he couldn't quite believe what he was seeing. But that wasn't surprising if his head was feeling the way hers was.

"Right," he said after a moment. "Let's go."

He still had his gun pointed at Madame Blotski, but it didn't seem necessary anymore. The woman stood in utter stillness, her arms wrapped tightly around her waist, as if she needed to hold herself together.

The eyes she turned onto Ry's face were dark with fear and pain. "You must kill me for my Oksana's sake. Otherwise how will he know that I did not just let you both go?"

Ry shook his head. "I can't—"

"You must. You *know* you must."

Ry put his hand in the small of Zoe's back and pushed her gently forward. "Go on ahead."

"What? No!"

He gave her another shove, hard enough this time to send Zoe reeling toward the door. Then he raised the Walther and pulled the trigger.

There was a *spfitt* sound, and Madame Blotski slumped to the floor.

Zoe whirled and started back into the room, but Ry gripped her arm and pulled her after him. She tried to wrench away from him, but he was too strong. She looked back to see that Madame Blotski was sitting up, holding a hand to her side, blood seeping out between her fingers.

"It's only a flesh wound," Ry said. "Let's hope that's enough."

35

ZOE RUBBED the steam off the café window so that she could keep an eye on the antiques shop across the Rue des Saints-Pères. Its wooden facade was painted a classy hunter green. Its name, Air de la Russie, was painted in discreet gold script above the door. A mesh metal grill still covered its dark plate-glass windows, though, while the other shops around it glowed invitingly in the gray, rainy morning.

"'M. Anthony Lovely, Propriétaire,'" Zoe said, reading aloud the smaller and even more discreet lettering beneath the shop's name. They'd scoped out the display in the windows before they'd come over to the café, and Zoe had been impressed. From what she could tell, the icons, Fabergé eggs, lacquer boxes, nesting dolls, and jewelry were all of the highest quality. Monsieur Anthony Lovely definitely knew his stuff.

"What an odd name. Anthony Lovely. I bet it was a kick and a half for little Tony, growing up with a name like that. It isn't Russian, or French either, for that matter. Hopefully he speaks English, because I hate it when people are jabbering around me and I can't understand a word. Not everybody speaks a gazillion languages like you do, Ry. At least I'm bilingual."

She stopped to draw breath and check her watch. "It's after ten already. What if he doesn't show?"

Ry stuffed the last of his croissant into his mouth. "It so happens I only speak twelve languages fluently, but I am functional in three more."

Zoe gaped at him; she couldn't help it. "You're shi—kidding me, right?"

"I kid you not. It's just a gift I happened to've been born with. Like having perfect pitch, or being able to multiply 1,546 times 852 in your head. Before I became a DEA agent, I was in the Special Forces, and the army treated me to a lot of immersion courses. The rest I picked up along the way.

"As for Anthony Lovely, the guy who recommended him said he's a British expat—from the Cotswolds, to be exact—so it's a good bet he speaks English. He's a lifelong bachelor, but straight, in his midseventies. Russian antiquities are his life, apparently, since he seems to have no other interests, and my guy says he hasn't missed a day at his shop in over forty years. He'll show."

"Okay." Zoe was still reeling over the fact that Ry spoke fifteen languages.

The waiter refilled their coffees in passing. Zoe rubbed the steam off the window again, then picked up her cup more to warm her hands than to drink from it. She was already wired to the max.

She looked up and caught Ry staring at her, an intense, almost fierce look on his face. "What is it? You've been looking at me weird ever since we sat down in here—"

A horrible thought suddenly occurred to her. She dropped her coffee cup back into its saucer and brushed her fingers over the front of her hair. "Please don't tell me I still have his blood on me."

He smiled. "No, you're fine. All scrubbed up nice and shiny."

After they'd left the Casbah, they hadn't dared go to a hotel, where they would have had to show their passports, but they used the cool public shower facilities called Mc Clean that were in the basement of the Gare du Nord railway station. Zoe hadn't realized how much of the ponytailed man's head had ended up all over her until she saw all the blood and gore swirling around the drain. Now, she couldn't think of it without feeling itchy all over.

"Well what, then?"

He shrugged. "It's just . . . You surprised the hell out of me back there at the Casbah. The way you saved our butts by going all ninja with a knife."

Zoe grinned at him, more than a little pleased with herself. "To be honest, it didn't happen like it was supposed to. I thought it would flip end over end like you see in movies, but it fell short and just kind of thudded."

"That's because the blade is curved. It ruins the balance." Ry reached for the check. Zoe watched as he pulled a wad of euros out of his jacket pocket. He seemed to have an endless supply of cash—a good thing, she thought, since all she had were a couple of now useless credit cards. If she hadn't hooked up with Ry O'Malley, she'd probably be in the hands of the French police by now, and then only if she was lucky. Otherwise she'd be in the morgue.

She said, "At least the ponytailed man is out of my life for good now, thanks to you. Madame Blotski said the man on the other end of the phone was a stranger to her, but she seemed pretty convinced he was *mafayi*, and what he said to her does sound like the sort of threat a *pakhan* would make."

"Yeah, I think we can safely assume Mr. Ponytail worked for Popov's son."

"He isn't going to stop coming after me, is he, Ry? Popov's son. His dad told him about the altar of bones, and now he wants it for himself and he's going to keep sending his *vors* after me until he gets it."

She hadn't realized she was clutching her coffee mug so tightly until Ry pried her fingers loose and wrapped them up in his big hand. "We've bought us some nice breathing room, though. It'll take some time for Popov's son to field another *vor*, and that guy's going to have to track us down. In the meantime maybe we can get a good lead from this icon guy on what and where is the altar of bones."

"And since Kennedy was killed because the KGB believed he drank from it," Zoe said, "maybe solving the mystery of the altar will show us a way to get rid of Yasmine Poole and Company as well. I still think she works for that guy in the railroad uniform who showed up at the end of the film to take the rifle from your dad."

"Yeah. I suppose it's possible she really does work for the CIA, but like you, my bet is on railroad guy. Whoever he is, though, he must have some serious juice, to—"

"O'Malley, look." Zoe grabbed his arm and pointed with her chin toward a man in a fedora and crisp gray suit who stood in front of the Air de la Russie. He carried a newspaper tucked under one arm and a Starbucks cup in one hand, and he had to set his coffee down on the shop's window ledge to pull a ring of keys out of his pockets.

"It's him. The icon guy."

━━━━━━━━

THEY DECIDED ON a cover: She and Ry were here in Paris on their honeymoon, but also to visit her grandmother, an émigré who came over from Russia during the glasnost era, and who'd given them the icon as a wedding present. They wanted to get it appraised, and perhaps insured, before they went back to the States.

"I'll act bored," Ry said. "Like this is your thing and I'm just along for the ride, humoring you because I want to jump your bones later on. That way he's less likely to feel threatened or intimidated by me. You be clueless, but eager to learn, which will get him to open up more. People like to show off their knowledge."

Zoe felt self-conscious, though, once they were in the shop and she was rattling off their story, as if she were reading her lines off cue cards. But Anthony Lovely didn't seem suspicious, only mildly curious as she took the icon from her satchel, unwrapped it from its protective sealskin pouch, and laid it on the counter.

The man caught his breath as the light from the shop's crystal chandeliers glimmered in the jewels and gilt paint on the Virgin's crown and robe.

"Why, it's . . . exquisite," he said, but Zoe thought he'd been about to say something else.

His hands hovered in the air over the icon, as if he yearned to touch it but didn't dare. "Yes, it is really rather extraordinary. I would like to examine it under more direct light. May I?"

"Please do. My grandmother said it's been in the family for generations. Didn't she, honey?"

Zoe turned to look at Ry, and her mouth nearly fell open. He had morphed into a completely different person—his face looked softer, emptier, as if he'd dropped about fifty points off his IQ. And although he couldn't make himself grow shorter or less buff, the way he slouched against the counter, his shoulders drooping, he didn't look nearly so tough and threatening anymore.

And, oh, boy—he was giving her this hot look, a very hot look, that clearly said he was picturing her naked right now. Naked and sex-sweaty, and lying underneath him—

Anthony Lovely cleared his throat. "Tell me, Mrs. . . ."

Zoe jerked her fascinated gaze off Ry and turned back to the antiques dealer. "Uh, Suzie Carpenter, with a *z*. My husband's name is Jake Carpenter. We just got married."

"Yes, so you said. May I ask, how extensive is your knowledge of religious icons?"

"Just that they're, you know, these religious things," Zoe said, hoping she sounded clueless enough. "But I want to know more, now that I've got one."

Anthony Lovely shifted his coffee and the folded-up newspaper farther down the counter and picked up a green gooseneck lamp from over by the cash register.

"Because of the veneration in which they were held by the Orthodox Church," he said, "Russian icons had to conform to strict formal rules, with fixed patterns repeated over and over again. There were severe repercussions for those artists who dared to deviate from the norm. Being whipped to death with a wire flail, for example."

Zoe shuddered. "Oh, but that's terrible."

"Indeed." Lovely set the lamp down on the counter. "Which is what makes this particular icon of yours so special—because its subject matter so completely violates all the rules, don't you see?"

He reached beneath the counter and brought out a box of thin plastic gloves, so the oil from his skin wouldn't get onto the wood. He took a black velvet cloth from out of a drawer, smoothed it out, then reverently laid the icon down on top of it.

Zoe felt a pang of guilt over the cavalier way she and Ry had been handling it, poking and prying and shaking it to see if it had a hidden compartment. She'd even jumped into the Seine with it.

"Normally," Lovely said, bending at the waist and adjusting his bifocals up, then down, then up again, "the Virgin is depicted holding the

Christ child in her arms, or with her hands folded in prayer. But instead, what we have here is a rather macabre drinking cup. Carved out of a human skull, no less."

"It is kind of creepy looking," Zoe said, with another shudder. "Do you think it has some special meaning?"

"To the artist, perhaps. The Church, I rather suspect, would have been horrified at the very idea."

Lovely lost himself in his thoughts for a moment, and his eyes, Zoe thought, were almost worshipful as he looked at the icon. *He loves this,* she thought. *Not only the icons—he loves Russia herself, her history, her dark and deep mysteries. He loves it all the way to his soul.*

He huffed a little laugh. "Yes, horrified indeed. And they probably would have looked askance at this Virgin, too, for she's not your typical, flat-faced saint who conforms to a dictated ideal. Rather, there's a mischievous, whimsical quality about her, don't you think? As if she has a secret she is teasing us with, only she will never tell. I have to believe the artist used a real person as a model. Her heart-shaped face and prominent cheekbones, the strongly arched brows. And her eyes, they are almost catlike—"

He stopped himself, looked up at Zoe, then back down to the icon. "How utterly extraordinary. The Virgin, she is . . . You two look enough alike to be sisters."

Slowly, he raised his gaze back up to Zoe's face, and she saw suspicion come into his kind eyes. "How long did you say this has been in your family?"

Zoe didn't dare look at Ry. "Oh, a long time," she said, her voice cracking hoarsely. "Grandmother never really said."

Lovely stared at her for several interminable seconds, then said, "I wonder . . . Is it mere serendipity you look so much like her, Mrs. Carpenter? Or do you perhaps believe she was a real woman, from a real place?"

A real place. Zoe looked down at the Virgin. She sat on a golden throne, and the throne floated above a lake that was shaped rather like a shoe. At the heel of the shoe was what looked like a pile of rocks. And at the toe end was a waterfall.

"Are you saying you think this lake really exists somewhere?"

"Indeed, I do." Lovely made a little circular motion over the icon with his hand. "We see the lake, the rocks, the waterfall, as if from above, a bird's-eye view. Yet the Virgin we see head-on, and out of perspective to everything else. It's as if the artist painted a map of a place he knew, his home perhaps, and then placed the Virgin on top of it."

"Did you hear that, honey?" Zoe said, turning to Ry. "He thinks the lake in my icon might be a real place. Wouldn't it be cool to go there and see it?"

Ry shrugged. "Whatever."

She turned back to the antiques dealer and beamed a smile at him. "Do you know where in Russia it might be, Mr. Lovely?"

Lovely smiled as well. "If the artist depicted the place where he lived, then it would be somewhere in Siberia. One can tell this from the paint he used, you see. The colors in the Virgin's robe, for instance, orange, vermilion, and turquoise, are distinctly Siberian. And applied with a sureness of touch I've rarely seen surpassed. Indeed, in the hands of a lesser master such colors might easily have assumed a primitive garishness of the sort we often encounter in folk art."

Zoe's heart pounded so hard with excitement, she was almost dancing with it. The icon was a map to a real place, a lake somewhere in Siberia. If they found the lake, could they find the altar of bones?

"The colors really are beautiful," she said. "And so vivid still, for being painted so long ago."

"It is all rather wonderful, is it not? The amazing freshness of the color is due to a technique of great durability called encaustic, in which the pigments are suspended in hot wax. It is a technique, by the by, which helps us to date it to around the time of Ivan the Terrible. That is, the sixteenth century."

Lovely stared reverently down at the icon, then he sighed. "The embossed silver overlay on the cup and the gold-leaf paint on the crown were added a couple of centuries later. Rather a pity, for it compromises the integrity of the piece."

"But what about those jewels on it?" Ry said. "Those've got to be worth something, right?"

"Ah, yes. The jewels." Lovely took a jeweler's loupe out of his suit pocket, put it to his eye, and brought his face so close he was within a millimeter of brushing noses with the Virgin. "I see that we have a diamond, onyx, iolite . . . ," he said, as he moved the loupe from one jewel to the other. "Fire opal, aquamarine, sapphire . . ." He ended with the largest jewel, the one embedded on the forehead of the silver skull cup. "Ruby."

He straightened, tucking the loupe back into his pocket. "Regrettably, they are all thoroughly modern. Post–World War Two, I would say, and of rather inferior quality and cut. The original jewels were probably removed by someone who needed the money."

My great-grandmother, Zoe thought. Lena Orlova. Had she sold the jewels to keep her and her baby alive in Shanghai during the Japanese occupation? Anna Larina had said Lena married a jewel merchant after the war. These later jewels had probably come from him.

But what had always seemed most strange to Zoe about the jewels was the way they'd been placed on the icon so haphazardly. Not only were no two of the jewels alike, but it looked as if they'd just been plopped down on a whim, with no thought for artistry or symmetry.

The Virgin's gold crown, for instance—why no jewels there? Yet in the sky on either side of the crown, floating up among the clouds, the artist had put a fire opal and an aquamarine. No jewels were on the Virgin's robe either, as you would have expected, but the iolite had been stuck in the middle of the pile of rocks, and the sapphire was in the waterfall.

It made no sense. The only jewel that seemed to be where it ought to be was the big ruby in the middle of the skull's forehead.

"So what are you telling us?" Ry asked, shifting his weight and slouching even more to lean his elbows on the spotless glass countertop. "Is the icon worth something, or isn't it?"

Lovely gave Ry's elbows a scathing look. "It is virtually impossible to put a specific value on such a unique piece as this. I can tell you that a well-preserved Siberian icon, circa early seventeenth century, recently went at Sotheby's for nine hundred thousand pounds sterling."

"Holy shit," Ry said, and Zoe almost laughed at the genuine shock she heard in his voice. Then she remembered her plunge in the Seine with nine hundred thousand pounds sterling worth of icon in her satchel, and that wild motorcycle ride through the streets of Paris, and she got a little queasy herself.

"Yes, quite," Lovely said. "And if you are interested in selling, then I might be able to put you in touch with a potential buyer. He lives just outside of Budapest, but he's a serious collector of Siberian icons, and an expert in Siberian folklore and artifacts. In fact, he—"

Lovely caught himself up and looked off into the distance, seeming to think about whether he wanted to say more.

Zoe decided to take a chance on leveling with the dealer just a little. "Mr. Lovely, I would never part with my grandmother's icon, any more than I would cut off my right arm and sell it, because it is a part of me, my heritage. But I would really like to talk to this man."

Lovely hesitated a moment longer, then nodded. "I have his card here somewhere."

He went to a drawer beneath the cash register and began to rummage through what to Zoe's eyes looked like several hundred business cards. "The odd thing is, he asked me once years ago to keep him in mind if I ever came across a Virgin holding a skull cup in her lap. It seemed such a strange request that I utterly dismissed it at the time. . . . Ah, here we are."

He brought the card to Zoe. "This should have everything you need. 'Denis Kuzmin, Professor Emeritus, 336 Piroska U., Szentendre, Hungary.' And a telephone number."

Zoe tucked the card in her back pocket, while Lovely carefully wrapped the icon back up in its sealskin pouch. Then he presented the pouch to her as if offering the crown jewels of England.

"Thank you for allowing me the pleasure, Mrs. Carpenter."

Zoe smiled back at him, feeling a little sad because she liked him, and yet she'd deceived him in a way, by not being herself.

―――――――――

"*Whooh,* boy," Zoe said, as the door to the Air de la Russie shut behind them with the tinkle of a bell. She was jazzed.

"The lake in the icon is a real place, Ry, way up in Siberia somewhere. And sixteenth-century. It's weird to think there was a Keeper who looked like me yet lived so long ago. I feel like we're finally getting somewhere, though. How did I do? Was I clueless enough?"

Ry drew in a breath to speak, but Zoe put a finger over his lips. "No, don't say it, O'Malley. I know I just left myself wide-open for a real zinger of a comeback there, but you owe me a free pass, remember?"

He wrapped his hand around hers, but he left her finger where it was. His breath was hot on her skin as he spoke. "You did good. You charmed poor Mr. Lovely down to his toes, then wrung him dry."

He kept hold of her hand, Zoe noticed, as they started to cross the street, heading back toward the café where they'd had breakfast.

She said, "And we also got the name of someone who might know even more. I hope Hungarian is one of your fifteen languages."

Ry grinned at her and rattled off something that to Zoe's ears sounded like the warble of a wren.

"Well, I trust that was at least polite—"

Zoe cut herself off, gripping Ry's hand tighter and pulling him up short. She leaned in close to him, pretending to nuzzle his neck and whispered, "News kiosk. On the corner."

He kissed her chin and tipped his head so that he could see the racks of newspapers out of the corner of his eye. "Oh, shit," he said, kissed her nose, her cheek. "This is bad."

Yasmine Poole had made good on her threat. Racks of newspapers ringed the kiosk, and every single one of them had their pictures plastered all over the front pages, beneath six-inch headlines that screamed TERRORISTES. They'd used her California driver's license and Ry's photo from his DEA badge.

Something like a premonition made Zoe turn just then and look back at the Air de la Russie. She saw Anthony Lovely pick up his coffee with one hand, while he shook open his newspaper with the other. The Starbucks cup stopped in midair, and his head jerked around to peer out the window.

"Really, really bad, Ry. Anthony Lovely just made us."

"I know you're scared," Ry said, his voice calm, and he smoothed the loose wisps of hair off her forehead with his fingertips. "But there's a metro entrance not far from here. We're going to walk there as if we haven't a care in the world, unless someone starts yelling. Then we run like hell."

36

Z OE HALF-EXPECTED Anthony Lovely to run out of his shop after them, yelling, "Stop, terrorists!" but he didn't.

They made it to the metro without any commotion at all. Ry stopped at one of the underground shops and bought her a large, plain black scarf—to cover her head, he said—but she barely registered what he was doing. She felt dazed. All those racks upon racks of newspapers with her face on them, branding her a terrorist. She wanted it to be happening to another Zoe, one whose troubles she could make go away just by turning off her TV set.

"We really need those fake passports now," Ry said, as he helped to tie the scarf around her head so that it completely covered her hair. "This guy I know, Kareem, he's got the soul of a Barbary pirate, but he's the best there is at forging documents, and his mother Fatama is a master of disguise. Their lab, though, is near the Porte St.-Denis. It's a Muslim neighborhood now, and it's been declared a *zone urbaine sensible*—that's a euphemism for a no-go zone, as in the cops won't go in there anymore, because of the riots and car burnings they've had there lately. So we'll need to take a few precautions, all right?"

"You take me to all the nicest places," she said, trying to smile, but it didn't come out right. She was scared, deep down scared. "Just don't leave me, though, okay?"

He cupped her face, tilting her head back so he could look into her eyes. "I'm gonna be right beside you every step of the way, Zoe. All the way through to the end. And you know I can kick butt, because you've seen me do it, maybe even better than you."

She managed to smile at that.

But when they came up out of the metro station, all her fear came rushing back, because it looked like a war zone. Blackened corpses of cars were everywhere, some still smoldering. Rocks, some the size of softballs, littered the street.

Zoe kept her head down and they walked quickly, Ry gripping her upper arm, and she knew his other hand was wrapped around the gun in his pocket. *This is his life*, Zoe thought. *This is what it's like all the time for him.* How could he bear it?

A rusty washing machine lay on the sidewalk, its guts spilling out, and they had to walk out into the street to get around it. A block later they had to go around a refrigerator.

"Why do they just throw their stuff out in the street like that?" Zoe whispered.

"They drop them out of the windows onto the heads of the firemen and paramedics."

Zoe now wished she hadn't asked. She lowered her head even more and tried to keep from breaking into a run.

They passed a burnt-out school, then ducked down the basement steps of a government housing project. The door at the bottom of the steps opened in front of them, as if by magic, just long enough for them to slip quickly through. Then it swung shut with a loud snap of a lock, and Zoe jumped.

They found themselves in one large room, half the size of a basketball court. On one side was an array of computers, printers, and hologram and embossing machines. On the other side were tables strewn with wigs, fake beards and mustaches, tubes of skin dye, palettes of paints, and pots of glue. And underneath the tables, on the floor, bin after bin of prosthetic noses, chins, ears.

A tall, bearded man, who was sitting at a computer table, spoke to them without turning around. "This morning I am eating my muesli and watching your face all over CNN, and I think to myself, 'Kareem, you are a fool. You should be charging him double.'"

"You do and I'll tell your mother," Ry shot back. "She always did say you'd come to a bad end."

A tiny, ageless woman in a beautiful, flowing blue hijab came up to

Zoe and took her hand. "Come. My name is Fatama. While the men drink tea and see which one has the smarter mouth, I will make you a new face."

—————————

FIVE HOURS LATER, Zoe was in the Charles de Gaulle Airport, staring at the metal pole barrier that isolated the passport control booths from the departure area. You had pass through them first, before you could take yourself and your bags through security, and the lines were long, snaking into the seating area.

Okay, you can do this, Zoe, she told herself. *You've got your ticket and your boarding pass in your hot little hand, so all you got to do is make it through security. You're going to walk up there and get in line, and smile at the man when he asks to see your passport, like you haven't got a care in the world.*

She joined the tail end of the nearest line just as her face popped up on the TV set that hung suspended from the ceiling above the lounge chairs. She couldn't read the French that was scrolling across the screen, except for that one horrible word. *Terroristes.*

Zoe ducked her head and turned away, as if the TV set itself might suddenly spot her and start blaring an alarm.

You can do this, Zoe. You can do this. . . .

But her feet seemed to have other ideas. Her feet left the passport control line and headed for a door sporting the ubiquitous blue silhouette of a woman in an A-line dress.

She stopped as the restroom door swung shut behind her and drew in a deep breath, feeling such an onrush of fear and despair it nearly drove her to her knees. How was she ever going to get out of this mess? The whole world thought she was a terrorist, but she didn't know what exactly they thought she had done. What the charges would be, or what chance she would have to prove her innocence.

But then, innocence or guilt, what did it matter? They would kill her long before she got to trial.

You can do this. She *would* do it. Her feet would go back out there and get in that line because she had to. Getting on the plane was her only option now.

She went to one of the sinks, turned on the tap, and splashed cold water on her face. She looked up and froze, startled by the stranger's face she saw in the mirror. A girl with short, spiked black hair dyed purple at the ends. Sallow skin and dark eyes the color of bruises. A ring piercing one eyebrow, a stud in her nose.

━━━━━

SHE WASN'T SURE how long she stood there, staring into the mirror. Her mind seemed to just drift away for a while. But then a loudspeaker high in the wall crackled something in French, snapping her back into the moment.

She tore her gaze off the punk-rocker girl in the mirror and shut off the tap. She dried her hands on her jeans because those blower machines were useless and headed for the door.

She was going to do this. She'd get through security and then she'd be home free. For a while, at least.

The lines were much shorter at the passport control stations now, only three people deep. Zoe hadn't seen Ry since they'd caught separate cabs to the airport, and had that ride ever been the loneliest hour of her life. But there he was, putting his carry-on onto the X-ray machine's conveyor belt. Fatama had put him in a salt-and-pepper wig and beard, and an old man's potbelly. He shuffled along, stoop-shouldered and looking crotchety, and it made her smile.

Then the smile froze on her face.

Four men of the French Sûreté Nationale were coming down the corridor. They carried submachine guns and scanned the crowd with narrowed, intense eyes. One of them had a piece of paper imprinted with the photographs of a man and a woman in his hand, and he was comparing it to the faces of those he passed. Zoe wondered if it was possible to faint from fear.

How can they recognize me? I've got purple hair and a gold stud in my nose.

Only one person was ahead of her in line now, a man wearing a maroon sweat outfit and with long, slicked-back hair that looked as if it hadn't been washed since Christmas. The man in the booth had already

given him his ticket and passport back, but maroon guy lingered, bab-
bling in French about God knew what.

Come on. Come on . . .

Zoe looked over her shoulder. The cops had turned off the corridor
and were coming right at her now, walking fast, one of them talking ex-
citedly into his shoulder radio.

Maroon guy laughed, said something more, and slapped his passport against his palm. Then at last, at last, he picked up his carry-on
and started to walk away. Zoe stepped up and handed her airline ticket
and passport to the man in the booth. She was Marjorie Ridgeway, from
Brighton, England. What if he asked her a question, though? Could
she fake a British accent? Her hair in the passport photo was short and
black, but it wasn't purple on the ends. Fatama had said that would be
too much; it would raise a red flag. Nobody ever looked exactly like his
or her passport photo.

The man in the booth opened her passport, looked at her photograph, looked at her, looked at her photograph. Behind her, Zoe heard
the crackle of excited chatter on the cop's radio.

The man in the booth was looking at her ticket now. Round-trip
to Budapest and back on Malév airlines, leaving at 1850 from Gate 15.
She'd bought a round-trip because one-ways also raised red flags.

What was taking him so long? Oh, God, now he was looking at her
passport again.

She heard a shout and the thud of running booted feet behind her.
She whirled, stricken nearly deaf and blind with fear. The cops were
coming right at her, and she started to raise her hands in surrender because she didn't want them to shoot.

Then they were running past her, through the throng around the
security machines, and out a door that led down to the tarmac.

She heard someone say, *"Mademoiselle?"*

She looked around to see the man in the booth, holding out her
passport and ticket. "Have a pleasant flight," he said, and smiled.

———

ZOE SANK DOWN into her seat, still shaking inside, sure she'd sweated off five pounds in the last five minutes. But she'd made it onto the plane, and Ry, too—she'd spotted him seven rows down, while she was stowing her satchel under the seatback in front of her.

She drew in a deep breath and looked out the window. The lights from the ground-control vehicles shone in red, white, and blue streamers on the wet tarmac. America. Home. She wanted to be back in San Francisco, curled up on the sofa in her loft with Barney and Bitsy purring away beside her, taking turns rolling onto their backs so she could give their bellies a rub.

She felt a presence beside her, heard a woman's voice, and she twisted around fast, nearly coming up out of her seat.

But it was only the flight attendant, who smiled and said, "I asked if you would like a magazine. I've only the one left in English. *Vanity Fair.*"

Zoe took the magazine, more to be polite than anything else. What she really wanted was a drink. Straight vodka, easy on the ice, thank you very much.

She started to slip the magazine into the seat pocket in front of her, then her eyes fell on the face of the man on the cover, and she nearly gasped out loud.

She couldn't believe it, it simply couldn't be, but it was.

It was the third man in the film, the one in the railroad uniform, the one who'd taken the rifle from Ry's dad, broken it down, put it in a toolbox, and then walked away with it, into the sunset. The flaring eyebrows, the pronounced widow's peak that pointed like an arrow to the hooked beak of a nose, the full lips that looked too Angelina Jolie for a man. He was much older now, nearly fifty years older, but it was still him.

The man who had helped to kill President John Fitzgerald Kennedy.

Zoe spread the magazine out on her lap with shaking hands. She read the subhead, and this time she did gasp out loud.

MILES TAYLOR, AMERICA'S KINGMAKER.

37

New York City

MILES TAYLOR picked up the steaming coffee his secretary had deposited by his elbow and took a sip, his mouth puckering. It was just the way he liked it, black and thick as tar pitch. He winced as he levered himself out of his favorite tufted brown leather wing chair and limped to the library window, bringing the coffee with him.

He looked down on Central Park and a grove of gray, withered birches. He spotted only one hardy jogger out on the path that wove through the trees. The street directly below him, though, was bustling with yellow cabs and scurrying pedestrians. The morning's snowfall had already turned to a sooty slush, and gray, saggy clouds hung low over the rooftops.

The whole damn world's gone gray on me. Gray clouds, gray trees, gray snow.

Yasmine. She should have called from Paris by now, called to tell him the Dmitroff girl had been found and dealt with and the film destroyed. Yet both the cell in his pocket and the telephone that sat on his massive antique partner's desk stayed ominously silent.

He hated this, hated not having control, hated having to wait for the ring of a telephone.

It's Nikolai, he thought. *The bastard's beat Yasmine to the girl. He's got the film, and now he's gonna try to use it. Either he'll bleed me dry, or he'll figure out a way to use me. Well, fuck that, because it's not gonna happen. Not this time.*

He thought back, so many years ago now, to the angry young man he had once been. And to the Russian who had come into his life and known just what it would take to buy his soul.

━━━━━━━

THE FIRST TIME he met Nikolai Popov, it was a crisp, sunny December day in 1951.

Miles had gotten a track-and-field scholarship to Boston College out of high school, but he blew out his knee going over the hurdles during his very first meet. So after that, the only way he could manage the tuition was to take just a couple of classes a semester, in between working construction jobs down at the harbor.

It was good times, though. He crashed with five other guys in a run-down Victorian apartment building on the edge of Chestnut Hill and lived off peanut butter and cans of pork 'n' beans. Got laid when he could, which wasn't often because the kind of girl that caught his eye— girls with class and money and pedigrees that went back four generations—they didn't often put out for schmucks like him.

Miles had this one Jesuit professor, Father Patrick Meaney, who was young and hip and a political activist, and who seemed to take a particular liking to him, claiming Miles was some kind of economic genius and pretending that he cared. One night, after his econ theory class, Father Pat invited Miles back to his place for a brandy, and to continue "our discussion on reflexivity in the marketplace."

To Miles's surprise, Father Pat had invited another guest over for a drink that night, too, a Russian he introduced as Nikolai Popov, who was supposed to be some sort of economic adviser attached to the Russian embassy in Washington. Miles figured the guy for a spy right off, though, because weren't they all spies?

The funny thing was, they did talk about reflexivity in the marketplace that night. At one point, Miles leaned back in his chair, pleased with the argument he'd just made—that the biases of individuals enter into market transactions, potentially changing the fundamentals of the economy—when he realized his professor had left the room and he was alone with the Russian.

"Poor Father Pat," Nikolai Popov said, as he leaned over to pour more brandy into Miles's glass. "He is in bad trouble with his bishop these days. It seems he may be consorting with some members of the Communist Party. Real card-carrying members."

"Like yourself?" Miles said.

Popov smiled and shrugged. "I foresee a reassignment in his future. To some mission in deepest, darkest Africa, I fear. What is it you Americans say? Better dead than Red?"

Miles waved away the idea with his glass, slopping brandy onto his hand. "Aw, most of that radical stuff he spouts in class—it's just for show. I doubt he really believes in half of it."

The Russian raised an amused eyebrow. "You think not? And what do you believe in, young Miles? Or for you, too, is it all just for show?"

"Nothing," Miles said, as he tried surreptitiously to wipe the brandy off his hand and onto his pant leg. "I don't believe in anything."

"Not anything?" Popov pursed his lips and tilted his head, as if he found the younger man quite amusing. It was starting to piss Miles off. "No, I think you believe rather wholeheartedly in money. The power of money."

"Money can't buy happiness," Miles said, not believing a word of it, of course, but then he rarely told people what he really thought.

"Enough of it can buy you anything."

Miles shrugged, conceding the point.

Popov took a sip of brandy, let the silence build, then said, "We have spoken of Father Pat's future, but what of yours? Boston College is a fine school, but it is neither Harvard nor Yale. And you will not get a position with a firm such as Wertheim and Company on wishing and hoping alone. You need connections. An in."

"I know people."

"Really? And how do you know these people, Miles? From parking their cars for them during summer parties at the Vineyard? From seeing them drop by your father's Oak Bluffs service station for a tune-up? These same people, who after your father deserted your family, didn't even think enough of your mother to give her a job cleaning their toilets."

Miles felt his face burn with shame and he hated the man for being able to do that to him. "Fuck 'em, then," he said, his lips stiff. "I don't need them."

"No, what you need is to *be* one of them, and that can never happen. You don't even exist for them. They drive up to your papa's service station in the summer, and you fill up the tanks of their big, fancy cars, and they don't see you. They look at you and give you money for the gas, but they never see you. You could drop dead at their feet, and they wouldn't give a shit."

Miles wanted to punch his fist through the guy's face, but he said and did nothing.

"That is why you stole the Kennedy boy's car that summer you were twelve," Popov went on. "You went for a joyride and wrecked it just a little, yes? But he sent a gofer down to the police station to deal with it, he didn't even press charges, and that rankled, didn't it, Miles? It rankles to this day. Because you took that car to make all of them see you, to prove you mattered, and yet . . ." Popov snapped his fingers. "*That* is how little you mattered."

Miles's mouth stretched into a travesty of a smile. "Who gives a fuck what happened when I was twelve? Someday I'm going to be richer than the Kennedys, richer than any of those arrogant assholes can hope to dream of."

Popov smiled that damn smile again. "And how will you accomplish that? You have a little over twenty-four thousand in the bank, which has come from playing the market—quite ingeniously I might add—with the few dollars you've managed to scrape together. But in the world you wish to enter, twenty-four thousand is pissing money."

"How do you know all this stuff? Just who in the hell are you?"

"Don't ask stupid questions. You know I do more for my embassy than advise them on which way the capitalist winds will blow when the markets open tomorrow. . . . As I was saying, you are about to embark on your career with a degree and twenty-four thousand dollars to your name. Not bad for a boy like you, who comes from nothing. But it is peanuts and you know it is peanuts. You know the only way to make real money is to have real money to begin with, like the Du Ponts have, and the Rockefellers and the Gettys."

"Okay," Miles said after a moment. "Why don't we cut through all the bullcrap, Mr. Popov? What are you willing to give me, and what do I have to do to get it?"

―――――――――――

WHAT ARE YOU willing to give me . . .

What Nikolai Popov had given him was the seed money, and the kind of insider trading, that he needed to play the markets in ways that really counted for something. Popov also gave Miles a mission: to search out and develop ties within the policy-making circles at the highest levels of the U.S. government. And once inside those circles, he was to feed whatever intel he came across back to Moscow. The deal served both men well. At least in the beginning.

Miles got filthy rich, and with each billion came a power and influence on Wall Street and within the corridors of Congress and the Oval Office beyond even his wildest dreams. In return, Popov had collected on his investment in the currency of all spies everywhere: information.

How many national secrets had Miles spilled into the Russian's ears over the years? Enough to get him hanged a thousand times over, and that didn't even count the murder of a president.

The grandfather clock in the corner began to strike, and Miles started so violently he spilled coffee down the front of his suit coat. He brushed at it with his hand, smearing it into the gray silk cashmere. He swore. Custom-made in Savile Row, it had cost him five thousand bucks, and even that ruinously expensive French cleaner his secretary took his clothes to on the Upper West Side might not be able to get the stain out.

Fuck this. If Yasmine didn't call in the next five minutes, he was calling Nikolai. Better to know right off if Nikolai had the film, and then he could exert some control over the situation.

It was almost funny when you thought about it. He'd watched it all go down, live and in living color, but the only images he could ever call to his mind were the still prints Mike O'Malley had made from that damn film. Of himself in that stupid railroad uniform, taking the rifle from Mike's hands.

Yasmine was right. He had believed the con was all his, that he'd played and manipulated Nikolai Popov and the KGB into carrying out the assassination. But when it came to Popov, he should have suspected that there were wheels within wheels.

Especially when Popov forced him to take part in the dirty work, by threatening to expose him as a commie spy if he refused. Putting him in the frame, figuratively. And literally, too, as it turned out. Thanks to O'Malley and that damn film.

Miles turned and limped back to the desk, stared down at the telephone. Black and simple, and checked by his security twice a day for bugs, its number known by only a handful of people in the world.

Ring, damn you. Ring.

———————————

IT DIDN'T RING.

He went around the desk and sat down, the leather of his captain's chair sighing softly beneath his weight. He pulled the telephone toward him, lifted the receiver, waited a few seconds more, then dialed the number of a telephone on the other side of the world that would also probably be plain and black and checked for bugs twice a day.

It rang four times, there was a click, but he heard no one at the other end of the line. No *"Da?"* or the more formal *"Zdraste."* Just silence.

"Nikolai?" Miles listened for the smallest intake of breath, for any show of surprise, but what he heard was soft laughter.

"Miles, is that really you? Of course it is you. But why are you telephoning after all this time? What do you want?"

"Can't an old friend call up to see how you're doing?"

"How many years has it been since last we spoke? Twenty-five, thirty? A loyal comrade falls out of favor and he is dropped like a—what is it you Americans say? A hot tamale? And now suddenly you are ringing me up to see how I am doing?"

"Potato," Miles said. "Dropped like a hot potato."

Nikolai blew out a long, sad sigh. "Since you are kind enough to ask after my health, I am alive. And at my age that is quite the accomplishment. Mostly, though, I am content to sit and look out at the lovely pond in my garden, at water so blue you cannot tell where it leaves off and the sky begins. Or rather I would be if it were not February and the pond was not strangled with ice."

Miles watched a pigeon fly into view, land on the windowsill, and then crap all over it. "You must be bored shitless."

Nikolai laughed. "Well, I do still dabble in a few things. On the occasion."

The pigeon flew off. Miles said, "Is that what you were doing in San Francisco? Dabbling? Because, if so, you've lost your touch."

For a second or two, all Miles heard was static. Hesitation on Popov's part? Or merely a hiccup with the satellite?

Then, "I am afraid you have lost me, Miles. I haven't been to your delightful country in years."

"Cut the crap, Nikki. I might be late to the party, but I know all about O'Malley's forty-nine-year bluff now. He never had the film. At least not for long. His woman ran off on him and took it with him, lo these many moons ago."

More static, then, "Here you are, America's Kingmaker, and I am but the son of a poor Russian peasant, yet I am, as always, one step ahead of you. Indeed, you are right, I knew all along about Katya Orlova, and that she had the film. And now you think that because she is dead, I must have it, and you are calling to see what my price will be."

"I don't care what your price is, I'm not paying it."

"But, my dear Miles, you are such a testimonial to the wonders of capitalism. Whereas I am forced to live off a measly government pension and the dubious charity of a son who is little better than a murderer and a thief. Surely you can spare a billion or two? You have so many."

"The thing is, I don't think you have the film, Nikki. I think your guy botched it and killed her before he could get her to say where she'd stashed it. Did you know that she was already dying of cancer?"

Nikolai heaved another mock sigh. "My man lost his temper. The bitch stabbed him with a whiskey bottle—can you believe it? It isn't like the old days. One simply cannot find competence in the assassination business anymore. . . . But you are right, of course, I do not have the film. At least not yet. I should have known better than to try to fool you, Miles."

"You've been fooling me from the very beginning, you bastard. Tell me about the altar of bones."

"The altar of what?" Not a second's hesitation this time, not even a second's worth of static.

"O'Malley talked about the big kill with his son the priest the day he died. He said you ordered it done because he drank from the altar of bones, and that made him dangerous to the world."

"Poor Mr. O'Malley. He must have been delirious, because I've never heard of this thing. This altar."

Miles hadn't expected to get the truth out of Nikolai. He could fly to St. Petersburg and try to choke it out of the man, and still he would get nothing.

"You're a lying sack of shit, Nikki."

"No, you are lying to yourself. You needed to believe it had everything to do with Cold War politics and money, but for you that was the least of it. You *wanted* him dead, Miles, and not for the millions you stood to make out of it. You wanted him dead because you hated him. He was the golden boy. Sun-kissed, rich, handsome, and meant for great things. And you couldn't bear it."

"No," Miles said, but he knew that it was true.

He laid the phone back in its cradle, breaking the connection without a good-bye.

A bare second later the telephone rang beneath his hand, and Miles jumped, his heart pounding.

Yasmine, he prayed. *Please, God, let it be Yasmine.*

38

R Y PULLED the rental car to a stop across the entrance to a narrow, cobblestoned street. They were in the heart of the Józsefváros district, a part of Budapest where decaying Hapsburg mansions rubbed shoulders with grim Soviet-era apartment buildings. And whores and struggling musicians shared the sidewalks with plumbers and electricians.

He cut the ignition and waited. The only sound he could hear was the ticking of the car's engine as it cooled. The empty street dead-ended into the wall of a cemetery. Ry did not like dead ends.

"Are you sure this is the place? I don't see anyone," Zoe said, just as the door to a nearby house crashed open and four enormous bruisers with shaved heads and hard, hooded eyes came out. It was the biggest house on the block, and its crumbling stucco had recently been painted a bright marzipan yellow.

As he watched the men come toward them, Ry raised his hands slowly and put them on the steering wheel. "Keep your hands out in the open, where they can see them."

"Oookay," Zoe said, and Ry heard the fear rising in her voice.

"They're not going to hurt us. They're just checking us out."

The men circled the car like dogs around a fire hydrant. They all carried guns in shoulder holsters under their coats, but they weren't acting as if they intended to take them out. Yet.

"The man we're meeting here," Ry said, "his name is Agim Latifi, and he's one of Eastern Europe's biggest arms smugglers. He's also one of the ugliest guys you'll ever see in your life. You ever seen a picture of a blobfish? Well, he's like that, only uglier."

Ry was joking around to put her at ease, but he was worried. It had been four years since he'd last seen Agim, and the French government was offering a reward of ten thousand euros for a tip leading to their arrest.

The goons finished circling the car. One motioned at them to get out.

They followed the men up the street. Ry heard a dog bark, then, from the open window of a house farther down the street, the incessant base beat of the Hungarian rap group Belga, singing "Az a Baj."

They went through the door of the yellow house, into a hall whose best days had been three centuries ago. Paint was peeling off the walls in strips, and the parquet floors were warped and stained. Ry could see no furniture anywhere.

With two men in front and two behind, they walked up worn marble stairs, through a pair of wood-paneled double doors, and into a dazzling, sun-filled room. Ry blew out a low whistle.

"Wow," Zoe said. "I feel like I should be wearing a ball gown and dancing the waltz."

Ry did a slow turn, taking in the deeply coffered ceilings and the garlanded friezes of carved and gilded fruit. "It was a ballroom once. He's restored it to all its former glory."

Before one of the floor-to-ceiling windows was a round table set with white linen, flower-patterned china, and a silver coffee service. A man sat at the table, reading the newspaper.

"Agim, you bastard," Ry yelled across the room. "Where are the violins? How do you expect Zoe and me to dance if you don't give us violins?"

Agim Latifi tossed the newspaper onto the floor and was out of his chair and onto Ry in three strides.

"My brother!" he shouted, wrapping Ry up in a bone-crushing hug. "It is fucking good to see you."

Ry could feel his face cracking into a big smile. His friend hadn't changed; he was still Agim.

Behind him, Ry heard Zoe mutter, "Yeah, he's ugly as sin all right," and Ry grinned to himself, because Agim Latifi looked as if he'd just stepped off the page of a perfume ad, with his head of thick, black curls, the dark, liquid eyes fringed with thick lashes, and a full-lipped mouth parted open to show off dazzling white teeth. He had on a white, silky shirt with flowing sleeves that seemed to go with the ballroom and was open at the throat to show off a lot of smooth skin tanned a golden brown.

"And this is your new woman," he said, turning to Zoe and hitting her with a smile that rocked her back on her heels. "I thought, Ry, my brother, from the way you described her to me over the telephone that she just may be your One. And now that I see her, I know it is so."

Ry felt his ears burn. He made a mental note to never again talk about love with a Kosovo Albanian over a bottle of ouzo at three in the morning.

"Miss Zoe Dmitroff, I am pleased to meet you." Agim leaned over, brought her hand up to his mouth, and kissed it. "I am Agim Latifi, and I would steal you away if you were not Ry O'Malley's woman. But I will behave, because although he is not my brother by blood, he is my blood brother. Do you understand what I mean by this?"

Zoe, still looking a bit dazed, said, "You've shed blood for each other. Your own and your enemies'."

Agim slapped Ry hard on the shoulder with the flat of his hand, and Ry felt it clear to the bone. "What did I tell you, brother? She is the One."

Ry opened his mouth to set his friend straight, then shut it. Some things were better off just left alone.

"This is a beautiful room," Zoe said.

"Thank you. I am restoring the house little bit by little bit. I think, though, that it will take me a lifetime and cost me several fortunes." He waved a hand toward the view out the window, of a garden choked with ivy and fig trees. "Perhaps I will tackle the courtyard next. They say that during the Soviet siege at the end of World War Two, many hundreds of Hungarian soldiers were buried in the courtyards throughout the city."

Ry looked around the room again, wondering where the money had come from. He thought he'd been exaggerating when he'd told Zoe that

Agim Latifi was the biggest arms smuggler in Eastern Europe, but now he wasn't so sure.

"Come," Agim said, linking his arm through Zoe's and leading her toward the table. "Let us have breakfast. There are small scones baked with cheese and potatoes, called *pogácsa*. And these," he said, as he pulled out her chair, "are sweet sponge cakes filled with cottage cheese and raisins. I suggest you take one now, Miss Dmitroff, before Ry eats them all."

Agim poured coffee in a thick black stream from the silver pot into their dainty china cups. Ry bit into a sponge cake and nearly swooned, it tasted so good.

"Now, to business," Agim said, "for I know you are short of time."

He bent over and took a wooden box from beneath the table. "First guns. You said you want trustworthy, not fancy, so I have for you two Model 19 Glocks. With two dozen ammo clips for each."

Ry took one of the pistols out of the box, already liking the feel of it in his hand, the way it slid right in and became a part of him, hard and cold and deadly. "The one thing about jet-setting around in this day and age is how much of a pain in the ass it is to get a new gun every time you hit a new place."

Agim grinned. "That is why it helps to know an arms smuggler."

Ry nodded with his chin at the box. "That's a lot of ammo. Were you expecting us to have to fight a war?"

Agim shrugged. "You are Americans. It is what you do."

Ry laughed. "Fair enough."

Zoe was checking out the other Glock, snapping back the slide, looking down the sights, getting a feel for the grip, testing the weight of the trigger pull. Agim watched her, smiling like a parent whose kid just aced her piano recital.

"As for this little trouble you are having with the French Sûreté Nationale, these accusations of terrorism . . ." Agim waved his hand through the air as if they were mere bagatelles. "My man inside Hungarian security tells me they have indeed received an official communiqué from Paris last evening warning them of your possible entry into this country. At the moment it is wending its way through channels, stopping at every desk to be read and initialed. You could live out your years and die an old man here in Budapest before they get around to looking for you."

"I don't need years, just a day," Ry said. But the trouble was, if the antiques dealer Anthony Lovely had talked to the French cops, and if Yasmine Poole had an in with them—and Ry would bet that she did—then she would know where they were headed. And she wouldn't have to wade through any bureaucratic red tape to be hot on their trail.

"Our meeting with Denis Kuzmin is set for this afternoon," he said. "What were you able to find out about him?"

"He is the son of a Budapest woman and a Soviet soldier who was part of the occupying army after the war. The father deserted the family and went back to his homeland when the boy was eleven. His mother was a gymnastics trainer for the Hungarian women's Olympics team throughout the Cold War years, so they didn't want for much.

"Kuzmin is in his sixties now, and a man of some wealth. Up until last year he was a professor of Russian folklore and mythology at our Eötvos Loránd University. Now he is retired and living in a small villa about twenty kilometers from here, on a hill overlooking the Danube and a little town called Szentendre. He was married once, years ago, and they had a son, but the marriage fell apart when the baby died of crib death."

"And he collects icons," Ry said.

Agim flashed a brilliant smile. "Indeed he does, my brother. He is famous for it."

Agim slathered clotted cream on a sponge cake and handed it to Zoe with a smile that made her blink. "There is one other thing you should know about Denis Kuzmin. There are rumors that before the fall of the Berlin Wall, he was an informant for the AVO. The Hungarian secret police."

Agim paused and looked off into the distance, thinking, then shrugged. "Perhaps his spying is the real source of his wealth, who knows? He would have been well paid surely for rooting out dissidents among the students and his fellow professors, listening for subversive remarks, since the seeds of revolution most often germinate within the universities. These people he informed on, they would have been sent to a 'psychological hospital' to be reeducated, but no matter what they chose to call it, it was only a sweeter word for prison. If the chance comes your way, my brother, you might want to kill him."

"We'd kind of like to stay under the radar while we're here, if we can help it," Ry said, reevaluating his first impression of Denis Kuzmin. In his mind he'd pictured a retired professor who pored over dusty old books and collected icons. But if he'd been an informant for the AVO, then he could be dangerous.

"You must have another cake," Agim said to Zoe. "Two is not enough. And while you eat, I will tell you the story of how Ry and I became brothers, since he probably did not think to tell you himself."

Zoe washed down the last bite of sponge cake number two with coffee and reached for sponge cake number three. "You've heard of the Silent Buddha?" she said. "Well, Ry could give that guy a run for his money."

Agim let loose a hearty laugh and slapped Ry on the back.

"The story begins four years ago in Kosovo," Agim said to Zoe. "When the bombs stopped falling. With the monster Milosevic gone, it was not long before you Americans and your allies discovered that the former freedom fighters you supported had turned the place into a drug smugglers' paradise. My people, the Kosovo Albanians, we make up what is called the Fifteen Families, and these families are now importing eighty percent of Europe's heroin. We call it *Albanka*. The Albanian Lady."

"I've heard of it," Zoe said, and Ry thought that given what her mother was, she probably knew more about Albanian Lady than she wanted to.

"One of the Fifteen Families was headed by a man named Armend Brozi," Agim went on. "The American drug enforcement agency set up an operation with their counterparts in Germany to bring this man down, and Ry, he was the one put in charge of it. He needed someone to go undercover, as you say, but the Fifteen Families . . . It is impossible for anyone not Kosovo Albanian to worm their way inside, you understand? For that, Ry chose me, and I did it willingly. No, hungrily."

Agim fell silent, staring down at his hands, which were balled into fists on the table. After a moment, Zoe asked, "Because it was personal?"

Agim swallowed, nodded. "I had a sister. Her name was Bora, which means 'snow,' and it was a good name for her. Not because she was pure—no, far from that. But because she was beautiful in the way that snow is beautiful when it is lying fresh and white and heavy on the rooftops of our village. Armend Brozi made my sister his whore, and when he tired of her, he turned her into a mule. He made her swallow condoms full of heroin and carry them in her belly through customs. On her last trip one of the condoms broke inside her, and she died on the filthy floor of a bathroom in JFK airport."

Zoe reached out to touch the back of Agim's hand where it lay on the white tablecloth. "Did you make him pay?"

Agim's smile was both sad and cruel. "Oh, yes, I made him pay. On the day when we took Armend Brozi down, Ry arranged it so that only I was there to kill him. He died like my sister died, slowly and in much pain. This is what Ry did for me, and this is why I call him my brother."

The room fell into silence, then Agim shrugged. "Afterward, it was too dangerous for me to be in Kosovo, but I had family here in Budapest and so this is where I came. Now I am getting rich selling guns to insurgents throughout the world, who buy them with the money they have made running drugs. Which makes me a hypocrite, but what can you do?"

———

LATER, AS THEY were walking back to where Ry had left the car, Agim snagged his arm, holding him back and letting Zoe go on ahead of them.

"Now that I have met her, Ry," Agim said in a half-whisper, his eyes glinting with poorly suppressed humor, "I can say this with absolute certainty. She is the One."

Ry kicked at a loose cobblestone. He wanted to kick himself. "Hell, Agim. I barely know her."

Agim shook his head, his face serious now. "You have learned more about her in these last two days than many lovers come to know of each other in a lifetime. She is your One. So do not be an idiot about it."

39

"MAN, IF these guys were going any slower," Ry said, fighting down the urge to lean on the horn as the ancient Volkswagen bus lumbered around the curve ahead of them, "they'd be traveling backwards."

"Uh-huh," Zoe said. She had the *Vanity Fair* open on her lap and was bent over it, staring at Miles Taylor's face, trying to crawl inside the man's head. Get inside his soul.

"At least they are taking in the view," Ry went on, as the road opened up to a stunning vista of wooded hills and the winding Danube River.

"I'm looking, O'Malley," Zoe said. "But I'm also thinking."

"Oh-oh."

"If America's Kingmaker once helped a Soviet agent assassinate President Kennedy, then what's he doing to the country now with all his power and influence and money? For all we know he might still be working for the KGB, or whatever they call themselves these days—"

"The FSB. Federalnaya Sluzhba Bezopasnosti."

She waved a hand. "Whatever. He can tell it to the judge after we expose him. But what I've been thinking is, how *do* we expose him? We could turn the film over to somebody in the government, like the CIA. But, oh, wait, the triggerman was one of their agents, who just also happened to be a KGB mole—"

A horn blew behind them. Ry glanced in the rearview mirror and saw a red Mini Cooper darting back and forth across the center line, wanting to pass both him and the VW bus, but not quite ballsy enough to try to do it blind.

"It's possible they found out my dad was a mole a long time ago," he said. "They might even know he was the man on the grassy knoll. But whatever they know now or knew then, you got to figure the minute the assassination happened, people started covering their asses all up and down the chain of command, from the CIA to the cops in Dallas, because they *let* it happen. Take the Secret Service, for instance. Never mind that they let the president ride around in an open convertible that day; as soon as the first shot was fired, the guy behind the wheel should've floored it and gotten the hell out of there. Instead, he practically came to a complete stop to look around, I suppose. Who knows? But that left Kennedy and everybody else in the car just sitting there like wooden ducks in a shooting gallery."

Zoe rolled the magazine up into a tight cylinder and turned to look out the window. "See, that's what I'm most afraid of, Ry. We give them the film, they tell us we need to consider what's best for the country, yada, yada, and then they turn around and bury it."

"Babe, they're gonna bury it so deep, the only way it'll ever see the light of day again is if some kid in China accidentally uncovers it while digging around in his backyard."

"While we'll spend the rest of our lives locked up in a cage somewhere."

The Mini Cooper honked again, and the VW bus retaliated by belching a cloud of black smoke and slowing down even more as they started around yet another bend in the road. Ry braked and forced his hands to relax their death grip on the wheel.

He said, "We could take it to the media. I know a guy who works for the *Washington Post* who's pretty good. He's smart, thorough, and not easily intimidated. And whatever his personal biases are, he seems able to keep them from bleeding into his stories."

They came out of the curve, and at last Ry saw straight road and no oncoming traffic ahead. He pressed down on the gas pedal and was within a split second of pulling out around the van when the Mini Cooper blew by them. The guy behind the wheel gave them the finger, and Ry thought, *Asshole.*

"What an asshole," Zoe said, and Ry laughed.

He said, "We could take the film to my guy, but the trouble is the film is only half of it. It shows who did it, but not why, and he is going to want to know the why before he breaks the story."

"And the minute he starts asking questions," Zoe said, "Miles Taylor is going to have him killed."

"Exactly."

They were quiet for a moment, then Ry said, "There is one guy I know who's powerful and connected enough in his own right that Taylor might have a hard time getting to him. Although, he might not have the juice to get the film exposed—in fact he wouldn't do it if he honestly believed it would hurt the country more than it helped."

"Who is this paragon?"

"Senator Jackson Boone."

Zoe whirled around in her seat to gape at him. "Oh, my God. You know Senator *Boone*?"

"Hey, don't swoon on me here."

"It's just . . . *Senator Boone*. People are saying he could be our next president, Ry. How do you know him?"

"From when I was in the Special Forces. He was my commanding officer."

Zoe laughed. "You know what I like about you, Ry? You not only speak fifteen languages, but everywhere we go you know 'a guy.' A guy who can get us guns. A guy who can make us fake passports. A guy who is a U.S. senator."

She unrolled the *Vanity Fair* and it fell right open to the Taylor article. Opposite the first page of the text was a photo display, and as she tilted it toward the sunlight that streamed through the window to get a better look, Ry repressed a groan.

The photograph that had her so obsessed was one of Miles Taylor standing alongside the president of the United States, awarding some inner-city educator the Freedom Medal. Behind them a small knot of people were grouped around an American flag, and a little apart from them, as if she'd deliberately stepped back to get out of the picture, was a woman in a bright red suit.

And, okay, maybe she had red hair, but you couldn't really tell because she had it up, and she was so far on the edge of the picture that half her face was cut off and the half you could see was out of focus. But Zoe was sure the woman was Yasmine Poole because she had on a red suit. As if there weren't a million red suits in the world. It had to be a woman thing, he thought.

And, of course, because she could read his mind, Zoe said, "I'm telling you, O'Malley, it's her. It's that same killer designer outfit she had on in Paris."

Ry bit the inside of his cheek to keep from opening his mouth, then said, "Hey, I'm with you, at least as far as Yasmine Poole working for Miles Taylor as his hit man, hit woman, whatever. I'm just saying the woman in that particular photo could be anybody."

Zoe studied the photograph a little longer, then closed up the magazine, put it in the side-door pocket, and uncapped one of the water bottles they'd stocked the car with. As they came around another bend in the road, she pressed her face against the window glass.

"This really is spectacular," she said. "But Strauss got it wrong. The Danube isn't blue, more like a dull, muddy brown."

"It still is blue most of the time. It's probably just got some runoff today from the melting snow."

He let a couple of beats go by, then said, "So Agim is one good-looking dude, wouldn't you say?"

Zoe took a swig of the water. "Really? I hadn't noticed."

Ry FELL IN love with Szentendre at first sight.

"It's almost too charming to be real," he said to Zoe. "Cobbled lanes, red-tiled roofs, brightly painted houses, quaint Orthodox churches. Look, they've even got horse-drawn carriages. I could hire a couple of guys to play violins, buy you one perfect red rose, and we could go for a ride in the moonlight—"

"It's February, O'Malley. Get a grip," Zoe said, but he saw she was smiling. "It's almost two. We need to find Professor Kuzmin's place. Agim said it was on a hill overlooking the river."

They found it easily, but Ry drove by without even slowing. He hung a right, then a left, so that they were on a street parallel and down-hill from the villa. He parked alongside a set of steps that led up to what looked like the wall of a cemetery.

They got out of the car, stretched out the kinks, and looked around them.

Zoe said, "I haven't seen any sign of Yasmine Poole yet. Have you?"

"No. But then we wouldn't."

Ry took the Glock out of the glove compartment where he'd stowed it while he was driving, slipped it into the small of his back, then stuffed the side pockets of his cargo pants with extra ammo clips.

"Are we going to be the Carpenters again? Jake the chauvinist pig and clueless Suzie with a z?" Zoe asked.

Ry shook his head. "No, the only thing the same is going to be the names. I figure this guy's spent years looking for your icon, and the min-ute he lays eyes on it, he's going to want it. If he thinks we're a couple of rubes, things could get nasty. They could get nasty anyway."

Ry took one last look around, then said, "Do you mind waiting by the car for a bit? I want to scout the villa before we go inside. Find the back way out, just in case."

"A plan B." Zoe was grinning and kind of rocking back and forth on the balls of her feet, and Ry thought, *Damn, in spite of everything, she's actually loving this.*

And he smiled to himself, because he was loving it, too.

━━━━━

PROFESSOR DENIS KUZMIN's villa—a two-story stucco painted a pale peach—sat behind a stand of cypress trees and a green wrought-iron fence. The gate was open to the gravel drive, and Ry slipped through without being seen. He circled around to the back and found a door that led out from the kitchen into a vegetable garden and a small apple orchard. On the other side of the orchard was a lane that led to the rear of a church.

He walked down the lane, past the church, and came upon a small cemetery of leaning stone crosses and crumbling monuments. A wall ran along one side of the cemetery, and on the other side of the wall, some stone steps. Ry looked down the steps and saw all but the front end of their rented Beamer, but no Zoe anywhere.

He trotted down the steps, still not seeing Zoe, panic uncurling in his belly. Then he saw the back of her, leaning up against the front bumper. He must've have made some noise because she stood up suddenly and whirled, a bottle of water in one hand, and a Glock in the other, pointed at his heart.

"Jesus Christ, O'Malley, what are you doing? I almost shot you."

"Sorry, I thought you . . . Sorry."

Ry drew in a deep breath and tried to get his racing pulse under control. He needed to get a grip here. He'd let Agim get inside his head with all that talk about the One, and now it was distracting him. And when you got distracted, you not only got yourself killed, you got the people who depended on you killed, too.

"Well, give me some warning next time. I'm a little jumpy here." Zoe slipped the gun back into her satchel. "So what did you find? Have we got us a plan B?"

Ry described the layout of the villa while he got out his Swiss army knife, opened the BMW's passenger-side door, and pushed the seat back as far as it would go so he could get at the center console.

Zoe peered over his shoulder. "What are you doing?"

"Disabling the air bags. I should have done it sooner. At some point we might need to haul ass out of here in a hurry, and if we end up colliding with something along the way, I don't want us to get hit with a faceful of nylon."

"That's probably illegal, what you're doing. But I won't tell."

"Hey, if I go down, sister, I'm taking you with me. Shit, I was afraid of this. I'm gonna have to cut the carpet to get at the control box."

"Fine, but when it comes time to take this sucker back to the rental company, you're on our own." She leaned over so she could stick her head in the car for a closer look. "If we do have to haul ass, though, can I drive?"

Ry laughed at the very idea.

THE DOOR TO the villa was opened by a rather attractive, but cold-eyed, blonde in her fifties, who told them she was the housekeeper and the professor was expecting them. As she led them across a spacious black-and-white-tiled foyer, Ry admired her legs and wondered if perhaps she was the reason why Denis Kuzmin had never remarried.

She showed them into what she called "the professor's library," a room full of sunlight, rich mahogany paneling, and walls of built-in bookshelves.

"What a lovely garden," Zoe said, walking up to a pair of French doors that opened onto a sloping green lawn hedged with hawthorn and azalea bushes.

The housekeeper didn't even crack a smile at the compliment. She said, "The professor will be with you shortly," and left, pulling the double doors to the foyer firmly shut behind her.

Ry took a turn around the room, but saw no other door. "I don't like it that the only other way out of here besides the door leading in from the hall is out through the front garden."

He stopped at the library table that served as the professor's desk. On the wall behind it hung a framed propaganda poster of Joseph Stalin—the famous one of the Great Leader posing with a little apple-cheeked peasant girl. "I wonder if he knows that Stalin ended up having that little girl's father shot," Ry said to Zoe.

"Maybe he doesn't care. Or, since he was an informer himself, maybe he just figures the guy deserved it."

Ry leafed through a stack of manuscript pages that sat next to the professor's computer. "It looks like he's writing a book. On medieval witchcraft in Siberia."

"Hey, don't knock it. For all we know, I might come from a long line of witches."

Zoe walked along the wall of shelves that held not only books but icons of all sizes, some so old most of the paint had worn off, others richly gilded with silver and gold. "He's got some good pieces," she said.

Ry was about to ask her how the professor's collection compared with her mother's when the double doors opened beneath the hand of a small, thin man who looked like central casting's idea of a retired college professor, complete with a red polka-dot bow tie, tweed trousers, and a sweater with elbow patches.

He held out his hand to Ry as he came into the room. "I am Professor Kuzmin. And you are Mr. and Mrs. Carpenter, I take it?" His English was almost accent-free, but he spoke slowly and carefully, as if he dreaded making a single mistake. "Forgive me, but I did not hear your car pull into the drive."

"We came on the HEV," Ry said.

"You climbed all the way up here from the train station?" Pale gray eyes, the color of cement, assessed them from behind thick tortoiseshell glasses, and Ry got the sense Denis Kuzmin sized people up at first meeting, then stood back and waited smugly to be proven right.

He smiled, showing teeth that were small and yellow, like kernels of corn. "Ah, but you are both so young and fit, and it's not too chilly a day for February. So what did you think of Szentendre's town square? Charming, yes?"

"A little too froufrou for my tastes," Ry said, "but my wife was charmed. She wants me to take her for a moonlit ride in one of those horse-drawn carriages."

Kuzmin chuckled. "A romantic sentiment, indeed, Mrs. Carpenter, but you might want to wait for more clement weather." He gestured at a sofa and a pair of flanking armchairs unfortunately upholstered in lurid green velvet. "Shall we sit by the fire?"

Ry paused on the way to study the large, framed print that hung over the mantel. *Kind of a weird thing to put up on the wall in your library,* he thought. But then the Stalin poster wasn't exactly conducive to happy thoughts either.

"I've seen the original of this print hanging in the Tretyakov Gallery in Moscow," Ry said.

Kuzmin sighed almost happily and rocked back and forth on his heels. The professor was about to launch into one of his favorite lectures.

"Ah, yes. Oil on canvas by Ilya Repin, *Ivan the Terrible and His Son Ivan on November 16, 1581.* It captures the moment after the Tsar Ivan, in a fit of uncontrollable rage, has just bludgeoned his son and heir over the head with an iron staff. The father kneels on the floor, cradling the bloodied body of his son. You see the lunacy in his bloodshot eyes, but also the horrible realization of what he has done. By contrast the face of the dead boy is calm, almost Christ-like in death. Fascinating, is it not?"

"And sad," Zoe said.

Ry didn't answer, for he was lost in that terrible moment captured by the artist. The tsar in priestly black, his son dressed in a robe of the purest white. The murder weapon, the iron staff, lying nearby, on the bloodred Oriental carpet.

"You seem particularly interested, Professor, in the more mentally deranged figures from Russian history," Zoe said, picking up from the mantel a silver-framed, black-and-white photograph of a gaunt, bearded man in a long black robe, seated at a desk before an open Bible.

An odd smile pulled at Denis Kuzmin's thin slit of a mouth. "So you recognize the Mad Monk, do you? Grigori Rasputin. Some argue that his influence over the Tsar Nicholas and his wife, Alexandra, led to the Bolshevik revolution and the fall of the Romanov dynasty. He variously has been called a saintly mystic, visionary, healer, and prophet on the one hand. And on the other, a debauched religious charlatan. Perhaps he was all those things, or perhaps—"

He cut himself off as the double doors opened and the housekeeper came in, carrying a tray loaded with three tall glasses, a cut-crystal carafe of water, and a squat, round bottle full of a dark brown, herbal-looking liquid.

"Ah, here is Mrs. Danko with some refreshment. Have you ever tasted Unicum? Some call it our national treasure, although the first-time imbiber might find it a tad bitter."

Bitter, hell. Ry had tried that stuff the last time he was in Budapest. It smelled like a hospital room, tasted like cough medicine, and the hangover he got after only two glasses had been truly spectacular.

"Maybe I'll have some water later, but I'm fine for now," Ry said.

The professor's face fell in disappointment. "Mrs. Carpenter?" he asked, picking up the liquor bottle and a glass.

Zoe flashed her brightest smile. "I'd love to try some, Professor, but I get a headache if I drink in the middle of the day."

He shrugged. "I hope you don't mind if I indulge myself without you."

The professor poured his drink, and they sat down, Ry and Zoe beside each other on the couch and the professor in an armchair. Ry noticed Denis Kuzmin couldn't seem to look at Zoe directly, as if he were afraid of meeting her eyes, of having her see too much in his. He could just be a chauvinist, Ry supposed, but he wondered if something more was going on.

"In your telephone call," Kuzmin said, "you told me you have acquired an icon that you wish for me to study."

"My grandmother gave it to us as a wedding present," Zoe said. "We were told there are often myths and fables attached to particular icons, and we wondered, since ours is so unusual, if maybe there's a story to go along with it, you know? And since this is your area of expertise . . ."

The professor's long, thin nose rose an inch or so into the air. "I have acquired something of a reputation in that regard. And, yes, indeed, some icons in times past had various mystical, even magical, properties attached to them."

Zoe took the sealskin pouch out of her satchel, deliberately letting Kuzmin get a look at her Glock while she did so, and Ry thought, *Smart girl*. But whatever the professor thought about her having a gun, he didn't let it show on his face, and Ry relished the cool, solid feel of his own Glock in the small of his back. He wasn't getting good vibes off this guy.

Zoe propped the icon up on her lap. The professor didn't gasp aloud the way Anthony Lovely had done, but Ry saw the corners of his mouth go white, and the hand that held his glass started to shake.

"Dear God, it's the—" He cut himself off, and Ry saw a vivid, almost gluttonous eagerness flash over his face.

He brought himself back with a jerk, downed a healthy swig of the Unicum, then asked, too casually, "Did your grandmother say how she acquired this particular piece?"

Ry could feel Zoe practically humming on the sofa beside him, and he knew just how she was feeling. His own toes and fingertips were tingling with excitement. What had Kuzmin been about to say about the icon? That it's the Lady? And if he knew about the icon, did he also know about the altar of bones?

"It's been in our family a long time," Zoe said, "passed down from mother to daughter. Grandmother likes to say we are blessed girl children, from a proud long line and none of us can be the last."

Ry got the sense that Katya Orlova had really said those words. Not to Zoe, for they'd never spoken, but to someone else. Anna Larina?

Kuzmin leaned forward, looking hard at Zoe now, as if he could use his pale eyes like lasers to dig into her mind.

"You are the Keeper," he said, and Ry felt Zoe go utterly still.

The professor sat back in his chair, obviously pleased with the reaction he'd gotten. "You wonder, how do I know this? Because I am not a fool. I see the Lady, I see your face."

Zoe cast a quick look at Ry, and he knew that she, too, was thinking again of that line in her grandmother's letter. *Look to the Lady* . . .

"Perhaps," said Professor Kuzmin, "I should start at the beginning. With my father and an event that occurred in the spring of 1936."

40

A T THE time, my father was serving in the GUGB, as the Soviet secret police called itself in those days. That makes him sound more
formidable than he was—a file clerk assigned to one Senior Lieutenant
Nikolai Popov, adjutant to the commissar of the Main Directorate for
State Security in Leningrad. What today we once again call St. Petersburg."

He paused, and his eyes grew moist. Was he remembering the father
who'd deserted him when he was only a boy of eleven, feeling the pain
of it still?

"My father . . . ," he said softly, then shook himself, sat up straighter
in his chair. "On this day I speak of, in the spring of 1936, my father is
busy shuffling papers when Senior Lieutenant Popov suddenly bursts
into the office, grabs him by the arm, and says they've an urgent mission,
a matter of vital importance to the security of the state. A secret cache
has been discovered in the attic walls of the Municipal Courts building
on the Neva embankment. Fontanka 16. You've heard of this?"

Ry said, "It's the address for what was once the headquarters of the
tsarist secret police. The Okhrana."

"Yes, a place to strike fear in the hearts of all Russians even on that
particular day, nineteen years after the Bolshevik Revolution. Certainly
my father is afraid, for it feels to him as if the very walls have absorbed
so much misery and terror and pain. But the walls hold something else
as well, for a small fire in the attic caused by faulty wiring has exposed a
hidden closet about the size of a phone booth. Within the closet are two
wooden filing cabinets filled with musty old dossiers."

He stopped to pour himself more Unicum, then got to his feet and went to stand before the Stalin poster. "Tell me, Mrs. Carpenter. Do you know what an agent provocateur is?"

"I have a general idea," Zoe said, "but why don't you tell me anyway. You lecture so well."

He turned back to her, blinking in confusion, not sure if he'd been complimented or insulted, and Ry hid a smile. Then the professor shrugged it off, said, "An agent provocateur is a spy who infiltrates revolutionary groups and tries to stir them up into doing things that end up getting them arrested."

Kuzmin left the poster and came to stand with his back to the fire. "During the time of my story, whispers are circulating that in the early months of the Bolshevik struggle Joseph Stalin himself had once secretly served the Okhrana as an agent provocateur. Not out of ideological principles, you understand, but rather as a means of eliminating his rivals."

Kuzmin stopped to toss back a healthy swig of the cough-medicine booze, shuddering a little as it went down. "So when Popov points to one of the cabinets in the secret closet and orders Father to search through it for any documents bearing the words *Steel Badger*, he suspects the mission might have something to do with this, that perhaps this Steel Badger was the Okhrana's code name for Stalin in his capacity as the agent provocateur."

"Not a very healthy suspicion for your father to have had in that place and time," Ry said.

Kuzmin's smile showed a flash of his yellow teeth. "Which is why he betrays nothing of what he is thinking to the senior lieutenant. My father believed always the way to survive was to know nothing, see nothing."

Kuzmin lifted his glass to his mouth, saw it was empty, and filled it again. "So, Popov sets to work sorting through one cabinet, while my father tackles the other, praying all the while his eyes never fall on anything to do with a badger of any sort. One dossier does catch his attention, though, because of a strange rendition he finds inside—a crude, hand-drawn sketch of an altar made out of human bones."

Ry heard Zoe draw in a sharp breath and thought his own heart might also have skipped a beat. But Denis Kuzmin, lost in his story, didn't seem to notice.

"It is such a macabre thing, the sketch, that it intrigues my father to look further, and beneath it he finds a report of a conversation that took place in a tavern in the fall of 1916, between an Okhrana spy and an extremely drunk Grigori Rasputin."

"The Mad Monk," Zoe said.

Kuzmin raised his glass in a mock toast toward the photograph on his mantel. "Mad? Perhaps he was. We do know that he was born in a small village in Siberia, where even from his earliest years he was known as a mystic and faith healer. He was also . . . well, to put it delicately, a man of considerable sexual magnetism."

Kuzmin flushed, then smiled weakly and went on, "Rasputin's power over the imperial family did not come through seduction, however, at least not seduction of a sexual nature. But rather through his ability to bring relief to their son, who suffered from hemophilia. Every time the boy Alexei had an injury which caused him to bleed, the tsaritsa would plead with Rasputin to come save her son, and save the boy he would. Now, how did he do this? Who knows? Some say he hypnotized the boy, some say he used leeches, while others believed it was through magic or prayer."

Kuzmin stopped to stare at the photograph, then looked up at the print of Ivan the Terrible murdering his son, as if the two men who'd lived centuries apart were connected in some way, Ry thought. The mad monk, the mad tsar.

"Which brings us back to the conversation in the tavern," Kuzmin said. "Rasputin told the Okhrana spy that as a young man, while wandering as a pilgrim across the Taimyr Peninsula in Siberia, he met and seduced a woman who was a member of a nomadic tribe called the *toapotror*. The magic people."

Ry looked at Zoe. He wanted to know what she was thinking, but her face was closed off now, even to him. She sat so utterly still, he thought he could count her every breath.

"One night after they made love," Kuzmin went on, "Rasputin's lover told him a dark secret. That she was the protector—the Keeper, she called herself—of a magic altar. An altar of bones. And that if he were to drink from this altar, it would make him immortal."

Okay, now we've gone off into woo-woo land here. The altar of bones was a fountain of youth, and if you drank from it, you would live forever? Ry thought he should be laughing, but the hairs on his arms were standing straight up, and a chill was curling up and down his spine. Zoe's face, he saw, had gone bloodless.

"You look skeptical, Mr. Carpenter," Kuzmin said, clearly pleased with the reaction he'd gotten. "Immortality? Eternal life? Impossible, you say. But Rasputin described in lurid detail how he worked his wiles on the woman, until one arctic night she led him to a cave whose entrance was hidden behind a waterfall on the shores of a forgotten lake, and inside the cave was an altar made of human bones. Rasputin claimed he drank from the altar that night. And he, at the least, believed himself to be immortal.

"What is more, he brought away with him a small vial of the elixir, or whatever you choose to call it. He said he had to be careful, though, because if it was exposed to sunlight, its magical properties would be destroyed. This was what he was using on the boy Alexei to cure his hemophilia."

"And yet both of them, the boy and the Mad Monk, were to end up dead within a couple of years of that night in the tavern," Ry said. "So much for the bone juice and living forever."

Kuzmin held up a finger, amusement creasing his long, thin face. "Ah, but you see that is the thing. It very nearly did make Rasputin immortal. Not long after that night in the tavern, a group of nobles, fed up with his influence over the tsaritsa, set out to kill him. They fed him cupcakes laced with cyanide, and when that seemed to have no effect, they emptied a revolver in his back, and when that failed to do the job, they clubbed him over the head, wrapped his body in a sheet, and threw him in an icy river. Four days later his body was recovered with his hands frozen like claws, as if he had tried to tear his way out from under the ice. An autopsy revealed the cause of death was not downing, or gunshot, or poisoning, but simple hypothermia."

"Dead is still dead," Zoe said, and Ry heard the anger and disappointment in her voice. He felt it, too. They'd thought they were on the verge of getting to the truth at last, and instead they'd been given a fairy tale.

"Somebody's pulling somebody's leg here," she said, "and since I'm a guest in your house, I'll be polite and assume it was the Mad Monk, pulling off a fast one on a gullible tsarist spy. Back in the States, Professor, we call that getting punked."

Kuzmin laughed. "You may be right, Mrs. Carpenter. Perhaps the spy was 'punked,' as you say. But the Okhrana took it seriously enough that they sent other agents to Siberia. They didn't find the lake or the cave, but they found instead a tribe called the *toapotror*, who told them a tale, about how there once was a shaman with talents so potent he could raise the dead. But one terrible day, the shaman was murdered. It was winter, and so his daughters took his body to a cave to await burial in the spring. But when they laid him down, his blood spilled onto the stone floor and turned into a fountain with magical properties.

"The daughters built a shrine over the fountain, and they called it the altar of bones. A folktale, certainly. But with some truth at its core, perhaps. For the *toapotror* claimed to know of people who drank from the altar and became immortal. But it also drove them mad."

A wry smile pulled at the professor's mouth. "I see by your faces that my credibility is now shot. Another quaint American expression, yes? But the magic people described in quite specific detail the symptoms of the madness they observed in those who dared to drink from the altar. Today, we call it megalomania. An obsession with power, the desire to dominate others, and the delusion that you can bend others to your will and change the world."

"All very interesting, and typical of many folktales," Ry said. "The Faustian bargain. You get your heart's desire, but only at a price. Your soul, or in this case, your sanity."

"Yes, yes, you scoff, but the Okhrana had in their possession secret documents going back hundreds of years, and they culled through them looking for any other mention of a Keeper and an altar made of human bones. There were many such stories, but my father only had time to read the one. From the time of Ivan the Terrible."

Ry looked up at the print over the mantel, he couldn't help himself. And he couldn't keep the hairs from rising up on his arms again. This was nuts, he didn't want to believe. And yet . . .

"It seems that a Keeper was also one of Ivan's lovers," Kuzmin said. "She loved him madly, or at least madly enough to break with her vows and give him some of the elixir. Supposedly all it takes is one small drop."

Ry saw the starkness come over Zoe's face again, and he knew she was thinking of her grandmother. Of Katya Orlova, loving and trusting in a man who turned out to be an assassin and a double agent. Giving the altar to her friend Marilyn, a woman she loved like a sister, but a woman who could be childlike at times, and achingly insecure. *A terrible crime was committed because I betrayed the altar's secrets. . . .*

Nikolai Popov and his father, killing Marilyn with an enema full of chloral hydrate. His father, standing behind the fence on the grassy knoll, a rifle in his hands, ready to murder the president because the KGB believed he had drunk from the altar of bones.

Ry shook his head, not wanting to accept any of this. It wasn't possible that Kennedy had been murdered because of a moldy, forgotten dossier and a Russian fairy tale.

Zoe started to wrap the icon back up in the sealskin pouch. "It's been fascinating, Professor, and you've been so generous with your time. But it's getting late—"

"No, wait," Kuzmin cried, coming half out of his chair, and Ry tensed, his hand starting to go for the gun at his back.

But then the professor eased back down again. His hand shook as he smoothed his thinning, red-gray hair. He drew in a deep breath.

"Forgive me, I became sidetracked and forgot to tell you the most important thing. What you came for, the story behind your icon. In his description of the cave and what took place that night, Rasputin spoke about seeing a jeweled icon sitting on top of the altar made of human bones. He said his lover called it 'the Lady,' and it was of the Virgin, holding not the Christ child in her lap, but a drinking vessel carved out of a human skull. And the face of the Virgin was the face of his lover. The Keeper."

Kuzmin leaned forward and Ry saw the desperation in his eyes, the hunger. "The Okhrana had the Mad Monk draw a sketch of the Lady's face. My father saw it in the dossier. There can be no doubt that the icon you are holding is the very one Rasputin's eyes gazed at inside the cave with the altar of bones."

"Maybe," Zoe said. She had, Ry noticed, never taken her hand out of the satchel after she'd put the icon away, and he knew she had it wrapped around the butt of her Glock.

"So what happened to your father, Professor?" Ry asked. "After that day at Fontanka 16."

"What? Oh, there were more papers within the dossier, but my father never got the chance to read them, for Popov suddenly slammed the door to his cabinet shut, stuffed a thin file folder inside his uniform tunic, and said, 'We're done here.' Then he saw my father was trying to hide something from him, and he said, 'What have you got? Give it over.'"

Kuzmin contemplated his empty glass, then said, "My father gave it over, of course. What other choice did he have? And so Senior Lieutenant Nikolai Popov left Fontanka 16 with two dossiers that day, and one of them had to do with an altar made of human bones."

Fat lot of good it did him, Ry thought. *All those years he spent searching for the thing, killing for it.*

"Did they never speak about it again?" Zoe asked. "Popov and your father?"

The professor snorted a bitter laugh. "Not hardly. Two days later, Senior Lieutenant Popov became Captain Popov, and Father was transferred out of the GUGB and into a regular army unit. One that was sure to be sent to the front lines during the war everyone feared was one day coming. He was lucky that was the worst that was done to him—"

Kuzmin snapped his fingers as if a thought had suddenly occurred to him. "My father drew from memory a copy of the two sketches he saw that day. Would you care to see them?"

He didn't wait for a response, but got up and went to a cabinet at the base of one of the bookcases. He dug a key ring from his pocket, opened the cabinet, and rummaged around with his back to them, then straightened and turned. He had a small, snub-nosed revolver in his hand.

He surprised Ry by laughing out loud when he saw the two Glocks pointed at his heart.

"Ours are bigger," Ry said.

"And there are two of them," Zoe said.

Kuzmin laughed again, then shrugged. "Well, I had to try, didn't I? I don't suppose you'd be willing to sell the icon? . . . No, I didn't think so. Perhaps your grandmother—"

"She's dead," Zoe said.

"Ah, yes, of course. For how else would you have become the Keeper? Yet I think she died without telling you much at all. I think you came here knowing even less than I do. And I have told you some, but not all."

He started to take a step toward them, but Ry stopped him with a look.

"We could become partners," Kuzmin said, his eyes shining, wet and pale like spit. "We could go together to Siberia. We could find the magic people, and they will know just by looking at you that you are the Keeper. They will lead us to the lake, to the secret cave. My God, a fountain of youth! Think of what we could do with it. Not only will we be immortal ourselves, we'll become rich beyond our wildest dreams by selling it to those who—"

A staccato of gunfire suddenly tore through the room from the garden. Flowerpots burst, the French doors erupted into splinters and shards of glass. Three red blossoms burst on Kuzmin's ratty old sweater, and a thin red mist sprayed the air as the bullets tore through his chest.

A split second later Ry saw a grenade sail through the shattered doors to land with a heavy thud on the far edge of the thick Oriental carpet.

He heard a sharp *pfffft* and threw himself on top of Zoe. They rolled off the sofa and onto the floor, just as the grenade exploded.

41

Thick, choking white smoke billowed around them. Ry's eyes and throat were burning up, he couldn't breathe. He choked, then his brain kicked in.

Not fire. Tear gas.

Zoe flailed underneath him, coughing, gagging. He rolled off her and up onto his knees. He still had his gun in one hand, and he grabbed her arm with the other, to pull her up with him. He saw her mouth open on a yell or a scream, then she choked and jerked away from him, scrambling on her hands and knees to the nearest armchair, clawing at the rug underneath it, as if she were a wounded animal trying to burrow into a hole.

He snagged her ankle; she kicked loose. He grabbed it again, tried to pull her out from under the chair. He yelled her name, but it came out in a croak. His eyes felt as if they were burning up inside his head, and every breath was like swallowing ground glass.

Gotta get us out of here, out of here now. . . .

Ry figured their attackers would give it another ten, fifteen seconds, at the most, for the tear gas to take full effect, then rush the library.

Gotta get out. . . .

He twisted his fingers in the denim of Zoe's pants and yanked hard. She came up fast and whirled, her eyes swollen, streaming tears, her chest heaving. Then he saw the Glock in her hand, and he finally got it. He must've sent her gun flying under the chair when he'd jumped on top of her.

He grabbed her by the shoulders and hauled her to her feet. "Kitchen," he rasped.

She nodded and ran half-blind toward the double doors that led to the foyer. Ry stumbled after her. He could barely see anymore. Ragged coughs ripped through his lungs. It felt as if he were breathing acid.

He glanced back at the shattered window through the white veil of gas. His swollen, blurred eyes saw a creature rise up as if from the black lagoon—tall and thick-chested, with bulbous, flylike eyes, a snakelike nose, and a long arm with a clawed finger pointing at Ry's heart.

Ry fired off a half dozen shots, his aim wild because he couldn't see. He heard the bullets hit wood and glass. The creature seemed to disappear in the smoke. Was he hit or just diving for cover?

A split second later a spray of automatic-weapons fire stitched the wall above their heads.

Not hit, or at least not so badly that he couldn't shoot. More bullets whizzed by, lower this time, shattering the lintel of the door. Chunks of wood and plaster flew through the air. The clouds of gas seemed to shimmer with the noise.

Zoe was having trouble with the latch. She twisted around and rasped something that might've been "Locked" or "Blocked." He pulled her out of the way and kicked the wooden panels into kindling with his steel-capped boot.

The pall of the tear gas followed them out into the foyer. Ry let Zoe get a couple of steps ahead of him, while he ran half-backward, covering their retreat.

The foyer dead-ended at a staircase, with two smaller hallways leading off on each side. Ry felt Zoe hesitate and he croaked, "Right," just as the creature from the black lagoon burst through the library's shattered doors, hitting the floor on a roll, firing his Uzi, but still aiming high.

Ry fired back as he rounded the corner into the hall and missed again because he couldn't *see* anything.

A swinging door was at the end of the long hall, and Ry prayed that it led into the kitchen. They were about ten feet away when it banged opened as if from the punch of a fist, slamming hard and loud against the wall. A big man wearing a black Kevlar vest and a gas mask, and with an Uzi at his side, filled the threshold.

For a sharp, suspended second they all three stood stock-still as if caught in a freeze-frame. Then Ry saw the barrel of the Uzi start to come up, but before his tear-gas befuddled and disoriented mind could tell his body to react, Zoe shot the guy right between his big, bulbous eyes.

The body had barely hit the floor before Zoe leaped over it and was into the kitchen, peppering rounds into the room, shattering crockery and glass in a staccato burst of noise.

Ry saw a blurred version of the door he knew from his earlier recon led out into the back vegetable garden. He headed for it and almost tripped over the sprawled legs of the housekeeper.

Her throat had been slit.

———————

THE COLD, CLEAR February air tasted better than beer and felt almost as good as sex. Ry's throat was swollen beyond talking, so he tapped Zoe on the shoulder and pointed the way through the apple orchard to the lane that led past the church, letting her lead the way again while he covered their backs.

They wove in and out of old tomato stakes, dead squash vines crunching under their boots. They were into the apple grove within seconds, and Ry could see through the trees the blurred steeple of the little Serbian church. Behind him, he heard a door bang and a spatter of Uzi fire.

They broke out of the trees and onto the lane. About thirty yards of open space were before the church and the cemetery's stone wall, and they crossed it at a dead run.

Ry got to the wall first, so he could help Zoe over it, but she managed it easily, vaulting on one hand like a gymnast.

———————

HE SQUATTED ON his haunches and leaned back against the rough stones of the wall, his chest heaving. Zoe knelt beside him.

She hacked phlegm out of her throat and started to bring a fist up to her eyes, but he grabbed her wrist, stopping her. "Don't rub." The words rasped out of his throat, which felt like coarse sandpaper. His own eyes were now swollen into slits and so clogged with tears he couldn't blink anymore. "Makes it worse."

The cemetery wall was maybe three and a half feet high and built of stones harvested from the nearby countryside, and from the way it curved out around the church, it was as effective as a hunting blind. With the wall as cover, one guy could keep an army pinned down in the apple orchard. Not forever, but long enough.

Ry popped up and saw a blurred black figure flitting through the apple trees, then another smaller figure in a maroon jacket behind and off to the left.

"Two. Still in the orchard," he said to Zoe, as he dropped back down. "Yasmine Poole, probably, and one of the guys from Paris."

"I killed the other one," she said.

He grinned at her. "Fucking A, you did."

He dug the Beamer's keys out of the pocket of his cargo pants and put them in her hand. He didn't want to tell her how badly he couldn't see because he was afraid she wouldn't leave him then. "You go get the car while I—"

Ragged coughs ripped through his chest, stopping him, but Zoe nodded to show she got it. He watched her take off across the cemetery, running at a crouch, weaving among the tombstones, satchel banging against her hip.

He took another look over the wall, still not seeing worth a damn, but he didn't need a dead-eye aim to buy Zoe the time she needed.

He thought about the guy who'd thrown the grenade, then rushed the library from the garden. That guy had fired his Uzi at them, but he'd aimed high, well above their heads. And the other guy, the one who'd been sent into the kitchen to cut off their retreat—he'd hesitated that split second at the door, long enough for Zoe put a bullet between his eyes.

And that meant Yasmine Poole wanted them alive. Probably because she didn't dare risk killing them only to find out too late that they no longer had the film on them, that they'd stashed it away somewhere between that apartment on the Île St.-Louis and here.

Ry smiled to himself because she wanted him alive, and he wanted her very dead. It wouldn't be enough, never enough, but killing her was the only thing he could do to avenge Dom.

He ejected the almost spent clip and slapped a fresh one into the butt. He gripped the gun with both hands, then pushed up far enough to brace his forearms on the wall. He waited until he saw another flash of movement, still in the trees, but closer now. He pulled and held the trigger, laying down a stream of fire, kicking up dirt and rocks, and shredding the weeds that lined the lane.

The sudden silence when he stopped was like the pall of a funeral home. Maybe five seconds went by, then he got a short burst of return fire. But it was just token fire, reminding him they had guns, too.

He laid down more fire, keeping them back in the orchard and out of the lane. He figured it would take Zoe three or four minutes to get down the steps and back up here with the car, but she beat his expectations because just then he heard the roar of the Beamer's engine.

Two seconds later it came whipping around the other side of the church, spewing dirt and gravel. Ry was over the wall just as it slammed to a stop. He yanked open the passenger-side door and dove in. Zoe gunned the motor. The Beamer's tires spun, then bit, and they sprang forward so fast the back of Ry's head smacked against the headrest.

He looked back through the rear window. He saw a blurred figure in black run out of the orchard into the lane, drop onto one knee, and shoot uselessly at the Beamer's disappearing tires.

<hr>

THE LANE DEAD-ENDED not much farther on, at the front gate of a gray stone manor house. A small road that led up into the mountains fed in from the left, and Zoe took it, taking the ninety-degree turn so fast the Beamer's back end fishtailed and the steering wheel shuddered in her hands.

Ry fumbled with his seat belt, taking two stabs to get it fastened because he could still barely see. The road they were on wasn't even two lanes wide, a backcountry road that hadn't been paved in decades. Trees whipped by the windows, then they hit a gap and Ry saw the river far below them.

Zoe braked a little to negotiate a hairpin curve, and Ry heard a sloshing noise, then felt something roll around on the floor at his feet.

Oh, sweet mercy. A water bottle.

He bent over, groped around, found it. It was nearly half-empty, but half was better than nothing. He straightened, twisted off the cap, then leaned his head back and poured the water into his eyes.

"Ah, God," he said at the soft, cool feel of it.

He looked over at Zoe, already seeing her a little better now. Her own eyes were puffy and bloodshot, and the skin on her face and hands was red, like a sunburn, but the tear gas hadn't seemed to hit her as hard as it had him. Funny thing was, although he'd been in a lot of hairy situations in his life, none of them had ever involved tear gas, and that was a really good thing because his corneal nerves and mucous membranes had reacted so badly to the lachrymal agent, he'd almost been blinded by it.

He opened his mouth to tell her he probably wouldn't have come even close to making it this far without her, when he heard the squeal of tires. He whipped his head around to look in the side-view mirror and saw a black Mercedes bearing down on them fast.

"We've got company," Ry said, just as an arm with an Uzi at the end of it popped out the passenger-side window, and the *ack ack* patter of automatic gunfire split the air. Ry saw bullets hit the tarmac behind them, felt one punch into the Beamer's undercarriage.

Zoe was already going too fast for the road, but she gripped the steering wheel tighter and poured even more gas into the Beamer's roaring engine.

Ry braced his shoulder against the back of his seat as they whipped around another sharp bend in the road. They were still climbing, and the way ahead of them was full of curves and switchbacks. There was no guardrail, just two feet of shoulder and then a plunge straight down in places, to rocks and thickets of trees, and far, far below them, the river.

Zoe took a blind curve at seventy miles an hour with a wing and a prayer, and suddenly the road ahead of them was filled with a giant hay wagon. Ry instinctively braced his hands on the dashboard and slammed his right foot onto a passenger-side brake that wasn't there.

Zoe didn't even slow. She jerked the steering wheel hard left, squeezing the Beamer between the hay wagon and a tangle of trees and boulders. One of them knocked off the side-view mirror, and something scraped the car's side with a shower of sparks. Ry caught a glimpse of the wagon's driver as they roared past—gaping mouth and wide, white eyes.

They went into another blind curve before Zoe could get back over to their own side of the road, and Ry prayed they wouldn't meet another car coming at them head-on.

He twisted around to look behind them, but the road was too curvy—he couldn't even see the hay wagon anymore, let alone the Mercedes.

Suddenly Zoe slammed on the brakes so hard Ry thought his brain had slammed against the side of his skull. He whipped back around and saw the big, black Mercedes blocking the entire road in front of them.

They screeched to stop, and for the length two heartbeats it seemed to Ry to grow eerily quiet, and the cloud of dust they'd stirred up settled back down like fine ash over the Beamer's hood.

Then Ry saw the barrel of an Uzi come up over the Mercedes's trunk, and bullets suddenly peppered the cracked tarmac around them and pinged off their front bumper and grill.

"Back up! Back up!" he yelled, but Zoe already had the Beamer in reverse.

She accelerated, going backward, until she got their speed up. Then she took her foot off the gas and jerked the steering wheel hard left. The car spun, tires squealed, grinding into the dirt and gravel, and the jagged slope of the mountain loomed up in front of them.

Now, now, now, Ry was shouting in his head, then she threw the Beamer back into drive, hit the gas, and straightened out the steering wheel.

They shot forward, and Ry looked back over his shoulder to see the maroon jacket come running around from the other side of the Mercedes and jump into the driver's seat.

"How in hell did they get ahead of us like that?" he shouted. "There must've been a small cut-though, a shortcut, we didn't see."

They were going back down the mountain now, back toward town, only way, way too fast. They headed into a curve, hit a gravel patch, and went into a wild, hard slide. Zoe turned into the skid, but it felt as if their rear wheels were just spinning on air. They kept sliding sideways, getting closer and closer to the edge of the road, onto the shoulder now, and Ry saw trees and rocks and then nothing but wide-open sky and certain death ahead of them.

Then at last the tires got traction. Zoe pulled the steering wheel hard right, and the Beamer's front end swung around, back onto the road where it was supposed to be, and all was right with the world again.

"Jesus God," Ry said.

He saw her glance in the rearview mirror, and she said in voice that was crazily calm, "They're back." Then she said, "Hang on."

They blew through a switchback, an S-shaped set of curves. As soon as they were out of it, Zoe took her foot off the gas, turned the steering wheel a quarter, and at the same time pulled up hard on the emergency brake. The Beamer spun around, tires shrieking and grinding, sending up a cloud of dust. She released the emergency brake and stepped on the gas as she straightened out the wheel, and they were headed up the mountain again just as the Mercedes came down it, whipping through the last curve in the switchback, going so fast it swung out wide, toward the edge of the drop-off.

Zoe took the inside lane, and the instant they were beside the Mercedes, she twisted the Beamer's wheel to the right and they rammed it hard.

The impact sounded like an empty metal drum thrown from a rooftop. The back end of the Mercedes skidded past them, spinning out of control toward the edge of the embankment, and Ry saw a flash of red hair in the driver's-side window.

For a single breathless moment, the Mercedes hung suspended, its back end on the road, it's front end out over thin air. Then it began to fall, almost in slow motion, tumbling end over end over end down the mountainside in a terrible noise of grinding metal, smashing glass, and human screams.

42

THEY STOOD at the top of the embankment together and looked down.

The guy in the passenger seat must not have been wearing a seat belt. He lay like a broken doll on a pile of boulders, his neck cocked at an impossible angle. Oddly, he still had the Uzi clutched in his hand.

The Mercedes had been stopped in its downward plunge by a thick grove of live oaks. Its front end was completely buried in leaves and branches, its roof nearly flattened. The stench of burnt rubber and hot metal drifted in the air.

Ry stared at the wreck for a long moment, looking for red hair and not seeing any. He walked down the road a few yards, until he found a place that wasn't so steep, then he headed down the embankment, half-jogging, half-sliding.

"Ry, wait," Zoe called after him. "Where are you going?"

"To make sure she's dead."

SHE WASN'T DEAD, but she would be soon. One of the oak branches had broken off and driven downward, through the windshield, impaling her through the chest.

Her eyes were glazed, emptying, and then they focused on Ry. She smiled, drooling blood. He saw her lips form the words before he heard them.

"Your brother, the priest . . . he died begging . . ." She made a gargling noise, as if she were trying to laugh only the blood was choking her. "Died begging . . ."

Ry's world blurred red around the edges, and he felt the blood shooting though the veins in his arms like tiny electrical currents. "Die, bitch," he said. "Die now."

She died. He watched the life go out of her and he wanted to pull the tree branch out of her heart so that he could ram it back into her again. Kill her all over again.

From a long way away he could hear Zoe calling his name. "Ry, stop. You can let go now, okay. Let go."

He looked down and saw that he was gripping the frame of the windshield, and it was buckled and jagged, and although he couldn't feel it, he thought he must be cutting himself because he could see blood running out from between his fingers.

Zoe wrapped her hand around his wrist. She didn't try to pull him loose, just gently held his wrist. "Ry, let go."

He let go, but only so that he could reach down inside the car. He searched through the pockets of Yasmine Poole's bloodied maroon suede jacket and found her cell, an iPhone.

He straightened and backed up a couple of steps. He scanned through the phone's history and saw that she'd called only one number during the last couple of days. He clicked on it, pressed send. The line, cell phone, whatever it was at the other end, rang just once before it was picked up.

"Yasmine?"

A deep male voice. Tough, but also anxious, and something else in there, too. Something sexual, maybe, but more than that. Tender?

"She's dead," Ry said. "So fuck you, Taylor. We're bringing you down."

Ry punched off and pulled back his arm to hurl the phone down into the river, then stopped himself.

He went around to the front of the car, pointed the phone at Yasmine Poole's impaled and bloodied body and snapped a picture. He found the e-mail address that went with the number he'd just called and sent the son of a bitch a little present.

Ry felt something touch his back. He whirled, his fist balled up around the cell phone, his arm half-cocked, ready to slam it into some-body's head, and he looked down into Zoe's face.

She was pale, her eyes dark with worry. "Ry? What are you doing?"

He drew in a deep breath, then another. The redness was starting to fade a little from the edges of his vision. "Miles Taylor. I heard something just now in the way he said her name. He cared for her. He—" Ry cut himself off, drew in another deep breath. "I'm okay. I'm going to be okay."

A smudge of dirt was on her cheek and he reached up to brush it off with his thumb, only he made it worse, because now there was blood on her cheek, blood all over . . .

"When I . . . Back in Galveston, in the church, you could still see Dom's blood. It was all over, and there was a chalk outline on the floor, where his body had fallen." Ry swallowed, closed his eyes, but he saw blood. Blood everywhere.

"I want that bastard to know how it feels, Zoe. I want him to *hurt*."

Ry realized he was still touching her and started to let his hand fall, but she wrapped her fingers around his wrist and held his hand against her cheek. Then she turned her head just a little, until the ends of his fingers were on her lips, and she kissed them softly.

"He will, Ry. He will."

BACK AT THE car, he said, "I can drive. You're probably exhausted, and my eyes are fine now."

She searched his face as she gave him the keys, but he was back off the ledge now, not so crazy anymore. Or at least no more crazy than usual. "I'm okay," he said. "Really."

She stared at him a moment longer, then she smiled and said, "I know." He felt that smile, felt the force of it, like a hot, wet gust blowing through him.

He pushed the driver's seat back, buckled up, adjusted the rearview mirror. He turned on some air. *Going through the motions, doing normal things, like a couple of tourists on a little day trip. A quiet, scenic drive along the Danube Bend.*

"It's weird," Zoe said, as if she'd been reading his thoughts. "I was fine during the middle of that wild chase, driving the car. I was in some kind of zone, not thinking or feeling, just doing. But now I can't seem to get my left leg to stop shaking."

She was rubbing her hand up and down her thigh, and Ry could see the tremor in her quad. "It's the adrenaline," he said. "Five minutes from now you're going to want to topple over."

She laughed, or rather tried to. It came out as more of a squeak. "Can't, O'Malley. No time. We got places to go, people to see, things to do. . . . What exactly *are* we going to do?"

Ry tried to think, couldn't, so he started up the car and pulled back out onto the road. "I haven't a clue."

They drove for a couple of miles in silence, then she shocked the hell out of him by saying, "I think we should go to St. Petersburg."

The funny thing was, he'd been coming around to the same conclusion. Reluctantly, though, because it was a risk. A big one. "Popov's son is in St. Petersburg."

She nodded slowly. "And that's why we got to go there and settle this. He had my grandmother killed for the altar of bones, and when that didn't work, he sent the ponytailed man after me. He would've got me, too, if you hadn't come back just in time, but that was luck, pure and simple, and we can't count on always being lucky. He's going to keep sending his thugs after me until he gets what he wants. I know guys like him—hell, my whole family's made up of guys like him."

"So what are you saying? We give him the icon and the riddle, say this is all we got, so good luck with it, bozo, and wash our hands of it?"

"Not on your life."

He glanced over at her. She had her chin up in the air and a hard look in her eyes, and he couldn't help grinning at her. But he said, "Okay, so say we find a way to get to Popov, or we deliberately let him get to us, and then we see what shakes out. But it's going to be really dangerous,

Zoe. The best we can hope for is that we come up with a plan where we control most of the variables, but no way are we going to be able to anticipate everything. And as someone once said, it's the unknown unknowns that end up getting you killed."

She flashed a cocky grin back at him. "Hey, how about a little confidence here, O'Malley. So far we've got America's Kingmaker and a Russian mafia boss after our asses, and we've managed to get ourselves branded as international terrorists. I say we're on a roll."

═══════════

IT FELT GOOD now that they had a plan, even if it was a half-baked, crazy plan, but Ry wasn't ready to stop and turn the car around just yet.

It was less than three days since he'd fished her out of the Seine—okay, she'd gotten herself out, but that was only a minor quibble. Three days, and for nearly every minute of it they'd been on the run for their lives. But now, for these few moments at least, the road ahead was empty of enemies.

He looked over at her. She still had that cocky tilt to her chin, but this time he didn't smile. He felt tight all over, in his chest and throat, so that for a moment he couldn't breathe. She was so damn tough and strong and smart, and he didn't know why, but those very things about her made him want to go out and slay dragons for her. Maybe just to show her that he could do it, that he was worthy of her, and wasn't that a thought?

A strand of hair had come loose from her clip. He reached over and tucked it back behind her ear, just to be touching her. "What are you thinking about?"

"The bone juice," she said. "I like that name you gave it. It fits. . . . How much of it do you think was real? That story the professor told us."

"I think the part about Nikolai Popov and the Fontanka 16 dossier was true. It's how he learned about the altar of bones in the first place. And we know the icon's real, so it's possible there's an altar made out of human bones in a cave somewhere up in Siberia. The rest, though, is just a myth, something an ancient people who lived a harsh life in a harsh land made up around the campfire one night, because it's hard to face the thought that from the moment we are born, we're already dying."

"I guess," she said, not sounding convinced.

"I'm beginning to wonder, though, if the KGB actually sanctioned the assassination, or if it was something Nikolai Popov pulled off all on his own. Think of who was involved: Popov and his two agents, who were both Americans. And Lee Harvey Oswald, their patsy, also an American."

"Uh-huh," Zoe said, but Ry didn't think she'd taken in much of what he'd just said. Her head was still in that cave in Siberia.

She said, "Does anyone know today exactly how Ivan the Terrible died?"

"Back in the sixties, when they were restoring the place where he was buried, they exhumed his body and did an autopsy. He died of mercury poisoning."

"So he didn't die of natural causes. He was murdered, like Rasputin was murdered, and look how hard it was to do even that. I remember reading about it in a history class, how they tried everything to get rid of him—cyanide, bullets, bashing him over the head, and finally dumping him in an icy river. It's one of history's great mysteries: Why he was so hard to kill? So what if the altar can make you immortal, Ry, in the sense that the only way you can die is if someone kills you, or you're in an airplane crash, or you get hit by a truck?"

Ry thrust his fingers through his hair. "You can prove anything if you never have to validate your starting assumptions. Okay, so a long time ago some witch doctor gets murdered and his body's buried in a cave. And by some wild coincidence when they stick him in the ground, a spring wells up, and then someone builds an altar out of human bones on top of it because, oh, hell, I don't know . . . maybe because bones were the only thing she had handy. But just because the altar and the spring exist, that suddenly doesn't make it into some kind of fountain of youth."

"But the riddles, the icon, all those generations of Keepers . . . Why would they do all that to protect a secret that isn't real?"

"It never had to be real, Zoe. They just needed to believe that it was."

SHE GREW QUIET after that, and Ry thought she'd fallen asleep.

But then she said, "Rasputin told the Okhrana spy that he saw the Lady icon sitting on top of an altar made of human bones inside a cave in Siberia. He also said he brought some of the bone juice out of the cave with him in a vial, that he was giving it to the sick boy, keeping him alive with it."

"Or," Ry said, "he could have just had a talent for using the power of positive suggestion. He was never able to actually cure Alexei's hemophilia for good, just bring him relief from the symptoms."

She waved a hand. "Whatever he did, it helped, so work with me a little here, okay, O'Malley? My grandmother gave Marilyn Monroe a green glass amulet in the shape of human skull and she called it the altar of bones. My great-grandmother Lena probably brought both the amulet and the icon with her when she escaped from the Norilsk gulag and made her way to Shanghai."

Ry tried to imagine doing such a thing, and couldn't. "She must've been one hell of woman. Tough and gutsy and smart. Just like her great-granddaughter."

He saw Zoe's cheeks flush, and she wouldn't meet his eyes. He wanted to tell her that he meant it, that he'd never before known a woman like her, and he wanted to know her better, deeper, and keep on knowing her and never stop.

"Anyway, the point I was trying to make wasn't all that earth-shattering," she said. "Just that even if we find the amulet, what's inside of it will have come from the altar, but it won't *be* the altar. The altar of bones is in a cave hidden behind a waterfall, on a forgotten lake somewhere near Norilsk."

"Do you want to go to Siberia now, instead?"

"No, St. Petersburg first. Then Siberia."

ZOE GREW QUIET again after that, and this time she did sleep. For about fifteen minutes, maybe, then she awoke with a start, her eyes a little wild. Ry saw that her thigh muscle was trembling again.

"You're okay," Ry said. "You're with me in the Beamer, heading God alone knows where."

"Oh." She scrubbed her hands over her face, then looked out the passenger-side window at the view far below them, of the Danube snaking around wooded hills and the red-tile roofs of another little village. "Not back to Budapest?" she said, apparently just now noticing which direction they were headed in.

"I suppose we are going to have to stop and turn around eventually." He let another half a mile click by, then said, "Not to change the subject, but that was a fine bootlegger's turn you did back there. Nobody can pull off that kind of fancy driving on instinct. You gotta be taught it, and you need practice."

She didn't say anything. In some ways she was the most open person he'd ever met. But he also sensed hidden places in her, like folds in the heart, where she hoarded her thoughts and feelings, and Ry got that. He wasn't all that good either at opening up the secret parts of himself.

She turned her face toward the window and he was about to just let it go when she said, "My father committed suicide the week before the start of my junior year in high school."

"I know. I'm sorry."

Her throat worked as she swallowed. "Thank you. . . . Anyway, my mother had already pretty much taken over the actual running of the family business by then, and I don't need to elaborate what the family business was since you were working for her."

"Anna Larina isn't you."

"Yeah? Nature or nurture. I guess with some families it hardly matters." Zoe laughed. Ry heard the bitterness and understood it, because for the last year and a half he'd been wondering the same thing. What parts of his father, the traitor, the assassin, did he carry around inside himself?

Probably more than he was ready to admit to right now. He'd joined the Special Forces right out of college, and they'd trained him to kill, just as his father had been taught to kill. Hell, at the time, his brother, Dom, had even accused him of signing up because he was trying "to out-tough the old man." Later he'd gone to work for the DEA, where he often volunteered for the hairiest undercover work because he got off on the excitement of it, the lying and the spying, the cat-and-mouse games, and he was good at them, too.

Just like his old man.

"By the time I was old enough to understand what was going on," Zoe was saying, "Daddy was just a figurehead, somebody to give the orders because the *vors* and captains and other sundry thugs would've balked at the thought of taking them directly from a woman."

Ry said, "They had to know who was the real brains behind the operation, though. I've joined a few gangs of one sort or another while undercover, and one of the first things you figure out fast is who's really calling the shots."

She shrugged. "I don't know. Maybe as long as Anna Larina allowed him to act the part of the *pakhan*, Daddy could fool himself into thinking he was the *pakhan*. He'd been molded for that life from practically before he could walk. To be the *pakhan*—it was what was expected of him, what he expected of himself."

Zoe went quiet again, thinking, remembering, and Ry let the silence fill the car until she chose to break it.

"He killed himself less than a week after Anna Larina pulled her infamous stunt with the head in the ice-cream tub. I've always thought that was why he did it. He knew only a true *pakhan* would have the toughness to do what she'd done, and he didn't have that sort of toughness. He knew that and he couldn't bear it, and so he killed himself."

She was sitting ramrod stiff in the passenger seat now, eyes straight ahead, chin in the air. She was trying to be so tough herself, Ry thought, and his heart ached for her.

"Anyway," she said, "Anna Larina crossed a big, bad line killing a top *vors* of the L.A. family, and Daddy was scared they would come after me in revenge. But I'd gotten this little red Miata for my birthday and I wanted to be out with my friends, go to Stinson Beach, to the Stonestown Mall, but Daddy was fixated on the idea they could get to me when I was in the car. He wanted me to take this course called Driving Techniques for Escape and Evasion, but I just rolled my eyes at him. Because I was sure I was God's gift and knew everything."

"You were sixteen."

She shook her head. "That's no excuse."

Maybe, Ry thought. And maybe not. When he was that age, he was sure he knew everything and was invincible in the bargain.

"On the day of his funeral," she said, "I signed up for that defensive driving course, along with shooting and tae kwan do lessons. I thought it was the one thing I could still do for him even though he was now gone. I could keep myself safe for him."

A moment went by, then it hit them both at the same time, what she'd just said, and they started laughing and then couldn't stop.

"Oh, God. Keep myself safe," Zoe said, finally winding down. "I'm kind of sucking at that lately, aren't I?"

Ry turned his head to look at her. Her cheekbones were flushed from laughing, her eyes bright. Her mouth was open and wet. Half her hair had come out of its clip and curled around the side of her neck. Cupping her neck just the way a man's hand might do, if he had it in his mind to tilt back her head so he could kiss that wet, red mouth—

A bang, loud as a cannon, rocked the car, and the steering wheel jerked in Ry's hands. He wrestled with it while he looked around wildly, thinking, *What the hell now?* Then he felt the chassis shimmy and heard the whop-whop of flapping rubber.

He pulled over to the side of the road and got out to take a look. Their left rear tire was in shreds.

"It must've taken a round from the Uzi," he said to Zoe as she got out to join him. "The bullet penetrated just enough to let the air out in a slow leak until it finally blew."

He laughed, feeling a little high after the big adrenaline rush. "I thought someone had lobbed a bomb at us."

She was feeling it, too; she was practically thrumming beside him. "You're telling me." She blew all the air out of her lungs in a big whoosh and lifted the hair off the back of her neck. "My leg's doing that twitching thing again, and I—"

He caught the back of her neck with his hand, pulling her face around to his, a little too rough, a little out of control. He kissed her and felt her gasp of surprise in his mouth, a warm, moist breath, and then she melted into him, opened her mouth to him.

They kissed, locked together, turning slowly, swaying. He ground himself against her belly. He was hot and hard for her and he wanted her to know it.

He was going too fast. He tried to gentle his kiss, but then she tangled her fingers in his hair and sucked on his tongue, pulling it deeper into her mouth, making love with their mouths, sucking, tonguing, and he was lost.

A hot, wet, gasping eternity later, he had her up against the Beamer's front fender, and they were fighting with the waistband of her jeans.

Zoe, her voice deep and rough, said, "God. I shoulda worn a dress," and Ry wanted to laugh, but he kept forgetting to breathe. She got a boot and her jeans and panties off one leg and that was enough. He had to be inside her now.

He gripped her waist with both hands, lifting her until her hips were braced on top of the hood of the car. He pushed her legs apart and thrust himself between them.

He felt her shudder, heard her moan, as the back of his hand brushed across her warm belly. He pushed a finger inside her. She was wet, hot, quivering, and he worked her with one hand while he wrenched desperately at his belt with the other, getting it open at last, at last, getting his zipper down, and all the while she was making little panting noises in his ear, "Hurry, hurry, hurry . . ."

And then her hand found him, gripped him so tightly he nearly came right then.

He went into her, hard, and nearly came again at the hot, tight feel of her. She clutched his shoulders and arched her spine, and her head fell back, and she screamed. He pressed his own open mouth against her wildly beating throat and pushed deep, then pulled almost all the way out of her, then pushed into her again and she met him, rose with him, and they found a rhythm, a beating pulse, their bodies rocking together, and the car rocked with them.

Ry's last coherent thought was *Oh, dear sweet heavenly Jesus . . .*

43

THEY SPRAWLED half on, half off the car in a tangle of clothes and she was looking up at him with sated eyes. Her mouth was wet, her lips slightly parted.

"Oh, my ever-loving God," she said, her voice hoarse, "that was . . ." Her eyes focused on his face and she grinned, a big, happy grin, and then she gripped his jacket with both hands, pulled him closer. He lowered his head to kiss her, felt her arch up hard against him, and he groaned.

He heard her shouting, "Oh, my God, Ry. Oh, my God," and then he realized her hands were now balled into fists, and she was heaving, trying to push him off her.

He jerked upright and staggered back. "What? What's the matter?"

"Oh my God," she said again, almost falling off the car onto her knees in the dirt as she tried to get back into her panties and jeans.

"Jesus, Zoe. What? Did I hurt you?"

She was tugging on her zipper. "Huh? No, it was great. You were great, and I really want to do it again. But I really, really need to look at the icon right now."

She gave him a quick, hard kiss on the mouth, then ran to get her satchel out of the car.

Well, at least I was great.

He turned around to pull himself together and zipper up, feeling both amused and abused. When he turned back around, he saw that she'd taken the icon out of its pouch and laid it on the Beamer's hood, using the pouch for a pad. She looked over at him, the color now high in her face. "You got to promise not to laugh. . . . It's just I've never come like that before and—God, this is really embarrassing."

"Hey." He slid his hand around the back of her neck and tilted her face so he could kiss her mouth. "It was the same for me, so I'm not going to laugh."

"Oh." Her eyes flickered up at him, then away. "I felt like I exploded inside, and I was lying there afterward, looking up at the sky and feeling like there were pieces of me floating around up there, a part of infinity now, and I thought, 'This is how it must have felt the day the world was created, like a kind of a cosmic organism,' and you said you wouldn't laugh."

"I'm not. Okay, maybe a little. But only because I love the quirky way your mind works."

"That's a good thing, I guess, because it's about to sound quirkier. . . . So I was thinking about the infinity of creation and my grandmother talking about infinity in her letter, telling me to look to the Lady, the icon. And then I thought about how ever since I first laid eyes on it in the griffin shop, it's been squirreling around in my brain that the way the jewels are laid out doesn't make sense. They aren't in the places where you'd expect them to be, like on her crown, or her slippers, or the hem of her robe, but instead they seem random. Then I suddenly realized they aren't random, at all. They form a pattern. Watch . . ."

She started with the ruby in the center and traced two circles on either side of the skull cup, lightly touching each jewel in turn. "It's a figure eight, lying on its side."

"The symbol for infinity," Ry said, and his pulse leaped at the thought of it.

"'Look to the Lady, for her heart cherishes the secret, and the pathway to the secret is infinite.' Infinite. Infinity. I think we were right all along, Ry. The amulet is inside of her, in some kind of secret compartment. And the jewels are the pathway to opening it."

Ry picked up the icon, looked at it closer, but he still didn't see any breaks or seams in the wood.

"It could be a spring-lock mechanism," he said, as he carefully set the icon back down on its pouch. "And the stones could work on the same principle as keypads do today. Push one after another in the right order and the lock will spring open."

"That's it," Zoe exclaimed, bouncing up and down on her toes, she was that excited.

She reached out with her finger, and Ry realized she was about to start pushing the stones willy-nilly. He grabbed her wrist. "Whoa, hold on a sec. The whole point of an infinity symbol is that it has no beginning or end. So where are you going to start?"

"With the ruby in the skull cup."

"Okay, that's probably logical, but then what? Do you go up and to the right, or up and to the left? Down and to the right? Or down and to the left?"

"So I got four choices. If one way doesn't work, I'll try another."

"Yeah? And what if the guy who designed this was a tricky bastard. He could've—"

"Why are you assuming it was done by a he? It was probably a she. A Keeper."

He held up his hands. "Okay, okay. I concede the point. It probably was a Keeper, but if she had a quirky mind like another Keeper I happen to know, she could have designed the locking mechanism so that if the jewels get pressed out of order, the spring jams and the lock won't open."

They both stared down at the icon a long moment. Then Zoe said, "Well, if that doesn't just suck."

Ry studied the face of the Virgin. It really was uncanny how much she looked like Zoe. Had a Keeper painted this herself five centuries ago and used her own face as the model?

"Do something for me, Zoe. Draw the infinity symbol in the dust here on the hood of the car. . . . No, don't look at the icon. Just do it without thinking. In fact, draw it with your eyes shut."

She closed her eyes and drew the symbol, starting in the center and going up and to the left, which was probably the last way he would have done it. He'd have gone up and to the right.

And maybe that just proved his point. If Zoe and the Keeper on the icon looked so much alike, then maybe they thought alike as well.

"I say we go with your instincts, babe," he said. "We've got a one-in-four chance of being right, and so far we've been beating the odds."

But now Zoe was the one to hesitate. "I don't know. . . . You said the whole point of an infinity symbol is that it has no beginning and no end—The riddle, Ry! It's in the riddle. 'Blood flows into the sea . . . Blood flows on into the sea without end.'"

She snatched up her satchel, opened it, pawed through more stuff than you'd find at a Walmart, and produced the unicorn postcard with a flourish. She turned it over and read out loud the riddle her grand-mother had written on the back even though they both knew it by heart by now.

Blood flows into the sea
The sea touches the sky
From the sky falls the ice
Fire melts the ice
A storm drowns the fire
And rages through the night
But blood flows on into the sea
                    Without end.

"This is it, Ry. This is it! Blood, sea, sky, ice, fire, storm, night—they all represent colors, in a way. Blood for red, sky for blue. And the colors match up to the jewels. Red ruby, blue sapphire. The riddle is the code."

"And your instinct was right on, too. 'Blood flows into the sea' . . . ruby to aquamarine. Up and to the left."

She grinned up at him, looking pleased with herself.

"Let's do it," he said, his voice a little rough. "I'll read the riddle one line at a time, and you press the stones. One at a time, nice and slow."

"Okay." She did a big inhale, exhale, then held out her hands and wriggled her fingers like a safecracker. "I'm ready."

"'The blood flows into the sea.'"

"Ruby to aquamarine," Zoe said, and slowly, carefully pressed first the ruby, then the aquamarine.

"'The sea touches the sky.'"

"Sapphire," she said.

"'From the sky falls the ice.'"

"Diamond."

"'Fire melts the ice.'"

"Fire opal . . ."

"No, *wait*," Ry yelled, and he grabbed her hand just as her finger was within a hair's breath of pressing down. "I think we almost blew it. We should've pressed the ruby again. Then the opal."

"The riddle doesn't say that."

"I know. But if we're making an infinite loop, then we're crossing back through the center, and the ruby is in the center."

She wiped her hands on the sides of her jeans. "Oh, man, O'Malley. I hope you're right."

She hesitated a moment longer, then pressed the ruby and the fire opal, firmly but quickly, as if she didn't want to think about it too much and lose her nerve.

"Okay. Now, 'a storm drowns the fire.'"

"Iolite . . ."

Ry had never heard of iolite, but the stone she pressed did fit the riddle's metaphor. It was a dark, purplish blue-gray color, like the belly of a thundercloud.

"'And rages through the night.'"

"Onyx." She pressed the multifaceted black stone then finished off the riddle with him: "'But blood flows on into the sea without end.' . . . Do you think that means we should push the ruby again?"

"Nothing's happened yet," Ry said, feeling a little sick inside, because he'd told her to press the ruby that second time. "So, yeah, go ahead. Push it."

She pushed, and they held their breath. Nothing happened.

Then there was a soft click and the skull's eye sockets slid open to reveal two holes carved into the wood. One was empty, but in the other was a tiny amulet of dark green glass shaped like a skull, and with a silver stopper.

It was exactly as Ry's father had described it, except it had no chain. Although the top of the silver did have a tiny loop for one. The amulet fitted so snugly into the hole that Zoe had to pry it out with her fingernails.

"Look, Ry . . ." She held the amulet between her thumb and forefinger and lifted it up, toward the setting sun. The glass was etched with runelike marks and was about half-full with a dark, viscous liquid.

"The altar of bones."

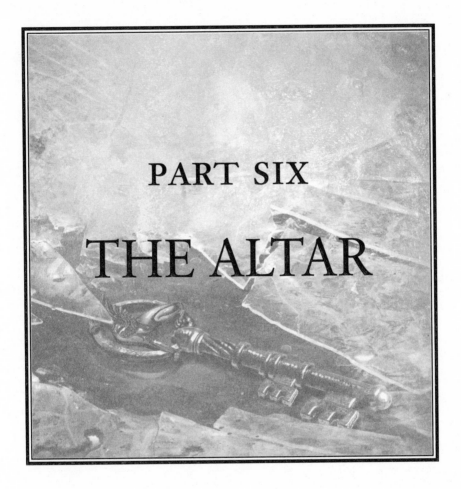

PART SIX

THE ALTAR

44

R Y LOOKED from the amulet to Zoe's face. Her lips were parted and her eyes gleamed as brightly as the sun-struck glass.

"Tell me you're not thinking about drinking from it," he said.

She shuddered. "God, no." But she lowered the amulet and cradled it in her hands against her chest, as if she were guarding it from him now, as well as the rest of the world. "But what if it's real, Ry? What if it could give us eternal life?"

"And make us crazy in the bargain?"

She shivered again, and Ry draped his arm around her shoulders, pulling her against him. It had grown cold now that the sun was setting.

"It's just a relic from the past," he said. "A piece of glass."

"With something inside of it, Ry. A liquid something."

"Which is still probably just some Siberian peasant's brew made of eye of newt and reindeer balls."

Zoe half-laughed, half-sighed. "You're right. At least my head tells me you're right. The Siberian peasant part of me feels all shivery inside just looking at it."

He hugged her tighter against him. "It gives me the willies, too. I think part of its power, what we're feeling, comes from knowing people have killed over it, are killing even now, but that still doesn't prove that it will make you live forever. Only that others believe it can."

She grew quiet, staring down at the amulet in her hands. Then she looked up at him, a teasing light in her eyes. "Okay then, O'Malley. Why don't you put your mouth where your money is? You drink from it."

"Can't. I'm allergic to reindeer balls."

She bit her lip to hold back a laugh, but it came out anyway. She leaned against him, laughing, and he felt the tension ease out of her. She turned her head into his neck, burrowed into him a moment, then pulled free, stood up on tiptoe, and gave him a hard, quick kiss on the mouth.

"What was that for?" he said.

"Being you."

He stared down into her upturned face. He wanted to make love to her again, slowly this time, deeply. He wanted her, every bit of her, so badly it scared him.

He took a step back, and she made a little jerking motion, as if she, too, had been caught up in the spell.

She looked away from him, up the empty road. The whole world was so still, so quiet, he could hear his own breathing, and hers.

"So," she said, her voice breaking a little. "What do we do now?"

"Go to St. Petersburg like we planned and hope like hell that before we get there we come up with a brilliant plan of how to deal with Popov's son without getting ourselves killed. Also, I know a guy there who teaches molecular biology at the university. He's probably got access to all kinds of equipment that could analyze the physical properties of whatever that stuff in the amulet is. We wouldn't need to give him the whole thing. Just a couple of drops."

"I don't know . . ."

"Or you could put it back into the icon and stash it in a bank vault in Switzerland. The choice is yours, Zoe. You're the Keeper."

She looked down at the amulet cradled in her hand. It didn't look so magical anymore, Ry thought. More like a cheap trinket you could buy in a Greek bazaar.

"No, you're right," she said. "We need to know what it is. People have been killed because of it. A president of the United States was assassinated because the KGB, or at the least Nikolai Popov, thought he drank from it, and I still can't quite wrap my head around that."

She stared down at the amulet, rubbing her fingers over the runelike etching on the glass. "I wonder what happened to the other one."

"The other what?"

"Amulet. There are two secret compartments in the icon, one behind each skull eye. So at some point there must have been two amulets."

"Maybe the other one went into the river with Rasputin."

"Yeah. . . . No, wait. We're being stupid. The missing amulet is the one my grandmother Katya filled with toilet water so that she could switch it with this one. This is the one she originally gave to Marilyn Monroe, the one with the real altar of— Ry, that's it."

She spun around to face him, her eyes bright, her lips parted and wet, and Ry almost lost it again right there. "That's *what*?" he said on a broken breath.

She started digging again through that bottomless satchel of hers. "You know how when you buy makeup at Saks, they're always giving you those little samples of perfume?"

"Yeah. That happens to me all the time."

She looked up at him, laughing. "Never mind, O'Malley, it's a girl thing. Just prepare yourself to be amazed at my brilliance, because I think I have an idea of how we can deal with Popov's son."

New York City

A COLD SWEAT bathed his face and he felt as if he were going to throw up, but Miles Taylor could not tear his gaze away from the horror that filled his computer screen.

Yasmine.

Her eyes were wide-open and empty, like a doll's, seeing nothing. Blood trickled out of the corner of her mouth, just a little blood really, nothing too terrible. Nothing like the blood farther down, where that . . . *thing*—what was it? A stake? A fence post?—pierced her chest. So much blood there, as if her heart had exploded.

His finger hovered over the delete key. He wanted to make it all go away, but he was also afraid to. As if by erasing this final image of her, as terrible as it was, he would end up erasing her existence from his mind.

From his heart.

Oh, God . . .

He curled his hand into a fist and pressed it against his chest. It hurt, it *really* hurt, as if he could actually feel it breaking. Feel it exploding, bursting, the way hers had burst, and he looked down, half-expecting to see his own blood splashing and pooling into his lap.

He squeezed his eyes shut, pressed his fist harder against his chest. A high-pitched whine filled his ears, like a flatline on a hospital monitor. It went on and on and on, a long, bloodred line stretching into infinity.

───────

HE SHUDDERED AND blinked, aware that time had passed, but he wasn't sure how much. Seconds? An hour? A century?

He saw his computer had gone to sleep. The screen was blank now, the photograph that O'Malley's whelp had sent him was gone. Gone, gone, gone. Yasmine was gone. As if, while he'd been off in a daydream, she had quietly and simply left the room.

He sat in a leather captain's chair before the massive mahogany desk in his library. Around him all was silent, and he had the strangest feeling that if he went to the door and opened it, the rest of the brownstone would have vanished and he would be staring down into an abyss. Yet the silence also had a weight and texture to it, as if he could feel it pressing like warm, wet palms onto his skin.

She's dead. My love is dead.

"Okay, Yaz," he said out loud into the empty room. "You're right. I won't let this beat me. I'll deal with it. I'll . . ."

You'll do what, Miles, you fool? Do what? What he wanted to do was bring her back. He wanted her *back.* If he wanted to, right this minute, he could pick up the phone and buy himself a villa on Lake Como, a Maserati Granturismo S, a van Gogh—except he already had all those things, and more. Okay, something bigger then, something both grand and catastrophic. How about start such a run on the world's biggest banking institutions that would bring down the entire global economy? He had the power and the wealth to do that, if he really wanted to. Whatever his heart desired, whatever whim he wanted gratified, he could make it happen.

But he couldn't bring her back.

"Christ, Miles, what a maudlin, pathetic cliché. Get a grip."

He wrapped his hands around the arms of his chair and pushed heavily to his feet. He stood for a moment, swaying, feeling light-headed and nauseated. That strange, high-pitched whine was back inside his ears again.

He jerked, shook his head. He'd been about to deal with something—what was it? Something that had come up right before he'd clicked open the e-mail from Yaz and that monstrous photograph had filled his computer screen. Something—

We're bringing you down.

The film, of course. The fucking film. O'Malley's kid and that old woman's granddaughter, Zoe Dmitroff—they had the film. They had to have the film because that was the only thing in this world with the power to bring him down.

Okay, so they've got the film. Now what are they gonna do with it?

What a stupid fucking question. They would give it to the media whores, of course. The government had a lot of reasons to bury it, but if Mike O'Malley's boy was smart enough to have gotten his hands on the film in the first place, then he was smart enough to have figured that much out. And the media . . . to them it would be the mother of all stories, the story of the millennium, and they would blast it around the world with the power of a megaton hydrogen bomb.

Panic ripped through Miles with such force he shook with it. He bent over and fumbled through the crap on his desk for the universal remote. He pointed it at the oil painting above the fireplace—a Jackson Pollock, not a van Gogh—and the painting and part of the paneled wall slid to one side to reveal a wide-screen digital TV.

The whining was now so loud in his ears he could barely think, and a terrible pain stabbed his head, right between his eyes, blurring his vision. His breathing was harsh and shallow as he clicked through the twenty-four-hour news channels. But they were all covering the story of the pretty blond coed who'd gone missing from the University of Wisconsin a couple of days ago. Nothing about the Kennedy assassination.

He left the TV on, but hit the mute button. Okay, this was good. This meant he still had time. Even if the O'Malley boy had already passed the film on to someone in the media, they would have to check it out first, wouldn't they? They would want to be sure it wasn't a fake before they aired it, and that gave him time.

Unconsciously he rubbed at the piercing pain in his forehead, but the whining had blessedly stopped. His mind felt clear now, as if he'd just sucked in a breath of pure oxygen, clear and cold and sharp as ice.

The only real proof that he was involved with Jack Kennedy's death was at the end of the film, when the camera had focused in on him taking the rifle from Mike O'Malley's hands. But that was the face of a man from almost fifty years ago, and who knew what kind of condition the film was in after all this time? Surely, if it ever came to trial, he would be able to buy a brigade of experts to testify in court that the man taking the rifle from the assassin wasn't him.

"Who you gonna believe, you or your lying eyes?" he said to the vacant-eyed talking head that now filled his television screen, but his words came out all slurry.

Well, fuck 'em—he didn't need them or their shit. He had so much money he could shred most of it into confetti and throw himself a ticker-tape parade down Fifth Avenue and still have enough left over to live like a king for the rest of his life. He could buy himself a tropical island and spend the rest of his days in a Margaritaville of warm sunshine and beautiful girls in string bikinis, and then, just because he could, because it would satisfy the black anger in his heart, he would get himself the most badass hit man he could find and send him after the O'Malley boy and that miserable old woman's granddaughter. Zoe Dmitroff.

God, did he want them dead. He wanted them *dead* the way Yasmine was dead, and he would tell the guy he hired to make their deaths long and slow and painful, and he would have it videotaped, too, yeah, and every night before he went to bed, he would watch the tape over and over, watch them dying over and over, and he would think of Yasmine, and he would smile—

Suddenly it felt as if a giant vise had grabbed his head and was squeezing it, tighter and tighter. He tried to reach out to keep from falling, but he couldn't lift his arm. He tried to take a step, but lurched instead, banging into his desk, knocking something off it. He heard it hit the thick carpet with a dull thud, but he couldn't see. It was as if a white, gauzy bandage now covered his eyes, and he tried to reach up to pull it away, but he still couldn't lift his arm.

His legs gave out from under him, and he pitched forward, banging his head on the corner of his desk as he fell to the floor. He tried to get back up again, but a boulder was on him, pressing him down. And the pain was so sharp and fierce, it felt as if a knife were slicing open his skull. Had Jack Kennedy felt pain like this when the bullet ripped through his head?

Miles blinked, and the white gauze fell away from his eyes. For a moment he thought he saw his son, standing by the fireplace, but no hate was in Jonathan's eyes this time. The boy's eyes were wet with tears, and Miles wanted to tell him to quit bawling, to be a man, but he couldn't get his tongue to work right. Nothing was working right anymore. Even his heart felt broken, and wasn't that a laugh.

Then suddenly his son was gone, and where his heart had been, Miles felt a gaping hole, a giant, sucking abyss of need. *I want*, he thought. *I want, I want. I want her back, I want it all back, every day, every moment of love and joy and sadness and misery—I want all of it back.*

45

Zoe stared at the ugly gray concrete building, its door nondescript except for the number 17 painted black on the milk glass of the transom above it. "This looks closer to a prison than a nightclub, Ry."

"The club itself is deep underground, in what was once a nuclear fallout shelter."

"How far underground?" Zoe asked, as a shiver of claustrophobia coursed through her, but Ry pretended not to hear.

She could feel the beat of the music blasting up from below through snow and the thick soles of her new fur-lined boots. The crowd waiting to get in was mostly teenagers. They drank from paper cups of vodka bought from a kiosk on the corner and sucked on harsh Russian cigarettes while they jiggled and stamped their feet, trying in vain to drive away the bitter cold.

"I thought you didn't want anyone to see us with your biologist," Zoe said. "In case we end up landing a pile of trouble in his lap." Actually Ry had said a *shitload* of trouble, but she didn't want to be indelicate in public. "Won't he stick out here like orange Day-Glo paint?"

Ry shook his head. His cheekbones were chapped pink from the cold, and his eyes glimmered in the harsh white light cast by the 1950s-era streetlamps. "We won't be meeting up with Dr. Nikitin in the club. That's where we're gonna let Popov's son, the *mafiya pakhan*, know we're in town."

"Oh, right. Him." Zoe shivered inside her new down parka. It was supposed to keep her warm up to minus fifty degrees and it was almost succeeding. "I almost managed to forget about the rotten schmuck for all of two seconds."

She couldn't believe they were doing this, even more that it had all been her idea. After that insane chase through the mountains above the Danube Bend, wild sex with Ry on the hood of a car, and then finding the altar of bones where it had been, with her, all along, hidden in the icon—she'd felt so wrung out and exhausted, she was asleep on her feet by the time they got back to their hotel in Budapest. She couldn't remember crawling into bed, although when she woke up late the next morning, she was in her underwear, beneath the covers, and the smell of freshly brewed coffee filled the room.

She didn't know how he'd managed to do it, or if he slept at all, but by the time she emerged from the shower, Ry had shopping bags full of the heavy-duty clothes they would need for a St. Petersburg winter laid out on the sofa, and on the coffee table a new set of fake documents, including visas to get into Russia.

"They're not up to Kareem's standards," he said, as she came up behind him. "But they'll get us in."

She let the towel she was wearing fall to the floor as she slipped her arms around his waist, pressing into him with her damp, naked belly. "You know, O'Malley, you're kind of handy to have around." She kissed him behind the ear, little nibbling kisses. Then one thing led to another, and—

"Come on," Ry said now, wrapping a gloved hand around her upper arm to steer her around a girl with platinum hair and kohl-smudged eyes who seemed to be swaying to the beat of her own inner music. "We're on the A-list, so we might as well cut to the head of the line."

They got a few dirty looks as they pushed their way to the door, where a bouncer in a dirty white quilted coat stood, feet splayed, arms behind his back. He looked like the Michelin tire man, only mean. He eyed them up and down, started to shake his head, then stopped when Ry pushed up the sleeve of his coat far enough to show the dagger tattoo on his arm.

The bouncer let them into a tiny foyer filled with a double-helix staircase that stretched up into an eerie blue-haloed blackness. "Uh, Ry," Zoe said. "I don't see any way down, except for an elevator over there in the corner that's no bigger than a Porta Potti."

"I'll be in it with you," Ry said. "Just shut your eyes."

Zoe snorted a scared laugh. "Like that's going to work."

Somehow—probably under the theory that if she was going to die, at least she wouldn't die alone—she let Ry maneuver into the tiny cage. She regretted it an instant later, when the door clattered shut, the low-watt bare bulb that was plugged into the ceiling dimmed even more, and the car plunged with a violent shudder.

It was an eternity going down, and Zoe spent it with her face pressed against Ry's chest to keep from screaming.

The elevator landed with another shudder and such a hard thud the lightbulb went out completely, and even Ry looked relieved to be out of it once the door finally rattled open. In front of them was a steel door outlined by pulsating green neon tubes and an old woman wearing a babushka and earplugs, who was there to take their coats.

The door opened into a large, square room with chrome-and-mirror columns, blue strobe lighting, and a broad band of twinkling pink lights that snaked across a midnight-blue ceiling like the Milky Way. The music, a painful mix of Russian techno and American hip hop, was so loud Zoe was surprised her eyes and ears didn't start bleeding.

She saw a few tables scattered about, but most of the people in the impossibly crowded room were dancing, their bodies grinding together in rhythm with the thumping techno beat. Suddenly the music switched to something softer—a Russian folk song, but with a touch of Harlem soul thrown in to sex it up, sung in a husky, melancholy voice. And on the far back wall a giant video screen came alive.

In the video a young man with the piercing, fanatic blue eyes of a martyred priest and the sex appeal of a movie star sang into a microphone as if he were making love to it with his song. He was dressed like a pirate, in a white shirt with billowing sleeves and a red silk sash tied around his forehead to hold back his shoulder-length blond hair. The neck of the shirt slashed open deep enough to reveal glimpses of a well-cut chest, and as he moved, Zoe caught the distinctive blue ink of prison tattoos.

Just then she felt Ry tense a little beside her and she turned to see a couple of security guards in black tie coming toward them. They stopped in front of Ry, and one of them said something to him Zoe couldn't hear, but Ry nodded, then he took her by the hand and they followed the men past the long, shiny black-lacquer bar and into a corner that was marked off with a red velvet rope.

Behind the rope, seated at a chrome-and-glass table and throwing back a tumbler full of vodka, was the beautiful young man still singing his heart out from the giant video screen. A couple of empty chrome stools flanked either side of him, but Zoe didn't realize that he was actually waiting for them, until one of the security men snapped open the rope and waved them toward the table.

The young man raised his head. Unlike in the video, he wasn't wearing the red sash, and she could see that the skin just below his hairline was marred by a raw, red scar. And those martyred-priest's eyes of his had fastened hard onto Ry's face.

He stared at Ry for a long moment, then leapt to his feet and came around the table to sweep Ry up in a big man-hug, thumping him hard on the back with bunched-up fists.

———

A BOTTLE OF Dom Pérignon and three fluted glasses appeared at the table, but the music was too loud for them to talk over. So they sat and sipped their champagne in silence, only from time to time the young man would lean over and drape his arm across Ry's shoulder and smile, posing for a seemingly endless clicking of digital cameras and cell phones from the people in the club.

Then after ten minutes or so of this, he abruptly pushed back from the table and got to his feet. Ry stood as well, holding out his hand. The young man started to take it, but then he pulled Ry into him for another fierce hug instead, and Zoe saw his eyes clench tightly shut as if he were in pain.

He said something in Ry's ear, and Ry nodded. Then they broke apart and the man disappeared into the crowd, one of the security guards close on his heels. The other jerked his head at Zoe and Ry for them to follow him through a small, narrow door behind the bar.

"I will return in a moment with your coats," the guard said, then the door swung closed, leaving them alone in a small room mostly taken up by a plush, white leather sofa. A huge plasma TV took up one wall; another was filled with rows of platinum records and framed CD jackets.

"Well, if Popov's son didn't know we were here before, he will soon," Zoe said, "Only about a hundred kids just took our picture with that singer. Who was he, by the way?"

"Sasha Nikitin. He's a big deal here in Russia, maybe not on the level of a Bono or the Boss, but getting there. He's a big enough celebrity, anyway, to cause a stir wherever he goes, and whoever gets seen with him gets noticed."

"Nikitin . . . Is he related to the Dr. Nikitin we're going to meet with?"

"Sasha's his son," Ry said, as the door behind them opened again, letting in a shuddering blast of music and the security guard carrying their coats under one arm and a pair of large-size men's boots in his hand.

"Should you choose to put your hand in your right pocket," the man said to Ry while watching them bundle up, "you will find a Beretta Px4 Storm, along with an extra ammunition clip. In your left pocket is the key to an apartment near the Pevchesky Bridge that I believe you know of. We'll let it be known where you will be staying, accidentally on purpose, you understand? So the *pakhan*'s men can find you."

"Yeah. Thanks."

"You might want to put these on now." The guard handed Ry the boots. "I've hidden the GPS tracking device in the left heel. We'll be monitoring it, so that once the *pakahn*'s men have you, we'll be able to follow it to where they bring you, but at a discreet distance, of course."

"How soon do you think he'll make his move?"

"Not before morning, I shouldn't think. We have inserted into the down lining of your coat a short-range voice transmitter. . . ." The security man paused, his forehead knotted in a frown. "As per your wishes, we won't move in for the rescue until we get the signal from you, and that worries me. You will be well searched for weapons, and anything else of that nature, before you are allowed in the *pakhan*'s presence. Which means you will have to improvise should trouble suddenly hit the fan, and there may not be a lot of time or opportunity to preserve your lives before we can arrive."

"I know," Ry said. "But there's no way around it. We need to talk to the man before you guys come in with guns blazing." He held out his hand. "Thank you for everything. And tell Sasha—"

"He knows," the security man said, shaking Ry's hand and cutting off whatever Ry had been about to say. "He said to tell you it is the least he can do for the man who gave him back his life." The guard paused again, cleared his throat. "You will find the entrance to the back tunnel inside the closet over there. It is a small hatch in the floor, beneath the filing cabinet."

"Tunnel?" Zoe said. "Oh, shit. And pardon my Russian."

———

THE TUNNEL WAS a little bigger than the laundry cute. Just. They were going to have to crawl through it on their hands and knees.

Zoe groaned. "I really hate this."

"I know. But look at it this way—it beats having to go back up in that death trap of an elevator."

Zoe gave a squeaky laugh. "You do have a point. So how far do we have to crawl down this thing?"

"Not far."

"You're lying through your pearly whites, O'Malley. I can tell. . . . I can do this, though. I can do it."

"Yeah, you can."

"Only do I have to do it now? Right this very minute, I mean?"

"Yeah, you do."

Zoe crawled down into the opening in the raw dirt, and it was worse than she imagined it would be. Thick wooden planks were fitted into the walls to hold back dirt that smelled wet and musty. The way a grave would smell, she thought, then wished she hadn't. Every ten feet or so, a bare, dim lightbulb hung from a wire that looped across the ceiling.

Her breath rasped in and out of her throat like rough sandpaper, her heart hammered in her ears, but somehow she kept putting one knee in front of the other.

Ry had lied, though. It was really, really far.

———————

THEY CAME OUT of the tunnel through a dummy sewer grate, into a small, triangular square with a bronze statue of the poet Pushkin in its center. A white Lada rolled along the curb and rattled to a stop in front of them, vapor spewing from its exhaust pipe—

Ry opened the back door for Zoe to get in, then climbed into the passenger seat alongside a small figure, so enveloped in a brown fur coat and matching hat that Zoe could barely make out a face.

"Zoe," Ry said. "This is Dr. Nikitin. Dr. Nikitin, Zoe Dmitroff."

Their gazes met in the rearview mirror. Behind a pair of thick bifocals, his scientist's eyes were round and liquid as a basset hound's.

"It's an honor to meet you, sir," Zoe said.

"The honor is all mine." He put the Lada into gear, and they lurched out into the street. "We will park in front of the Ploshad Vosstania metro station," he said to Ry. "As if we are waiting there to pick up a friend. That way we can talk here in the car without drawing attention to ourselves."

As they turned a corner, a blast of cold air blew up Zoe's pant legs. She looked down and saw the snowy street rushing by through a hole in the floorboard. She turned sideways and drew her legs up onto the seat, tucking her knees up under her chin. The car smelled of boiled cabbage and the pine-scented air freshener that swung from the rearview mirror.

They drove for about five minutes through dark and mostly deserted streets before pulling up in front of a large, domed-roof building, ringed by a bright necklace of streetlights.

Nikitin lit up a foul-smelling cigarette. "Did you just come from my Sasha's nightclub? I have heard that you can get ecstasy pills there out of a vending machine."

Zoe caught the flash of Ry's smile as he turned to look at the older man. "It's possible, but I didn't see any."

Nikitin shrugged. "He won't let me come check it out for myself. He says the style is not to my taste."

"It's modern," Ry said. "And loud."

Nikitin grunted. "So, tell me . . . where is this thing you wish for me to analyze?"

"I've got it back here." Zoe dug into her parka for the clear glass ampoule with its rubber stopper that Ry had bought in Budapest, along with the eyedropper she'd used to take a tiny drop of the bone juice from the amulet. In the semidark of the hotel bathroom, the juice had been the color of swamp water. But now, as she handed the ampoule to Dr. Nikitin, she was more than a little spooked to see the bone juice was glowing a bright, iridescent red.

Ry was spooked by it, too. She could see it in his face.

"Interesting," Dr. Nikitin said, peering closely at the ampoule through the thick lenses of his glasses. "Where did it come from?"

"A cave in Siberia," Ry said. "The people there believe it's some kind of fountain of youth. That if you drink one drop of it, you will live forever."

"Interesting."

"Could it be real?" Zoe asked. "I mean, is it possible? Scientifically?"

"Theoretically, perhaps. But it is highly unlikely given the complexity of the aging process. All the genetic and lifestyle factors, the hundreds, possibly thousands, of individual factors in our cells and organs that affect our longevity."

Dr. Nikitin gave the ampoule a little shake, and Zoe would have sworn the red iridescent goo glowed brighter.

"Because of its phosphorescent property," Nikitin went on, "it is understandable that a primitive people would imbue it with special powers. Perhaps one day a witch doctor or a healer mixed it with some herbs and the patient recovered. And a legend grew from there."

"But you'll analyze it for us anyway?" Zoe asked.

"I could analyze it, certainly, but my area is in developmental biology. Who you should really have take a look at it is a biochemist. There is a woman I know with the Institute of Bioregulation and Gerontology who has done some experiments with the longevity genes in *Caenorhab-*

ditis elegans—that is, roundworms. Nearly transparent little things, are roundworms. You can see their heart, neurons, and other innards clearly through a microscope. They are a favorite of Olga's because of their simple anatomy and because they have a minimal number of genes. I would like to include her in our discovery, if I may. Her expertise would be invaluable."

Ry shook his head. "I don't know. . . . How much do you trust her?"

Nikitin looked surprised by the question. "We have been lovers on occasion. Why would— Ah," he said, interrupting himself to answer his own question. "You need her to be discreet because there is danger involved. Because if a man truly believed there was such a thing as a fountain of youth, he might kill to get his hands on it."

"He has killed," Ry said.

Nikitin stared at Ry for another long moment, then nodded slowly. "I can take the subway home. You might have use for a car while you are here."

Nikitin slipped the ampoule into the pocket of his fur coat, but he made no move to get out of the Lada. "It has just occurred to me," he said after a moment, "that if such a thing as a true fountain of youth existed, it could be a terrible thing to let loose upon the earth. Overpopulation, wars, famine . . ." He shuddered. "How often has mankind seen our salvation in something which turns out later to be the means of our destruction?"

He turned to look at Ry, and Zoe saw a sadness come over Nikitin's face. "When you were in the nightclub, did you see my son?"

"Only for a few minutes. There was no chance for us to talk."

"But he looked well?"

"Yes, he did. Very well."

"His music—it, too, must not be to my tastes, for I admit it makes my ears cry out in pain. Yet he's made himself rich and famous with it. Anything he wants he can have. . . ."

Nikitin looked away, through the windshield at the dark and cold Russian night. "But that place where you found him, the place you saved him from—he had fear etched into his soul there, etched like acid into stone. Will he ever recover from it? That is the question I ask myself, and cannot answer."

46

⸙

THE OPEN cast-iron railings of the Pevchesky Bridge were throwing spiky shadows onto the river ice when Ry pulled over to the curb and killed the ignition. The Lada's engine sputtered on out of spite for a few seconds more, then finally died.

"You've stayed here before?" Zoe said, as she got out of the car. She tilted her head to look up at the tall, elegant cream-stone building. "With Sasha?"

Ry shook his head. "Sasha's lover lives here. She inherited it from her grandfather, who was quite the Communist Party apparatchik in his day."

He slipped his arm around her waist and pulled her against him. She looked up into his face, and soft, feathery snowflakes fell from the night sky into her eyes and open, smiling mouth.

"I've been told," Ry said, "that the bed in the master bedroom came from one of the Tsar Nicholas's palaces."

THEY FELL ONTO the postered bed with its rose silk canopy, mouths together, trying to tear off all their clothes at once. It was like it had been on the hood of the car, coming at them, coming over them, hard and fast. He nearly strangled her with her bra, funny really, but their need was so urgent, so vital to what they were and what they were becoming to each other, that there was no laughter, no attempt at anything other than coming together as quickly as possible, joining into one.

When, at last, they were quiet, lying beside each other, replete and at peace, she said, "You almost yelled down the ceiling."

He tried to laugh, but it came out as an exhausted sigh. "Maybe, but you were louder, the loudest scream I've ever heard. I hope we don't get arrested."

She snuggled against him. "Thank you, Ry."

"For what?"

"Being you and finding me."

He felt the need for her build again, and this time they took it slowly, touches easy and unhurried. He kissed her mouth, her breasts, her belly, kissed all of her, lingering, and she screamed again.

———

LATER, THE ROOM dark, lying within the crook of his arm, she said, "What did you save Sasha Nikitin from?"

Ry's hand was idly caressing her breasts, then toying with the green-skull amulet she'd worn on a chain around her neck since Budapest.

"A prison in Tajikistan," he said after a moment. "I was on a mission there, Operation Containment we called it. Trying to put some kind of dent, no matter how pathetic, in the flow of Afghan heroin into Russia. One night things went all to hell, and we ended up having to bust one of the smuggling rings on the fly. But the wrong guy got killed, and I got hauled in by the local cops and thrown into a jail cell that was already packed like sardines in a can with forty other men. Sasha was the youngest, just a kid, and he . . . He had this heart tattooed on his forehead."

"I've seen *vors* with teardrops and daggers on their faces, but never a heart. Why that?" she asked, because prison tattoos always had a meaning.

"Because of what they'd done to him. They'd turned him into a sex toy for any man who wanted him."

Zoe closed her eyes, not sure she wanted to hear any more now, but he went on, "In a Tajikistan jail they make the ink for the tat by burning the heel of a shoe and mixing it with urine. They'd made Sasha use his own shoe and piss. They even made him pay off the tattoo artist by . . . well, you can guess."

Zoe nodded, swallowing around the thick lump in her throat. "But how did he end up in such a place? His father's a scientist, a professor at the university here."

"Drugs. He got himself hooked bad on the poppy juice, and then he got it into his head that he could finance his habit by doing his own smuggling. He got caught trying to drive a vegetable truck full of two hundred kilos of heroin across the border."

She felt Ry shrug in the dark. "I don't know. I guess I felt sorry for the kid, so when I escaped, I brought him with me."

Zoe thought it was probably a lot more than that, but she let it go.

"He wasn't in very good shape, so I had to bring him all the way back home here to St. Petersburg. Soon as he could, the first thing he did was get that heart taken off his forehead. They had to dissolve his skin with magnesium powder to do it. It must've hurt like hell."

She turned her head into Ry's chest and kissed him, relishing the rise and fall of his breathing beneath her lips. "Ry? Are we going to get out of this alive?"

Every other man in the world would have lied to her then, but not him. "Either we take Popov's son out tomorrow, or he takes us out."

"If I have to, I'll give him the bone juice. But only if I have to."

The arm he had wrapped around her back tightened its grip. He kissed the top of her head. "Do you think you can find the nightclub again?"

"Yes. But why—"

"Sssh." He put his finger against her mouth. "If you make it through this and I don't, I want you to promise me that you'll go to Sasha. He'll take care of you. He'll see that you get back home."

She shook her head. "If you don't make it, then I don't want to either."

"Yeah, you do. Nobody wants to die."

She thought suddenly that she could feel a heat coming off the amulet where it lay between her breasts. She sat up, pulled off the chain, and held it out to him on her open palm.

"If this really is a fountain of youth, then maybe if we drink from it, Popov can't hurt us. Can't kill us, at least. One drop and we could live forever—"

"No." He curled her fingers around the amulet and pushed it away from him. "No."

"Okay, then." She shrugged, pretending not to care, but she was shaking inside. From temptation, and a terrible fear. *Nobody wants to die.*

She looked down into his hard face. "I don't know how you do it. How you've lived this kind of life for so long."

His face didn't soften then either, but he said, "I don't know if I can do it anymore. If there is a tomorrow after tomorrow, and another tomorrow after that, then I want all those days and nights to be full of moments like this." He reached up and cupped her cheek, his fingers wiping away tears she hadn't known were there. "I want you."

She leaned over and kissed him, softly at first, and then the kiss turned hard, and this time as they made love, she tried to make herself remember every moment of it.

They fell asleep in each other's arms.

———

RY CAME AWAKE suddenly and sat up. The moon had risen, filling the room with a silvery light. He reached for her, but she was gone.

Then he saw her standing in the bathroom doorway, wearing one of his T-shirts. A man in a black jogging suit stood close behind her.

He had the blade of a knife pressed to her throat.

47

LIGHT FLOODED the bedroom with the flip of a switch, and a second man came through the door. He, too, was dressed in a black jogging suit and Adidas athletic shoes—the uniform of a *vors* in the Russian mafia. Only this guy had jazzed his up a notch. Three gold chains and an enormous gold baptism cross hung around his neck.

"I like your look, *dolboy'eb*," Ry said to him in street Russian. "Real classy. Do you plan on being buried in it?"

"You're the dickhead, dickhead. I'm the one with the gun, so shut up and get dressed." The *vor* tossed a duffel bag onto the floor. "In these clothes, not your own, and be quick about it. The *pakhan* does not like to be kept waiting."

Ry shook his head slowly back and forth. "I'm not doing a thing until you tell that rutting goat over there to take his knife off my woman's throat."

"Grisha, take your knife off her throat."

"But, Vadim—"

"*Do it.*"

Grisha gave the other man a sour look, but he lowered the knife and took a step back. His black eyes focused on Ry, a sneer curdling his mouth. "Move, bitch," Grisha said, and slammed the flat of his hand into Zoe's back so hard he sent her sprawling.

Ry came off the bed, hard and fast, but he was stopped cold by the poke of a gun barrel in his belly.

Vadim brought his face right up to Ry's, so close Ry could see the blackheads on his nose and smell the boiled cabbage on his breath. "One more inch and you die. One more fucking word out of your mouth and you die."

"Ry, *don't*."

Zoe scrambled to her feet and held up her hands, palms out. He could see the fear in her eyes and knew it was for him. To get his hands on the altar of bones, Nikolai Popov would need Zoe alive and cooperating, but if Ry started looking as if he was more trouble than he was worth, he'd get a bullet in his head.

"I'm all right, Ry, really. He didn't hurt me." She bent over to pick her bra and panties from off the floor, but Grisha grabbed her arm. "Put on what we brought you, and nothing else."

For a split second longer, Ry thought about trying to take the other man down, gun or no gun, but that was the testosterone talking—he could feel it, pumping along with the hot blood through the veins in his neck.

He raised his spread hands and backed up a step. "Okay, okay. I'll shut up and get dressed. But I want her left alone."

Vadim smiled, showing off the diamond chips embedded American-rapper-style in his two front teeth. "We won't kill her unless the *pakhan* says kill her. Then? We kill her."

———————

THE CLOTHES IN the duffel bag were more black jogging suits and Adidas shoes, along with a couple of cheap parkas and some wool hats and gloves.

"Don't we get any bling to go with our new outfits?" Ry said, once they were dressed.

Vadim dangled a pair of handcuffs from his left pointer finger. "This is the only 'bling' you're gonna get, except maybe for a bullet in the head. So shut up and put them on."

Ry snapped the metal bracelets around his wrists. Either they only had the one pair of handcuffs, he thought, or they didn't consider Zoe much of a threat.

It was snowing, the dark streets deserted, but a chauffeured black Mercedes SUV waited for them at the curb, engine running. Grisha opened the back door, shoved Zoe inside, and climbed in after her. Then the Mercedes suddenly shot forward before he'd finished shutting the door.

"Hey!'

Ry started to run after the car—not so easy to do on a street packed with snow and with your hands in cuffs. It was pointless anyway. All he could do was watch as the red taillights grew slowly smaller until they turned onto the Pevchesky Bridge and disappeared into the darkness.

Vadim came up beside him, wheezing from that little bit of a run. He had his gun out again and this time he looked as if he really might use it. "What are you doing, asking to be shot? The *pakhan* said come in separate cars."

"Then where's ours?"

"It will be here when it gets here. Now get out of the fucking street before you get run over by a snowplow."

They waited, then waited some more. This wasn't good. Why separate cars?

Vadin fished a Bic lighter and a pack of cheap Russian cigarettes out of the jacket pocket of his jogging suit. He lit up, took a deep drag, then coughed up half a lung.

"Those things'll kill you," Ry said.

"Fuck you."

A snowplow crunched by, and lights came on in the apartments across the street. Vadim began to jiggle up and down on his toes. His lips and nose, even the tips of his ears, Ry noticed, had turned blue with the cold.

"What?" Ry said. "The *pakhan* doesn't pay enough for you to buy a coat, not even a cheap-ass parka like this one you gave me?"

"I'm from Siberia. In Siberia this is not cold. In Siberia this is spring."

Ry's nerves were on the screaming edge by the time the second Mercedes SUV showed up.

Their driver made a U-turn and drove off in the opposite direction from the one Zoe's car had taken, and for the first time in his life Ry felt literally sick with fear. Not so much because he knew he could be riding to his death—although that was not a pleasant prospect. But what would happen to Zoe now if she had to handle what was coming on her own?

Their driver took them through a dizzying maze of streets lined with decaying palazzi of long-dead merchants and noblemen, mixed in with fitness clubs, espresso bars, and a Porsche dealer. Trying to ditch a possible tail, Ry supposed. Not that they needed to. Sasha's security men had positioned themselves well back to keep from drawing attention to themselves, counting on the GPS in the heel of Ry's boot to let them know if he and Zoe were on the move. A brilliant plan, except that Popov had anticipated it, and now the boot was still back at the apartment, while he and Zoe were now headed God knew where.

Every ten minutes Vadim lit up another foul cigarette, filling the SUV with a greasy yellow cloud of smoke. Eventually the eclectic neighborhood gave way to blocks of crumbling Soviet-era apartment buildings and rusting factories. The snow was coming down hard, stacking up on the windshield faster than the wipers could flick it away.

About an hour out of St. Petersburg, they crossed a set of railroad tracks and ran out of asphalt. They were deep in the country now, lurching over frozen ruts through a wasteland of pines and rocks.

Ry was beginning to think he'd fallen into some existentialist hell, then out in the middle of nowhere they came upon an old cemetery. The driver slowed and turned down a narrow lane, lined on both sides by the cemetery's tall stone walls. They drove for about a mile, and then the lane dead-ended in front of the ruins of a large brick building.

"Once we get out, take yourself and the car up to the farm," Vadim said to the driver, as the SUV crunched to a stop on the fresh layer of snow.

The frigid air felt good after the smoky stuffiness inside the Mercedes. Flakes, soft and thick as down, fell from a black sky overhead, but Ry's internal clock told him it would soon be dawn.

He thought the brick ruins were once a slaughterhouse because of the bronze sculpture of a bull that stood guard next to the building's wide, arched doorway. A lone, bare lightbulb cast just enough light on the yard for him to pick out the remains of what looked like a cattle chute sticking up out of the snow and a rusted-out hay baler.

There was no sign of the other SUV, nor of any living thing. And, worse, no other fresh tire tracks in the virgin snow.

Oh, man, O'Malley, this isn't good. This is not good at all.

Vadim poked him in the side with a Beretta. "You speak good Russian for an American. Do you know the word *grokhnut?*"

Literally it meant "to bang," but it had another meaning as well. "If you were going to shoot me," Ry said, "you'd have done it by now."

Vadim grunted a laugh. "Does it comfort you to think so?" He pointed with his gun. "Go over there, beneath the light."

With Vadim close on his heels, Ry walked toward the wide, arched entrance into what had probably been the slaughterhouse's bleeding and gutting area. A long time ago fire had destroyed part of the roof and blackened the brick walls, but as he got closer, he could see someone had pulled an old, turquoise trailer house inside and set it up on cinder blocks.

"That's far enough," Vadim said, and Ry felt the burn of cold steel in the side of his neck, the wash of hot breath against his cheek.

Ry stood unmoving, the gun at his head. A long moment passed, and then another. They seemed to be waiting for something—but what? It was so eerily quiet, you could almost hear the snow falling.

Here, the stench that permeated the air around the ruins was more pronounced, the old, sour smell of blood and rotting entrails, overlaid by a newer, more pungent stink—like a combination of cat pee and rotten eggs.

He had a good view of the old trailer house now, and the litter of KFC tubs and pizza boxes around it. But he also saw empty cans of paint thinner, stripped lithium batteries, used coffee filters, and empty cold-tablet blister packs. Propane canisters with blue, corroded valves were stacked up on one side of the trailer's front door. On the other, a pile of rotting bags full of ammonia nitrate.

In other words, everything you would need to make methamphetamine.

A crank lab was usually a hive of activity, but at this one there wasn't a tweeker in sight. Yet although the place looked deserted, Ry knew it wasn't abandoned, because under the low aluminum roof of the trailer's patio extension, he could see two picnic tables loaded with row after row of mason jars filled with cold-medicine tablets soaking in muriatic acid.

And those babies are cooking all right. He could actually see the fumes rising in waves out of the open mouths of the mason jars. *One spark, and this whole place could blow to smithereens.*

"Nice little meth lab you all going on in there," Ry said.

Vadim was silent for a couple of beats, and the gun at Ry's head didn't waiver. "I am beginning to suspect you are *mussor*. I think you know that word, as well, huh? How do you say *mussor* in American?"

"Garbage."

Vadim laughed, because it was also Russian-mafia slang for "cop." "I thought you would know it."

At that moment, Ry heard what he'd been hoping, praying for—the steady hum of a powerful car engine turning down the lane from off the main road, the crunch of tires over snow. He felt Vadim stiffen behind him.

"Now, *mussor*," said Vadim, "it is time for you to die."

Ry started to spin around, throwing up his arm to knock the gun away, but he was too late. His head exploded in a white, hot flash, and then there was nothing.

48

THE *MAFIYA* thug, Grisha, had told her they would be bringing Ry to the meeting place in a separate car, but she didn't believe him, even though the alternative was unbearable.

The litany of a prayer ran through her head over and over. *Please God don't let them kill him. Please God, don't let them kill him. . . .*

After an eternity of driving aimlessly around the city, and then another eternity through a dark, arctic countryside, they turned down a lane that ran alongside a cemetery. The car's headlights picked up crumbling brick walls, then Zoe saw a black Mercedes SUV just like theirs pull out and head down a narrow road that led away from the ruins.

"There, you see," Grisha said. "Vadim and your lover have made it here ahead of us. I told you not to worry."

Zoe said nothing. She was filled with a strange fatalism now, and she pressed her hand against her chest, where beneath her clothes the green skull amulet hung from its silver chain. It would happen now, she thought. Whatever *it* was.

As they rolled to a stop, Grisha reached out and grabbed Zoe's wrist. Instinctively, she tried to pull away, but his fingers were like a vise, and then she realized he was only snapping handcuffs on her, as they had done with Ry.

He reached across her lap to open the car door. "This is the old Rach'a slaughterhouse," he said, with a strange, secretive smile that made her skin crawl. "You will wait for the *pakhan* inside."

Icy snow stung her cheeks as she got out of the car. The cold in the city had been bad enough, but this far out in the country it was a biting, living thing.

Grisha wrapped his meaty hand around her upper arm and half-pushed, half-dragged her toward the ruins, while their car drove off, taking the same side back road as the other SUV.

Zoe had to look down at her feet to keep from slipping on the rutted, icy snow, so it wasn't until they were almost at the gaping, arched doorway that she saw the body.

And the man standing over it with a gun in his hand.

———————

"No!" Zoe screamed, and tried to run, slipping and flailing over the icy snow. Grisha snagged her around the waist, lifting her off the ground, and still she screamed, *"No! No! No!"* and her legs thrashed at the air.

Ry lay on the ground, a pool of blood staining the snow by his head. What she could see of his face looked as cold and white as marble. Already a thin layer of flakes dusted his coat and hair.

Vadim said, "Get her inside, then help me get rid of this dead *dolboy'eb*. He's too big for me to drag off by myself." And he gave the body a kick in the side to emphasize his point.

Zoe clawed at the arm that held her and screamed again, and it was as if the scream tore all of her breath out with it. She went limp, and the world around her blurred into a white haze. She was barely aware as Grisha carried her into the ruins.

He flung her into a straight-back wooden chair that sat in front of a gray metal table. He unlocked one of the handcuffs from around her wrist and refastened it to one of a pair of eyebolts embedded into the tabletop.

He started to leave, then turned back. "Life is as cheap as the price of a bullet. Remember that when you talk to the *pakhan*."

Zoe barely registered what Grisha said, or that he left her. She couldn't see Ry's body from here, but her mind was filled the image of his blood staining the snow, so bright and red and wet.

She wasn't sure how long she sat there alone. She didn't dare let herself think beyond the need to take one breath and then another and not scream.

The cold penetrated the horror first, then the stink—like cat urine, only worse. The single dim light over the doorway didn't penetrate far into the shrouded, cavernous ruins. She saw old graffiti spray-painted on the crumbling walls and a lot of trash scattered about, but no cats. Someone had pulled a ratty old trailer inside the crumbling walls, and the worst of the smell seemed to be coming from it.

A patiolike extension ran out from the trailer's aluminum roof, sheltering a pair of picnic tables that sagged beneath the weight of dozens of old-fashioned mason jars. Around the tables were piles of rusting cans and hundreds of what, oddly, looked like old coffeemaker filters. Obviously, Zoe thought, the trailer was being used for something, but at the moment all of its windows were dark.

She was alone, handcuffed to a table in the dark and foul-smelling ruins of a slaughterhouse, while Popov's men went off to get rid—

Zoe forced herself to breathe, one single breath and then another.

She heard a man curse out in the yard. Grisha? Then the clank of metal slapping against metal. An instant later a bank of electric stadium lights flared on, nearly blinding her.

When the bright spots that danced before her eyes finally faded, she saw Ry standing in the arched doorway.

"What?" came a rich baritone voice from out of the darkness behind her. "You don't believe in miracles?"

———

A TALL, SILVER-HAIRED man in a long sable coat emerged from the shadows, picking his way through the rubble that littered the floor, but Zoe was barely aware of him. Ry was alive, alive, alive. . . . Blood, too much blood, covered one side of his face, and he swayed on his feet, but he was here, she could see him with her own two eyes.

She stared, stiff and unmoving, not daring to believe, not even daring to breathe. *If I could touch him*, she thought, *I would know he was real*, and she started to stand up, but the handcuff stopped her, jerking her back down into the chair.

She wondered why he wasn't coming to her, then she realized Vadim was behind him, with his Beretta pointed at the back of Ry's head.

"Ry," she said, her voice breaking over his name. "I thought . . ."

"She thought we had killed you," the *pakhan* said in English made thick by his accent. "It was a little charade we played, so she would fully grasp, deep in her gut, that you are about as useful to me as a hangnail. And just as easily disposed of."

Grisha came back through the archway just then, and the *pakhan* said to him in Russian, "Good. You're still here, as well." He waved his hand at Ry. "Help Vadim handcuff him to the table across from the girl. No need to be gentle if he doesn't cooperate."

Vadim grabbed Ry by his coat and hauled him to the table. Grisha kicked out a chair for him to sit in, and he sat. Vadim unfastened the cuff that was on his right wrist and refastened it to one of the bolts. Then Grisha backed up a couple of steps, folding his arms across his chest, while Vadim stepped to the side and lit up a cigarette.

Blood was all over Ry's face from a deep gash high on his forehead, his coat dark with it. "You okay?" he asked her softly.

Zoe tried to answer but a sob caught in her throat, so she nodded instead.

"What a touching little reunion this is," the *pakhan* said, as he stepped between them. "And how tedious for the rest of us. It hurt, though, didn't it, my dear, when you thought him dead? I want you to remember that feeling. Remember it well."

He let that sink in while his eyes, sharp and hooded, studied Zoe intently. She stared back, trying not to show her fear of him. He was a Popov all right, for he was the spitting image of the man in the film, who had almost fifty years ago used an umbrella to signal to Ry's father that President Kennedy's limousine was coming into rifle range. He had the same handsome face, with its wide mouth and Slavic cheekbones, the proud nose. The same startling blue eyes beneath thick, rakish eyebrows.

"This moment does have a feel of the inevitable about it, does it not?" he said. "A fate that cannot be denied." He raised a long, fine-boned hand and brushed the back of it once, lightly, across her cheek. "How like my Lena you are. I would know you anywhere."

"You touch me again," Zoe said through clenched teeth, "and I'll bite your hand off."

He cocked an eyebrow, as if he were shocked, shocked that she would say such a thing, but he did take a step back, out of reach of her teeth.

"What do you mean by 'my Lena'?" Ry said, and Zoe was relieved to hear the strength in his voice. Then the sense of his question penetrated her brain. *How like my Lena you are*, Popov's son had said. *My* Lena.

But Lena Orlova had been his father's lover, and that was over seventy years ago. Long before this man could possibly have been born.

Zoe shook her head. Something was wrong here. She looked up into the lean, handsome face. Some wrinkles were around his eyes and at the corners of his mouth, and the skin along his jawline sagged a little. His hair was gray but was still thick and full, not even thinning a little at the temples. This man couldn't be older than in his midfifties. But he had called her great-grandmother "my Lena."

And then she remembered what Katya had told Ry's father: *She gave it to him to drink, and so he thought he knew all its secrets. He thought he would be able to find it again, but he was wrong, and he's been searching for the altar ever since. Hungering for its power.*

No, it couldn't be true, Zoe thought, yet it also explained so much.

"There never was a son," Ry said. "We're looking at the man himself. Nikolai Popov."

49

THE *PAKAHN* lifted his shoulders in an elegant shrug. "Ah, yes, another charade, I'm afraid. But one that became necessary after a time, when all my contemporaries began losing their hair and their teeth and their memories, while I barely seemed to change at all. I was going to start looking younger than their children before long, so I retired from the world for a while, and when I reemerged, it was as the son I never had. For, sadly, although I've had many women in my long, long life, I didn't marry until 1964, when I was well into my sixties. And then, when my wife and I had a child, it was only a daughter."

"My God," Zoe said, "just how old *are* you?"

A sly, triumphant look came over Popov's face. "In a little over a month I will celebrate my one hundred and twelfth birthday. But then I drank from the altar of bones, so I have many, many more years yet. An eternity perhaps?"

His voice trailed off for a moment, and to Zoe, his eyes seemed to glow as if a fire raged inside him. "The altar is real," he said. "A true fountain of youth, and I am living proof of it."

Ry slouched back in his chair. "Yeah, we can see the bone juice worked on you just fine. You're a hundred and twelve years old and crazy as a loon."

Popov's face hardened, and a killing fury came into his eyes. They'd been speaking all this time in English, but now he said in Russian, "You will hit him, Vadim. Once. Make him feel it."

Vadim took the cigarette out of his mouth, tossed it on the floor, and slammed his fist hard into Ry's face.

Ry's head snapped back, and a film of fresh blood misted the air. He breathed hard for a moment, then shook the hair out of his eyes. He spat out a glob of blood and grinned. "Is that the best you can do?"

Vadim rubbed off the sting on his bunched knuckles. "I know you said only once, *Pakhan*. But I beg permission now to disobey you."

Popov made a tsking noise, shaking his head. "You remind me of your father, Agent O'Malley. He, too, had that tough swagger and the smart mouth. Although now that I remember it better, Mike was not so full of the swagger that night we killed poor Miss Monroe."

"Must've really felt good to be you that night," Ry said. "Killing a woman half your size, and a drugged one at that."

Popov merely smiled. "Did your father ever tell you that we saw her naked tits? They were all you could ever imagine."

A laugh, half-hysterical, spurted out of Zoe's mouth. "This is insane. You are insane. There, I've said it—so what are you going to do now, have your pet goon give me a smack in the jaw? You killed a president of the United States, you killed Marilyn Monroe. You even killed your own daughter, and, yeah, Katya Orlova was your daughter, and you know it. And why? So you could drink from the altar of bones? But you've already been there, done that. So why would you need more?"

"Because he's still aging," Ry said. "Much more slowly than the rest of us, maybe, but he's still getting old. He looks in the mirror and sees the crow's-feet coming on little by little, the sagging skin, the fading hair, and if he's still getting old, then that means he's dying. And he wants it to stop."

"Ah, God," Popov said on an explosion of breath. He tilted back his head and shut his eyes, then breathed out a hollow laugh. "You couldn't be more wrong. I don't want it for myself. I want it for my grandson. For my Igor, who is dying. . . ."

POPOV MADE A sudden jerking movement and looked away, as if he suddenly realized they could see his pain and might be reveling in it.

"My daughter married and had a child," he said after a moment, then he paused and his mouth pulled into a wry smile. "My legitimate daughter, I should say. . . . And she had a child, a son. He is twenty-one now. Twenty-one! And he has alveolar soft-part sarcoma." Another twisted smile. "A mouthful of a disease, is it not? 'A rare and always fatal form of cancer,' the doctors told me that day. I didn't want to believe them."

Popov turned back around, and the desperation on his face now was as disfiguring as scars. "It began with a tumor in his thigh. 'Cut it out,' I told the doctors, 'take the whole leg if you have to, but get it out of him.' In the end, they did take his leg, but the cancer had already metastasized to his lungs and brain. They gave him a year at the most to live. That was eight months ago, and now he swallows OxyContin like breath mints for the pain. He barely weighs a hundred pounds."

"I'm sorry," Zoe said.

"Sorry?" Popov choked over the word. "Your sorry has no place in this. It is too puny. He is my Igor. My *Igor*, and I love him more than anything on this earth, more than my life. If God would let me die in his place, I would."

"But you can't die," Ry said, "so you kill for him instead."

"Nothing, no one else matters, but Igor. The altar of bones is the only hope he has left. It has given me a hundred and twelve years so far, and I feel and look like a man of what? Fifty-five? I've never been sick for a day since I drank from it, not even a sniffle. It worked a miracle on me, and it will work a miracle on Igor."

Popov focused on Zoe's face and she saw the hardness and cruelty come over him, like a steel curtain slamming down. "You are going to take me to the altar of bones, and I will use it to save my Igor. Whether you do so willingly or unwillingly—it does not matter."

Zoe felt tears press against her eyes. This story of his Igor slowly dying, the pain she could see in Popov—it all seemed real, but, *Remember, trust no one*, her grandmother had written. *No one. Beware the hunters.*

"Why do you need her?" Ry said. "You already tricked your Lena into taking you to it when she was a nurse at Norilsk. You know where it is, so what's been stopping you from going back?"

Popov slashed his hand through the air. "Do you think I *haven't* been back to that cave dozens of times? An avalanche buried the entrance, and Lena along with it, and it took three days and fifty *zeks* to dig out the snow, but the cavern was still there, behind the frozen waterfall, and the altar made out of human bones was inside, with the spring bubbling away underneath it."

He stopped, and a faraway look came into his eyes. "I was out of my head with fever and near death when she brought me to the cave. The altar of bones was in the gruel she fed me, one drop, that's all she needed to save me, but I never saw where she got it from. I thought it had to be the boiling spring—why else would they have built that altar made of human bones on top of it?"

He blew out a ragged laugh. "God in heaven, I must have carried away dozens of bottles of the noxious stuff. From the spring at first, and then later from a pool that was in the center of the cavern. From the spring and the pool, and every other bit of moisture dripping from the ceiling and oozing out of the walls, and none of it did a thing. I tried it out on the desperately sick and the dying, and afterward they were still sick and still dying. I had a dozen scientists study it and they all told me it was only water. Well, water polluted from the nickel mining, but water nonetheless. And Lena . . . ?" He snapped his fingers. "*Poof.* Gone into thin air, from a cave whose only way in or out had been buried for days beneath a mountain of snow."

He braced his fists on the table and brought his face close to Zoe's. "So one thing I do know for a certainty. That altar in your little Keeper cave, the one built above a spring and made of human bones, the one that anyone can see with his own eyes . . . that altar is a lie. The real altar of bones is something else, somewhere else, and you are either going to tell me where it is or take me to it. Your choice. But those are the only two choices I am giving you."

Zoe's eyes were steady on his face. "You can give me a hundred choices and it wouldn't matter. I don't know where it is. Maybe my grandmother Katya knew, but you hunted her down for most of her life and then you killed her before she had a chance to tell me."

"Yes, you are right. I hunted her for years, but she was like her mother, Lena—good at escaping from seemingly impossible traps. When my agents found her little girl, Anna Larina, in an orphanage in Ohio, I was sure I had her then, that she would not stay away from the child forever, but I was wrong. All those years I watched and waited for her to seek out the daughter she'd abandoned, and to meet you, her granddaughter, but she never did. So wary, she was, and so clever, until the end when the cancer got her and she grew careless. Or perhaps merely desperate to pass her knowledge on to the next Keeper before she died."

He stared at Zoe hard for a moment longer, then straightened, shaking his head. "That is why I think you are lying to me. Playing me, as you Americans say. You are the Keeper now, and you know where the altar is, because the Keeper always knows where it is."

He turned away, as if dismissing her, and Vadim, who'd understood nothing of the English words, must have taken this as his cue because he straightened and said, "Now, *Pakhan?*"

"Yes."

"What?" Zoe cried. She tried to get up again, but the handcuff still held her fast to the eyebolt in the table. "What are you going to do? Don't hit him again. Please."

"She's begging you not to hit him, Vadim," Popov said in Russian to his enforcer, and the two men shared a laugh.

———

RY WATCHED AS Vadim lit up a fresh cigarette, drawing on it deeply, seeming to relish the burn of the smoke as it went down his throat, and Ry felt that first lick of fear because he knew what was coming.

He also knew he could take it because he'd lived through much worse. But Zoe—he could tell by her face that she had no real idea of what was happening, and he ached for her because he knew she would blame herself afterward.

Vadim laid his Bic down on the table, took a couple more deep drags off the cigarette, then stared at its glowing red tip and smiled.

"Hold him down."

Ry heard a step behind him, and Zoe shouting, *"No, don't,"* but it all happened so fast. A thick, heavy hand gripped the back of his head, pulling it back, exposing his neck, and an instant later he felt the burning cigarette sear like the fire of a thousand suns into the right side of his throat.

He trapped the yell of agony that rose up inside of him through a sheer force of will. *Jesus God, it hurt.* He could smell his own skin sizzling.

Through the pain shrieking in his head, he heard Zoe screaming, and the rattle of her handcuff as she tried to pull it out of the table with brute force. Then he thought it must be over, because Zoe stopped screaming and Popov's face appeared before his watery vision.

"My great-granddaughter seems to be in some considerable distress, Agent O'Malley. She must truly be quite fond of you."

Ry fought to get his breathing back under control. He was bathed in a cold sweat and he wanted to puke. The ravaged nerves in his neck had been shocked into silence for the moment, but he knew the pain would come back any second now, and with a vengeance.

"You want her to make something up just to get you to stop?" Ry said. "Listen to me, she doesn't know where it is."

"I think she does. And after we have hurt you enough, she will tell me."

"Oh, for God's *sake*," Zoe shouted. Such pure female exasperation was in her voice, both men stopped glaring at each other to look at her.

Her face was wet with tears, but fury was in her eyes, and Ry loved her for it. "For someone who's supposed to be a hundred and twelve, you sure haven't evolved much," she said to Popov with the best sneer that Ry had ever seen on any mouth, and he loved her even more. "Do you get your jollies off of torture?"

Popov looked taken aback, then his lips twitched, as if he were genuinely amused. "A small jolly perhaps. But then Vadim can do much worse damage than a cigarette burn or two. Much, much worse. He does this thing with a pair of bolt clippers. . . . But if you tell me now how to find the altar, it won't have to come to that."

"I don't *know* how to find it—"

Popov turned and snapped his fingers at Vadim. "Again," he said in Russian. "Do it on an eyeball this time."

"No, wait. Stop," Zoe cried. "Oh, God, *stop*."

She was tearing frantically at the collar of her parka, and for a moment Ry thought she was choking. Then he realized she was trying to dig out the green-skull amulet. "I'll give it to you, okay? I'll give it to you, only don't hurt him any more."

She finally got the chain off from around her neck. She held the amulet tightly in her fist, hesitating, as if even now she was having a hard time letting it go. Then with an abrupt movement she slid it down the table toward Popov.

He trapped it with his hand before it could fall to the floor. "What is this?"

"You know what it is," Zoe said, still breathing hard from her fear and her fury.

Popov held the amulet up to the light, turning it over and over in his long fingers, studying it carefully.

"I don't know where the altar of bones is," Zoe said. "I couldn't even tell you how to get to the lake or the cave if my life depended on it. But that gooey stuff inside the amulet came from the altar. At one time there were two of them hidden inside the Lady icon. Katya gave one to Marilyn Monroe. That's the other one. And if that story about your dying grandson wasn't all just one big, fat lie, then I hope you get your miracle. But only for his sake."

"My miracle . . ."

Popov's fingers closed around the amulet, locking it up in his fist, and Ry saw the knuckles whiten. Then the Russian looked at Zoe, but if he felt anything for his great-granddaughter, it didn't show on his face.

"Well now, my dear," he said. "That wasn't so hard, was it? But then few of you Keepers have ever been any good at keeping to your sacred duty, if history is anything to judge by. You give your secrets up so easily, as easily as you spread your legs, and for why?" He laughed. "Love."

"I hope you rot in hell," Zoe said.

Popov smiled. "No doubt I will. But not for a long, long time yet."

50

Nikolai Popov put the amulet around his own neck and stood before Zoe, looking down at her. He reached out to touch her, but she flinched away from him. So he let his hand fall back down at his side.

"Why the sad eyes, my dear?" he said. "You will come away from this with your life. And your lover's life, too, because you have proven your devotion to him so sweetly."

He paused, as if he expected a thank-you, but when she said nothing, his face hardened. "I know you also have the Kennedy film, and that I will let you keep. I don't care what you do with it. I never wanted it, in spite of what Miles Taylor thought. You could release it in every multiplex across your large, obscene country if you like. Of the three of us involved in the assassination—four, if you count that fool Oswald—I am the only one still breathing—"

"Miles Taylor is dead?"

Popov laughed at the look of shock on Ry's face. "As good as. You kids should really watch more CNN. Your Kingmaker had a massive stroke this past Saturday, and he is now in what they are calling 'a permanent vegetative state.' He can neither move nor speak, and a machine does his breathing for him. Whether there is any awareness in what is left of his brain"—Popov lifted his elegant shoulders in a shrug—"who knows?"

He turned abruptly away from them. "Vadim?"

Vadim, who was just reaching for the lighter he'd left on the table, straightened back up. He took the unlit cigarette out of his mouth and said, "Yes, *Pakhan?*"

"You may uncuff them now, then call up to the farm and have one of the cars brought down here to take them back to the city. . . . What?" he said, at Zoe's look of surprise. "Are you still thinking I am going to have you whacked, as they say in your silly American *mafiya* movies? My very own great-granddaughter?"

And Ry knew, from the spark of pure malice he saw flash in Nikolai Popov's eyes, that the man had every intention of having them killed. That the orders had in fact, been given to his two enforcers well before this final charade had even begun.

POPOV DOFFED HIS head in a mocking good-bye and headed toward the back of the ruins, and the deep shadows behind the trailer. The meth was really cooking like mad now, Ry saw. Visible fumes were rising out of the open mouths of the mason jars filled with cold-medicine tablets soaking in muriatic acid.

One spark, and this whole place really could blow to smithereens.

All he needed was the spark, and Ry knew where he would find one. But he also needed to keep Popov here, in the slaughterhouse with them, until Vadim unlocked their handcuffs and he was free to make his move.

"I want to know why you waited," Ry called out to the *pakhan's* departing back.

Popov stopped and turned around. "Why I waited for what?"

"You told my dad the president had to die because he drank from the altar of bones and that made him dangerous to the world. Yet you waited fifteen months after Marilyn gave the amulet to Bobby before you came to that conclusion. Why? What happened that made you decide he had to die?"

Popov looked up at the ceiling, as if the real truth were to be found up there. "Why, why, why. Such a simple question, and so I will give you a simple answer. I did it for my country. Or rather for what my country was then. The Union of Soviet Socialist Republics."

This surprised Ry, although he knew it shouldn't have, and Popov laughed. "What, Agent O'Malley? Do you think only you Americans are capable of patriotism?"

Ry heard a stifled curse, and he glanced over at Vadim. The *vor* was patting down the pockets of his jogging suit, the unlit cigarette dangling from his lips. *Please, God*, Ry thought, *don't tell me he's lost the keys to my cuffs.*

"So are you saying you killed Kennedy because of the Cuban missile crisis?" Ry said to Popov. "He forced Khrushchev to back down, he humiliated your country, so you decided to make him pay?"

"Make him pay? Mother of God, boy. This wasn't some sandlot game we were playing. You weren't alive then, so you don't know what it was like. They called it the Cold War, but it wasn't cold. It was a hot war and we were winning it. We were *winning*. Africa, South America, Southeast Asia—we had people's revolutions going on everywhere, like little brush fires. Too many for the West to even hope to put out."

A brightness had come over Popov's face, as if a fire had suddenly ignited inside him. His eyes burned with it, and Ry thought he was getting a glimpse of the man he had been when he was procurator general of the KGB in Moscow.

"But there was always the risk one of our brush fires would start a conflagration that could erupt into a nuclear war," Popov went on. "It was the fear lurking in all our hearts, that someday an American president or a Soviet premier would decide a line had been crossed, that he had to take a stand, to be a man. Or maybe he would simply lose his mind one day and push the red button, and our world would be gone in a radioactive flash."

Vadim still hadn't found the damn key, but at least, Ry saw, Grisha had unlocked Zoe's cuffs. She stood up now, rubbing the red marks they'd left on her wrists.

"The night we killed Marilyn Monroe," Popov was saying, "she told your father and me that she'd given the amulet to Robert Kennedy, to give to his brother. But there was no way of knowing whether the president ever got that silly bitch's little gift, let alone whether he ever drank from it. So I waited and I watched him. He had Addison's disease, so I waited to see if he got any better. And I watched him for signs of . . . of the dark side of the altar."

"Because you'd already seen those signs in yourself?"

This time Popov's laugh was a little too wild. "How could I have seen it in myself? I had been one of Joseph Stalin's pet spies. Whatever lines of sanity and morality there are in this world, I crossed them long before I drank from the altar of bones."

"Here's the fucker," Ry heard Vadim mutter under his breath, and Ry's thumping heart slowed a little. *Soon now. Soon.*

"So I watched and I waited," Popov said, "for any signs that your President Kennedy ever drank from the altar. And what is one of the first things to happen? He cuts a deal with Sam Giancana of your Italian *mafiya* to assassinate Fidel Castro. They put poison on Fidel's cigars—can you imagine such a crazy thing as that? 'This truly is the act of a madman,' I thought to myself at the time, but I did nothing. Because the only certain and permanent solution I could think of was to kill the man, and although you might not believe me now, it was a path I was truly loath to take. But then there came the crisis he made over our missiles in Cuba, where he went right to the brink, and yet still I did nothing."

The cuffs were off at last. As Ry stood up, he brushed his hand across the table and palmed Vadim's lighter, slipping it into his pocket.

Popov was on a roll now, as if it were a relief to him to finally be able to explain to someone why he had committed one of the great crimes of the twentieth century.

"He pushed us to the brink of nuclear war, and still I did nothing. Then one day Miles Taylor, my mole inside the administration, passed along a top-secret document to me, and I saw that it was a detailed plan for an American invasion of North Vietnam, already set for the following spring. Sixty thousand combat troops, with full air and sea support, were to hit the beaches south of Haiphong harbor and sweep towards Hanoi. While your air force would nuke the rail and road passes between North Vietnam and China.

"I am holding this document in my hands, reading how your president intends to escalate from a few inconvenient advisers in South Vietnam to a full-blown war with the North and with China, and with us Soviets, as well. It was sheer insanity. And that was when I knew the dark side of the altar had truly taken hold of him. That for the sake of my country, for the world, he had to go."

An invasion of North Vietnam? Nuking the passes? It seemed unreal to Ry. Truly insane—and wasn't that a laugh? Yet, when you thought about it, after Kennedy's death those "advisers" *did* escalate into an invasion of a sort, although into the southern half of the country, not into the North.

While Popov was talking, all of Zoe's attention had been on Ry, letting him take the lead. He held out his hand to her now, and she came to him. He put his arm around her waist and drew her to him. Popov and his two goons didn't seem to care.

"So you decided all on your own," Ry said, "that President Kennedy had to go. And you had my father and Miles Taylor to help you pull it off. The brilliance of the plan, the reason why it worked, was in its very simplicity."

Popov looked pleased at the compliment. "If you involve too many people in your conspiracy, someone always ends up talking, either to save his own ass or because he just can't help himself. Even so, I never anticipated your father would have his woman make that damn film. He outsmarted me there. Miles Taylor was going to be useful to me for many years to come, but your father? From the moment he pulled the trigger, he was dispensable, and he knew it."

"Like Lee Harvey Oswald."

"Ah, yes. Poor Lee Harvey. Why am I always forgetting about him? But then he was never a real part of it, except as a patsy. You know the type. In Russia we call him the elephant-in-the-parade man—the one who follows the elephant with a shovel and a pail full of shit. I fed him a beautiful story about how Castro wanted revenge for the poisoned cigars, then I sent him off to make history."

Popov laughed again, and Ry thought he looked positively entranced with himself now—the star of his own movie. "And what a history it turned out to be," he said. "Imagine that a single bullet from a clunky Italian-surplus bolt-action rifle could change direction several times in order to kill the president and wound the governor of Texas. A pity our poor Oswald didn't live long enough to marvel and gloat at what a crack shot he was that day."

"And Jack Ruby, the man who in turn gunned Oswald down in the basement of the Dallas police headquarters—I take it we have you to thank for that? Snipping off loose ends, were you?"

"Of course. Like your father, Lee Harvey Oswald was a dispensable commodity."

While Popov talked, Ry had edged himself and Zoe farther from the table and closer to the slaughterhouse door. He could see that it had grown light outside, and it was no longer snowing. Feeble rays of sunshine filtered through gaps in the crumbling walls.

Ry casually put his hand into his coat pocket, found the lighter, and flipped open its lid. He pushed down on the gas lever and pressed the pad of his thumb on the striker wheel. He said, "I remember reading about the Warren Commission's 'magic bullet theory.' You must've gotten a good laugh out of that."

Popov was getting a good laugh out of it now. "Magical bullet, indeed. But what turned out to be even more magical was the top-secret document Miles Taylor had given me. It was only later, long after our big kill, that I found out the document was a forgery. An exceedingly well-drawn forgery, but all lies nonetheless. Miles, and some other members of the Kennedy administration, had been pushing for an escalation of the fighting in Vietnam because of the millions to be made in Defense Department contacts, but Kennedy was balking. Vice President Johnson, though, seemed quite amenable to the idea. Miles must have decided that the easiest way to get those defense contracts was to arrange to have the vice president become the president."

Popov laughed again and shook his head. "Miles, the devious bastard—he used me to do his dirty work for him. I had *made* Miles Taylor, I shaped and molded him, and so I thought he was my creature, that I owned him. It was arrogant of me, I know, and in my arrogance I swallowed that phony document of his hook, line, and sinker."

"You thought you were so smart," Zoe said, startling everybody because she'd been quiet for so long. "And yet you were wrong about everything. The document was a fake, but so was the amulet, because the real one, the one with the altar of bones—Katya got that one back. You're wearing it now, around your neck. The amulet Marilyn Monroe gave to Bobby that day was filled with toilet water, so even if his brother did drink from it, he was never going to lose his mind and push the red button."

Popov raised his eyebrows at Ry. "This is true?"

"Yeah, Popov, it's true," Ry said. "It turns out you were played all over the place, every which way there is."

The Russian thought about it for a moment, then threw back his head in genuine amusement. "What a joke on me. A joke every which way, no? . . . And now I really must be going. As you American's say, have a good life."

Ry waited until Popov had turned and was walking away, out of earshot, then he pulled Zoe tighter against him, leaned his head close to hers, and spoke softly as if he were giving her comfort, "Do you remember Paris and the Drano bomb?"

Zoe nodded.

He gave her a little squeeze. "Straight out the door, babe, and don't look back."

Zoe nodded again.

Vadim, Ry saw, must suddenly have figured out that the cigarette dangling off his lower lip wasn't lit, because he was patting the pockets of his jogging suit looking for his lighter. Popov was almost at the trailer house now, nearly abreast of the picnic tables with their lethal brew.

But suddenly he stopped short and turned back.

"You think it is so terrible," he said, "what I have done to possess the altar of bones so that I might save my grandson's life. But Katya herself would have understood. Did you know, Zoe, my dear, that when your mother, Anna Larina, was four years old, she was stricken with leukemia? She was given only weeks to live, but a year later not only was she still alive, she was as healthy as any child of her age. And in every test they ran on her, they could fine no trace of the cancer. The doctors were at a lost to explain it. They called it a miraculous recovery."

Zoe shook her head. "I don't . . . What are you saying now?"

The smile Nikolai Popov gave her was full of spite. "Just that I thought the sacred duty of the Keeper was always passed down from mother to daughter. Yet Katya skipped Anna Larina and gave it to you.

Ask yourself why she would do that, Zoe. Ask yourself why your mother didn't die when she was four like she was supposed to."

———————

THIS TIME WHEN Popov left them, he kept on going.

Ry watched him take one step, then another, purposeful steps, mission accomplished, and Ry waited, waited until the man was walking past the trailer house again, alongside the picnic tables and the mason jars full of cooking meth.

He waited one more second, two, then yelled, *"Now."*

Zoe ran all out for the door, just as Ry jerked the lighter out of his pocket and hit the striker wheel.

Nothing happened. He hit it again, then again. Got nothing but puny sparks. He saw Vadim and Grisha scrambling to get out their weapons, saw Popov spin around and pull a gun out of the pocket of his sable coat. Ry prayed as he'd never prayed before in his life and struck the wheel again. And again.

Suddenly the wick caught, bursting into a bright blue-yellow flame. Ry threw the burning lighter onto the picnic tables, then ran for the door. He heard two shots, rapid-fire, one after another, but nothing hit him. Then he heard a loud whoosh, and a blast of hot air hit the back of his neck. He looked over his shoulder as he ran—the picnic tables had become a giant fireball.

He saw a curling tongue of fire leap out, like a giant fist, and grab Popov. The man screamed and screamed as the flames enveloped him, shooting up the length of his sable coat, wreathing and billowing around his face.

Ry's last view, as he went through the door, was of the flames spreading from Popov to the trailer house, and to the stacks of propane tanks and bags of ammonia nitrate, and he ran harder, desperate now, because any second that stuff was going to blow and send everyone to hell.

He was out in the yard, looking frantically for Zoe, not seeing her. Then, oh God, oh God, there she was running about ten yards ahead of him, moving fast, long, hard strides, and he pushed harder to catch up with her. She didn't know, she couldn't know—

He tackled her, slamming her down into the snow-covered ground, covering her with his body as best as he could, his arms over their heads as the world exploded behind them. The air disappeared, sucked out of their lungs, and time seemed to stop. Then bricks and shards of sheet metal and glass rained down, and hot, roaring flames shot up into the sky.

51

R Y ROLLED off Zoe and got up onto his knees. She lay facedown in the snow, unmoving, and he felt a split-second's panic before he saw the back of her parka moving up and down with the force of her breathing.

He started to reach for her, but she pushed herself up, spitting snow out of her mouth and rubbing it out of her eyes.

"Are you okay?" he said, although he knew she couldn't hear him, because his own ears were still deafened from the force of the explosion.

He looked back at what was left of the slaughterhouse. Flames still shot up from the rubble, and roiling brown smoke billowed into the air. Anyone still inside when it blew, he thought, could never have survived, and he didn't see anyone else about. He remembered Vadim ordering their driver to take the SUV up to "the farm," and he wondered how far away that was and how many of Popov's men were there.

He touched Zoe's arm, and she looked up at him, still blinking the snow from her eyes. "Can you run some more?" he shouted at her.

She nodded, and he wrapped his hand around her arm, helping her to her feet. The lane that led to the main road was too exposed, so he looked around and spotted a small gate in the cemetery wall. The gate was padlocked shut, but it was old and rusted, and one kick with his boot broke it open.

They wove in and out of snow-draped tombstones and monuments, heading away from the gutted, burning meth lab. They stopped at the top of a small rise and looked back. The fires had gone out, but thick brown smoke still lay over the ruins like a shroud. Ry searched for any movement, for any sign of pursuit, but he saw none.

Then, as they started down the other side of the rise, Ry noticed the small group of people gathered around a freshly dug grave. And parked next to them, a hearse, the smoke from its exhaust blowing out into the cold morning air.

"Babe," he said, "I think I see our ride back to St. Petersburg."

———

Riding in the back of the hearse was weird, but warm.

They lay side by side, Zoe cradled in the crook of his arm. She turned her head and lightly kissed the cigarette burn on his neck. "I know you said not to give up the amulet too quickly or he might get suspicious, but if I'd known—"

"Sssh. It's over now, and he's dead. Roasted and blown to smithereens. I'm just sorry he took the altar of bones down into hell with him."

"He took the amulet with him," Zoe said. "Not the altar of bones."

He pushed himself up on one elbow so that he could look into her face. "But last night . . . Wasn't the juice still in the amulet, then? When did you—"

"Right before Popov's goons showed up. That's what I was doing in the bathroom." She grinned up at Ry. "It was a good plan, if I do say so myself."

"Better than good. It was brilliant." He kissed her on the mouth, then lay back down beside her. "And the best thing about it was that it worked."

Back on that mountain road above the Danube, when she'd showed him the little sample perfumes, she'd told him of her idea then—to pawn a fake altar of bones onto Popov by transferring the bone juice into one of the perfume vials and putting mineral oil in the amulet. The consistency of the mineral oil was close enough to the real thing, as long as you didn't know it was supposed to glow in the dark.

Zoe stirred in his arms. "Do you think Igor's real, that Popov really had a grandson who's dying of cancer?"

"I don't know. His pain seemed real enough. But then I know from my years as an undercover narc that sometimes you can play a part so well, you can even talk yourself into believing it."

"He wasn't really going to let us go, was he?"

"No. We were loose ends that needed snipping."

Her breathing slowed and quieted, and he thought she'd fallen asleep, then she said, "Then maybe what he said about my mother was a lie, too. What he implied. That Katya gave her the bone juice when she was a little girl because otherwise she would have died of leukemia."

Ry hesitated a moment. "Remember I told you how I researched your whole family last summer, when I was trying to find your grandmother? . . . Anna Larina's 'miraculous' recovery was such a big deal back in 1957, it made the front page of the L.A. *Times*."

Zoe shuddered. "It kind of creeps me out, thinking about it, but it explains a lot. Why she looks young enough to be my sister. And why she is . . . what she is."

"Don't think about it, because it doesn't matter. You broke free of her a long time ago."

Zoe was quiet again for a while, then said, "The altar of bones is real, Ry. He was a hundred and twelve, yet you saw how he looked. The altar did that to him."

"It also made him crazy, and in the end it couldn't keep him from dying. Whatever the altar did to him, it didn't make him immortal."

"Popov was convinced it was never in the cave," she said. "But it's there. He just didn't know how to find it."

"And you think you can?"

"I'm the Keeper, so I have to try."

"It *would* have to be all the way up in Siberia, though," Ry said. "And it's the goddamn middle of February."

She laughed and snuggled deeper into him. "That's why I'm bringing you with me, to keep me warm. At least we've run out of bad guys to come after us. Popov was blown to smithereens, Yasmin Poole was skewered, and apparently Miles Taylor is now a turnip. We won't have to worry about being chased all over the place and shot at every time we turn around."

Ry wasn't so sure about that, but he said nothing.

The hearse rocked over the ruts in the road. In the distance he heard the wail of a train whistle. "We must be getting close to civilization," he said. "The first thing I'm going to do when we get back to the apartment is take a long, hot shower. A loooong, hot shower . . ."

Ry hoped she would ask him if she could join him, but she said nothing, and then he realized her breathing had slowed and quieted. She had fallen asleep.

He turned his head and rubbed his mouth over her hair.

52

New York City

MILES TAYLOR couldn't stop himself from screaming every time someone came near him, even though it didn't do any good because nobody could hear.

The screams were all inside his head.

They thought he was a vegetable. He heard the doctor tell his daughter that, the one and only time she had been to see him since the stroke. "Persistent vegetative state," the asshole had said, and Miles had done lot of screaming then, oh, yeah. Inside his head. *You fucking ignorant bastard, where'd you get your degree, Podunk U? If I understand every fucking word you're saying, how can I be in a state where there's no cognitive function? Hunh? Answer me that, asshole. Answer me that.*

Miles slept a lot; there was nothing else to do. Every time he woke, it would take one sweet, exquisite instant for his mind to catch up to the hell he lived in now. And then he would remember and he would scream and scream and scream.

He wanted to die. He prayed that he would die.

Lately, when his doctor or one of the nurses would come into his room, that's what he would scream at them. *Let me die, please. For the love of God, pull the plug and let me die.*

But they never heard him because he couldn't open his mouth or move his tongue or work his throat. *If a man screams and no one hears him, does it even happen?*

He had round-the-clock care, four nurses who bathed him and did other things too humiliating to even think about. He loved them, and he hated their guts.

The new girl—her name was Christie—had a whore's mouth and long, wine-red hair. A few days ago, he began to dream about her. Exhausting, erotic dreams. *Doctor, Doctor, can a man still shoot his wad even if he can't get it up anymore?*

Today, Christie was on the afternoon shift, and he found himself waiting for her with such excitement it almost hurt. His eyeballs—the only part of him that he could still move—were riveted on the open door. He'd heard her voice earlier, out in the corridor, so he knew she was here, but the hours crawled by and she wouldn't come, wouldn't even pass by his door so that he could see her. It was as if she sensed in some way how desperate he was, and she wanted him to wait. To suffer.

He was beginning to wonder if there was more to her than her mouth and that red hair that reminded him of Yasmine Poole.

A little meanness, maybe?

He fell asleep waiting for her and awoke with a start. She was leaning over him, her face only inches from his, and he felt a strange tingle on his left cheek. What had she done to him? Pinched him, poked him? Kissed him?

"Are you in there, Mr. Taylor? I think you are. No one else does, but I do."

Yes, yes, he screamed, so ecstatic with joy he was nearly delirious. *I'm here, I'm here. Oh, God . . .*

The girl leaned closer to him, lowered her voice. "You thought you were such hot shit, didn't you? Mr. Hot Shit Billionaire. I read all about you in *Vanity Fair* and the stuff you did to other people to make all that money. How people lost everything because of you, and all you could say was 'Fuck 'em.'"

No, you don't understand. It's all just a game, and if you want to be somebody, if you want to matter, you've got to play the game. The money isn't even real, just numbers in computers. Just ones and zeros. Not even real . . .

"But now it's your turn to experience hell on earth, Mr. Taylor." The girl oh so gently caressed his cheek. "And you know what I say to that?

I say, fuck you, Mr. Taylor. Fuck you. And I want you to know that I'm going to be taking extraspecial care of you from here on out, because I want that hell to go on and on, for a long, long time."

She straightened and glanced over her shoulder, checking out the doorway. Then she turned back around and slapped him hard across the cheek, where a moment ago she had touched him so sweetly.

Tears filled Miles Taylor's eyes and the girl smiled, a smile that was pure mean, but he didn't care. She couldn't know his tears were ones of joy.

Hit me again, he screamed, over and over inside his head. *Hit me again.*

Because you wouldn't hit a vegetable, would you? Vegetables couldn't feel, they couldn't think, so why would you bother to hit a vegetable?

Hit me again, hit me again, hit me again.

53

Norilsk, Siberia
One week later

Zoe watched the giant red digital clock on top of the Norilsk Nickel headquarters building click over another minute: 12:19.

"Our mystery woman's late, Ry. Are you sure this is the place? 'Cause right now there ain't nobody out here but us freezing chickens."

Ry just looked at her and waved a Polartec-mittened hand at the bas-relief sculpture built into the corner of the building above their heads—a big bronze guy, shirtless, muscled, his square-jawed face set hard with purpose, wielding some sort of shovel. Chiseled into the base were the words THE BUILDERS OF NORILSK.

"I know, I know," Zoe said. "There can't be two builders' monuments in the city. It's just . . ." She hunched her shoulders as a blast of frigid wind sent ice crystals dancing in waves down the wide, nearly deserted street. She wanted to give up and go back to the hotel. She wanted to be warm.

The mystery woman was a mystery because they didn't know a thing about her, not even her name. She'd telephoned their room late last night, said two sentences: "I can take you to the lake you search for. Be at the builders' monument on Leninskiy Prospekt tomorrow at noon," then hung up before Zoe had a chance to so much as draw a breath.

The whole thing was surreal, but then surreal was what Zoe had come to expect of this strange frozen place almost two hundred miles north of the arctic circle. Norilsk was a closed city, and the policy was strictly enforced. No one, not even Russians, let alone foreigners, could come here without an official invitation and special authorization from the FSB intelligence service.

It took some time and a lot of money, and even Ry wasn't sure how Sasha managed it, but he finally got them the documents they needed. There'd been a scary half hour upon their arrival, though, when the police boarded the plane, confiscated their passports, and led them off for questioning. They were posing as potential investors from a Montana nickel-mining company, and Zoe let Ry do all the talking since the only thing she knew about nickel was that it was a coin worth five cents.

Then there was the two-hour bus ride into the city in the dusky gloom of a polar night, the sun barely above the horizon even in the middle of the day. They rode past ghosts of trees with blackened, barren trunks, and factories and smelters that spewed black, smelly smoke into the air. Past oily pools of stagnant water so toxic they couldn't freeze even in the subzero temperatures. It was amazing to think this sprawling, polluted city of two hundred thousand souls and blocks of massive Soviet-style buildings began life as a prison camp cut out of the icy steppes, and that her great-grandmother Lena came from here.

These are my roots, Zoe thought with a shiver that only partly came from the cold. It was such a hard, frozen, ugly place.

After they checked into the one decent hotel, they'd spent a day studying topographical maps and satellite photographs at Norilsk's city hall. There were hundreds of lakes all over the Taimyr Peninsula, but not one shaped remotely like a boot. For four more days they'd walked the ice-encrusted streets, going into shops, restaurants, nightclubs, even a couple of bowling alleys, asking of anyone who would listen how to get to the lake with the waterfall.

Nothing, zilch, nada, zip. Until last night's phone call.

Zoe thought of how Boris, the griffin shop man, had spotted her great-grandmother Lena in a noodle shop in Hong Kong and knew right off that she was a Keeper because she had the face of the Lady in the icon. Had that happened again, with herself and the mystery woman? Surely some magic people were still left in the area. Was the mystery woman one of them?

Zoe stamped her feet to keep them from turning into frozen stubs.

This street, Leninskiy Prospekt, was the main drag and was well-lit enough for her to see there wasn't a soul around now for blocks. At least the buildings here were painted a cheerful, if rather gaudy, orange and yellow, unlike the rest of the city, which was all washed-out shades of gray and brown.

She checked the time on the Norilsk Nickel building again: 12:24. Almost a half an hour late. The woman wasn't coming.

Zoe stamped her feet again and clapped her mittened hands together for good measure. She looked up and read the inscription on the base of the sculpture for the umpteenth time, and she must have sighed out loud, because Ry said, "Be patient. She'll come."

"I was just thinking, whoever this particular 'builder' person was, he couldn't have built anything in Norilsk. Even with pecs like his, you're not gonna sashay around this place without a shirt. You'd be a Popsicle in five seconds. And I've got purses back home bigger than that itty-bitty shovel— Hey, look, Ry, that car's slowing down. Please, God, let it be her."

A silver sedan with a broken right-turn signal pulled up to the curb halfway down the block from them, but the figure that got out was so bundled up against the cold, Zoe couldn't tell whether it was a man or a woman. Whoever it was reached back into the car and came out with an oversize and obviously heavy attaché case, then carried it into a nearby bank.

Zoe sighed again and looked back up at the digital readout on the Norilsk Nickel building, but the time had flipped over to the temperature. Minus thirty-nine degrees. *Somebody made that up*, she thought. *If it were a real number, we'd be dead, and—*

"Here she is," Ry said.

Zoe followed his pointing mitten to a small, slender woman wearing a black fur hat and an ankle-length black coat getting off an ice-crusted city bus. She made a beeline for them, her stride purposeful, confident.

The long, white wool scarf she'd wrapped around her neck obscured part of her face, but as she got closer, Zoe was surprised to see she was young, barely out of her teens.

She stopped in front of Zoe and stared at her as she loosened the

thick scarf. Zoe saw a pale face with translucent skin and delicate fea-
tures. Her eyes were gray and full of curiosity.

She said in fast-flowing Russian, "Sorry I'm late. The buses are always breaking down in this weather. Great-uncle Fodor saw you two
days ago. He said he overheard you chatting up Ilia the baker in her
shop, and that you've come from America and were asking about the
lake with the waterfall. And that you're the very image of the old photograph we have of Lena Orlova, who was the last Keeper. At least we
thought she was the last . . ." Her voice trailed off as she studied Zoe
some more.

"Lena Orlova was my great-grandmother."

The girl nodded, her eyes sparkling. "Most think Lena was the last
Keeper because she was killed before she could pass on her knowledge
and anoint a new one. She was a nurse at the prison camp here, and she
was killed by the guards when she tried to help the poor *zek* who was her
lover to escape. But there've always been a stubborn few who wanted
to believe in the rumors that she got away, for it was too good a story
not to be true, was it not? And here you are, living proof. Are you the
Keeper now?"

"Yes. My grandmother Katya, Lena's daughter, she . . . anointed me."

"Good. That is how it should be." The girl turned abruptly and
looked up at the builders' monument. "I hope you don't think this Soviet
poster boy is anything at all like the men who built Norilsk."

Zoe would have blinked at this abrupt change of subject, but she was
afraid her eyelids would freeze shut. "Not hardly. I mean, who would go
to work in this place without even a shirt?"

"It's not so much the scarcity of clothing as the abundance of robust
flesh. The men who built Norilsk were prisoners, who were fed just
enough so they could stay alive and work, and they worked until all that
was left of them was bones. When they died, they were buried together
in mass graves, and every year to this day their bones come back to haunt
us. In June, when the winter breaks, the melting snows churn them up
from out of the ground, only everyone pretends not to see them."

"But you don't pretend," Zoe said.

The girl smiled at her. "No. Because that would be denying them all, wouldn't it?" She pulled her wool scarf across her face again. "Come with me now, out of this cold, and we will talk."

━━━━━━━━

SHE LED THEM into a small, blessedly warm restaurant with two surly waiters and a dozen low, ugly Formica tables. They all ordered cups of teeth-rottingly sweet black Russian tea.

"My name is Svetlana," the girl said, "but do not tell me yours if it is different from what is on your official documents. I will simply call you cousin, for if you are Lena Orlova's great-granddaughter, then that would make us cousins of a sort, many times removed. Great-uncle Fodor says I am sticking myself out on a clothesline by even speaking to you, but I had to see you with my own eyes. And to help you if I can, because as I told Great-uncle Fodor, it is the duty of the *toapotror* to help the Keeper when we can."

"I am very grateful to you," Zoe said. "In your phone call last night you said you can take us to the lake we're looking for?"

Svetlana nodded solemnly. "I will take you, but only as far as the waterfall. After that, you are on your own. You are the Keeper, and only the Keeper is allowed to approach the altar of bones. I would rather have all my teeth pulled than go into that cave anyway. None of our people wanted me to come to you, they're afraid you will destroy the altar or betray its secrets to the world since you are not really one of us. Even if you were born of *toapotror* blood."

"They're wrong. I am one of you. I have come a very long way to prove that I am one of you."

"Yes, you are tough, otherwise you would not have made it this far, and that is what I told Great-uncle Fodor. There aren't many of us magic people left, you understand, and of those who are, most are old and tired and set in their ways. They do not know the Grammies from Google." Svetlana paused, drew a deep breath, and lowered her voice. "I said for you not to tell me your name, Cousin, but it and your face are all over the Internet. They say you are terrorists, but I know that is a lie. You are being hunted, as the Keepers often are, and I will do what I can to help you. But I think we should also pray to the Lady to protect you."

"I really am grateful for your help, Svetlana, but if it means putting you in danger—"

She waved a hand. "Never mind that, I am bored with being safe. Besides, I live in Norilsk, where there is acid in the snow and we kill ourselves with every polluted breath we take."

She shrugged and drank the rest of her tea as if it were fine ambrosia rather than syrupy sludge. "Now, the fastest way to get to the lake this time of year is by snowmobile. My cousin Mikhail, who is smart enough not to ask questions, has a couple of Arctic Cats we may borrow."

She paused and looked hard at Ry, and Zoe didn't think she was happy about him at all. And Ry, probably sensing as much, had been keeping quiet.

"If I don't trust him," Zoe said, "then I may as well not trust myself."

"Because you sleep with him? Other Keepers gave up the altar's secrets along with their hearts. It never ended well, if the stories are to be believed."

"Maybe because the only stories that got told were the ones with the bad endings. The ones where the Keepers fell in love with rotten assholes, who should never have been trusted past first base to begin with. But who's to say there haven't been Keepers who trusted good guys, guys who were never going to betray them, not for love nor money? You'd never hear about them because there'd be nothing to tell, and . . . And I know I've got a point in there somewhere, and it's a real zinger, too."

The girl surprised Zoe by joining in her laughter. "How can I argue with such logic? Except to say you are the Keeper, so you will do what you will do, anyway." Svetlana gave Ry another once-over. "He's a big and strong one—I'll say that for him."

A pale-faced waiter had appeared to pour more tea into Svetlana's empty cup. She raised it and toasted them. "It is poison, I know, but drink up. You will need the warmth." She looked at Ry yet again, and this time she gave him a fleeting smile. "One of Mikhail's Cats is a two-seater, so you can bring him along if you want. They heat up, by the way, the seats on the Cats. And there are hand warmers, too. Can you imagine such a luxury? Drink up now, drink up."

The tea was awful, and they drank every drop.

54

ZOE STARED up at the waterfall that shot out of the bluff above their heads in waves of ice and jagged spiky icicles.

"It almost doesn't look real," she said. "It's like some god came along and zapped it, freezing it solid in midair, in a single instant of time."

"This is Siberia," Svetlana said, "where everything is always frozen solid. Except maybe for five minutes during the first week in August. . . . All right, I am joking. But only a little."

Svetlana looked up at the tall, wide pillar of ice, and Zoe thought a shudder crossed her face. "There's barely an hour of daylight left and a snowstorm is coming, so I must leave you now, my cousin of sorts. The cave with the altar of bones is behind the waterfall, and you should stay inside there overnight. Your Cat's got a GPS system, but it doesn't work here in the canyon, and even back out on the tundra it's easy to get lost in the snow and the dark. And this is the starving season. The wolves will be out."

"Thank you," Zoe said. "For everything."

Svetlana smiled at Zoe, then looked at Ry and gave him a flicker of a smile as well. "In the compartment behind the seats on your Arctic Cat, I put a couple of space blankets, some sausage and cabbage rolls, and a bottle of Kalashnikov. The blankets are good at keeping a body warm, but the vodka is better."

Svetlana cast another, fleeting glance up at the waterfall. "I should go now."

"We'll bring the Cat back to Mikhail's no later than tomorrow morning," Zoe said. "Will you be there? I'd like to talk with you some more, about the magic people and my great-grandmother, and your great-uncle Fodor, all those stories you've heard."

Svetlana nodded. "Yes. If you wish, I will be there."

For a moment Zoe thought the girl would embrace her, but then she only nodded again and turned away.

———————

THEY WATCHED THE Arctic Cat cut away from them across the frozen lake, kicking up a rooster tail of snow.

"I think she was warming to you a little, O'Malley. There at the end."

He didn't smile, and he was quiet for so long, she said, "What? What are you thinking?"

"That this shouldn't be a test of your feelings for me. I don't see it that way and I don't want you to see it that way either. Tell me to wait out here by the Cat, and I will. No questions asked, and no resentments either."

She took him by the arms and turned him around to face her. "There is no halfway here, Ry. Not with me."

He stared down at her, his eyes dark with some emotion she couldn't read, except it seemed to be shaking him to the core. But all he said was "All right, then. Let's get it done."

He took her by the hand, but now Zoe held back.

She stared up at the huge, rippling pillar of ice. "All of this . . . it's just so hard to believe we're actually here. When I first heard the story about Lena Orlova escaping from the gulag, trekking across Siberia all the way to Shanghai, and all the while pregnant with her lover's child, I thought it sounded so beautifully sad and romantic, like something out of *Doctor Zhivago*. But the truth turned out to be nothing like that at all, did it? What really happened here was brutal and ugly and cruel."

"Not all of it," Ry said. "She survived, and that was a brave and wonderful thing. She survived so that this day, this moment, could happen. When you, her great-granddaughter, could come back to the place where it all began and see it through. Full circle."

Zoe swallowed hard and nodded. "Because I am the Keeper now."

But she wondered how she would find the altar of bones in a place Nikolai Popov had searched so many times. And if she did, then what? What would come afterward, because once she found the altar, she would become its Keeper in fact as well as in name. The altar's secrets would be her secrets then, to keep or to betray.

Ry touched his forehead to hers. "You had an incredible burden laid on you, Zoe, from out of nowhere. And you know what? You haven't faltered. You've got grit and a brain." He lightly touched his palm to her chest. "And a huge heart. I am very proud of you. Now, let's find the entrance to this damn cave so we can do what we came to do."

"Did she say wolves?"

He laughed. "I'd kiss you, but I'm afraid our lips would freeze together."

55

ZOE STARED at the impossibly small gap between the two sheets of rock that made up the face of the bluff. "Sweet Mother of Jesus, Ry, this can't be it. I mean, there's no way we're fitting through that. It's impossible. There's got to be another entrance somewhere else, and we're just not seeing it."

But it had taken them forever to find even this slit in the rock face. When they'd first walked out onto the ledge behind the waterfall and looked head-on at the front of the bluff, their eyes had seen only a solid wall of rock. It wasn't until they walked all the way out to the end of the ledge and looked back did they realize that two sheets of rock were actually overlapping each other.

Zoe leaned forward just far enough to peer into the narrow crevasse. It was too dark to tell how deep it went, or whether the entrance to the cave really was at the other end of it. It could lead to nowhere, or just drop off into space. "Nope. Uh-uh. No way. It's too narrow. An anorexic goat would get stuck in there."

"I'll go first," Ry said. "If it's wide enough for me, then you'll get through. I know you hate tight places, and believe me, this doesn't look like loads of fun to me either, but it's what we got to do."

"I know, I know. But what if you get stuck?"

"Then go get some dynamite and blow me out."

"This isn't funny, Ry. I'm really, really scared. My mind knows it's irrational, but my body isn't getting the message." Her heart was already racing so fast, she thought she could feel it whapping against her ribs like the wings of a trapped bird.

"I know, babe. Look . . ." Ry turned sideways and sidled into the overlapping gap in the rock face. "It's wider than it looks. A lot of what you're seeing is an optical illusion."

"Maybe . . ."

Ry held out his hand to her, palm up. "We'll do it together. It's the end of the journey, Zoe. This is the last step."

"Yeah, but does this last step have to be such a bloody narrow one?" she said with a shaky laugh. She grabbed his hand, though. Then she turned sideways to match him and put one foot and half her body into hell.

"That's good," Ry said. "I won't let you go. Now, shut your eyes and concentrate on breathing. In, out. In, out."

Zoe closed her eyes and breathed. In, out.

Ry took a step, bringing her with him, then another step. In, out. In, out.

"Imagine you're in the middle of a football field," Ry was saying, "and the field's in the middle of a huge, empty stadium, and there's nothing around you but space, wide-open space, everywhere you look."

Zoe couldn't picture the field, her mind felt too full of white noise. Her ears were ringing with it. Red dots danced in the darkness behind her closed eyes, and she fought down a sudden, desperate urge to open them.

Her left boot stepped on a loose stone causing her ankle to buckle underneath her. Instinctively she brought her free hand up to steady herself and it knocked against something hard. Her eyes flew open, and she was staring at a wall of solid rock not more than an inch from the end of her nose.

The white noise in Zoe's head flared up into a single loud, penetrating scream. *Get out, get out, get out.*

She tried to pull her hand out of Ry's grasp, but he held on. "Eyes shut and breathe."

She squeezed her eyes shut, so hard it hurt. Her breaths scraped in and out of her throat, burning, and her chest felt as if it were going to explode. She wanted out, out, out—

"Talk, Zoe."

"Huh?"

"Talk about whatever comes into your head. Babble away. It'll soothe my nerves."

Zoe made a little yelping noise that was supposed to be a laugh. "Like you've ever had a nervous moment in your entire life, O'Malley. Ever since that night I crawled out of the Seine and you shot me with that tranquilizer gun, it's been one hairy moment after another for us, and yet you go about saving our asses and knocking off the bad guys like it's just la-di-da and all in a day's work with you. It's enough to give us normal people an inferiority complex—"

Her bottom brushed against something hard, startling her. She tucked it in, and the front of her anorak scraped against the rock in front of her. *Oh, God . . .* "Ry? It's getting narrow. Really, really narrow."

"We're here."

Slowly, Zoe opened her eyes. Enough light still penetrated through the gap in the rock for her to see that they stood at the top of a flight of narrow steps cut into the sheer side of what looked to be a bottomless pit.

Ry took a step toward the edge, and pebbles scattered, hitting the cave floor below them. Okay, not bottomless then.

"I know I should be scared spitless about going down into that," Zoe said, whispering for some strange reason. "But after surviving that the slit-in-the-rock-from-hell, I feel like I could tackle those steps while turning somersaults."

Ry grinned at her as he pulled a flashlight from his pocket and aimed it down into the cave. "It's actually not that deep," he said, and he, too, was whispering. "Fifteen feet, maybe twenty at the most."

The climb down, while steep, turned out to be easier than it looked. At the bottom they found a kerosene lantern hanging on a hook. Ry took it down and gave it a little shake. "It feels full."

Zoe didn't bother to ask him if he had something to light it with; she knew he would. The man was always prepared for anything.

She watched while he held a butane lighter to the lantern's wick, and it caught. He lifted the lantern and together they turned in a slow circle as the light moved over the walls of the cave. It was round, nearly perfectly so, and it wasn't all that big, maybe twenty feet in diameter. An evil-looking oily black pool took up most of the middle, and across the pool, against the far wall, stood an altar made out of human bones. A hot geyser bubbled beneath it, enshrouding it in a soft veil of steam.

"The altar of bones," Ry said.

"But not *the* altar. If Popov was telling the truth about that, and there's no reason to think he wasn't. It's creepy, though, to think all those bones were once people. I wonder who built it and why."

"To worship some ancient god or goddess, maybe? But it also could have been set up as a decoy all along, to make people like Popov, people who manage to get this far, believe they've found the source of the bone juice, when the real altar of bones is somewhere else."

"Yeah, but where?" Zoe said. "I don't see anything else down here that it could be, except maybe the pool. But besides being too obvious, Popov claimed he had that tested, too, and the pool isn't it."

Ry cast the lantern light over the walls of the cave again. Water dripped into the pool from the ceiling, making a melodic *plop, ploppity, plop* noise. Zoe saw stalagmites, a few rotting pieces of wood, the remains of a campfire, and a battered metal bowl. Etched deep into the stone walls were the crude outlines of seven wolves, each one chasing after the other, in an endless loop around the cave.

"The wolves . . ."

"What?" Ry said.

"It was what my grandmother wrote at the end of her letter. Something about not treading where wolves lie. Maybe these wolves carved into the wall are some kind of clue to where the real altar is. Another Keeper riddle."

"I don't know. They aren't lying down, for one thing. But solving riddles got us this far. How much of your grandmother's letter do you still remember?"

"Not all word for word, but big chunks of it. Let's see. . . . The first part was about no time left and the hunters closing in on her, and how she stayed away because of them, the hunters, only now she was dying . . ."

It suddenly hit Zoe then, what exactly her grandmother must have felt while she was writing her letter, maybe because Zoe had been living it herself these last two harrowing weeks—feeling that no place on earth would ever be safe for you again, no one you met could ever be trusted. But for her grandmother it had been worse because she'd had to endure it alone. For years.

Zoe blinked back tears and went on. "There was something about ignorance being no shield against danger, but how she dared to put only so much in her letter, and this next part I remember exactly, because I read it a gazillion times."

She closed her eyes. She could see the Cyrillic script of her grandmother's hand, blue on white paper . . ."'The women of our line have been Keepers to the altar of bones for so long, the beginning has been lost in the mists of time. The sacred duty of each Keeper is to guard from the world the knowledge of the secret pathway, for beyond the pathway is the altar, and within the altar is the fountain of—'"

She cut herself off, opening her eyes. She stared hard at the altar, but that seemed to be all it was—an altar fashioned out of human bones. "For beyond the pathway is the altar," she said again.

"Yeah," Ry said, "but unfortunately, the pathway seems to be a secret pathway."

"She mentioned the pathway again later, though, when she wrote about the icon. Remember, 'Look to the Lady, for her heart cherishes the secret, and the pathway to the secret is infinite'"

Zoe walked up to the altar. She saw that the table part of it was also made out of bones, whole flat bones such as scapulas and skull plates, and parts of other bones that had been carved and then fitted together like jigsaw pieces.

"That story Rasputin told the tsar's spy in the tavern that night," she said, as Ry came up beside her. "He claimed he saw the Lady icon sitting on top of an altar made out of human bones. So at one time the Lady was here, on top of this altar. 'Look to the Lady, her heart cherishes the secret, the pathway to the secret is—'"

"'Infinite,'" Ry said. "Infinity. The symbol for infinity."

Zoe bent closer over the altar top, looking for the infinity pattern in the bones—the figure eight lying on its side—but it was all a jumble. Ry took a step back, to look at the altar's front again, and eventually she did, too. "It's all just a jumble, Ry. I see skulls, femurs, fibulas, tibias, but in the end it all adds up to just a bunch of bo—"

"*Skulls,*" Ry said. "Look. There are seven of them, like there were seven jewels that made up the infinity pattern on the icon."

And as soon as he said it, the sleeping figure eight made by the layout of the skulls on the front of the altar jumped right out at her. "I see it, Ry. I see it. So what do you think? Do we press on the skulls like we did with the jewels?"

Ry grinned at her. "Yeah. I say we go for it."

Zoe knelt down in front of the altar. She started with the skull in the center, as she had with the icon's jewels, pressing into its smooth forehead with the heels of her gloved palms. She went through the pattern, up and to the left, pressing each skull in turn, and remembering to hit the center skull again on her way through the middle of the eight.

But when she got to the last skull, she stopped. "I know it doesn't make any sense after all the really bad stuff we had to live through just to get to this point, but I think I'm more scared right now than I've ever been in my life."

"No, I get it," Ry said. "The mystery of what's on the other side of the locked door at the top of the stairs can be an incredible lure, up until the moment when you're faced with having to open it. Then the fear of what might be on the other side can stop you in your tracks."

Zoe rubbed her hands up and down her thighs. It was probably impossible in the subzero cold, but inside her gloves, her palms felt as if they were sweating.

"All right, all right," she said to herself. She drew in a deep breath, laid her hands on the forehead of the seventh skull, and gave it a good push.

"Nothing's hap—"

A terrible grinding noise shattered the silence of the cave, seeming to come at them from everywhere at once. Zoe reared backward onto her butt, then nearly burst out laughing because Ry had crouched and whirled toward the front of the cave as if ready to go all kung fu on whatever might be coming to get them.

The grinding noise stopped abruptly. There was a moment of dead silence, then a whirring noise started up, like a fan with a leaf stuck inside it.

"*Look.*" Zoe grabbed Ry's arm as the rock wall behind the altar split open and began to slide sideways, taking the altar with it.

They stared as, inch by inch, the rock creaked open, revealing a narrow, arched hole that opened into darkness. But not a complete darkness. There was, Zoe realized, a weird, pulsating red glow to the blackness beyond.

Ry snatched up the lantern and headed for the crude opening in the cave wall. Zoe scrambled to her feet and caught up to him.

He stopped just inside, holding the lantern out in front of them. Pale, yellow light cut through the darkness, and Zoe gasped.

They stood at the entrance to a small, round chamber, less than six feet in diameter, and it was empty except for the dolmen standing in the middle of it. Three big, flat rough slabs of stone, put together to form an altar, like something you would see on the field of Stonehenge. And seeping up from out of the rocky floor beneath it, like coagulating blood, was a phosphorescent red ooze.

"We've found it," she whispered.

Ry said nothing. His face was hard, intense, as he stared at the dolmen and the red ooze seeping up from the rock beneath it.

The ooze formed a small pool that was slowly trickling out into the cracks and crevasses in the stone floor. Etched into the floor in front of the pool were three wolves making a circle, noses to tails, chasing each other through eternity.

Don't tread where wolves lie.

A sudden image flashed in Zoe's mind, of Boris the griffin shop man holding one of the keys to the unicorn casket in his hand and saying, "Clever, is it not? But then the Keepers have always been clever at devising riddles to keep the altar safe from the world."

On some instinctive level Zoe felt Ry start to pull away from her, to go the dolmen—

"*No!*"

She grabbed his arm, jerking him back the instant before his foot came down on the circle of wolves.

He half-turned to her. "What—", he began, then his eyes focused behind her, and he flashed a sudden, brilliant smile.

"*Pakhan,*" he said. "What took you so long?"

56

M OTHER?"
    Anna Larina Dmitroff stood on the other side of the crude
opening in the cave wall, where the altar made of human bones had once
been. Snow dusted her mink hat, the mink collar of a long quilted coat,
and caked the soles of her fur-lined boots. She held a Glock 37 pistol in
her hand, pointed at her daughter's chest, but her eyes, every fiber of her
being, seemed riveted on the dolmen and the iridescent red ooze that
lay beneath it.

"The altar of bones," she said, awe and a hot, hard desire roughen-
ing her voice. "I knew you would lead me to it eventually. All I had to do
was wait and be patient."

Zoe shook her head. "But how could you know where . . . ?" A terrible coldness suddenly washed over her, but she wasn't going to believe
what she was thinking. She couldn't believe it, because it would kill her.

Slowly she turned to look at Ry, and it felt as if she were moving
underwater. "What did you mean, 'What took you so long?' You were
expecting her?"

"I work for her, remember? She told me to seduce you, to worm my
way into your trust, and you would lead us to the altar of bones. I gotta
say you weren't much of a challenge, Zoe."

The pain in her heart was so fierce, she thought she would faint
from it. *God*, what a fool she'd been. Trust no one, not even the ones you
love. But like so many Keepers before her, she'd fallen in love and that
love had betrayed her and made a lie out of everything she believed in.

"I hate you right now, Ry O'Malley. I hate you enough to kill you."

"Oh, for God's sake, Zoe," Anna Larina said, tearing her gaze off the altar with a visible act of will. "You can be so obtuse at times. Can't you see he's improvising? Trying to make me think he isn't the puissant traitor I know him to be. He might have been expecting me, but that lovely smile of welcome he gave me—it was all teeth and no fire. Isn't that right, Sergei?"

Ry let out a deep breath and shrugged. "It was worth a shot." He turned to Zoe and gave her a weak smile. "Sorry, babe."

The wave of sheer, blissful relief coming on the heels of so much pain brought burning tears to Zoe's eyes. "I think I still hate you, Ry. For scaring me like that."

"Are you two done?" Anna Larina said. "As for how I knew where to find you . . . I figured you would eventually end up where our family's rather macabre history began, so I decided to come to this frozen hellhole directly and skip all the drama in between. I knew you were in town five minutes after you checked into the hotel. Did you really think I was going to let you get away with taking what's mine? I'm the one who should be the Keeper. The altar of bones belongs to me."

"The altar isn't yours, and it doesn't belong to any one Keeper either. Our job is to keep it hidden and safe from—"

"Your *job*?" Anna Larina laughed a little too wildly. "Are you getting paid by the hour?"

"Keep it safe," Zoe went on, "from people like you. And if you've come to drink from it, you may as well not bother. It only takes one drop, and you've already had yours."

"What are you talking about?" Anna Larina said, but Zoe had seen something flicker across her face. Secret knowledge, and a sick sort of triumph.

"Oh, I think you know. Your miraculous recovery from leukemia when you were four. The fact that when you look into a mirror, you see a face that doesn't look a day over thirty."

"Then imagine all the money I'll save over the years on Botox and plastic surgery. All the more for you to inherit, Zoe, my dear. Except, oops, too bad for you, I'm never going to die."

"Unless someone shoots you," Ry said. "And there's always stabbing, drowning, and death by garrote."

Anna Larina made a little tsking noise and shook her head. "Sergei, Sergei. For a dumb *vor*, I thought you showed some promise, yet what a disappointment you have turned out to be. The last man to betray me ended up with his head in an ice cream carton. Regrettably I don't have the time to get creative with you. But rest assured, I will get you."

"Unless I get you first."

She laughed again, as she pulled off her mink hat, shaking out her hair. "What are you going to do, throw a rock at me? Since I doubt you have a gun in your pocket. The only way you can get to Norilsk this time of year is by plane, and they have no problem with profiling here in Russia. Foreigners, especially Americans, are automatically suspect, and liable to be strip-searched at any time. Even a dumb *vor* like you wouldn't risk getting caught with so much as a toothpick in his possession."

"Yet somehow you managed just fine," Zoe said, but it was all bravado. Her mother was right. No way could they have carried a gun onto the airplane, and Norilsk seemed to be the one city in the world where Ry didn't "know a guy."

"I am a *pakhan* in the Russian *mafiya*, darling. I could probably get my hands on a suitcase nuke, if I wanted one badly enough. It is not that hard when you own half the damn country."

She made a little movement, as if she was going to step inside the chamber with them, and Zoe felt Ry tense. She knew what he was thinking: If her mother got close enough, there might be a chance for one of them to go for her Glock.

But although Anna Larina's eyes were riveted on the altar again, she didn't come any farther into the little chamber. The red ooze seemed to be pulsating now, brightening, dimming, brightening again, and Zoe saw the naked greed blaze to life on her mother's face.

After a moment, no more, Anna Larina tore her gaze off the altar and focused all her attention back on them. "You, Sergei. Put the lantern on the ground, nice and slowly, and if I even think you might throw it at me, my daughter gets a bullet in the heart. That's good. . . . Now, starting with you, Zoe, I want both of you to come out here and join me in this lovely cave. Baby steps, though, dear. Nice and slow."

Zoe led the way through the hole and into the cave. Anna Larina backed up as they came toward her, careful to keep a safe distance between them and the pistol pointed steadily at her daughter's chest.

"Very good, children. Now, get over there. On the other side of the pool."

"You should have tried to break into the movies when you were in L.A., Mother," Zoe said, wanting to get her talking, distracted, to buy them some time. Although time to do what, she didn't know. "What with that little acting job you treated me to in your library, pretending you'd never heard of such a thing as an altar of bones in your life."

A brittle smile stretched her mother's lips. "You were not always the chosen one, Zoe dear. The morning before she dumped me off at the orphanage and left me forever, your dear, departed grandmother told me about this wonderment she called an altar of bones. She said it was hidden in a cave deep in Siberia, and if you drank from it, you couldn't die, and that made it dangerous. She said the women of our family were called Keepers, and they kept the altar hidden from the world. A sacred duty passed down mother to daughter since the beginning of time. What drivel."

Yet as Zoe watched, her mother's face seemed to soften and she became lost in the memory of those last moments with a mother who was about to walk out of her life forever.

"But I was only nine," Anna Larina went on, "and you know how kids are. All I was interested in was how an altar could be made out of bones. I think that's what stopped her from telling me the rest of it—she was afraid I wouldn't understand or that I'd forget. She did show me the icon, though, of a Virgin Mary holding a skull cup in her lap. She said a Keeper during Tsar Ivan the Terrible's time had created the icon as a way to keep the altar's secret."

"No wonder you collected them all these years," Zoe said. "I thought it was because they were beautiful and it made you happy just to look at them. Your icons seemed to be the only thing in this world you really cared about, and even that was lie."

Her mother's mouth curled into a sneer. "I swear, Zoe, you positively drip sentimentality at times. They were an investment, nothing more, while I searched the world over for the only one that really mattered to me. When Mother didn't come back, I thought she'd died and the thing had been pawned or sold. I thought she'd died. . . ."

She's still that little girl, Zoe thought. That little girl waiting at the orphanage for a mother who never came back. And when Katya passed her over to make her granddaughter the Keeper, it must have felt as if she'd been abandoned all over again. *Only she doesn't know why. Katya told her about the altar and that she would be the Keeper one day, but then she took it all away and give it to me, and she can't understand why her mother would do that to her. She doesn't know why.*

"I thought she'd died," Anna Larina was saying, fury and pain in her eyes as she glared at her daughter. "But all this time she was saving it for you."

"You're wrong about her," Zoe said. "What you're thinking about her. She never hated you. She left you in that orphanage to keep you safe from the hunters, and she would have given you the icon later, she would have made you the Keeper, but . . ."

"But what, Zoe? I'm beyond giving a shit why the old bitch did what she did, but you seem to need the catharsis, so go on."

"You were her little girl and you were dying, and she couldn't bear it. So she gave you the altar to drink, even knowing what it would do to you. One drop and you would live. But one drop would also make you crazy."

"I don't . . . What are you saying?"

Zoe almost took a step toward her mother, wanting instinctively to comfort her, but the pond was between them now. And the gun still pointed at her, unwavering, deadly.

"She's saying the altar of bones is a real fountain of youth," Ry said. "But there's one disastrous consequence to drinking it, and I think you already know, deep in your heart, what that is. All these years, while the face in your mirror barely changed, you've felt the crazy growing and twisting inside of you, consuming you. You might stay forever young and beautiful, *pakhan*, but the price you're paying is your sanity. Without your knowledge, without your consent, you're paying the price. And it will only get worse. Every year on this earth is going to cost you another piece of your mind."

Anna Larina shook her head. "No, that's a lie. Some kind of trick to get the altar away from me, and it's not going to work."

"Haven't you ever wondered," Zoe said, "why your mother gave you the altar because you were dying, but never drank from it herself? The reason why she didn't make you the Keeper was because she saw what you've made of your life. You're a *pakhan* in the Russian mafia. How much more depraved and crazy—"

"I am not crazy!" Anna Larina shouted, shocking even herself. But then she shrugged it right off, even gave a little laugh. "Well. That might've been just a little too telling. And you can stop your smirking, Sergei, because it doesn't matter. You two can think what you want. I'm taking what is mine."

And then what, Mother?

Zoe couldn't see how her mother was going to let them leave the cave alive. Ry she would kill on principle alone, because she was the *pakhan* and he had betrayed her. But would Anna Larina really kill her own child? What lived inside her now? Was it a disease, or was it evil?

Whichever it was, it didn't matter. Because as she looked from her mother's soulless face to the barrel of the Glock, then back to that face, Zoe knew in her gut that this thing couldn't be dealt with or rationalized with or bargained with or wished away.

Yet still she tried. "Mother, please. Why are you doing this?"

"Why?" Anna Larina's laugh was wild now, out of control. "I should think it's obvious. Why don't you tell her, Sergei? You're standing there, suddenly silent as a bloodsucking leech, probably plotting how you're going to leap across the pond and wrest this gun from my hand. Explain to my naive daughter what I could possibly want with the altar of bones."

"Besides the fact that you're batshit crazy? Money and power. The usual suspects."

"Bingo, and give that man a prize. Think of the billions of dollars people spend every year in the vain attempt to fool their mirrors. Botox, face-lifts, liposuction, tummy tucks—all to look younger than they really are. To convince themselves, in spite of all evidence to the contrary, that with every breath they take, with every minute that passes, they are not dying."

Zoe realized that while her mother was talking, she was also backing toward the opening in the rock wall. The chamber beyond it was glowing red like a beacon now, pulsing, pulsing . . .

"Nobody wants to believe that the wonderfulness that is their wonderful, exceptional self will just end. Simply dissolve into nothingness," Anna Larina said, and backed up another step, then another, her voice rising with excitement, anticipation. Passion. "Imagine what the rich would pay, what they would give up to me, in return for not having to face their nothingness. And I could choose who to bless and who to damn. I would be God."

Zoe saw the white flash shoot out of the muzzle of the gun barrel, a split second before she heard the report of the shot.

Ry grunted and fell face forward, into the black, oily pool.

ANNA LARINA HEARD the echo of her own voice, *God . . . God . . .* along with the gunshot, bouncing against the rocky walls, as she whirled and ducked through the opening in the wall and into the red, pulsating chamber.

But then almost against her will, as if she didn't really want to know, she looked back, and she saw Zoe trying to haul Ry out of the pool by the back of his coat.

Yes, that's my girl. I knew you'd try to save him because that's what you do. So get him to a hospital, before he dies, only he's probably going to die anyway because I aimed for his gut, to make him suffer, make him hurt. Take him away, though, Zoe, and leave the altar to me, and later on we'll figure out just what we're going to do with you.

The altar of bones . . . It looked like blood on the floor, shiny, viscous. She thought it even smelled like blood, and it seemed to be calling to her, drawing her into its beating, red heart.

She went toward it, her eyes on the prize, on the power. She didn't see the wolves on the floor.

She stepped into the circle they made, and the world seemed to fall out from underneath her. Something was wrong with the floor, the stones were disintegrating like sand beneath her feet.

Anna Larina screamed and screamed as she fell back, falling down into blackness, falling forever, and above her, so very far away now, she saw the pulsing red light. It was very bright now, lighting the darkness in a strange swirl of color, as if reaching for her, and she wanted to scream for it to save her, but it didn't even slow her down.

And then, in the instant before she hit bottom, she saw, silhouetted by the bright glowing red light, the tons of rocks and boulders coming down on top of her.

57

Ry, please . . .

He was so heavy, so unmoving. *Please, God. Ry, don't you be dead on me, don't you dare be dead.*

Zoe dug her fingers deeper into the folds of his coat and pulled with every bit of strength she had. It was enough to keep him from sinking to the bottom; it wasn't enough to get him up and out of the pool.

"Mother, damn you. Help me," she shouted.

For a moment Zoe thought her mother might have paused and looked back, but then Anna Larina kept going, through the hole and into the glowing red chamber.

Zoe felt Ry thrash beneath her hands, heard him cough. She sat back on her heels and pulled again, sobbing his name, while he clawed at the rocky ledge of the pool, and then he was out, streaming black water, shuddering with every harsh breath. He rolled over and half sat up, bracing his back against a stalagmite, pressing his hand to his right shoulder, and Zoe saw blood seep out between his fingers.

Then she heard her mother scream.

Zoe's head jerked around, and what she saw didn't seem real. The ground beneath Anna Larina's feet had disappeared. "Mother!" Zoe shouted, horrified, wanting to run to her, to save her, but she couldn't let go of Ry. For an instant, her mother seemed to hang suspended over a gaping abyss, and then she plunged, and she was screaming, screaming.

Her mother's screams seemed to turn into a high-pitched whine, and the whine got louder and louder as the ground began to vibrate and then to shake.

"Get out!" Ry shouted above the noise that was now like a train bearing down on them.

Zoe tried to grab him, to wrest him up onto his feet, but he pushed her away from him. "No. I'll slow you down. *Go.*" And he shoved her again, harder.

"I'm not leaving you, you idiot!" Zoe screamed. She knocked his flailing hand aside and covered his body with hers, as dirt and bits of rock rained down on them.

She thought, *I'm going to die*, and she was engulfed by a terrible sadness. It was too soon.

———

GRADUALLY THE GROUND stopped shaking and the terrible shrieking noise became a low rumble and died.

Slowly, Zoe lifted her head off Ry's chest. "Is it over?" she asked, more of the gods than of him.

But something in her already knew that it was over, that this was the final riddle. Rocks and boulders and debris now filled the hole where the chamber with the altar of bones had been. To protect the altar from the world, it had been taken from the world forever.

An image filled Zoe's mind then, of her mother in that last instant before the ground opened up and swallowed her. She'd had her back to Zoe, her face riveted on the altar, and even as she was falling to her death, Zoe knew she hadn't been able to look away.

Ry groaned, and Zoe rolled off him fast, suddenly afraid that she'd made his gunshot wound worse, throwing herself on top of him the way she had. He looked bad. The hand he had pressed to his shoulder was now covered in blood. Already his eyes looked glazed, feverish.

He did still have the strength to get to his feet, though. And she could never have said how she did it, but somehow Zoe got both herself and him squeezed through that slit in the rock without her freaking out completely. She was more scared of the thought that her mother had brought some of her *mafiya* goons along with her as backup, and they were now hidden among the trees that bordered the lake, ready to open fire with their semiautomatics.

She had no choice, though. Ry's wet clothes were freezing on him. She had to get him warm or he would die of hypothermia before she could even get him to a hospital.

———————

Ry was barely conscious by the time they staggered out from behind the frozen waterfall. The lake felt eerily still and was almost completely enshrouded by the creeping night, only a wisp of blue polar light still clinging to the snow-sodden clouds. She bore as much of his weight as she could as they slogged through the snow to where they'd left the Arctic Cat, her eyes scanning the ice-crusted pines and piles of boulders, her body braced for the flash of gunfire.

We made, we made it, her mind sang in a singsong as Ry fell into the Cat's rear seat, grunting from the pain.

But then Zoe felt, more than saw, a flash a movement among the trees and she whirled. She stood frozen, her eyes straining against the encroaching darkness, but all was still.

A white hare darted out from behind a tumble of rocks. Zoe started to let out a breath, then she caught it again.

Eyes.

A pair of yellow eyes floating close to the ground, and then another, and another.

And then the wolves began to bay.

. . . this is the starving season. The wolves will be out.

Oh, God. Please, dear God . . .

"Key's in the ignition," Ry wheezed. "Start it up. Turn on lights. Should scare them off. Need the blankets, Zoe. Cold."

Zoe leaped on the Cat, started it up, turned on its headlights, and the pack of wolves, which had already begun to slink onto the lake, turned tail and ran back into the trees.

Zoe got the vodka out first, and Ry's teeth knocked against the bottle as he drank from it with his free hand. His other hand was still pressed against his shoulder, but the blood had now soaked his coat to the knees.

As Zoe tore open the space blankets and wrapped them around Ry, her frantic eyes searched the shoreline for the wolves. She couldn't see them anymore, but she could feel them, moving through the darkness, getting close again.

Ry was having trouble catching his breath, she thought she could practically see the life draining out of him. *But you're gonna get him to a hospital, Zoe girl, and then he'll be all right. They'll take the bullet out and—*

"Something's wrong," Ry said, his voice a bare rasp. "Bitch only shot me in the shoulder. Shouldn't feel this bad."

Zoe finished tucking the second blanket under his hip, then leaned closer into him to be sure he heard her. "You're going to hang on for me, Ryland O'Malley, you hear me? I'm getting you to a hospital, so you're going to hang on."

"Bone juice," he said, his breath wheezing in and out. "Don't give it to me."

"I'm not going to let you die. I'm not."

"No altar of bones. No matter what. Want you to swear . . . sacred promise . . . you won't."

Zoe shook her head, feeling her tears freeze on her cheeks as soon as they hit the air. "Ry, you can't expect me . . . I love you."

"Then swear on that. Swear it."

A sob tore out of her, so hard it wrenched her chest. "Okay, I swear it. On my love—"

A wolf lunged at them from out of the darkness. Zoe screamed and instinctively flung the vodka bottle at the beast's head. He shied away at the last second, snapping and snarling, then the entire pack whirled and disappeared into the darkness again.

Zoe nearly fell in her panic to get into the Cat's driver's seat, and then the horrible thought hit her—she'd never driven a snowmobile in her life. *What if . . . what if . . .*

The wolves had regrouped already and were coming back. She jerked the front end of the Cat around, shining the light full on them, and they backed off again, but not so far this time, and she could see the hunger and the killing instinct in their yellow eyes.

"Ry," she screamed. "How do I drive this thing?"

But he must have passed out because he didn't answer.

Suddenly, a loud crack, like a rifle shot, exploded above their heads, and something came hurtling at them from out of the sky, stabbing into the snow barely a foot in front of them—

A giant icicle, the length and width of a man's forearm.

Zoe stared at it in horror for a suspended second. Then the whole world seemed to explode above her, as the giant frozen waterfall broke apart, raining deadly blocks and spears of frozen ice down on top of them.

Zoe searched frantically for a gearshift, something . . . then she saw a button next to the ignition. She pressed it and the Arctic Cat shot forward.

Just as the head of the frozen waterfall broke free of the bluff and came crashing down in a mountainous avalanche of ice and snow.

THE FIRES FROM Norilsk's smelters lit up the blue-black arctic sky, silhouetting the smokestacks.

The first factory she hit, on the outskirts of town, looked shut up and abandoned. Then she spotted a couple of men huddled around a fire they'd built in an old oil drum. They squatted on their haunches, holding hands wrapped in rags out to the flames, and they barely looked up, even when she nearly drove the Cat right through them before she was able to wrench it to a stop.

"Hospital?" she croaked, and tiny icicles shattered and fell from her eyebrows and the front of her hood.

One of the men, who had a red sock cap pulled nearly to his eyes, said, "Go seven blocks, then go right. After that you keep on going and going and going. It's out in the middle of nowhere, only it's so big you can't miss it once you *are* out there. I'll give it that. They say it's the biggest hospital in Russia. It's a thousand beds, they got, so—"

The Cat's skis ground on the ice-coated pavement as she shot forward, craning her head around to look over her shoulder at Ry. She could barely make out his face, he was so covered with snow. He'd passed out long ago, and now even his eyelids looked blue.

58

STEAM HEAT blasted out of the vents in the east surgical ward's waiting room, but Zoe couldn't stop shivering. She sat on the edge of a hard plastic chair, staring at the locked double doors, terrified of what was going on behind them.

She'd driven the Cat right up to the emergency room, and after that it had all been a blur. They'd loaded Ry onto a gurney, stuck IV tubes of blood and other fluids into his arm, and covered his face with an oxygen mask. They'd asked her for his blood type, but she didn't know it. They asked her if he was allergic to any drugs, but she didn't know that either. She didn't even know for sure how old he was. She felt as if she knew him down to his soul, so how could she not know those things about him?

Then they wheeled him away from her so fast there was no chance for her to kiss him or even touch his hand, no chance for her to tell him he had to come back to her. After a while she was brought here to wait, and here she'd been, alone and waiting for a thousand years.

Once, a woman wearing a white polyester pantsuit and carrying a clipboard came into the room just long enough to give her a plastic zipper bag filled with the things they'd taken from Ry's pockets: wallet, cell phone, a key to their hotel room, cigarette lighter, flashlight, miniature tool set, a coil of wire, and what might be a set of lockpicks. *Typical O'Malley. Always prepared,* Zoe thought with a watery smile that turned into a sob, and she crushed the bag to her chest as if it were a lifeline tossed to her, a part of him to see her through this endless waiting that went on and on and on.

She was about at the point of banging on the doors and screaming for someone to tell her what was going on when they swung open, and a middle-aged woman in bloodstained scrubs strode through. Zoe got stiffly to her feet, her heart pounding, nauseated with fear. She tried to read what was coming in the woman's face, but all she saw was exhaustion.

"The bullet entered and exited cleanly," the surgeon said. "There was some muscular damage, but he should recover full use of his shoulder with the proper therapy."

Zoe's voice was hoarse, as if she'd spent these last hours screaming. "So he's going to be all right then?"

The doctor seemed to hesitate a second, then said, "As these matters go, the operation was relatively easy. What's worrisome is the virulent bacterial infection that has invaded his system. I understand he fell into a pool of stagnant water right as he was shot?"

Zoe nodded numbly. Had she told someone that during the controlled chaos down in the emergency room?

The surgeon shook her head, sighing. "The water, the earth, the air we breathe here—it's all filled with untold amounts of toxins. Our smelters release two million tons of sulfur dioxide alone into the air each year. We have endless acid rain, no plant life, no birds, and the heavy-metal pollution has become so severe it is now economically feasible to mine the very soil we walk on." She shook her head again. "One really should not live in Norilsk."

"But I thought you . . ." What was she saying? "Is he going to die after all?"

The doctor hesitated again. "His situation is extremely critical. And, yes, to be frank, he very well might die from this infection. As I said, it is a highly virulent and toxic bacteria. However, the next few hours should tell us more. He's getting a high-dose antimicrobial therapy of vancomycin, chloramphenicol, and sulfa drugs to interrupt the viral process. Much depends on the resistance factors of this particular bacteria and the strength of the patient's own immune system."

Zoe thought there had to be a million questions she should be asking, but her mind felt frozen. And the surgeon, her duty done, was already turning away.

"Doctor, wait. . . . Can I see him now?"

"I'm afraid that's out of the question at least for the next couple of hours. He's in recovery, after which he'll be moved to the ICU, and then we shall see how he is doing at that point. The nurse will keep you informed."

"Thank you," Zoe said, but the doctor was already disappearing behind the swinging double doors.

Zoe walked aimlessly to a window that looked down on a nearly empty parking lot and a strange forest of rusting concrete pilings thrusting up out of the snow. The plastic bag full of Ry's stuff trembled in her hand. At first she thought it was her own nerves finally letting go, then she realized Ry's cell phone was vibrating.

Zoe stared at the phone, unsure of what to do. Should she answer it? It was one of the prepaid cells they'd picked up in St. Petersburg, so who would even know the number?

Her hands shook a little as she unzipped the plastic bag, took out the phone, and flipped it open. "*Da?*"

There was a pause at the other end, then: "Miss Dmitroff? This is Dr. Vitaliy Nikitin."

Zoe let out the breath she'd been holding. "I'm sorry, Dr. Nikitin, but Ry is unreachable at the moment."

"It is a bacterium," he said, excitement in his voice.

"What?"

"The red phosphorescent, viscous fluid that you gave me to analyze. It is a bacterium. Rather to be more specific, it has the genes of bacteria, but also of archaea, which is the most primitive of microorganisms on earth. It is most fascinating."

There was a brief pause, then he lowered his voice almost to a whisper as if he were afraid of being overheard, "Miss Dmitroff, I think it could be real. A true fountain of youth."

It took a moment for Zoe's brain to catch up, to remember that the night she'd given Dr. Nikitin the small vial of bone juice to analyze was back in the good old days, when they still thought the altar of bones was mostly a quaint Siberian myth.

Nikitin, though, seemed to take her silence for disbelief. He said, "Remember I told you that Olga . . . that is, my colleague, Dr. Tarasov of the Institute of Bioregulation and Gerontology, has done some experiments with the longevity genes in roundworms. There is a regulator gene in the worms called daf-2, which controls as much as a hundred or so other genes involved with aging. You can think of the daf-2 as like an orchestra conductor leading the flutes and the violins and the cellos. Each instrument plays its individual part, but they all must also play in concert. Do you understand, Miss Dmitroff?"

"I think so."

"Because of the nature of the folklore that has grown up around the red bacteria, we decided to inject it into the cells of a few dozens of the roundworms, just to see what if anything would happen, and to our astonishment we observed that the bacterium transported genetic bits of itself into the worms' daf-2 genes, mutating them. You could say it made the daf-2 a better orchestra conductor. Suddenly we saw the violin cells rejuvenating themselves, cleansing the worms of built-up toxins, repairing the harm done by free radicals. We saw the flute cells enhancing the worms' metabolism, improving fat transport and food utilization, keeping them fit, stronger. We saw tuba cells fixing broken DNA, cello cells fighting off bacteria that cause infection, and so on. I am vastly oversimplifying it, but you could say the worms' daf-2 now has all their longevity genes playing in near perfect harmony, keeping them from aging. Forever alive, perhaps, although that remains to be seen."

Zoe's heart and breathing had both seemed to stop at the words *fighting off bacteria that cause infection.* "Dr. Nikitin, are you saying the alt—that the red bacteria changes your DNA so you're better able to fight off infections? Even really bad infections?"

"Indeed. The worms' natural immunity systems have been boosted to such a level that they can zap an infectious bacteria dead, to mix my metaphors. Like a laser gun in one of your space-war movies."

For a moment Zoe felt as if the earth had dropped out from underneath her and she was hurtling through space. *Don't give it to me. . . .* She had promised him she wouldn't. On her love, she had promised. But that was before the doctor had said an infection was killing him, before she knew for a certainty that the altar of bones could . . .

All it takes is one drop.

"Unfortunately," Nikitin was saying, "we discovered almost too late that once exposed to light, its properties began to deteriorate. We have barely a tenth of a viable cc left, yet obviously more observation is needed. Right now we can see *what* it is doing, but we don't understand *how*, and we must be able to do that if we are ever to have hope of being able to replicate and produce it within a laboratory. I need more of it, Miss Dmitroff. Do you understand? I must have more."

"There isn't any more."

"But you are in Siberia now. Didn't you tell me the fountain originated in a cave there?"

"It's been destroyed. The cave, everything—it's all gone."

A long pause, then he finally said, "That is most unfortunate." But Zoe could hear the skepticism in his voice. He wasn't a stupid man.

"Dr. Nikitin, there was more to the legend than just the fountain of youth. A dark side. It is said that those who drank from it in the past became megalomaniacs. So if the bacteria gets inside you and does what you said, your life might go on forever, but you'll live it crazy."

"No specific component of the human genome has been identified as a link to that kind of psychosis. To megalomania. But even if what you say were true, if the red bacteria does cause other genetic mutations that compromise the mind in some way, there might be a way to separate the two effects. Keep the positive, counteract the negative."

Zoe was staring, unseeing, out the window at the black night, but suddenly she focused on her reflection in the glass. The pale blond hair, the broad forehead, and wide-spaced, tilted gray eyes. The Russian cheekbones and pale Russian skin. Her mother's face.

How much of her is in my blood and flesh? In my cells?

Nikitin was now saying something about mitochondrial DNA, but Zoe interrupted him, "Are your roundworms inheriting it? Are they passing on what the red bacteria does to their genes? Like if a female roundworm was given some of the bacteria and it altered her longevity genes, and then she had baby worms . . . Have the baby worms' DNA been altered, as well?"

"The *Caenorhabditis elegans* are hermaphrodites, but I understand the point of your question. While it is true that some genetic mutations are replicable, this one appears not to be."

Zoe laid her head against the glass as the relief washed through her. Her mother's face, but not all of her mother's genes. Please, God, not the mutated ones that had kept her forever young and turned her mind to poison.

"Miss Dmitroff, if you do in fact still have some of the red bacteria in your possession, I beg that you reconsider. Think of what this could mean to mankind, to the world. Most disease is the result of general aging. Heart disease and cancer are the big killers, with strokes, Alzheimer's, diabetes, and opportunistic infections claiming most of the rest. Parts wear out and begin to act in ways that cause symptoms of disease. But the fact remains that science has not yet discovered an indisputable biological expiration date for human life. If our parts could be rejuvenated, if they could be replaced, if built-up toxins could be removed, then the bulk of the diseases that kill us would never develop in the first place."

He paused, but Zoe said nothing. Her attention had been caught by a flickering blue light far off down the long road that cut across the barren tundra from Norilsk.

"In the meantime," he went on, "we shall see how long our DNA-mutated worms live, or if they ever die at all. Yet even so, I would not call it the gift of eternal life. For one can still die if hit by a truck, or by a plane crash or a mugger's knife. So, no, not eternal life. But rather *infinite* life, in that the cells might be able to go on reproducing themselves infinitely—"

"Dr. Nikitin, something has come up. I'm going to have to go."

Zoe shut off the phone and dropped it into her pocket as she watched the flashing blue lights of a Norilsk police car turn into the parking lot below.

———

Of course they would call the police. You don't come into a hospital with a gunshot wound without their calling the police.

Zoe knew she would eventually have to deal with the legal fallout of the bullet in Ry's shoulder, to come up with a plausible lie, but she wasn't ready yet. She didn't want to get trapped coming out of an elevator, so she took the fire stairs down four flights to a deserted lobby. She paused just inside the door, long enough to see two cops get out of their patrol car and go around to the emergency entrance.

Outside, the wind was blisteringly cold, swirling the snow into a gritty, icy mist. She huddled along the side of the building for what felt like a thousand years, waiting until the cops came back out and drove off.

When she was sure they were gone for good, she took the elevator up to the surgical ward again, but she didn't go to the waiting room. Instead, she crept up and down the hallways, peeking into rooms, until she found Ry.

For one heart-stopping moment she thought he was dead—his face looked so waxen, his lips bloodless. He lay in utter stillness, with IVs snaking out both of his arms, connected to machines that beeped erratically.

All it takes is one drop.

I swear it. On my love.

The icon and the film were in a safe-deposit box in a bank in St. Petersburg, but all that was left of the altar of bones Zoe had with her now, in the pocket of her parka. In a little sample perfume vial wrapped up with a tissue that she'd put into an Altoids tin to keep it from getting broken or exposed to the light.

Slowly, her heart thundering, she took out the tin, cradling it in her hand. She was afraid, so very afraid that if she got too close to temptation, if she so much as touched it, even with fingers thickly padded with Gore-Tex and fleece, then she would be burned by it. It would consume her.

And yet she couldn't stop herself.

She snapped the tin open, tipped the wrapped perfume vial into her palm, and closed her fist around it.

She stared at Ry's face. She could drop the little vial on the floor right now, she thought. Crush it under the heel of her boot. If she destroyed it, its dark legacy would forever be gone, along with its shining, seductive hope.

If she destroyed it, Ry might die, and if he died, she didn't know how she could bear it

If he drank from it, he would live. It was that simple. Live not just today or tomorrow, but for all the years of her own life, and then how many more? She would never have to suffer the pain of losing him. But even as the altar saved him, it would also change him, change him perhaps into someone she could no longer love. And if he ever found out that she'd given it to him, she knew he would never forgive her. Then what would either of them have?

She could feel the pulsating heat of the altar even through the thickness of her glove. She could see it's red phosphorescent glow leaking out around the tissue and her clenched fingers.

All it takes is one drop.

But she'd sworn. On her love.

EPILOGUE

Jost Van Dyke, British Virgin Islands
Five months later

Y EAH, YEAH, yeah," Zoe said, laughing as Barney let go with another indignant meow. "I can see you're starving. All fifteen blubbery pounds of you."

Zoe was in the galley making flying-fish sandwiches for lunch, while Bitsy slept on the sofa in the cabin and Barney curled around her feet, alternately purring and meowing because they'd run out of cream cheese yesterday and starvation was now imminent. To Zoe's relief, both Barney and Bitsy had taken to life on the ketch as if they were born to it.

Zoe hummed to herself as she arranged the sandwiches beside the potato chips on the new, bright red dishes they'd bought in Road Town. She set the dishes on the beautiful teak shelf that divided the galley from the living area, so cozy and colorful, and just like the ketch's previous owner, Aisle Briggs, a Scottish expat who'd lived on Tortola for nearly thirty years. He was so proud of his magnificent boat that both she and Ry were afraid he might cry when he signed over the ownership papers. But it was time, past time, he'd told them, for him to go home to Galloway and see what his dippy relatives had been up to while he was gone.

Zoe ran her hand over the satiny wood, thinking of the great deal Aisle had given them, because they were newlyweds, he'd said, and because they were just beginning their charter-yacht business and he was sure they would succeed with his "beauty." Had he guessed that it was more than the simple desire to run a charter business that had brought them here to the Virgin Islands? Guessed that their lives were now brand-new as well?

She glanced out the galley porthole and spotted Ry in the silver dingy, bouncing through the waves toward her. He was wearing only low cutoff jeans, a sleeveless white T-shirt, a Boston Red Sox baseball cap, and flip-flips on his big feet. He looked brown and healthy and beautiful, and she sure hoped he'd remembered mayo for the sandwiches and Barney's cream cheese.

Zoe grabbed the plates and brought them up on deck, just as Ry killed the motor, letting the dingy drift up to the yacht's port side. He'd only been gone a couple of hours, but he beamed up at her as if he'd been away at sea for a year.

"Got both the mayo and Barney's cream cheese. The little greedy Gus."

"Thank God. He's been meowing all morning, in between giving me dirty looks to let me know what he thinks about a charter yacht that doesn't have any cream cheese in its galley."

"Foxy had the TV on down at the Bar and Grill," he said as he tossed her the mooring line. "The stock market nose-dived over nine hundred points yesterday. They had to suspend trading, and everybody's panicking. Your hero Senator Jackson Boone was on CNN, talking about how it could impact the election."

"He's not my hero." She laughed. "Okay, maybe he is a little."

She had met the handsome, charismatic senator in a room at the Watergate Hotel one night last March. It had just been the three of them, she and Ry and the senator, and Ry had turned the film over to him then, trusting him to do the right thing with it. But so far there had been nothing about it on the news anywhere, and maybe that was for the best.

He *had* used his juice to get them taken off the terrorist watch list, though. So at least there was that.

Ry handed her the canvas sack full of groceries, then climbed on board. "I'm telling you, everyone on the island was in Foxy's, glued to the TV. I thought I was going to have to offer Jigger a bribe to get him to open up his store."

Ry planted a wet, sloppy kiss on her cheek. "So, babe. What's for lunch?"

THEY ATE THEIR flying-fish sandwiches, with mayo, and drank two Painkillers from Foxy, his specialty rum drink that was more lethal than dropping acid, he liked to say. They spent the afternoon sailing, Ry steering the helm with one hand and his toes, Zoe nestled in the crook of his free arm. The water was turquoise beneath a clear sky, the wind soft and warm on their faces.

"Sasha Nikitin called while you were onshore," Zoe said. "He said he wanted to curse you for sticking him with that gig in Norilsk."

With the help of Svetlana and her cousin, they'd concocted a story to explain Ry's gunshot wound—that he'd been hit by a stray bullet from the gun of a caribou poacher. A story the police hadn't believed for a minute. In the end Ry had bought them off by offering to use his influence to get Russia's most famous rock star up to Norilsk to give a concert there.

"At least I didn't promise them he would show up in winter," Ry said.

Zoe remembered the hideousness of minus thirty-five degrees in Siberia and shuddered at the very thought. "He gave me a message from his father, too. The roundworms finally died, but not before lasting three times their normal life span. A hundred and twenty-five days. That's the equivalent of four hundred human years, if the bone juice works on human DNA the way it worked on them, that is. What's more, he said the roundworms kept their youth, wriggling happily to the very end. He wants to publish a journal article about it, but he's afraid no one will believe him." She twisted around so she could look into his eyes. "He's going to try to replicate it. He thinks he might be able to get us humans up to living a hundred and seventy-five to two hundreds years, and with no crazy gene."

She thought about the icon, sitting right now on a shelf in the cabin below them, with what was left of the altar of bones back in the secret compartment behind the skull cup's right eye.

"All through the centuries," she said, "the Keepers kept the altar hidden from the world because they didn't think the world was ready for it."

He brushed the wisps of windblown hair back off her face. "You think the world is ready now? I just wasted fifteen minutes of my life watching a bunch of talking heads posturing and pontificating and politicizing over the dire straits of the global economy. The governor of Arkansas, or maybe it was Kentucky, got caught in bed with a hooker yesterday. Some terrorists set off a bomb in a bus stop in Rome, and North Korea's saber rattling again. Human nature doesn't change, Zoe."

"No, I guess not."

She watched two seagulls swoop down for dinner, cutting the surface of the water like sharp knives, then she sighed and settled back into the crook of his arm.

She hadn't realized she'd gone so quiet for so long until she felt the brush of his lips on her cheek. "What?" he said.

"That night in the hospital in Norilsk, after you were shot, I snuck into your room and stood by your bedside, and all I could think about was how I didn't want to go on living if you didn't."

"You were going to give me the bone juice."

She nodded. Her throat felt tight, and an ache was inside her that was both relief and a remembered horror. A horror that she knew she might one day have to face again.

"I was going to put it into one of your IVs. But before I could, the doctor came in and told me your vitals were starting to improve, and that she thought you would make it. I know I promised, I swore it on my love. But when faced with the actual thought of losing you, I would have done anything, sold my own soul and yours, to have you live."

"I don't blame you for that. I probably would have done the same thing had it been you. We're human, Zoe. Our hearts take over our heads and keep us from considering the consequences."

"Oh, no, Ry, I considered the consequences. And I realized the only one I cared about in that moment was whether you lived or died."

"Then maybe that's your answer right there. Think about this moment, right here, right now. The sunset's got the sky all purple and pink and orange, the wind's so soft and sweet it makes you ache inside, and you're in my arms wearing nothing but a bikini and a tan and looking more lethal than any of Foxy's Painkillers. Do you think this moment would feel so wonderful, so, I don't know . . . precious, if we knew all our tomorrows were infinite? If we knew there would be another hundred trillion moments just like this one, how much would we care?"

He turned her around to face him, and she saw the love on his face, and she knew what he meant about a thing being so soft and sweet it made you ache inside. "I think what makes life matter, what makes it *good*, is knowing that someday we'll die. Maybe death is God's joke on us, but I think it's also his gift. We have our allotted time and then it's over. It's up to us to make it meaningful and special."

She leaned into him and brought her lips to his, softly at first, like the wind, and then deeper, harder, hungrier. "All I know," she said when at last they came up for air, "is that for however many days we have, I'm never gonna let you get away from me, Ry. After all, I'm the Keeper."